ALONE ON THE DARKSIDE

ECHOES FROM THE SHADOWS OF HORROR

John Pelan

RoC

A ROC BOOK

ROC
Published by New American Library, a division of
Penguin Group (USA) Inc., 375 Hudson Street,
New York, New York 10014, USA
Penguin Group (Canada), 90 Eglinton Avenue East, Suite 700, Toronto,
Ontario M4P 2Y3, Canada (a division of Pearson Penguin Canada Inc.)
Penguin Books Ltd., 80 Strand, London WC2R 0RL, England
Penguin Ireland, 25 St. Stephen's Green, Dublin 2,
Ireland (a division of Penguin Books Ltd.)
Penguin Group (Australia), 250 Camberwell Road, Camberwell, Victoria 3124,
Australia (a division of Pearson Australia Group Pty. Ltd.)
Penguin Books India Pvt. Ltd., 11 Community Centre, Panchsheel Park,
New Delhi - 110 017, India
Penguin Group (NZ), cnr Airborne and Rosedale Roads, Albany,
Auckland 1310, New Zealand (a division of Pearson New Zealand Ltd.)
Penguin Books (South Africa) (Pty.) Ltd., 24 Sturdee Avenue,
Rosebank, Johannesburg 2196, South Africa

Penguin Books Ltd., Registered Offices:
80 Strand, London WC2R 0RL, England

First published by Roc, an imprint of New American Library,
a division of Penguin Group (USA) Inc.

First Printing, September 2006
10 9 8 7 6 5 4 3 2 1

CONTENTS

ALONE ON THE DARKSIDE

AND OUR TURN TOO WILL ONE DAY COME

By Brian Hodge

They're the phone calls we hate most. That unnerving two a.m. jangle that drills your gut the way a dentist drills a tooth. If you've been out of college for longer than a year, nobody has anything to tell you after midnight that you want to hear.

And could you bring a shovel? I can't find ours.

Things like that least of all.

Yes, I went to college. Took a year or two longer than it should have. I had a habit of arguing with professors. Except for the extended trip back to the auld ancestral homeland—a given, in our family, a rite of passage that somewhere along the way seems to have lost most of its original significance—college was the farthest away from home I'd ever gotten for any length of time.

Otherwise, thirty-eight miles—that's it. I rolled down the mountains, bounced across the foothills, and had just enough momentum to make it as far as Boulder. Not a bad place to land, really. It put a little distance between me and where I grew up, but not so much that I didn't have a ready sanctuary close by in case I ever needed it. In case I had another of those phases in which I couldn't quite trust my eyes and ears.

The drive back up? I've never minded it in the day. At night, that's something else. Get past a town called Lyons and the spine of the North American continent starts to wrap around you. The road winds. A lot. Cliffs tower on one side while gorges yawn on the other. Narrow, as gorges go, and not terribly deep, but enough to swallow your car and leave you broken on a rocky streambed below.

When the settlers of the New World left their homes in the Old, it was only natural that they look for things that would be a reminder of what they would never see again. The Dutch who founded New Amsterdam, later to become New York, were drawn to Manhattan because the encircling rivers there reminded them of the lowland waters back home. Germans who made it past the Mississippi found, another hundred or so miles west, a region around the Missouri River that seemed very much like the Rhineland.

And the Scots from whom my sister and I descended? They had to go farther before they were satisfied. Occasionally I've wondered whether it was blind chance or ordained fate that drew them up into the Rocky Mountains until, at the site of what would one day become Estes Park, they looked around at the peaks and crags, and knew that here was as passable a substitute for the Highlands as they were ever likely to find.

While staking their claims in a world that could be as

hostile as it was unfamiliar, these immigrants couldn't have helped but take comfort in whatever semblances of home they could find. I've always understood that.

What I never really thought about was what they might have brought with them.

She was waiting for me outside the front door: Noelle sitting on the ground with a candle. I didn't know if the candle was for her benefit, to keep her occupied, or for mine, so I wouldn't trip over her in the dark. This house sits on the edge of town, up against the old scar where pines were cleared to make room for cattle, so you can't see much here at night. There are no streetlights here. There never have been. There probably never will be.

Not much of a street either. More like a neglected road and a pervading sense that what happens around these old pines and aspens stays within them.

My sister Noelle's candle was a big, fat pillar brimming over with melted wax. She took hold of it and tipped it, poured the molten wax over her hand, over the crust already there, turning her hand as it ran, cooled, hardened. She must have done that when we were kids, although now wasn't the moment to ask. There were times when we were growing up that I wondered how her hand got so chapped-looking—only ever the left one—and just as often in the middle of summer as the dead of winter.

"Brandt," she said. The name of her ex-husband came out of her as if it had been lodged deep, had to be yanked out, skewered on the barbs of a fishhook. "He killed her. He's killed my baby."

It cut the legs right out from under me. Down on the ground, hugging my sister, feeling that if I didn't have her to hold on to, I'd just keep falling, up to my clawing fingertips in clotted earth.

Should I lie, to pound home the sense of tragedy? Prattle on about what a little beauty queen my niece was, radiant and full of poise and charm beyond her years? That's what sells the grief: the image of a potential that people can recognize at once, without having to look deeper or think; someone they want to wrap their arms around and protect from every bad thing until she's old enough to fuck.

Except my niece wasn't a cute child. Not on the outside. It was like she'd taken the least appealing attributes from both parents, then made the worst of them. Maybe she would have grown out of it, duckling into swan, but probably not. So this is what she would've grown into: a homely young woman ignored by the world, except for the parts that she touched directly because she loved the world anyway. Six years old and already, on some level, she knew what lay ahead, so she'd begun to prepare. Bugs and plants and mammals, Joy just couldn't get enough of them . . . especially the herds of elk that ambled through Estes Park every autumn rutting season. I adored her all the more for it—that hopeful, melancholy spark of awareness.

So did her father. That's what I want to think: that he loved her more than he simply hated losing. Loved her enough to break into his one-time home and try to take her away into his new world. Except he didn't love her enough to do it competently. In the middle of the night, the haste with which he was trying to get the job done . . . Maybe she didn't realize who it was, just that she was draped over some man's shoulder—and that was how you made the news, as long as you were cute enough. No wonder she fought. Six years old and groggy and still she sent a grown man down most of a flight of hundred-and-twenty-five-year-old stairs.

In a just world, Joy would've landed on her father, not the other way around. He would have broken her fall instead of her neck.

Noelle's hand was starting to look truly deformed. I should've blown out the candle, except that would've left us in the dark, and just hearing her cry would've been worse somehow than seeing her.

"A shovel—did you bring one?"

No one could blame her for not thinking straight. What jury would fault her for finishing the job on her ex-husband that the stairs had started? What cop wouldn't have coached her, however subtly, to spin her story to eliminate her culpability? Okay, she took the big iron fireplace tongs to the back of his skull—so?

"You didn't do anything wrong," I told her. "There's nothing to bury here."

I'm more familiar than I would like to be with how, even in the most crushing moments of their lives, women can look at you as though you're the biggest fool they've ever seen.

Noelle peeled the wax from her hand and snuffed the candle, then stood and, like a wraith, turned and walked toward the front door.

This house. We've always lived in this house.

It was built by ancestors who died when my grand-parents were young, by that first generation of immi-grants who came and saw and set down roots, sinking them deep in the cool, mist-dampened earth.

This house. Sprawling and dark, its timbers hug the land as if it had come to a respectful truce with the hills and trees, rather than trying to defy them. When it was new, could anyone have looked at this house and not seen that it was built by people who were determined to dig in, hunker down, and stay? Could anyone have failed to recognize that these were people who would love the land and reserve their wrath for neighbors who might op-pose or try to cheat them?

It's their blood that flows through my veins, even if these people couldn't be much more remote if they were characters from myth. Their names were spoken with reverence even in my own lifetime, during my first few years, with my grandparents living in their own wing of the house.

We've always lived in this house. But there was never the remotest chance that it could one day be mine. It's al-ways been passed down to the daughters.

Tradition like that, you change it at your peril.

As for the boys, I suppose we learned to never ask why.

Inside the house, Brandt lay where he'd died. He had managed to get up and stagger away from where he'd landed at the foot of the stairs, but appeared not to have made it far before Noelle brained him.

"I hit him once to keep him still right after it happened. So he wouldn't get in the way while I was taking care of Joy," Noelle told me. "Then . . . when I knew . . . I must have come back and hit him some more."

The back of his head was buckled and broken, mostly intact but smashed in like the shell of a hard-boiled egg. His face seemed to have shifted, displaced from the inside, his eyes protruding and his jaw jutting crookedly. Everything a head could leak had oozed out of one orifice or crack or another.

The fireplace tongs lay nearby, a huge, iron scissors-like utensil ending in curved pincers big enough to grab onto burning logs. This contraption had fascinated me as a boy, one of those things that you instinctively know has a history, has been gripped by generations of hands, as much a part of the fireplace as the flat, blackened stones of its hearth. I would imagine our great-great-grandfather pausing in negotiations with someone who had come to buy cattle or sell him horses, stooping before a blazing fire and using the tongs to wrestle the biggest log into place. I imagined him standing up straight again without setting the tongs aside, instead flexing their heavy, hinged handles and clanging the pincers together to knock loose the ash—once, twice, three times—but eyeing his guest in such a way as to tell him that this display was really to demonstrate that my family had a long reach.

I can only think that this forefather would've been fiercely proud of Noelle.

What about Joy, though—would he have thought much of her? Her ungainly little body, her inquisitive scrunched-up monkey face? He probably would have, for her love of animals, but even if not, one thing mattered much more: She was one of ours, and she'd been taken from us by a thief in the night.

I'd always sensed that, both here and in Scotland, our family was no stranger to feuds and blood.

Joy lay on the sofa where Noelle had put her, still wearing her pajamas, pale blue and full of Dalmatians. My sister had straightened her head so she would look like she was only sleeping, but then there was that awful bruise down the side of her neck.

I knelt to hold my niece, and remembered so much, and never until this moment knew which of my feelings for her had outweighed the other: love or pity.

Noelle leaned against my back, her freshest tears on my shoulder.

"You should start digging," she said, finally. "One for each of them. Near the tree line. Anywhere along there should be good. And not too deep."

"Wouldn't *in* the trees be better?" I still wasn't sure why we were going through with this. Maybe I would strain and sweat a while before she came to her senses and realized, no, that's not the way we handle things in this day and age. "Not so . . . in the open?"

"They need to be away from too many roots," she said. "So you really never knew? You never actually saw anything before, or figured anything out on your own?"

Whatever that implied, I had to tell her no, I must not have.

"I want to stay in here with Joy as long as I can. But

not with *him* around." She pointed at Brandt. "Can you get him out back on your own?"

I found an old blanket that would do for dragging him. Didn't much want to touch him to get him onto it, though.

But the fireplace tongs fit his neck just fine.

It wasn't until I was old enough to not care that I realized our family was different in some ways. Like my grandparents, and the flashes of memory that I swear I have of my great-grandmother, although everyone says I was too little when she died to have remembered anything.

In virtually all the families I've known, or heard friends reminisce about, it's the grandfathers who like to scare you—all in fun—while the grandmothers sit back and shake their heads and *tut-tut* and warn the grinning old men that they're going to give the children nightmares.

In our family, it was the other way around. Which isn't to say that our grandfather couldn't play the game, it's just that our grandmother was the one to send us off to sleep burrowing under our blankets and watching for shadows. Bedtime stories—if Noelle and I heard this one once, we must've heard some variation of it two dozen times.

My grandparents—your great-greats—they wasn't poor when they come over. Not like so many of 'em back then, especially them scraggly Irish. No, they had a nice tidy sum that had come down through the family. Always been wealth in cattle. And there always will be.

But back then, there wasn't no planes to fly in, the way there is today. Back then, if you had a long trip you needed to take, you had to do it slow, no matter how fast you wanted to put some distance between you and wherever you was coming from. So to cross that wide old ocean, they had to get on a big ship. That was the only way in them days. It was one of them big pretty ships like the Titanic, *except older and not as fancy, plus this was one of the ones that didn't sink.*

So it was big and pretty enough, all right, but it was slow. Some of 'em took about a week to cross the ocean, but that's if you got a captain on board that knew his business. Not all of them captains did, you know. Some of them captains were just as dumb as rocks and didn't even have the good sense to realize it, so they'd get lost and the trip might take a little longer. And some of 'em took a lot longer. They might be out there a month or two. And some of 'em never did find their way into port, so they must still be out there today, sailing 'round and 'round and not even knowing it, maybe not even knowing they've been dead most of this time too. Terrible, just terrible.

But the voyage our family come over on was one of the regular-length ones, or near to it. Except it was long enough for what usually couldn't be avoided on trips like that. People died during the middle of it. Nothing sinister about that, just sad, from natural causes. It's bound to happen. You get that many people together on one boat, especially when they're packed together the way them Irish traveled, and some of 'em are bound to turn toes up. They show up sick and near to dead already, and the strain of the trip finishes 'em off. Or they show up not too bad off and might've survived the crossing, except for breathing somebody else's sick air, and the combination takes its toll.

Now, they couldn't just give them poor folks a burial at sea. It wasn't like the Navy. Their families was right there, and if the sailors had've dumped them bodies over the sides and let the waves take 'em, the families would've raised holy hell. Maybe there would've even been a mutiny, and throats would've got cut, and that wouldn't've been good for anybody. So what they done was wrap them bodies up decent and respectful, and box 'em up in crates, and put 'em way down in the hold, in the bottom of the ship, where it was nice and cool and they might keep a little fresher.

Except what do you think they found after they got to port and it was time to give them families back their dead?

It was only a surprise the first time. All the other times I knew what was coming. I kept hoping that somehow the story would turn out differently for a change, and this part never did.

That's right—there wasn't any bodies left. Just the biggest of the bones and some old dried stains, and the tore-up shrouds, and the holes in the crates where they'd been pried into.

But our family was lucky. They was healthy and strong when they stepped on the ship, and they stepped off the same way. And down that gangplank they walked, your two great-great-grandparents, and my own momma, just a girl then, and my two uncles, and the two babes in *arms that my grandma and momma held close and wouldn't ever let another soul see, and nobody kept asking once it was explained how sickly the pair was.*

And that's how we come from Scotland to America, so you could grow up in this big house and lay there in that nice bed.

Then she would kiss me good night and turn out the light.

There were many other stories that she told my sister and wouldn't tell me, and worse, had instructed Noelle that she was to *never* share them with me, under penalty of . . . Well, I never knew what that would've been either.

At first I believed Noelle, that for some reason I'd been excluded. Then I refused to believe her at all, figured she was just being malicious, only trying to make me *think* I'd been excluded—looking for that wounding edge the way siblings do. Because she never once cracked and uttered a word of what those other stories were about. That isn't natural. If she'd had anything, wouldn't she have let it slip? Teased me with a few hints?

I'm not sure when I reverted and started believing her all over again.

Maybe soon after our grandmother was dead, and our mother had indisputably assumed the mantle of matriarch, with Noelle grown old enough to feel weighed down by secrets and obligations, and her hand looking chapped sometimes, but only ever the left one, and just as often in the middle of summer as the dead of winter.

*　　*　　*

Like the opposite of a grave robber working by moonlight, I put shovel to earth and broke the soil.

A few yards in front of me, the pines and aspens rose in a dense, murmuring thicket, poured full of night. Their tops were black cones against the sky, sometimes swaying as if to swat down the stars, blind the only witnesses. Behind me was the house where we've always lived, vast and dark, lights showing in only a couple of windows. Such a big house for so few people these days, with both our parents gone.

And in between, closer to the house than to the tree line, stood the stout wooden post that supported the iron bell. Just as we've always lived in the house, the post has always stood there—replaced each time it grew weathered and weak—and the bell has always hung from it, as much a part of each generation as the fireplace tongs.

I'd never dug a grave before, let alone two. Noelle had stressed that she wanted plenty of space between them. To dig them side by side would have been an insult to Joy and the way she'd died. It would have given Brandt more consideration than he was due, either on the earth or under it.

No doubt there are men for whom grave digging feels like honest work, or the last kindness they can show the dead. There was none of that for me and my shovel. We were accomplices, guilty of something I couldn't specify, although it mattered less here than it might have elsewhere. It may have been wrong, but down deep I knew that the greater right was to stand with family.

One adult, one child . . .

The thing about graves, I learned, is knowing when to

stop. Six feet under is the rule of thumb, and even though I wouldn't be digging that far—not too deep, Noelle had said—I knew even that wouldn't feel far down enough. Things like this, they feel as though they should be buried deeper.

Behind me, nearer to the house than to the graves, the bell seemed to watch, to make sure it was all done properly.

At just past three feet, the shovel blade scraped something hard and unyielding, although it didn't feel big. Easy to pry out of the hole, caked with earth like a flattened dirt clod, and wash off with the bottled water I'd brought from the kitchen.

Even in the moonlight I could tell what it was. It was corroded by perhaps decades underground, but so thick and sturdy it was still mostly intact: a gigantic belt buckle of brass or iron. Just the kind of thing a man might wear if he had a lot of cattle and not much taste.

It should've been a bigger surprise to think, finally, that I hadn't really known my family at all. But it wasn't.

During the years I spent growing up, I couldn't think of a single occasion, with any certainty, that I'd heard the bell ring. A time or two, maybe, or three or four, late at night—the sort of event you can't be sure whether it really happened or whether you'd dreamed it. The sort of thing you might ask about over breakfast, like any boy trying to satisfy his curiosity without going too far, making someone angry. And of course they never got angry, my parents. They would just look at each other, blank and quizzical, as if to silently inquire of each other how

I could ever have gotten such an idea. Then they would tell me no, no, the bell hadn't rung. How could it? The bell was just for show, remember. The bell wasn't for ringing.

And it wasn't, so far as I knew. It was the only bell I'd ever seen that spent its life with a sleeve secured over its clapper. A thick old leather sheath with an intricate weave of ancient rawhide that laced up one side, and whose tip, like some kind of strange condom, was stuffed with fresh-shorn wool.

I would've been only a toddler the afternoon my great-grandmother caught me staring up at the bell with helpless longing. The time they tell me I would've been too young to remember, so I must be making it up.

"Don't you ever ring that bell there just to be ringing it," she warned me, as if I were tall enough to even try. "Do that, and you just might look down to find your toes gone."

The holes were dug, the bodies placed inside—Joy's lowered with tender care, Brandt's rolled in the way you'd kick a can to the gutter. All that was left was to replace the upturned earth. Because Noelle never had come to her senses. She was adamant: *This had to be done.*

So I did it, and night was kind, keeping me from seeing the soil in much detail. I imagined that mingled within the two mounds, in each shovelful, there must have been other trinkets: buttons and rings and boot nails and scraps of rotted leather. But as long as I didn't notice bones or teeth, I could tell myself that those pale glints were bits of glass, chips of ceramic.

"Thank you. So much," Noelle told me after it was done. "You should go now."

"That's it? Just *go*—like that?"

"It would be better if you did."

"I'm not some hired hand," I said, and thought of my niece in the ground. "Family, *that's* who comes out in the middle of the night, no questions asked." Thought of the little girl to whom, last Christmas, I had given a telescope, and how much she'd loved it, even though she quickly grew bored with looking at the sky and instead wanted to turn it on the earth, the woods. Looking for her cherished elk and whatever else that roamed. "Is there something that makes you more family than I am?"

"So what if there is? That doesn't have to mean it's a *good* thing." She wiped dirt from my cheek. "So please . . . just leave now and be glad you grew up sheltered."

"I didn't grow up sheltered, Noelle. I grew up being lied to. Sheltered is when you're blissfully ignorant. Lied to, that's when you know there's something not right, but everyone you trust tells you you're imagining things. Tells you so often that one day you're just not sure when you can believe your eyes and ears, and when you can't. Was that somebody's idea of doing me a favor? Because there were some years there that I was pretty well unemployable."

"There was always money. You never had to worry about that."

"Aren't you even listening? Isn't that kind of beside the point?"

That was the remark that made me decide to shut up, no matter what. For a woman who's just buried her only child, the point is whatever she says it is.

Noelle draped both hands onto my shoulders, on the verge of . . . something. Tears, yes, always those, but now more, as if she wanted to tell me something, but didn't yet dare to. She had looked this way so many times while we were growing up that I was used to it. Or just decided that I was imagining it.

Gran's not here anymore to punish you if you tell me anything, I almost said, and any other night, would have. It wasn't that I knew for sure Gran used to do anything. It's just that I started to wonder where Noelle had picked up the bit with the hot wax.

"Okay. Stay," she said. "You can't say you weren't warned."

She went for the bell, hanging from the post with its clapper sheathed, and in the near-dark Noelle untied the complex knotwork of the rawhide lacing as though her fingers had always known how.

She struck the bell then, a short but consistent pattern rung three times and left to hang in the predawn chill, like so many recollections from dreams that they'd never entirely managed to convince me weren't real.

Here's one that never happened either: There was this boy, see, who grew up in a mountain valley on the edge of a one-time resort town whose main streets had gradually become clogged with touristy kitsch. But the past was never entirely out of reach there. On a prominent hill, presiding over Estes Park like a dignified old mayor, stood the rambling Stanley Hotel and the ghosts that called it home. Below, sometimes all but forgotten, were even older pockets of time, bygone traces of the trappers and hunters and prospectors and ranchers who settled the valley first, fighting—sometimes to the death—for their rights to take and make, as settlers always do.

The boy's roots went very deep here, even if he was too young to know it at the time.

He must have been four, maybe closer to five, because his sister was still in the crib that summer. Even today he remembers that part quite clearly, and how attentively their grandmother used to watch over her as she slept. There were times the old woman seemed to see everything, but not while she was tending the baby. This, and their father and grandfather's habit of retreating to the den after dinner, was what finally gave him the courage to slip outside one evening. Because lately he'd been wondering where their mother disappeared to this time of evening.

At first he looked for her up and down the empty road, trying to push back the gnawing sense of dread he got whenever he wondered what would happen if one evening she never came back.

He tried behind the house next, past the muffled bell hanging from its post like a poison fruit he was already too intimidated too touch, and followed his instincts into the pines and aspens. They were as good a place to walk alone as any. There seemed to be no end to them; that their depth was unknowable, and you might walk and walk for days, yet never come close to emerging on the other side.

Her back was to him when he first spotted her in a cluster of trees going dark with pooled shadows, as she sat upon a sun-bleached fallen log. Before her, obscured by the log, he could see the upper curve of a dark bulky stone. Her hair was long then, halfway down her spine. For a moment, he stood and watched. Her elbows were thrust out behind her, as if she were holding something close to her body. Whatever it was, it seemed to be squirming.

Pretty soon, he started forward again, to close the gap between them.

It was inevitable that she would hear him eventually. Even a woodland filled mostly with evergreens can be a noisy place to walk. She whirled, her hair like a lashing whip, her eyes fixing on him first with fright and then with fury and, if his memory could be trusted, something he later identified as guilt.

His gaze lowered to the bundle in her arms—the wrinkled pink-gray skin that seemed to bristle with coarse dark hairs, and the conical face whose spade-like snout was clamped over her exposed breast. Surely he hadn't imagined the little peg teeth; why else would he have wondered if they hurt? Surely he hadn't imagined the way it seemed to sense his mother's abrupt distress, and pulled away to open its mouth—inside, the roof was ridged and spotted—with a squall like that of a bear cub.

When the stone before his mother rose with a shudder and a thick, wet snort, he turned and ran.

She was all smiles the next morning. Made him his

favorite breakfast—waffles and bacon. Told him what an imagination he had, that she'd only been out there with Noelle, in a small threadbare blanket, the same blanket she used to carry him out as a baby too, to nurse him within the trees so that he would learn to love nature and its bounty. Like everyone in the family.

He ate his waffles. He let her stroke his hair. He decided to try harder to believe.

"I guess if you take most any family that has old money coming down through the generations," Noelle said, "the farther back you go, the more likely you are to find that so much of what they have is built on the bodies of people who got in their way."

We were sitting on the wide, open porch along the back of the house, where we used to play as children and dream of the adventures the world held for us. It had been a long night, and the sky was beginning to lighten with pink and blue and orange, just enough dawn to make out the pair of dark mounds near the tree line.

"We were never the Hearsts or the Rockefellers—not even close," she said. "But there still were bodies."

The last echoes of the bell had faded minutes ago, but I thought I could still hear them, pealing across the open ground and ricocheting among tree trunks.

"It started in Scotland, but not even Gran was sure how far back it actually went, or who was the first. I mean, Gran used to tell me stories about those parts too. But not long before she died she told me that she'd made up parts of them herself, because she had to tell me something. It was easier than admitting she didn't know. You can't tell little kids stories without people in them."

If the look on Noelle's face some mornings had been anything to go by, there were stories you shouldn't tell kids at all.

"So let's call her Jenny, okay? Our great-great-great-whatever-grandmother. And even though she was a good woman, she always turned a blind eye to what her father and grandfather and brothers and uncles and husband did: stealing cattle—those big, shaggy Scottish cattle that look like walking carpets—and sometimes killing the rightful owners *and* their men when they came to get them back. Or killing other thieves that tried to take what they'd stolen first."

Stolen fair and square, I imagined our grandmother saying. I could hear none of her voice in Noelle's hollow recitation, my sister murmuring her way through this as if she'd waited so long it finally seemed to involve some other family. Except I still couldn't help but think of the words that Gran might use instead, the old woman forcing herself between us even though she'd been dead for years.

"So Jenny had seen enough men in her life get hanged for murder by sheriffs, and wanted to do something about it before it reached her own sons. Only she was enough of a pragmatist to realize that she couldn't stop them from following the same path if that's what they meant to do. So instead of trying to prevent . . . Jenny turned to the cleanup."

By now, long minutes after the bell had rung its last,

I could hear something heavy crashing through the still-darkened woods.

"God knows how she did it. How she managed to find them. And then how she managed to communicate with them. It's not like they speak, you know. But when you're looking in their eyes . . . you see something there that gives you the impression that some part of them is listening." Noelle kept watch, her eyes as dead now as the daughter we'd buried. "I don't know, maybe I'm giving them too much credit. Gran never said so, but more than once I've wondered if we weren't only descended from cattle thieves and killers, but a witch too."

From out of the trees, where the dawn had not yet reached, they came: six dark shapes, thick and low to the ground, like boars, their round, muscled shoulders and backs bouncing along with eager purpose.

"They're called yerd-swine," Noelle said. "They like to dig into graves for food. And these are ours. They've always been ours."

They attacked the fresh, shallow graves with snorts and squeals, sounding not quite like any hogs I'd ever heard—like if you listened closely enough to the grunting, you could make out the rudiments of voices. And they were ravenous, burrowing into the mounds and churning through earth with forelimbs that I was too far away to see, with too little light yet, but their snouts, their claws . . . the soil flew as though they'd been made for this and nothing else.

You can watch things that hold you rapt with fascination even as they sicken you. And so it was, here and now. Because I began to understand. They weren't merely ours; we were theirs too. Just as the murderous blood of our fathers ran through our veins, the milk of our mothers ran through theirs. They would demand it as part of their bargain.

"So Jenny, whatever her name really was, she went out in secret to these *things* that her neighbors felt nothing but dread for. However she managed it—and I don't think I ever want to know—she turned them into allies. Then she came home and demanded of the men left in her family that if they took another's life, she had to know about it immediately . . . and that she would take care of it. At least that's the way Gran told it. More or less."

Over at the mounds, they were shoulders-deep and going strong.

"Why wasn't I supposed to know any of this?" I asked her.

"That's just how it all came about. Having a way to get rid of the bodies . . . quickly, completely . . . It only made things worse, in a way."

Yes. I imagined that it did. It gave our forefathers a license to kill. Made them arrogant, maybe even prolific. I could imagine sons, brothers, uncles, cousins, drunk on ale and their own impunity, battering on Jenny's door in the middle of the night, their saddles draped with the corpses of those they'd killed on the road after some trivial insult in the taverns.

"So you—all the men in the family, I mean—weren't supposed to know until there wasn't any way to avoid it," Noelle said. "Gran loved men, I know. But she didn't have a very high opinion of your self-control."

Over at the graves, they'd reached the bodies. Noelle snapped out of her muted trance and buried her face in her hands.

"I can't watch it. Not this time," she said, and the slammed door off the end of the porch was the last I would hear of her for hours.

So I stayed to do my family duty, because while Noelle hadn't said so, I suspected that this was a vital part of the process; that *they* expected one of us to remain and bear witness, remembering the covenant between our species, our clans.

So I stayed, and watched as they ferociously tugged the bodies halfway from their graves, to feed on what lay helpless and exposed, then tug a little more to expose that too. I listened as their tusks ripped through skin and muscle, to the bursting of tender organs, to the grinding of their teeth on bones.

It was clear to me now, finally, Gran's old story about our family coming over on that ship: what was really swaddled in the blankets and what they'd grown into, what they'd bred. I'd always thought we'd come because this was the land of opportunity, and maybe that's really how my ancestors saw it . . . but only after they'd done things so terrible they could no longer remain on the far side of the ocean.

So because of their sins, I watched, listened, as their youngest descendant was ground into gristle.

We too were a part of the old bargain. Noelle hadn't said this either, but didn't have to. She'd been raised to believe, obviously, that there was no other way. Why else would she turn her daughter over to *this?* I could imagine the things our grandmother must have told her, things that Gran maybe even believed herself: *You've seen them things dig, so don't think you could ever get away. They got the smell of you in their noses, you know, and they was fed on the same milk that you suckled from your momma, so there's no place you could go that they couldn't sniff you out and dig their way to, someday.*

And still, I loved her.

It all explained some things—why I had never once visited the graves of my grandparents—but called so many others into question: If my mother, after the cancer took her, had really donated her remains to science. If my father, the day he left, had truly left for the reasons he'd said, and why he hadn't tried harder to take me with him.

And because I knew so much more now about where and what I came from, I had to wonder who I would kill. If it ever came to that.

BELINDA'S COMING HOME!

By Eddy C. Bertin

WEDNEYSDAY.

Dear Diary. I hope you're not mad at me. It's been so very long since I told you anything. But you know, Mom says that diaries are silly. That only little stupid girls write stupid things in silly diaries. That's really dumb. Sometimes I think I really hate Mom when she says things like that. It's just to hurt me, I know. She knows she hurts me, but she says it anyway. Why? I love Mom and I love Daddy. And I love you, dear Diary. Maybe most of all. I can tell you everything. Everything!

That's why I have hidden you, dear Diary. I know Mom has been snooping, she's been reading you. Reading the very secret things I've told only to you. You know I am not a little dumb stupid silly girl. I've hidden you very safely. Mom won't find you. I hope she thinks I threw you away. Then she'll stop looking for you. I don't want Mom to read what I only told to you. Those are OUR secrets. Mom has no business with them. None at all.

So you don't have to be mad at me. I've hidden you very safely. In the back of my closet. Under those old books of Belinda and me. To make sure, I put a mountain of dolls on top of them. No way Mom's gonna search there.

The light is out in my room. I'm under the blankets, like in a tent. I use my *Star Wars* light. Mom can't see the light under the bedroom door. She thinks I'm fast asleep. Now I can talk freely to you.

I think Mom hates you so much because Daddy once gave you to me. Mom always hates things I got from Daddy. Like Teddy. I never told you about Teddy. I was too sad at that time. He was such a lovely puppy. I loved him very much. Daddy gave him to me last year at my birthday. Teddy was so small and all black with curly hair. So sweet. I bought a little collar for him with his name on it. From my own pocket money, I did. Two weeks later, he was gone. Mom said he had run away. But I know better. Teddy would never run away from me. He know our house was his house. Jennie saw it all. Jennie is the girl next door. She's a bit older than me. Daddy was at his office. I was at a matinee at the movies. Jennie said a white car came to our house. And a man in uniform who rang the bell. Mom gave Teddy to that man and I never saw my puppy again. When I told Mom, she got very upset. She said I was a liar and a bad girl. She said Jennie was lying too, and she would speak with her parents. Jennie never spoke to me again after that.

Then there was that beautiful music, *Swan Lake*.

Daddy gave it to me, long ago when I still went to ballet class. I know Mom broke it. It was no accident, as she claims. It was a record, you know. One of those old big discs which I had to play on that ancient thing, a grammo-something. Daddy sometimes uses it to play very old jazz music. He calls it vinyl records. One day it was partly melted. Mom said I had left it lying in the sun. That isn't true. Mom bought me a CD with that music. I have never put it in my player. It's lying in a drawer. With the melted vinyl disc.

I never told Daddy about *Swan Lake*. Maybe he would get very angry at Mom. It happens. Then they have a very loud argument. So loud that it scares me. After a time Mom always begins to cry. Then Daddy says he's sorry. That makes Mom cry even harder. She's an expert in crying whenever she wants to. And she always gets her way. Sometimes Daddy thinks it's my fault that he got mad at Mom. Then he gets mad at me. And so it's always my fault.

Everything is always my fault. Always. I think I should've never been born. Then they could only get mad at each other. That's why I never dared to tell everything, that time with Belinda. It would've been my fault again. I couldn't stand them both being mad at me.

If Mom would find you, dear Diary, she would destroy you. Tear you apart or burn you. I know. That's why I only get you out of hiding now and then. To tell you something really important. When Teddy was gone, that was important too. But I was so sad then. I couldn't tell you. But now, dear Diary, surprise!

BELINDA'S COMING HOME!

Yes, it's true. They haven't really told me yet. I over-heard them talking in the kitchen. They didn't know I was there.

Belinda's coming home. This very Saturday evening! Maybe they want it to be a surprise for me. So I pretend I know nothing. I do love Belinda so very much. Now she's finally coming home. She's been at that school so long. I know I won't be able to sleep tonight. But I will not give away anything. I have reread what I told you in the past about Belinda, dear Diary. I won't betray any-thing.

I'm so happy. I could dance!

THURSTDAY.

I have not hidden you after last night, dear Diary. Well, not far away anyway. I need you close now. I know I will have much to tell you now that Belinda's coming home. Important things.

But right now I feel sad. You can't help me, dear Diary, you only listen to what I tell you. You understand what I'm writing down. As if I was really speaking to you. My writing is my speaking. Words have trouble coming out of my mouth. But writing is like speaking. It goes slower. I have a very good memory. I can remem-ber very long sentences. And difficult words. But when I try to really say them, it goes all wrong. My tongue ob-jects. My lips close. I start mumbling. My writing speaks only to you. But of course you never answer.

The teacher comes three times a week. He once said something very beautiful. I always remembered it: Not eyes but words are the mirror of the soul. There, I said it with my pen. In once sentence! Now tell me again that I'm dumb!

You, dear Diary, are my speech, my words. So that makes you my soul, right? You know that I'm really very smart. Mom doesn't know. Daddy doesn't know. He always says I'm his lovely smart daughter. But he doesn't mean it. He loves me, but he lies to me. Why else won't he let me go to a normal school? Why do I need a teacher at home? Because Daddy has a lot of money?

But that's not why I feel sad. They had another fight. Mom and Daddy. Mom sent me away, to my room. But I sneaked down the stairs. Listened at the door. I know that's bad. I couldn't help it. Because it was about me and Belinda. So I had to know.

They still haven't told me she's coming home. Daddy was very angry. He spoke with that quiet and hard voice. Hard and cold as a knife. He always uses that voice when he's very very angry. Mom was crying again. I hate it when she cries because she wants to get her way. They said horrible words to each other. I was afraid they might really hit each other!

I don't understand grown-ups. Yesterday I was so happy. Mom was happy too then. Now they're fighting again. Why? They should both be so happy that Belinda's coming home. Away from that awful school. But that was what they were fighting about. About Belinda. I couldn't understand it all, dear Diary. Sometimes they spoke very quietly, then they were yelling. But I have a very good memory, as you know. I'll tell you what I understood.

Daddy said: I don't want her here in this house do you hear me I don't care what the doctor said I don't want your goddamn freak in this house with Karen not now not ever.

Mom cried and yelled: But I want her back you fucking asshole I want her back she's my child.

Then Daddy yelled so hard I couldn't even hear Mom crying. So loud that surely even the neighbours must have heard it: I should've kicked you out years ago you slut you and your fucking freak I should've thrown you down the stairs you and your lover boy should've broken his neck when I caught you then all of this never would've happened.

And then Mom got ice angry. I call it that. When she stops crying and her voice changes. It gets cold and sharp. As if she thinks about every word before she says it. She no longer yells. Every word is cold and clear and smells of hatred: But you didn't you didn't dare shorty with your soft dick you were so glad to brag with your snotty friends that you could do it you were fucking happy that I got pregnant and it didn't matter that she wasn't yours you only started hating Belinda after Karen was born then it was all Karen here and Karen there and my Belinda could go fuck herself.

Then I stopped listening, dear Diary. I'm making spots on your pages. I'm sorry. I'm crying. I can't help myself. I told you all I heard. As I heard it. But I don't understand it. I can't ask anybody. Then I would have to tell about you. I can't do that. They would laugh at me. They would say I'm dumb. Maybe I am. Why else don't I understand what they mean?

Because when I sneaked away from that door below,
Daddy said something else. I didn't get it all. He spoke
very soft then: . . . retard . . . needs all the love of her
parents. That wasn't about Belinda. Daddy said that. And
it was about me, me, ME!

Then Mom said: You know who the retard is. With
that cold voice of hers. And Daddy hit her. I heard the
loud smacking sound as I hushed up the stairs.

I'm scared. I'm alone. Teddy is gone. Belinda is gone.
Mom and Daddy hit each other! Do they still love me? I
love them. Even Mom.

Maybe it'll be better when Belinda gets here.

FRIDAY.

At last they have told me, dear Diary. They really told
me Belinda's coming home tomorrow evening! Finally
we'll be together again. It seems like ages since we saw
each other. Mom never let me go with her. When she
went to that school to visit Belinda. She'll be taller now,
I think. She was always taller than me. She already had
a bra when she left. But now I have one too! Yep. Mom
said I had to wear one. I find it rather stupid. My titties
aren't that big. Not much more than oranges.

Of course Belinda is two years older than me. Years
ago hers were already bigger than mine now. Her nipples
also, so very pink and pointed. Always jiggling loose
under her sweater. Till she began to wear that bra.

I'm so happy she'll be back. We love each other so
very much. Now we will play together again. As in those
days. I have put all our dolls in rows, as then. In front of

our big dollhouse. Daddy made that himself in the shed in the back of the garden. Where we never were allowed to enter. Daddy keeps his gardening tools there. He always said we might hurt ourselves there. I've put all our favourite books and comics in neat stacks. Belinda will be so glad. It will be as if she never left.

I don't understand why Mom is still mad at Daddy. She wears her angry face all day. Daddy isn't happy either. Mom says he's tired from his job at the office. But I know that isn't the reason. It's about Belinda. Daddy said to Mom that Belinda's a freak. They often use such difficult words when they fight. I looked it up in the dictionary when Mom was upstairs. It says that a freak is an abnormal person. Like the vendor at the corner shop. He has a strange growth on his hand. It looks like a sixth finger. Or like people with three legs. Or the Elephant Man. I saw him in a movie on the telly one night. He was a nice man but so horrible to look at. Or like two children who are grown together. With their heads. Sometimes they have only one head and two bodies.

But Belinda is not like that at all! She is so very normal. Two eyes, two hands, two legs, two titties. One nose and one mouth. I don't understand why Daddy would call her a freak. Sometimes grown-ups use weird words when they mean something else. Maybe I have misunderstood. I am smart. But sometimes even smart people misunderstand things. When they know that, it proves that they are smart. I could ask Daddy to explain it to me. But I don't dare. I never get any answers when I ask about Belinda. Daddy might understand that I had listened at the door. Then he would be very cross with me.

He would tell Mom and she would be mad too. She is always very quickly mad at me. She never got mad at Belinda. Why can't she love us both? I think she blames me for Belinda being away. At that school. But why? Is it because she already had Belinda before she met Daddy?

That is no reason to hate me as she does. I know what she says to Daddy. I know what retard means. But I am not! No matter what she says. I cannot speak very well. But I can read and write. I can write very well. You know, dear Diary. Sometimes it's difficult when they're long words. Then I write very slowly and carefully. And I do get them right. I am a good pupil, the teacher once said so to me. He said I am doing very well. So you see! He is a teacher, he knows.

I don't like playing outside with the other children. They aren't nice, not at all like Belinda. Sometimes they are really nasty. Sometimes they laugh at me. They tear at my hair, my clothes. Last time there was that boy, pimple-face Tom. He lives two streets farther. He grabbed my titties under my sweater and pinched my nipples. Then he tried to kiss me. Imagine! He was slobbering like a dog, his mouth all wet. And they all just laughed. Till I hit him on his nose. When I came home with blood on my sweater, I told Daddy. He went and had a talk with Tom's dad. Tom never bothered me again.

The kids broke one of my prettiest dolls too. One Belinda loved very much. I hope she won't miss that doll when she gets here. I buried the doll behind the shed. And said a little prayer for it. I had a very bad dream last night, dear Diary. About that dead doll. It was all

smashed into little pieces. The doll was bleeding everywhere, also between its legs. There was a hand with big
scissors carving between those legs. Till there was a big
hole there and more blood kept on pumping out. I got
sick. I thought I was going to vomit. Then I woke up. I
couldn't go back to sleep. I kept on seeing that doll. Only
now it had Tom's face who had been at my titties. I
started sweating, I felt very strange. I felt very hot, as if
I had a fever. And I got all wet down there. I was tossing
and turning in bed. I kept on seeing Tom and that lump
in his trousers. I went to the bathroom and dried myself.
When I touched myself down there, it got all tingly. As
that time when my fingers touched an electric plug. But
different. It felt weird but nice. As with Belinda when we
slept together. Very close together, all cuddly and warm.
Just the two of us.

Maybe she won't miss that one doll. There are so
many of them left. And it's been years since then. I have
been thinking about that. I can't remember how long it's
been. And I wonder. Do Daddy and Mom think it's my
fault Belinda was sent away? Is that why Mom hates
me? Why Daddy sometimes is mad at me? But I haven't
done anything. I haven't told. Well, not everything. It
was Belinda. She always dared more than me. When
Dan said he would show it to us, it was Belinda who
laughed. Who said he didn't dare. But he did. And he let
us play with it. Then when it began to rise and grow, we
laughed. It was so funny. But then Belinda began to act
weird, she got all red in her face. Then Dan grabbed
under her skirt and they made me turn away. But I looked
anyway and I saw it all, what they did. Everything! That's

what I told, I had to. Daddy was very angry and Mom got all white. I thought she was going to faint right there. When they took Dan away on that stretcher. He didn't say anything, he was more pale even than Mom. I felt so scared then. I tried to tell it all, but the words wouldn't come. Then they took Belinda away to that school. I haven't done anything wrong. I only told what Belinda had done, nothing more, nothing more! My mouth refused to tell the rest. It wasn't my fault at all!

Daddy and Mom told me very quietly. As if they thought I wouldn't be glad for Belinda to come home. Of course I'm glad. I'm very happy, and so excited!

SATURDAY MORNING.

They have left, to get Belinda. Finally, finally! I know she won't be mad at me because I told some of the things she did with Dan. Besides, everybody could see it in her face. And it was years ago.

I've done some checking. It wasn't easy. I'm not very good with numbers and years. But I have kept all my birthday cards. In a big paper box under my bed. I am not seventeen years old. I looked through all the cards I got through the years. From Daddy and Mom and Belinda. Tell me again I'm a stupid retard! I can SEE which ones are true and which are false. I just compare the ones Belinda gave to me before she left. I know her handwriting so well. Then I look at the cards Daddy and Mom signed with Belinda's name. The ones they said she had sent me from that school. I know she never sent me a card from there! But I acted as if I believed them. The last real card from Belinda she gave to me when I was twelve. Then she was fourteen. Five cards with fake handwriting. So she has been at that school for five years. That long! Why did she never send me a card herself? Or answer one of my letters? I wrote so many to her but I never got one back. Why did they never take me with them when they went to visit her?

Because they didn't want me to! That's why! Mom hates me because what I said about Belinda. And Daddy always gives Mom her way. He always says I'm his daughter. But he never really protects me against Mom. Mom always talk about Belinda. Only Belinda counts. As if I don't exist. As if I'm not her daughter. Still, I love Belinda. That scares me. What if she doesn't love me after that time?

Dan's gone too. His parents moved away shortly after . . . that.

I wonder what kind of school Belinda went to. They were talking about it when they left this morning. Very softly so I didn't get much of it. I just heard Daddy say something like: fully normal progress, and: no more problems.

Normal? What problems? Why can't grown-ups say it like it is? Why don't they tell me? I want to understand, dear Diary, but they make such a big secret out of it. They act as if I don't understand anything. As if I do everything wrong. Why normal? Belinda's always been normal. Or does he mean she can talk again? Would that be it, Diary? That would be wonderful.

It will be so marvellous when they get here with Belinda. My sweet sister, my sweet Belinda. I've put all our dolls in bath. Dried their hair and brushed it. Put all new clothes on them. They look lovely. Belinda will be delighted. We'll reread our favourite books. I wonder if they had books like ours at that school. We'll have fun together. Then together in bed we'll whisper in the dark. Just as if nothing happened. We'll be nice to each other and play those little games Belinda taught me. Those games which made me feel tingly and good.

Belinda will understand. Why I had to tell things about her and Dan. I hope they taught her to speak again. Not like that time with Dan. Sitting there screaming with her mouth wide open, but making no sound at all. Her lips moving but no words coming out. Moving her hands like butterfly wings. But she couldn't say anything, so I had to take care of that.

I do hope she can do better now. Does it take five years to learn to speak again? Belinda is older, but maybe she's not really as smart as I am. Maybe she needed so much time.

Anyway, I'm sure she still loves me. Maybe she never got my letters. Or maybe Mom and Daddy never gave me her letters. It doesn't matter now. Soon she'll be with me again. So happy. So happy!

SATURDAY AFTERNOON.

I read what I wrote this morning, dear Diary. I'm crying again. I can't help it. I feel so miserable. Belinda's home but she doesn't love me. She hates me. She hates me! I was so glad when she came in. I almost didn't recognise her. She's grown so much. She looks so much older. That dress she wears, that makeup. It makes her look like Mom. She acts absent. I heard Daddy use that word. As if she isn't all here. As if part of her is somewhere else. She speaks, but only a few words. In very short sentences. As if it gives her trouble. I would think after five years she'd do better than that.

I showed her our room. Our dolls. All the dolls said hello when she came in. But it was as if she didn't hear. I'd gone to all that trouble. Washing the dolls and dressing them up. Making them pretty for Belinda. She didn't look at them at all. She didn't even notice that one of her favourites was missing. I told her about our books and how much fun we would have together. She didn't smile once. It was so weird. The way she didn't seem to hear what I was saying. The way she looked at things. Her head making shaky little movements, as a bird does. She kept her hands clasped together. All fingers into each other. When she looked at me, she got a fine wrinkle between her eyes. As if she was trying to remember me. She doesn't speak to me. When I kissed her, she was standing there as stiff as a doll. In that silly grown-up dress. I think it's supposed to look joyful. All flowers in strong colours melding together. But it makes her look so old-fashioned. She is not the Belinda I remember. She is a strange grown-up woman. She's gotten huge tits. She wears panties.

When I touched her arm, she really shivered and drew back. I thought: That's the homecoming. After five years in that school everything here is strange, like new. When we were alone, in the circle of our dolls. I told her about before. How sweet and nice we were to each other. Our whispers in the bed. What we did together in the dark. How we slept afterwards, huddled together, so warm and soft. How much we loved each other. I really begged her to say something to me. To know she still loved me.

And then she said those things to me. With that weird, cold voice of hers. A voice like Mom's. Not loud but so very cold. Words I can't write down, dear Diary. Mean, filthy words. Each word cut me like an ice pick. So mean, so cruel! Then she just turned and left me with our dolls. My dolls.

I don't understand, dear Diary. Why would she say that I was mean and nasty? What's wrong with her? She hates me as Mom hates me. Then Daddy came up and he wasn't nice either. He asked what I had said or done. But I had done nothing! He'll start to hate me too, like all the others. You must help me, dear Diary. I feel so alone. I'm scared. All our dolls are in the corner now. All their heads are with me, in bed. They keep me company. They weep with me.

SATURDAY NIGHT.

Everything's fine now, dear Diary. Oh, I'm so glad it all worked out right. Belinda's not here with me. She sleeps in the spare bedroom. Where Mom sometimes sleeps after a fight with Daddy. Belinda didn't want to sleep with me. That hurts very much. But I understand. It's been so long. She has to adapt. That's what Daddy said when Belinda was out of the room. She has to get used to us again. After five years. Maybe she couldn't love me after that thing with Dan. But it was for her, wasn't it?

Because I loved her so much. My sweet Belinda. I'd do anything for her. Then and now.

I'm smart. I've been thinking about it after I stopped crying. At that time I thought maybe it's like a hunger. Belinda used to bite me. When we were playing in bed, you know, in the dark. It was fun. Her small, sharp teeth biting in my neck and shoulders. Never hard, you know, just for fun. Sometimes she began panting very hard then.

As she did with Dan. When he showed his and then grabbed under her skirt. Then, when Dan was lying op top of her and they were moving and shaking. She bit him too, on his ears and lips. Making funny gasping noises. When they stopped and he rolled away on the grass. Just lying there with his eyes closed. Breathing very hard and his thing in the open. Wet and still stiff. I thought she'd like to have it forever. Maybe we could use it to have fun together.

So I went into the shed and got the scissors Daddy used for cutting the flowers. And I cut it off. Gave it to Belinda. She liked to bite what she loved. So I put it in her open mouth. It went so easy, so quick. Then Dan sat up and started screaming. Belinda started screaming too, but her mouth was full. There was blood everywhere. I never thought there would be so much blood! She started waving with her hands like mad. Grasping at my hands, and so I put the scissors in her hand. The way she acted made me scared and I ran away.

Then all those people came. Dan was very white and very still. I don't know if he was dead. And Belinda was choking on Dan's thing in her mouth. The red dripping

from her mouth like spaghetti sauce. When they took it
out of her mouth, she kept on screaming without making
any sound. That scared me even more. They asked all
those questions. I just shook my head. But they persisted, especially that nice lady in uniform. Finally I told
them a few things about what Belinda and Dan had been
doing. I said that it scared me and I ran away. They asked
me where Belinda had gotten the scissors. I didn't know.
Had she been fighting with Dan? I didn't know. So finally they let me alone.

Now Belinda can talk again. But mostly she keeps
silent. The only thing she said was that I was sick. When
I mentioned Dan, she started shaking her head. She put
both hands to her ears. She didn't want to hear. And she
looked real funny as if she was trying to remember
something. Then she just walked away from me.

Is it possible that she doesn't know? That she has forgotten it? Maybe at that school they taught her to forget
everything. Then she doesn't remember that I did it because I loved her so much. That I only wanted to do her
a favor. That hurts.

I think she's just an egoist. No more. She just thinks
of herself. She doesn't care about me. She refuses to
touch me. She won't even look straight at me. Maybe
she thinks I'm silly too, like the others do. It's Mom and
Daddy's fault. They sent Belinda to that school. They
made her hate me.

Only Belinda was really nice to me. Belinda was mine
till Dan came along. I only wanted her to love me more.
Even when she and Dan were doing it. They saw me
watching and they laughed. But I wasn't hurt. I wasn't

ashamed. I was happy for Belinda because she liked it. I thought if that is what she wants from Dan, I'll give it to her. As a present.

I know now that I made a mistake. I don't know what I did wrong, but I did something wrong. I'll fix it. I'll make her love me again. She kicked at our dolls, she didn't look at our books. She didn't notice all our birthday cards. But I don't care. She can't have changed that much.

Once she understands how much I need her, she'll come back to me. Mom and Daddy did this to her. They sent her away. They never took me along to visit her. No wonder she's angry with me. She thinks I have forgotten her all those years. That isn't true. I have always been thinking about her. I'll make her understand that.

SUNDAY EARLY MORNING.

Mom and Daddy were fast asleep. They had been talking for a long time before they slept. It all went so easy. I used a chair to get to the knife rack in the kitchen. I just took the biggest one. It's almost as long as my forearm. Then I took it upstairs.

I was very quiet and careful. I had to be very fast too. Didn't want to wake them. But they slept so deeply. First Mom, then Daddy. After I had done Mom I had to wring the knife because it stuck. But I got it out without waking Daddy. He just snored and turned over in his sleep. It was a messy job, all wet and sticky afterwards. It was hard work and it took some time. But I think I managed it quite well. Now Belinda will know how much I love her. I took a shower first before I went to Belinda's room.

She was sound asleep. She looked so restful and lovely. I arranged all the heads of our dolls on her bed, around her. Very quiet, very careful. But she didn't wake up. She was snoring softly. Then I put those of Mom and Daddy between the doll heads. On the spot of honor so she will see those first when she wakes up. It wasn't easy, they kept falling over. I had to use a spare pillow to support them.

Now I'm sitting in a chair beside Belinda. It's hard writing in the dark, dear Diary, but I manage. Soon it'll be light. I wait for Belinda to wake up. For the big surprise.

I have Daddy's here. It looks like Dan's but a bit bigger. I've cleaned it under the faucet. When Belinda wakes up, I'll put it in her mouth. So she can bite on it as with Dan. I can't wait to see her happy, shining face!

THE CHEERLEADERS, THE GEEK, AND THE LONESOME PINEY WOODS

By d. g. k. goldberg

Amber looked up from her glossy magazine, "It says here that even ugly girls secretly think they're pretty." I felt like the room was tilting and that I'd swallowed a lump of lead; my body couldn't contain the unbearable heaviness. I kept smiling.

Amber stretched out a tanned leg and squinted at her bright orange toenails. They resembled candy corn. "This polish doesn't work, does it?" Amber had a fall of shimmery, sunlit hair that framed her unremarkable round face. Her lithe figure topped with two cupcake breasts made up for the angry red pimples peeking and winking, twinkling like stars beneath a layer of makeup. She was blond. That said it all, didn't it?

Tiffany continued meditating in the mirror, licking her lips and flinging her hair this way and that. The cheerleader flick. "It's okay. The polish." Tiffany didn't even glance at Amber's toenails.

"What do you think?" Amber rolled over on to her flat tummy and stretched like a tigress.

"Nice polish," I said. I hated her. It rose in my throat like hangover vomit, it squeezed my guts, it coiled in my belly like a snake ready to spring out of my mouth and spew venom at her. I hate hate hated her, and I hated the world where she was pimply but pretty, where something—I didn't know what—was wrong with my olive skin, and frothing mad black hair, and wounded Madonna cow eyes, and all the other bits and fits of me that weren't blond, weren't perky, weren't right. I wanted to smash her face in. It was hot in the bedroom—poisonously toxically hot, like radiation poisoning—and the air smelled of hair spray and bubble gum and Shalimar.

Amber rolled her eyes.

Bitch. Edible bitch with her Halloween candy toes and her cupcake breasts. She had soft, pink nipples—I saw them last night when she shrugged off her sweater and popped on her stupid flowered nighty. She hadn't turned modestly to the wall like most girls, just pulled off one set of things and pulled on another. Casually. But not really casual. It wasn't as if she didn't know. Bitch. Homecoming Queen bitch, even with pimples. Pimples plus pink nipples. What was it they said, the boys who smoked behind the gym? Oh, yeah. They said that virgins had pink nipples, and that when a girl started screwing they turned brown. Yeah, right. I thought of my horrible coffee-colored nipples and winced. "Really, the nail polish is cool," I said, wondering that my hatred didn't run out of my mouth and drip down my chest, staining my shirt.

"No, Josey," Amber said. "Do ugly girls secretly think they're cute? You should know." She twisted around and sat yoga-style on the ruffled bedspread. Everything in her room was pink.

"Not really," I said, blinking back tears. It was cringe-makingly, throat-closingly awful. Shame blistered my skin. Sweat flooded my armpits. Breathing became difficult. "No, we really don't." I didn't fault her for it. It wasn't like I didn't know that I was the ugly friend. I knew it was almost time for me to gather my stuff and trudge on toward home: Amber and Tiffany were expecting boys.

I stuffed yesterday's sweater and the oversized t-shirt that I slept in into my book bag. I picked up my toothbrush and hairbrush from the corner of Amber's dresser.

"Are you sure that, like, deep inside or something, you don't think you're cute? Like that girl in the movie who practices sexy looks in the mirror when no one is around?" Amber ran her fingers through her silky blond hair.

I concentrated on breathing. In. Out. My muscles, particularly the ones in my neck and shoulders, felt tight. I stared at the corner of Amber's bedspread, memorizing it, pretending that I'd have to take a test on stuff in my friend's room. Describe the bedspread in fifty words. Rank the hand mirror, nail polish, trash can, and stuffed animals in order of price and coolness. I always did well on tests.

"What movie?" Tiffany opened a bag of Skittles and started lining them up according to color. "I can only eat primary colors," she said. "It's like a candy diet."

"You know," Amber persisted. "That movie with what's her name in it. You know, Josey, don't you?"

"No," I said. My cheeks felt hot. Damn. I prayed that I wasn't blushing. "Don't know what movie that might have been."

Amber sighed dramatically. "I thought you always remembered everything. Hey, can I borrow those earrings you had on yesterday?"

"No problem," I said. I pulled them out of the small zippered compartment on my book bag.

"Thanks."

Amber admired my earrings in her ears, turning her head from side to side and staring into her blue, blue eyes in the mirror while I slunk out the door.

I should have called home to see if Mom could come get me.

I needed to get out of that house.

Away.

Book bag thumping against my side I stomped down the sidewalk. I enjoyed the crunch of acorns. I wanted to smash Amber's face in. I swallowed hard and kept walking. I thought about some pictures I'd seen in driver's ed of gross accident victims, their faces smears of hamburger meat with a few lonely teeth clinging to cavernous mouths half-open in shock. I clenched and unclenched my fists. I didn't really want to smash her face in. I wiped my hands on my jeans. I didn't want her blood and snot on my hands. I didn't want her teeth falling onto my flesh.

I kept walking toward home.

Maybe if I hit her with something, a tire iron or something. I went weird and jerky at the thought. I didn't want the mess of splattering Amber all over me. I felt like blood and stuff—gross stuff—would spew all over me if I kept thinking these thoughts.

The air was heavy. I started to sweat. Blondes never seem to sweat. It's the dark, nasty girls like me who sweat and smell and have to spend half their money on panty liners to soak up the odd little secretions and smells we can't quite scrub off, have to spend money on shameful things—wax for our upper lips, hair remover for our thighs. Blondes seem to scarcely even menstruate, they're always so cool and clean and crisp and always smell nice.

A car sped by—a Honda Civic, Jason's car. He's Amber's almost-boyfriend; another guy was with him. I stood on the corner waiting to cross—a gawky geek, book bag slung off one shoulder hunched over to hide my almost flat chest. I gnawed on a cuticle and watched the car. It seemed that Jason looked at me and smirked. I may have imagined. I must have imagined—they went by so fast that I really couldn't know what he looked like. But I somehow knew that they were talking about me, talking and laughing and saying horrible things.

What I knew best was the sound of tree branches scratching my bedroom window when the wind blew; the abrasive patter of the all-night DJ on the local alternative rock station; the crazy, breathless ladies who

called talk radio in the wee hours to complain about bira-
cial couples or claim that Martians were invading their
subdivisions; the thick, heavy cotton of sweat and sleep
that sprawled across the South until the first frost bent
the skeletal remains of tomato plants in the backyard.

I stayed up late most nights. Reading excessively.
Doing homework that my teachers forgot to assign. If I
couldn't be pretty, it I couldn't be blond, if my nipples
were wrong and my skin too sallow, I could still be
smart. The smarter I was, the safer I felt.

It didn't fix everything; it didn't fix anything. I always finished tests before the rest of the class. I had to:
getting everything right in half the time made the rest of
them twice as stupid. In English, after I finished the
midterm in a remarkable twenty-three minutes, I sauntered across the room to put my paper on Mrs. Flodder's
desk.

Kurt sat next to me.

He'd sat next to me all year.

I think he tried to copy my tests.

He had soft brown hair that swooped over his forehead, and I wanted to brush it back with my hand. He
was tall enough that I felt small sitting next to him. I
knew just where I would come to if he'd held me: the
spot right beneath his collarbone. When his shirt escaped
from its buttons, I could see his smooth flesh, taut across
the bones. I wanted to press my lips just beneath his collarbone.

When I sat back down, ready to stare at the clock for
the remainder of the class, Kurt whispered, "Josey, I just
noticed something about you."

My heart hamstered in my chest. I was certain that the pounding was audible. I knew I was shaking. "Oh," I said, my throat closing.

"Yeah, you have a really flat butt. It's not like a girl's ass at all. It's weird—when you walked to the front of the room, you looked just like my kid brother."

I stared at the clock. It was like that dream everyone is supposed to have where they are caught in public naked. I have never had that dream. He was dating Tiffany.

My parents worried. I felt their worry descend the stairs and hover in the corners of the kitchen where I sat night after night listening to the radio and reading. Worry more like a jinn or a malevolent kelpie swayed Hasidic in the kitchen. An entity, their worry, a dark oppressive dangerous thing. A constant reminder of my anomalous oddness, my lack of friends, my not-well-roundedness. What were these horrid things, and how had they come across the centuries to fester in a Southern suburban kitchen? Poltergeists thrive on adolescence, feeding on teenage energy and angst. Or maybe I poisoned the air around me.

I could have told my parents that it would all be okay, that one day all the cheerleaders would be chipmunk-cheeked soccer moms ferrying their children hither and yon while I did great things—wrote a novel, cured cancer, and sculpted a pietà. But the worry knew better—it knew that in life rewards come to the already rewarded, that student council presidents run corporations and cheerleaders morph into marketing executives clicking through corridors on spindly stilettos and charging thousand-dollar pocketbooks without peeking at the price. The worry knew that I'd graduate summa cum something, and end up strangling in some labyrinthine civil service bureaucracy, while all the well-rounded kids lived in McMansions and ran the world, or at least the city.

I scribbled poetry and computer code in my note-books, endless notebooks with neat handwriting and train-wrecked dreams. Mostly I dreamed of justice, of something awful happening to Amber and Tiffany, of fairytaling into a swan—a blond, breasted swan.

My parents worried and bought me a car. Ever prag-matic, Amber and Tiffany allowed me to tread along in their wake as long as I had gas money. I pulled into Amber's driveway, almost clipping the huge Fraser fir that her parents decorated with lights each Christmas. Amber took her own sweet time prancing down the driveway from the family room door, the heels of her boots absurdly high, her skirt riding up the expanse of her thighs. Amber slid in shotgun and flicked the radio over to a top forty station. "Kurt and Jason are meeting us in the parking lot of Wendy's, but we have to pick up Tiffany first." A zit pierced her makeup like the mark of Cain. She was very blond.

I backed out slowly. "Christ," she said, "you drive like a librarian." She popped a breath mint into her mouth.

Tiffany was waiting at the edge of her parents' yard. "Hit it," she said squirming into the front seat, smashing Amber against me. The scent of Shalimar mingling with the sharp smell of twilight, heavy, wanton and wanting, the sky reclining into the tops of clawed pine trees, the streetlights blinking on sleepily, awakened by the silent exit of the sun. Tiffany lifted her arm onto the dashboard and squinted at her watch. "We need to hurry."

Amber's leg was warm against mine. "Nice earrings," she said. "Tiffany, look at Josey's earrings. Doesn't she have the coolest stuff?"

"Yeah." Tiffany giggled. "Cool."

I allowed myself to feel a tiny ember of warmth, as a faint ghost of something like acceptance made a sudden guest appearance in my life. I stopped at a yellow light. I usually didn't, and I immediately regretted it. More librarian driving. But I wasn't in a hurry—I wanted to prolong the moment—didn't want to reach Wendy's where the boys were waiting for the delivery of the blondes, and I'd once more slide into oblivion, and once more be the ugly friend.

The light changed. Two left turns, and I pulled into the parking lot. Jason and Kurt were leaning against Jason's car. Tiffany hopped out and climbed into the backseat. Amber slid out and went over to Jason, giving him a pornographic kiss. It seemed choreographed. "We're taking both cars," Kurt said as he opened the back door and moved into my car to embrace Tiffany. "Head out to the rock."

I sighed and turned up the radio, hoping that it would drown out the slurping noises of Kurt and Tiffany sucking face in the backseat. I kept stealing glances at them in my rearview mirror. Arms and legs going this way and that, like some strange multiarmed beast, flashes of flesh, the high-pitched sounds of forced giggles. I drove down the highway out of town.

I followed Jason's taillights. Amber's head had vanished. The car seemed to contain only one person.

I wondered why no one had mentioned stopping to get beer or anything, but the noises from the backseat made me feel like an interloper in my own car. Fine then, drive out to the rock and do God knows what while they all get it on. Why in the hell did they even want me to come with them? The road darkened. Just past a boarded-up store that nobody remembered ever being open, I took a sharp left down a dirt road. Took the corner too hard, and my back end nearly fishtailed. The car went *bump bump bump* through the mud and potholes. Tiffany squealed, and Kurt murmured something disgusting and boyfriendish to her. Yeah, tell her everything is fine, I could take this thing right into a tree.

High beams on, I hit the brakes hard. Tiffany thumped against the backseat. "Sorry." I cracked the window; the air was heavy with the scent of pine, long-leaf pines, Carolina hemlock, tiny scrub trees covered in kudzu making weird monster shapes in the fringes of the car's headlights. I crept along, trying to stay on the road. Following the dirt that snaked through the trees until the half-road ended, I pulled up next to Jason's car. He and Amber were sitting on the hood. I cut the lights and got out.

Amber came toward me, a can in her hand. She held it out to me. I was sure it was beer, that all of this was just us going to the rock to drink a six-pack. I took a swallow; it was some kind of diet cola.

THE CHEERLEADERS, THE GEEK, . . .

"It's really awful," Amber said.

"It's not so bad," I said and leaned against the trunk of a pine tree, the bark prickling through my shirt.

"It is awful. You don't know yet." Amber made that sound confident girls make—halfway between "tch" and a sucking noise—when someone else is being totally lame.

I winced. I had thought she meant that the soda was awful. I was always doing that: getting things wrong and feeling like the butt of a joke.

"Come on," Jason said.

Amber and I followed him with Kurt and Tiffany slightly behind us, their arms around each other, wobbling like some odd, two-headed creature. I slipped on some wet leaves and bruised my palms. Stigmata. I wondered what they'd say if I held out my hands and said "stigmata." They wouldn't have a clue what the word meant—they'd all just give a look that suggested that I once again had said something stupid.

We squeezed through trees grown dense and stubborn, until we reached the crest of a small hill. Jason inched down sideways, holding out his hand to assist Amber as she picked her way down in her absurd heeled boots. She'd ruin those damn boots, and her mom would get her another pair. I tried getting down the slippery slope, skittering like a drunken crab, and fell on my ass. Kurt picked Tiffany up and carried her down the hill caveman style, while I tried to brush the grit off the seat of my jeans. We passed through a stand of pines, crunching beer cans beneath our shoes, and emerged into a clearing dominated by a huge gray rock.

Jason lit a candle. Oh no, not another dreary pseudo-séance where we try to summon a dead Cherokee chieftain or an abused slave girl buried with her master's bastard child. According to the fools I went to school with, every inch of North Carolina is either a slave graveyard or an ancient Native American holy site.

"Let's go around to the other side of the rock." Jason cupped his hand around the candle.

I scrambled over the rock, tearing the flesh on my injured hands. When Amber, Tiffany, and I were on the far side, Jason and Kurt sat above us on the rock, their legs dangling and their faces rendered spooky by the candle-light.

Kurt pulled out a handgun and laid it on his lap.

"It's not that we don't trust y'all," Jason said, "but we're in deep shit, and we need some help. But we can't let it look like y'all helped us out of your own free will, because then y'all might get arrested."

Amber grabbed my arm, digging her nails into my flesh. Tiffany made a whimpering noise. My mouth went dry. I thought I heard an owl.

"You see," Jason continued, "we sort of robbed a store, and we've got to go on the run and we had to say good-bye, and we figured that with Josey's car we'd have a head start on getting out of here. We knew you'd lend us your car, Josey, but we couldn't have it look like you were a . . . whatever it is."

"Accessory after the fact," I said. I sounded like I was answering a classroom question. My tongue felt thick in my mouth.

"Keys," Kurt said.

Tiffany moaned. Amber gripped my arm tighter. My chest hurt.

"We need your keys, Josey."

"Oh, right." I handed them over.

"Now, we need to make it look like y'all are innocent. So line up against the rock with your backs against it," Jason said.

I heard a click, like Kurt was doing something with the gun.

Amber, Tiffany, and I obediently pressed ourselves against the rock. It was surprisingly cool.

"So y'all can't even see what direction we take off in, we need you to shut your eyes," Jason said.

Obediently, I shut my eyes.

"Okay, now we need to get a real head start so that y'all are safe. So keep your eyes shut and take off your shirts and hand them to us."

I didn't think. I couldn't swallow. I jerked my shirt off and raised it over my head for Jason to grab.

Then I heard laughter. A huge wall of laughter crashing against me. Amber's squeals, Tiffany's giggles, Kurt and Jason laughing so hard they snorted.

I opened my eyes.

Neither Amber nor Tiffany had taken off their blouses.

"Oh my God, oh my God," Amber said. "That's just the funniest damn thing ever. You really believed it. Oh my God."

I snatched my keys and my shirt, then ran around the rock and up the hill. Their laughter swelled around me like a vicious sea. I didn't even put my shirt on until I was safely in my car with the doors locked.

I managed to smile weakly when I passed Amber or Tiffany in the hallways at school. I changed my college plans—screw Chapel Hill, I needed to be as far away from North Carolina as I could get. I did what most disgruntled Southern outcasts seem to do; I went to school up North and felt sad and transplanted. I longed for the smell of pine needles and the evening coo of doves. But during vacations, I hated home. I slunk around my parents' house, dreading trips to bookstores because I might run into someone I'd known in high school. I could still hear the laughter.

Unlike most bitter southerners I never even started writing a novel. I became a scientist—a botanist, a suspect profession in a state where tobacco had changed from being king to being a pariah.

When I did write, it was scientific papers primarily about the immediate and critical threat posed by the hemlock woolly adelgid (*Adelges tsugae*) in the Southern Appalachians, a nasty little booger that's decimating Carolina hemlocks. I had odd moments of cheering it on whenever a particular stand of trees put me in mind of my horrible high school humiliation. I'd be hiking through the Great Smokey Mountain National Park and come across a cluster of hemlocks denuded and dying and find myself thinking, "Good, goddamn you. Die. All of you die." Then, I'd shudder and wince. It wasn't the trees that had hurt me.

I trudged through the forest occasionally slipping and

bruising my palms following the path of the adelgid, documenting the damage.

Late in the evening, I sat on my porch. During the spring and fall I strained against the laughter, until I sometimes heard the crackle of luna moths abandoning their cocoons. Then, lighting a candle, I sometimes saw those fairylike moths, their wings luminous, flittering off to mate and die. The adult luna moth doesn't eat at all; it only lives in its beautiful fey incarnation for about a week. It mates. It dies.

I'd learned a lot from nature. So I had no friends, no lovers, and I certainly didn't bother with high school reunions. Twice a year, the sound of luna moths escaping cocoons drowned out the laughter that had become my constant companion.

Laughter like tinnitus filled my ears as I sat on the porch waiting for moths. Instead of a moth, I thought I saw something ethereal—a shape like a girl hovering near a hickory tree, weaving in and out of the branches. Too much time alone. I drank a beer and stared at the spot where I thought I'd seen something. Nothing. Just darkness and a noise that could have been an owl.

The next time my mother called, she mentioned that Tiffany had died of breast cancer. Someone from my high school class reunion committee had called Mom soliciting money for a scholarship fund in Tiffany's honor. I didn't make a donation.

The laughter wasn't quite so loud.

I was rotated out of the hemlock project and put on a team cataloguing the over one thousand flowering plant species in the park. When I couldn't politely avoid it, I went into Gatlinburg with the folks I worked with, for a few beers. Even the most tourist-infested, bad-cover-band bars couldn't drown out the sounds of laughter. I always managed to leave early, and drove home along winding roads with the sound of laughter accompanying me. Sometimes I wondered if my hatred had become the cancer in Tiffany's breast. I hoped that it had.

After a particularly horrible week of slogging through mud to photograph plants, and a terminally boring evening of expensive beer, I woke up late. I staggered onto my porch to find that I'd clipped my mailbox when I'd turned into my drive. Must have had a bit more to drink than I thought. I checked my car; I'd given the driver's side door a huge dent. Odd: I didn't even remember it. All I recalled about the drive home is that the laughter seemed to have faded a bit.

Like a dutiful daughter, I called home on Sunday. I only half listened to Mom. I was straining to hear the laughter. It sounded odd; something had changed. "It really was horrible," Mom said.

"What was?"

"Haven't you been listening? You remember Amber? You were best friends with her all though high school. She went right through the window of her SUV; it smashed her face beyond recognition. No one knows what made her go off the road. It's horrible. She left two little children."

"Horrible."

The laughter remained. Deeper. Male. Like the laughter of frat boys playing who-can-nail-the-ugliest-girl; like the wheezing, snorting laughter of a salesman explaining how he stiffed the lap dancer with a phony credit card number; like the blistering sound of Jason and Kurt when I'd stood goose-pimpled and shirtless in the cool night air.

I didn't wait to talk to Mom when the laughter next decreased. I got on the Internet and checked the obituaries in my hometown paper. Kurt had been a cop. Killed in the line of duty trying to apprehend a robber at a convenience store. Now *that* was funny.

I lived with Jason's laughter. It was like having a friend.

I went back to my solitary pursuit of a plan to defeat the adelgids. I wrote a paper studying the potential for biocontrol with *Pseudoscymnus tsugae* as opposed to horticultural soap. My research was well received, and I got a chance to present my findings at a conference of arborists and botanists in my hometown. It was my first trip home in years.

After my presentation, I left the convention center and drove through the uptown area to Morehead Street and followed it to Dilworth, then I parked beside a Starbucks. Charlotte didn't seem like home anymore. It could have been any city in America with Starbucks, Holiday Inns, and Nordstroms erupting against the red clay and blocking the view of pine trees. I took my coffee—some odious, funky brew with odd flavors shoved into it—outside. I could barely hear the laughter over the sound of passing cars.

The patio bled into the sidewalk. I waited for my coffee to cool, and watched a jogger pass. I stared across the street and saw a bedraggled man, his clothes flapping scarecrowishly around his scrawny body. He stopped to pick up a cigarette butt from the pavement. Weaving slightly, he braced himself against a telephone pole and lit the scavenged butt. He jerked a bit, then stuck his finger in his mouth. I thought I heard him say, "Fucking splinter."

Still weaving, he stumbled into the street and was nearly hit by a car. He staggered on. As he approached, I could see his bloodshot eyes, matted filthy hair, and yellow teeth. He muttered something unintelligible. I chucked some change onto the pavement and watched him scoop it up eagerly before the lurched down the road, barely able to walk.

I still heard the faint sound of Jason's laughter.

I smiled and sipped my coffee. I hoped that I would hear his faint laughter for many many years.

SENTINELS

By Mark Samuels

Inspector Gray's involvement in the affair was due to a combination of ill fortune and the photographic cover of a London "urban legends" paperback called *The Secret Underground*. He should not really have been in that part of London at the time, but had been forced to stay late in the office and complete a batch of gruelling paperwork, required by his superior the following morning. Had he driven past a matter of seconds before, he would have seen nothing. After all, he was off duty and his main concern was to get back to his dingy flat in Tufnell Park, sink a few glasses of whiskey and forget about that day.

He planned to lose himself in some cheap and trashy horror paperback from his little collection. The TV had broken down months ago and instead of replacing it he found that he had got into the habit of reading musty book relics from the '60s and '70s, with their yellowing, brittle pages and lurid covers. Gray fancied himself something of a connoisseur when it came to the covers; in fact he felt himself in opposition with the old maxim about never judging books by them. He harboured the conviction that those featuring a weird photographic composition were invariably superior to those that had artwork depicting the tired-cliché symbols of horror: skulls, snakes or gothic castles for example.

In fact, he had come in for some jokes at his expense back at the Yard over his choice of reading matter. Most of his colleagues talked about little except what they'd watched on TV the night before, often sleazy porn videos that they'd "borrowed" from the Obscene Publications division. They'd taken to calling him "The Weird Detective" behind his back; on one occasion he'd turned around sharply to find a group of constables miming having vampire fangs by putting their index fingers at the corners of their mouths. Gray made sure thereafter that he wasn't seen reading any of his books during the little time he had for lunch. Instead he read one of the broadsheet papers as he consumed his sandwiches at his desk. His alienation from his colleagues caused him pain and he suspected that the department would run more smoothly were he not there.

What Gray saw as he passed by in his car appeared to be some sort of stunted, emaciated creature peering through the trellis gates of Kentish Town Underground station. The thing was only around four or five feet tall and dressed in ragged black overalls. Its face was obscured by a mass of dusty shoulder-length hair.

It was gone one a.m. when Gray passed the Underground station, and it had been closed for only a short time. He had pulled over to the side of the road and looked back in order to see whether the apparition was still there, but there was no sign of it at all. Doubtless, he thought, his colleagues back at the Yard would have

laughed at what he thought he'd seen; too many of those
damn books he read. But Gray felt his heart racing in his
chest. He could not dismiss the thing that easily from his
mind. What he'd seen was no product of the imagination. It had really been there.

Although the station was closed, it might not yet be
deserted. Once the train service finished, there were still
staff working on the platforms and in the tunnels. An
army of cleaners called Fluffers made their way along
the lines and scoured them for debris. All manner of lit-
ter had to be cleared away: beer cans, half-eaten junk
food, newspapers, even tumbleweeds composed of skin
and human hair. There were also the Gangers—the en-
gineers who checked track safety. Perhaps Gray had simply glimpsed one of those overnight workers having a
break, one whose similarity to the uncanny thing on the
front cover of *The Secret Underground* was nothing
more than a trick of the light.

Nevertheless, what he had observed remained in his
thoughts, causing uneasy dreams when he finally slept:
dreams of endless subterranean tunnels and of a gaunt silence punctuated by a distant rustling or whispering
noise. Had he not seen whatever it was at the station (or
whatever he *thought* it was), the case that came to his attention afterwards might not have seemed significant
and worth pursuit.

As he sat at his desk the next morning, sipping at a
cup of vile instant coffee, Gray flicked through the case
files in his in-box. He had a feeling that had become increasingly commonplace during the course of the last

few months. It was that the investigations to which he had been assigned were effectively a waste of effort. The assault that he'd suffered months ago during the arrest of Montrose the serial rapist had left him hospitalised for weeks and resulted in internal ruptures that would, he had been advised by the surgeon, require a much more sedate lifestyle. The Yard had done the best they could under the circumstances and found him a role, albeit deskbound, but although his initial assignments had been current, Gray discovered that as time passed he was being asked to examine cases that had little chance of being solved. The bulk of these were missing persons.

Scarcely sociable before, Gray had turned further inwards after the beating. It had affected his mind just as much as his body. Somehow he had allowed his old friends to drift away, and found excuses not to keep in touch with them. He felt himself to be little more than an empty shell, and contact with others only served to reinforce the impression. The Yard offered Gray counselling to help him come to terms with the trauma caused by the Montrose incident, but he found the idea even more repellent than his doctor's suggestion that he take a course of antidepressants. When fate worked upon him, he intended to adapt to it and not resist. Even so, he felt like a missing person who had himself been assigned to trace other missing persons.

Gray ran his tongue over his scalded lips, again cursing the too-hot and foul-tasting coffee, when his attention was taken up by a communiqué that had come in only a few hours earlier. Although a missing persons report is not usually filed until some days after a disappearance (except where children are involved), this one had been fast-tracked due to there being no question of the subject having absented himself deliberately. The missing individual was a tube train driver (or "operator" as they were now called). His name was Adam Drayton. The curious thing was this: he had abandoned his train between the Camden Town and Kentish Town stations on the Northern Line. It had been the very last service of the night, due to terminate at High Barnet at one thirty a.m. Moreover, if there had been any passengers in the carriages then they too had vanished.

Early in the morning a replacement driver had shunted the train into a siding. On the front of the case file a joker in the office had scrawled the words "Mary Celeste Tube? A Case for the Weird Detective?" with a marker.

But Inspector Gray, through some bizarre coincidence, was one of the few people who would recognise the name "Adam Drayton" in another connection. For it was also the name of the editor of that outré book of urban legends published under the title *The Secret Underground,* whose cover preyed upon his mind.

Gray spent the afternoon interviewing Drayton's colleagues in the staff mess room of the train depot just outside Finchley Central station. This was where the tube drivers spent their time between shifts, sitting around drinking coffee, smoking their cigarettes and reading newspapers. They were a talkative bunch, although the inspector could not help noticing their mistrust and fear of him as a representative from an outside authority.

Some of them even seemed to believe that Drayton's disappearance was an internal matter and should be left to the union to investigate. Outside interference, whether from the law or elsewhere, was certainly not welcome. Still, there were one or two who retained a sense of individuality and were able to realise that Gray had not come in order to apportion any blame, merely to discover what may have led Drayton to act in the manner that he did.

One of the drivers, Carlos Miguel, a Castilian, was particularly communicative. He had settled in England after leaving Madrid in the early 1990s. He had been almost alone in befriending Drayton, who had been regarded by the others as an oddball whose political views were not sufficiently radical. Miguel was a tall, distinguished man in his forties with a shock of jet-black hair and a neatly trimmed moustache. He had shared Drayton's enthusiasm for the recondite, and whilst the others talked of union activities or the football results, the two men had retreated to a corner and held their own discussions.

Had Gray not been aware of Drayton's editorship of that paperback *The Secret Underground*, he doubted that he would have achieved quite the same rapport with Carlos Miguel.

"So," the Spaniard declared, "you know of *el libro de Drayton*."

"Yes," Gray replied, "I think it's a bit garish, but the cover's particularly—"

Miguel cut in.

"*Señor*, you know that Drayton only applied to become a train operator so that he could travel the tunnels of the Northern Line and examine their mysteries?"

Gray looked blank and shook his head.

"Well," Miguel went on, "you must understand that it would not be mistaken to say that he was obsessed with them. Drayton told me that the Northern Line has the longest continuous Yerkes tunnel on the network—over seventeen miles long. The stretch between East Finchley and Morden. Also it has the deepest. At Hampstead nine hundred feet below ground. He had numerous theories about what was down there; *fantástico, no?*"

"Speculations, rumour, hearsay," Gray responded, "amounting to nothing more than fiction. He was just an editor of a horrible book of urban legends. I confess that the parallel between his disappearance and obsession is striking, but—"

"*Perdón, señor*, but it is more than that simple fact. Drayton was my friend; it was in me that he felt he could confide. *Las estaciones fantasmas,* you know of them? In English: "the ghost stations"? North End, City Road, South Kentish Town and King William Street? These were what obsessed Drayton."

"The abandoned stations?"

"*Sí*, abandoned. *Pero* in Drayton's eyes, *no*. 'Taken over,' he would have replied. No longer safe to use. *Señor*, if you are operating the last train on the line it is easier to slow down when you wish, no? Perhaps while travelling through one of those stations, and even bringing trains to a complete stop. There are not so many passengers and they are too drunk or sleepy to complain at that time of night, *tú comprendes?*"

"Are you suggesting that Adam Drayton stopped his train and got out at one of these ghost stations?"

"Como una polilla atraída por la llama. . . . "

"I don't understand."

"Like a moth drawn to a flame."

That evening, once Gray had got back to his cramped flat in Tufnell Park, he sat down in his easy chair with his copy of *The Secret Underground*. He flicked back and forth through its brittle yellowed pages, glancing at them over and over again. The book was divided into several chapters, each specialising in a subterranean urban legend: "Cases of Posthumous Mutation in London Cemeteries"; "Derelict Reverse Skyscrapers 1936–1957"; "Mass Disappearance of Persons Sheltering in the Underground During the Blitz"; "Graffiti or Occult Symbolism?"; "Suppressed Eyewitness Accounts During the Construction of the Underground Railways 1860–1976"; "The Fleet Line Extension to Fenchurch Street Must Be Halted"; "Secret Bunkers or Extermination Centres?"; "The Deep-Level Platforms of the Proposed Express Tube: Why They Caused Insanity"; "The Hidden Shafts that Connect Subterranean London."

There was one paragraph in the final chapter that seemed to be the inspiration for the uneasy dreams Gray had experienced.

Most of the city is now underground and not above the surface, and I scarcely need list its innumerable tunnels, subterranean car parks, cellars, crypts, bunkers, basements, vaults, passageways, and sewers. Every building in London has an underside buried deep in the earth. Beneath our feet are the ruins of Anglo-Saxon Lundenwic and of Roman Londinium. The contemporary city will, in time, be swallowed up. This neon and concrete labyrinth will become an Atlantis of catacombs. The higher we build up, the deeper it is necessary to build down in order to support the structures above. All the nightmare sewage that we pump into the depths, all the foulness and corruption, the abortions, the faeces and scum, the blood and diseased mucus, but mostly the hair: what a feast for those underground beings that exist in darkness, and shun the sunlight! Those things below hate us and have every reason to do so.

His attention kept jumping from the text to the series of bizarre black-and-white photographs throughout the book. Quite where Drayton had obtained them was not made clear; they were not credited. They may even have come from his personal collection. What they showed was this:

Front cover: a blurred humanoid figure seen from a passing tube train whose face is almost completely covered by its hair. Between the strands there seems to be a mouth lined with sharklike fangs. The haggard creature is backing into a siding, away from the light.

Page 18: a photographic record of a series of exhumed graves with empty coffins whose bases had been torn apart.

Page 33: a blueprint of a forty-five-storey subterranean

reverse tower with access shafts radiating from it in all directions, some leading to burial grounds, others to sewers, etc., bearing the legend "North End (Hampstead)."

Page 49: what appears to be a series of bloody, smeared handprints on the white wall tiles of British Museum station during its use as an air-raid shelter circa 1941.

Page 87: human bones, including a skull, photographed lying alongside the tracks of an Underground tunnel.

Page 102: graffiti scrawled (in charcoal?) on the side of 1972 Mk. 1 train stock that reads "THE HUNGRY CANNOT SLEEP," "WE CRAWL THROUGH GRAVES," "THE DARKNESS BEHIND YOUR EYES" and "BELOW THERE IS ONLY PAIN."

Page 126: a sewer chamber choked by vast quantities of hair, hanging from a curved ceiling of Victorian brickwork.

It was relatively easy for Gray to obtain a search warrant in order to enter the disused South Kentish Town station. Although aboveground the building was now occupied by a massage parlor where once the ticket hall had been, all the subterranean shafts, corridors and other passageways were still owned by London Underground. Since their abandonment, there had been no reason to maintain them and parts of the former station were unsafe. In order to gain access, Gray had to agree to be accompanied by a track maintenance engineer who worked on that stretch of the Northern Line and who was familiar with the site.

This engineer, John Heath, arranged to meet Gray outside the massage parlor at the corner of Kentish Town Road and Castle Place. Gray parked his car directly in front of the building and was struck by the fact that its exterior still had the appearance of an Underground station, lacking only the familiar sign displayed outside. Hanging around in front of the entrance to the newsagent's was a small man in a yellow safety helmet and boilersuit. He carried a heavy bag with a subcontractor's logo on it. His hands were entirely covered with a thick layer of soot. Doubtless it was the man who been assigned to assist Gray.

Heath looked just like a throwback to the 1960s. His hippie-length hair was brittle and gray as dust. Over his mouth and nose he wore a loose protective mask. He also wore a pair of John Lennon–style glasses with thick lenses that made the eyes behind them look liquid. He was really quite horribly ridiculous.

After Gray had produced his police ID, the two went inside, and Gray explained their purpose to the owners of the massage parlor (who seemed relieved that the search was not connected with what went on at their premises). Then Heath, consulting a map of the structure, led Gray down into a storage cellar at the back of the establishment, where access to the emergency stairs could be gained.

The old lift shafts were useless. Their cages and all the workings had been removed back when the station was closed in 1924, but the stairway to the upper lift landing and the emergency staircase to the lower lift landing were passable. The entry doors were padlocked; Heath sought and tried several keys drawn from his bag before he found the correct ones to use.

"They," Heath said, his voice muffled by the baggy mask covering his mouth and nose, "told me why you want to get down here. Anyway, it's pointless. We already looked for Drayton. All you're doing is putting yourself in danger."

"I'll be the judge of that," replied Gray. "Just get on with it. You do your job and I'll do mine, OK?"

"Watch your step as we go. These old passageways are treacherous. Even if you don't wind up falling into a ventilation shaft, you might stumble in front of a passing train. Hear the noise?"

As he unlocked the door, there came from far below in the depths the sound of carriages rumbling along distant tracks, followed moments later by a powerful draught of musty air.

Heath chuckled. He turned on a powerful torch and aimed its beam along the stairway and around to the dark green tiled walls at the turn ahead. The steps were littered with debris.

Gray was amazed at how familiar and yet how strange their surroundings appeared. Like any Londoner, he had used the tube system on innumerable occasions and had passed through the subterranean mazes of many stations, though always when they were illuminated by overhead strip lighting, with hurried passengers making their way to or from a platform. But here the darkness was in control and every echoing footfall reinforced the grim feeling of total isolation. And yet it was only the withdrawal of light and of other people that created this feeling: actually, it was just the same as any other tube station would be after the services had stopped running. Except that this was no temporary interruption to be resumed in the morning. This really was what Carlos Miguel called *una estación fantasma*.

"Did you know Adam Drayton?" Gray asked in order to break the gaunt silence between the sound of passing trains.

He could only see the back of Heath. The engineer's slightly hunched form crept downwards along the steps, apparently intent solely upon what he was doing. But he finally responded after what seemed to be a considered pause.

"Oh yes," Heath said, "I knew *of* him all right. He was legendary on the Northern Line. Kept stopping his train at odd places and holding up the services. Only worked at night, when it didn't matter so much. The union stepped in to stop him getting the sack—said he was worried about safety."

"Safety?"

"The union said it was faulty signals that were to blame. And strange noises on the track. Made him cautious. Better to be safe than sorry. 'Go slow is preferable to taking chances.' That's what the union said."

They had reached the bottom of the stairway and emerged onto the upper lift landing. The tiles here were a grimy cream and red colour. In the circle of light cast by Heath's torch, Gray caught glimpses of advertising posters from the early 1920s that had been left up on the tiled walls of the corridor ahead: LIFEBUOY, BOVRIL, OXO, WRIGLEY'S and GUINNESS. Another tube train roared through one of the tunnels below, and the accompanying blast of air flapped the torn parts of the posters.

"What do you know about the disused stations here on the Northern Line? Have you seen the others for yourself?" Gray asked.

"I know something. I've been in them all at one time or another. They have a bad reputation. The most significant is North End or the 'Bull & Bush' as the train operators like to call it," Heath responded.

"Why significant?"

"The floodgates, y'know." said Heath, "Instead of the tube station that was going to be there in 1906 they developed it into a central command centre. Certain stations on the network have the gates, but they're all controlled from North End. Reckon the building goes down more than a thousand feet, though only the higher levels were initially used. It was started in the 1940s so they could stop the entire Underground system being flooded. Most of the gates were individually controlled before then."

"How could the whole system be flooded?"

"If the Nazis had dropped a bomb in the Thames, the tunnels under the river could have collapsed. Within ten minutes the Underground system would have been completely filled with water and submerged, y'know. Well, that's what they said. Later on, in the early 1970s, they built a second zone of gates just outside stations like Shepherd's Bush, Aldgate East and Bounds Green, before where the tracks emerge aboveground."

"What have they got to do with flooding?"

"Nothing. But they thought people would go mental when the three-minute warnings went off, and try to run along the tracks into the train tunnels to escape from Soviet atom bombs. Well, you get the idea. . . ."

By now they'd reached the emergency spiral stairway, which led much further downward to the lower lift landing. It was considerably steeper than the previous stairway, and Gray kept a hand against the wall as the two men descended. Their footfalls echoed as if ghosts were following close behind.

"Talking of weird stuff like that, you know about the Sentinel train?" Heath asked. He didn't wait for an answer before continuing with his topic. "First stop King William Street station along the abandoned spur, runs down to Borough without halting, then reverses up the Bank branch of the Northern Line. Only stops at the ghost stations along the route, nowhere else; goes on to City Road, right here to South Kentish Town, then back via Camden, before terminating at the deepest of all: North End, under Hampstead Heath. Anyway, I told you about that one, didn't I? The Sentinel lets the inspection crews examine the stuff the public never sees. Company doesn't leave the traction current to the rails on overnight, so a diesel locomotive pulls the old F-stock carriages. The train has a free run on the deserted tracks. Happens once a week or thereabouts. Every tube line has its own Sentinel."

"Are you pulling my leg?" Gray replied testily, "That's straight out of Drayton's book. It seems to me you must have read it."

They'd reached the lower lift landing.

"This passageway leads to the north and southbound platforms," Heath said, "but they're long gone."

Were the idea not totally ridiculous, Gray could have mistaken his companion for something dressed up in a boilersuit in order to pass as human. His colleagues at the Yard would have laughed at his suspicion. But he could not shake off the impression that, in the darkness, Heath's appearance was genuinely similar to the figure that Gray had glimpsed peering out of the trellised gates of Kentish Town station. That was only a few nights ago and one stop along the Northern Line from this ghost station. He'd seen it with his own eyes and the experience was not drawn from the pages of a crazy book like *The Secret Underground*. Gray could easily believe that this character Heath had not just read the volume but had stepped out from its pages into life.

"You didn't answer my question," Gray said. From his coat pocket he drew a packet of Benson & Hedges cigarettes.

"What one was that again?" Heath snuffled.

"The one about having read *The Secret Underground*." Gray responded as he jammed one of the smokes between his lips and touched the end with the flame from a battered old Zippo. A faint smell of petrol wafted from the lighter. He drew on the cigarette and exhaled, sending curling blue smoke across the beam of Heath's torch.

"Oh, that . . . look, you can't smoke down here. It's dangerous."

"Do you see any NO SMOKING signs around? Anyway, I'm sure your mask will protect you."

Heath paused and regarded the glowing tip of Gray's cigarette. He finally came back to the point.

"Yeah, I've read that book. I know it by heart. It's a favourite of mine."

From further back along the passageways, Gray thought he detected a rustling noise, like a pile of leaves dispersed by the wind. But before he was able to tell from which direction it came, the racket of a passing northbound train drowned it out. Gray thought he heard Heath muttering. It sounded like ". . . big-mouth . . . Miguel . . . he's sorted . . ." but most of these words were also lost in the roar.

It was obvious that Heath knew something about Drayton's disappearance, and may even have had a hand in it. Perhaps he also was dangerously obsessed with all those ghost stations and had come to regard Drayton as his rival. In any case, the place to interview Heath was back at the Yard, not here and now. Gray's back and stomach ached; the old ruptures were playing up again. It was time to get back to the surface. There was nothing down here that was of any use to his investigation. Besides, although Heath was small, Gray feared that he was dealing with a lunatic.

There was that damn rustling again, like leaves! It sounded closer this time. Heath seemed not to notice it though, and coldly regarded Gray smoking his cigarette, glaring through narrowed eyes that swam behind the thick lenses of his glasses.

"Well," said Gray, "I've seen everything I want to see here. Let's get back to the surface."

"All right," Heath replied, "but you ain't looked yet. To come all this way and not look at it would be a waste of my time and yours."

"Look at what exactly?"

"Over there in the corner. Thirty yards, right up against the wall." Heath flashed the torch's beam onto what appeared to be a large pile of rags. "Go and see. I already know what it is. I'll stay where I am. In case you're worried, like."

As he got nearer, Gray glanced back to make sure that Heath made no attempt to creep up on him. What he believed was a pile of rags was in fact a body slumped in the angle between wall and floor, its face turned towards the tiles. The back of its skull was smashed in. Dried blood caked the matted hair. As he turned the body over, Gray guessed that its face would be unfamiliar; he expected it to be Drayton, whom he'd never seen. But it was the Spaniard, Carlos Miguel. Heath had not moved an inch whilst Gray examined the corpse, but something living dropped from the darkness of the ceiling onto the police inspector, and the impact drove him crashing to the floor.

His head struck the concrete and he blacked out.

Gray awoke in a tube train carriage. He felt nauseous with pain as consciousness returned. He ran his fingers over his head and found half a dozen scratches and wounds around his face and on the back of his skull. There was a stabbing pain in his stomach, and he was aware of feeling wet around the seat of his trousers. The fall had reopened some of his old internal ruptures, and blood was leaking out of his lower intestine.

Although wracked with pain, he forced himself to take in the details of his surroundings. He was on a moving train, one that hurtled through the tunnels at breakneck speed.

The floor was littered with prostrate bodies. Some were hanging by their necks from knotted leather straps attached to the ceiling rails. All had been recently murdered and bore signs of mutilation. There were dozens of the corpses packed into the carriage. Their limbs protruded at misshapen angles from the humps of flesh and clothing. Extreme terror and pain marked their facial expressions. The body of Carlos Miguel lay amongst the charnel crowds. Like the Castilian, Gray had been left for dead.

Somehow he'd come to be a passenger in a carriage that appeared to date from, he guessed, the 1920s. The carriage lights were single bulbs housed in Art Deco glass oysters, with a very wide aisle running between the longitudinal seating. It must have been antiquated rolling stock, for there were advertisements from that far-off decade above the windows, and the Underground map showed routes such as the Hampstead and Highgate Line, the City and South London Railway and the Central London Railway. Back then the Victoria and Jubilee lines had not even been thought of, let alone built. Moreover, the map was like a complicated tangle of spaghetti and not modeled on the famous Beck circuit-board design.

Struggling to his feet and clutching the pole at the end of the seats, Gray stood in a daze for a moment, rocking with the motion of the train. His wristwatch showed one twenty a.m. He'd been out cold for well over eight hours. His left trouser leg stuck to the inside of his thigh, where the stream of blood oozing from his rectum had partially dried. He picked his way through the corpses and found that he was trapped in the last carriage of the train, and the connecting door to the penultimate carriage had been welded shut.

Gray crept back to a seat and peered through the window to the tunnels outside. Suddenly the train entered a platform, without slowing, and he pressed his face to the glass, to try to make out the station name as it flashed past. The light from the interior of the carriages projected enough illumination for him to see the signs for Chalk Farm. It also just made visible the stunted, faceless forms that lurked in the shadows of passageways further back. Forms that shunned the light, but which followed the progress of the Sentinel with malefic glee, whispering deafeningly to themselves in the darkness.

Gray had no doubt that the train would terminate at North End, and that the inner and outer gates were closed right the way across the Underground network, once the Sentinel had completed its journey. He harbored the notion that these gates served a purpose quite different from the official one, and were used to prevent escape along the tracks to the surface. Drayton had described many pieces of the jigsaw in his book *The Secret Underground*. Gray had not fitted them together until it was too late, and would finally solve the mystery in the labyrinthine reaches of an industrial Sheol.

In his mind's eye, he saw a vision in which the disparate chapters of Drayton's book merged to form a coherent explanation of what was happening. It was an explanation involving a series of derelict reverse skyscrapers, one of which was beneath North End, whose ultimate depth was probably over a thousand feet; a structure populated by beings who were sometimes bored with the repast foraged by using the smaller tunnels that led to the cemeteries and burial grounds across London. Could it be possible that the feasters had absorbed some of the characteristics of the corpses upon which they preyed, as in cannibalistic folklore?

He thought of an abandoned train and its driver . . . *como una polilea* . . . of a man called Heath with thick eyeglasses, his face obscured, and who knew as much as Drayton himself. . . .

And he thought of the ghost stations on the Piccadilly Line, the Central Line, the Metropolitan Line and all the others; doubtless each service had Sentinels operating that night.

Dedicated to A. C., London Subterran

REEL PEOPLE

By Patricia Lee Macomber

Gus Aiello sat in his favorite seat in the Arcade Theater. Row eleven, aisle seat, at just the right angle to see the screen; just the right position for the sound to engulf him perfectly. Bogey held court up on the big silver screen and the popcorn had just the right amount of butter on it. For a guy like Gus, life just didn't get much better than that. He had no idea that he was about to be a witness to murder—or at least he would have been, had he turned his head just a little to the left.

The Arcade Theater had gone through ten owners and even more names since Gus Aiello was a boy. In fact, it wasn't even called the Arcade Theater anymore; not by anyone but Gus. Change didn't come easy to Gus. He hated the new name just as much as he hated the new seats. Back when it had been billed as "the rocking chair theater," life had been good and a guy's rear end didn't fall asleep before the end of the movie.

The Arcade still showed old movies, and the popcorn was still made using real oil with real fat and real flavor. The floor was clean enough that his feet didn't stick to it, and the crowd was always small. True, there weren't ashtrays in the arms of the seats anymore, but the old movies turned on an old projector, and the screen was the very same original one that his grandparents had watched movies on, back when a guy always took his girl out on date night.

Gus was a third-generation cop, tough as nails and blessed with a keen sense of curiosity. Like his dad and his grandfather before him, Gus had collared his share of murderers and car thieves. Once, he had had the good fortune to stumble onto a serial killer. He still had the plaque and the medal he received while working with the Feds on that one. Yea, the Feds had had all the fancy equipment, but it had been he, himself, Gus-freakin'-Aiello, who had made the bust. He still had the knife scar on his chest to prove it.

As seriously as Gus took his work, he also took his leisure time seriously. This was his time, and he was enjoying the hell out of the Bogey movie. Never mind that he'd seen it at least a dozen times. He still loved it, and it was his time, after all. He turned off his cop senses and scooted down in the seat. Yea, it was wrong to put your feet on the seat backs and he'd have yelled at any kid for doing so. But still. . . .

He was focused on the movie, and nothing outside that mattered to him at the moment. Thus, he had no idea what was happening across the aisle to his left. It was outside his field of interest. He watched Bogey and Bacall to the very end, and then he picked up his trash and left the theater before the lights even came up.

From there, it was a seven-block walk to his house, a small arts and crafts–style place he had once shared with his parents, once shared with a wife, and now begrudgingly shared with a picky bassett hound named Fred. He sent Fred into the backyard while he made ready for bed. Then it was in between the crisp white sheets, and off to dreamland.

In the morning, Gus once again tossed Fred into the backyard while he completed his morning ablutions. Ever since Donna had passed, he'd begun kicking Fred out of the house several times a day in the hopes that the stupid mutt would eventually wander off, but not only would the damn dog not leave, he'd park his butt on the top step of the back porch and howl to be let in. Gus hated that dog more than anything, or so he'd have people believe. But Donna had loved Fred dearly, and somehow Gus saw it as his responsibility to take care of the dog until the end of his days. . . or the end of Gus's, whichever came first. It had given him purpose in the early days, when he couldn't seem to find an excuse to climb out of bed without Donna there to prod him.

Gus walked the same path to the station every morning, stopping at Edna's Diner for coffee and the stereotypical donut. On the corner, in front of the Rexall, Gus paused to drag a paper out of the machine. He scanned the headlines as he walked, the donut only a sticky memory and the coffee finally cool enough to drink. And so the morning routine was completed when he arrived at his desk and slapped the paper down on the stack of reports he had been meaning to file for nearly a month.

"Morning, Gus. How's things?"

Gus lifted his chin and turned his head to the right, proffering a thin smile to Stan, the first-year detective who occupied the desk next to his. Stan was a nice enough guy, a good enough cop. Still, it wasn't a job of passion for Stan the way it was for Gus, and so Gus considered him to be just marking time. "Things're good."

Gus slid his tush into the divot in his chair, and scooted up under the desk. In his mind, the conversation with Stan was over.

Stan did not share that sentiment. "Quite a shock about Denby, huh?"

"What about Denby?" Karl Denby had run the general store in that town ever since the death of his father some ten years prior. Gus wasn't exactly friends with Denby, but somehow he had taken it for granted that the man would always be there, behind the counter or washing fruit in front of the store, for as long as Gus needed him to be.

"Dead. Man! Don't you even read the papers you buy?" Stan let loose with a laugh that was more giggle than chuckle; definitely more feminine than any man should allow.

"Dead?" Gus frowned and let his eyebrows meet in the middle, "How?"

"Throat cut. Right in the middle of the theater last night."

Gus's back slammed against the worn back of the chair, which groaned in protest. "No. I mean, that can't be right." He swallowed hard. "What time?"

"During the nine o'clock show last night. That Singer kid found him when he set to cleaning up after the show." Stan slipped into his own chair, and took a cursory glance at his pristine desktop.

"No," Gus repeated, as though it would negate the whole thing. "I was in the theater last night. Sat through the whole show. I didn't see a damn thing."

"Well, I'd say your trusty cop senses are slipping then, man. Somebody slit his throat slicker'n shit. There was blood all over the seat and the floor. I've never seen so much blood."

"You were there? In the theater?" Gus leaned forward, his elbows grinding into the desk as he put more weight on them. God, he needed to gain some weight.

"Sure. I pulled the case."

Gus was out of his chair in a second. "The body's at the morgue?"

"Hell, they've done the autopsy already." Stan waved a thin stack of papers in the air and smiled.

Gus took the papers from Stan, using nearly enough force to be considered rude, just enough to be considered urgent. He sat down again slowly, brows still knitted as he scanned the papers. "Right-handed killer, kitchen knife, cut from behind. Time of death between nine thirty and ten."

"Yes indeedy-do. And nobody saw a damn thing. Including you, apparently."

Gus's gaze shot to Stan, and he frowned more deeply. Stan was irritating at best. Just then, Stan was asking for a good cuff across the head. "You need any help on this, you let me know."

"Will do, pal-o." Stan reclaimed the autopsy report, grabbed some more papers off his desk and headed down the hall. "You have a nice day now, Gus."

Too cocky. The man was just too cocky for a rookie

detective wannabe. It made Gus's temples throb and his jaw clench. The only way to fix that situation was to catch the killer before Stan did. Hell, Gus didn't have any cases going at the moment. He had some time.

The next night found Gus back in the theater. Oh, he didn't expect to find the killer returning to the scene of the crime or anything. He just wanted to see things for himself, and he wanted to do so without giving the impression that he was stepping on Stan's toes. There had been no murder weapon left behind, no fingerprints at all, and nothing in the way of physical evidence. Not so much as a hair on the seat back. Gus found that odd, but understandable. What wasn't understandable was the fact that he had been in the room when the murder had occurred and he—a trained cop—had seen and heard nothing.

Gus arrived at the Arcade a good half hour before the movie started. He spent the time checking out the seat, the floor, every inch of the theater surrounding the murder site. He had come in confident that he would find something Stan had missed. He left empty-handed and frustrated. The Singer boy doubled as janitor and ticket-taker, and he named off every single person who had entered the theater the night of the murder. He also confirmed that the rear theater exit had been stuck shut for close to twenty years. Gus walked home and put himself to bed in a huff. Even Fred, watching over his sad basset eye-folds, frowned.

Night after night, Gus returned to the theater. Part of him believed the old adage that criminals always return to the scene of the crime. Part of him just had a gut feeling that Denby's murder wouldn't be the last. So, in the flickering light of the old projector, under the giant watchful eyes of Tracy and Hepburn, Gus watched the crowd.

People filed in, and Gus recognized every one of them. It wasn't hard to know everybody in town when there were only some eleven hundred bodies. The lights dimmed, and the movie started. Somewhere along the way, the bloodied seat had been removed and replaced with a clean one. That selfsame seat was now occupied by Mr. Perry, owner of the local hardware store. It was the hat that gave the man away. It was from the thirties, and as crisply creased a fedora as Gus had ever seen.

Halfway through the movie, as Gus watched Mr. Perry nap, someone entered the theater and sat behind the man. Gus hadn't actually seen the man enter, but suddenly there he was, sitting board-straight in his seat and staring at the screen. Gus scooted higher in his own seat and turned a bit, so he could watch the man and still give the appearance of watching the movie.

The stranger was quite thin and apparently very tall. His hair was wild and stuck out on the sides and the front. In the back, it was mashed down as if from being pressed against the back of a chair. Gus couldn't see the man's face, but he got the impression of wrinkles.

The movie forgotten, Gus kept his eyes glued to that stranger. The man had done nothing suspicious, but the hairs on the back of Gus's hands stood on end, and somehow he knew something was about to happen.

As sure as if he had seen a preview of coming attractions, the man leaned forward, placing both hands on the back of Mr. Perry's seat. There was a flash of light off of something metal in the man's right hand and Gus put one hand on his gun, nearly convinced that the man held a knife. The second flash clearly showed a ring, something large and with a lot of stones. Gus put his hand back on the arm of the seat and settled down a little.

That's when it happened. In one not so quick but fluid motion, the man leaned forward farther, slipped one hand into his jacket, and grabbed Perry's hair with the other hand, pulling the man's head back over the seat and exposing his throat.

Flash! The light from the screen lit the blade like a headlamp, and Gus was out of his chair like a rocket, his hand already on the grip of his gun as he bolted across the aisle. Then the man did the strangest thing. Just as Gus reached the first seat across the aisle, the man twisted the blade in the air, letting it flash in Gus's eyes almost as if he wanted Gus to see it. Then he brought the knife down, making a quick, clean slice across Perry's throat.

Gus felt as though he were moving through molasses. He was only two seats away from the man now, gun drawn and screaming at the top of his lungs. "Freeze! Police! Bring up the lights. Turn on the goddamn lights—now!"

There was the sound of feet scurrying, as people moved away from that area of the theater and clustered together for comfort. The man stood upright again, let go of Perry's head, and tipped an imaginary hat at Gus using the tip of the bloodied knife.

Gus was about to grab for the man when the lights

flashed on. Just like that, without the passing of a heart-beat or the blink of an eye, the man was gone.

Someone behind Gus screamed. The manager ran in from the left, and Gus was peripherally aware that the projectionist was peering down on the scene through the small projector window. Perry was quite clearly dead. His throat was cut deeply, and his head lolled to the right. Given the way people were staring at him, Gus had no doubt that they suspected him of being the murderer. Gus looked over the back of the seats. He dropped to the floor and peered between the seat supports, looking for any sign of the escaping murderer. He was simply . . . gone.

Four hours were spent giving his statement and searching for evidence that night. No sign of the man was ever found. There wasn't one shred of physical evidence, not one other witness who had seen the man enter or leave the theater. The only thing that was accomplished that night was that the case was turned over to Gus, a mixed blessing if ever he had seen one.

Gus spent the next day interviewing relatives of the deceased and everyone he could think of who might have seen the stranger around town. By the end of the day, he was convinced that neither victim had had an enemy in the world and he, Gus, was the only man alive who had seen the mysterious stranger.

Now the feeling that the killer would strike again was stronger than ever. For the life of him, Gus couldn't find a motive for the murders, but he supposed that the man might just be some sort of serial killer. Something in the way the man had tipped his imaginary hat with the knife made Gus think that the killer was trying to attract his attention or rub his nose in it. It made his blood curdle.

Gus returned to the theater every night, but it wasn't until a week later that the killer appeared again. A pattern was developing, at least in Gus's mind. The killer struck only once for each movie that was shown and he never struck on the first night that movie was shown. It was almost as if each movie had to run at least once before the killer *could* strike. Gus had no idea why that might be, but he had seen much stranger habits in killers before.

That particular night, Peter O'Toole graced the silver screen, and the crowd was thin. Aside from Gus, there were only four other people in the theater, and two of those were in the balcony making out. No one sat in the offending seat, perhaps because they considered it cursed. Gus himself felt sure that the man would only kill victims in that one seat, but he had no idea *why* he was so sure. If nothing else, tonight's events would decide Gus's theory, one way or the other.

Halfway through the movie, when Gus was convinced that the night was a bust and he should just go home, a portly woman with spectacles and a white dress slipped through the door and into the seat in question. Part of Gus wanted to yell at her to get out of that chair, to save herself. The cop part of him wanted her to stay so the killer would show up again. He was ready this time, and he wouldn't need to dash across the aisle. He was seated only three seats down and one row behind where the killer had appeared.

Just like clockwork, the tall man suddenly appeared, materializing right in the middle of Gus's view of the screen. One moment he wasn't there, and the next he was. Gus wasted no time, took no chance that the man would be able to slit the woman's throat and disappear again.

He'd had his gun drawn, cocked, and resting in his hand on his lap the whole time. The second the man appeared, Gus leaped from his chair and thrust out the gun. "Hold it right there!"

Something very strange happened just then. As Gus watched, the man flickered, much in the same way that a worn old movie reel will flicker. His movements sped and slowed as though something were dragging at his particular reel. For one half of a heartbeat—so brief a time that Gus doubted completely what he'd seen—the man actually flickered out of existence. Then he was back.

That quickly, Gus shook off the shock of it and dove. He threw himself across two seats and over the back of one, arms wrapping around the killer's thin form and dragging him downward, toward the floor as Gus fell first onto the row of seats in front of him and then to the wood floor.

The woman in the offending seat screamed and backpedaled across the row. The projectionist stopped the film and threw on the house lights. For a brief moment, Gus fancied that he felt something of substance in his arms. Then it was gone.

He lay on the floor alone, among a spray of popcorn and open air. No doubt, all the wide eyes staring at him meant that they thought him to be quite insane. But one thing was for sure: he had gotten a very good and clear look at the killer's face.

Gus hauled himself up from the floor and dusted himself off with his free hand. When he turned his attention to the small gathering of people before him, he was shocked to see them staring at his gun and backing away. He quickly holstered the weapon, shaking his head as he picked a piece of popcorn out of his hair.

"It's okay, I'm a cop. You all know I'm a cop." He swallowed hard, suddenly feeling nearly as crazy as they must all have thought him to be. "Did anybody see anything? Anyone?"

"Just you doing the fandango across the row of seats," hollered the smart-ass from the balcony.

"Swell." Gus sighed and adjusted his jacket. "There was a man, right here. It was the same man who was standing right here on the night Mr. Perry was killed. He was about to kill this woman." Gus turned to point at her, but the old woman was gone, too. "There was an old woman here. She had on a white dress. She came in late. Anybody know her?"

They all shrugged, and the smart-ass from the balcony laughed. "I think you're losing it, Gus man."

The tone of that remark reminded Gus a little too much of Stan. He thrust one finger in the air toward the balcony and yelled. "I know your father, young lady. He's not going to be too pleased when I tell him where and how you got that mark on your neck!"

The girl smacked Mr. Smart Ass on the arm and turned to leave, no doubt trying to beat Gus's bad news back to daddy.

Gus's eyes were drawn back to the screen. The projector had been left on, the reels frozen in place and the same frame stuck on the screen as if painted there. As Gus watched, the image began to burn, sending shadow-smoke spirals across the screen as Peter O'Toole slowly melted into oblivion. Gus cocked one side of his mouth into a sardonic grin, and then turned and left.

"How would you feel about going to the movies with me tonight, Stan?" Gus grinned a little bit. He wouldn't allow himself a full smile, despite the smart remark he could sense was going to follow.

"Well, really, Gus! I don't think we know each other well enough for that." Stan batted his eyes and giggled.

"Shut up, asshole!" Gus laughed. Okay, so sometimes Stan really was funny. He had a way of growing on people . . . like mold or moss.

Stan turned serious for a moment, a phenomenon that Gus had seen only once before. "This have anything to do with those murders?"

"Yeah, it does. But I need an extra body, so to speak."

Stan stared at him, rendered speechless for the first time since they'd met. Then, very slowly, he sighed, "Okay."

"Where do you want me?" Stan asked, fussing with the crease of his pants.

"Right there," Gus stated simply, pointing to the offending seat.

Stan gaped. "You know what they call that now, don't

you? They call it Murderer's Row. I'm not sitting in the death chair. No way!"

"Stan, how long have we known each other?"

"A little under a year now. Why?"

"Do you think I'm a good cop?"

"Well, yeah. Sure. You're a good cop."

"And a good cop wouldn't put anyone's life in danger, would he?"

"Well, no." Stan pocketed his hands and frowned at his shoes. "Where are you going to be?"

"Up there." Gus jerked his thumb toward the projectionist's booth.

"So, I'll be down here, all on my own?"

"Don't worry. You'll be perfectly safe."

"How can you be so sure?"

"Because this time, the murderer's coming after me. Now, here's your popcorn, and here's your soda." He clapped Stan on the shoulder, and used that motion to shove him down into the seat. "All you have to do is sit back and enjoy the show."

Gus left before Stan could protest. The fading sound of Gus's one squeaky shoe drove home the fact that Stan would soon be alone in the theater. Gus had planned it that way. Nothing made him happier than giving old Stan the heebie-jeebies. Well, maybe catching a killer, but . . .

Gus opened the door to the projectionist's booth and offered Jefferson a smile. Some people were just meant for simple, meaningless jobs, others embraced them. Gus had the distinct feeling that Jefferson loved his

work, and that he might well be the premier projectionist in the world. Gus respected that.

"We all set?"

"You betcha. Now, you have to turn on the bulb first,
get it focused with this knob here." Jefferson twisted the
knob, and the lens moved in and out. "Once you've got
it in good focus, you start the reel turning with this knob.
And you can use the same knob to stop the reels turning,
but I gotta warn you that if you leave the lamp turned on
without the reels turning for too long, you're gonna burn
the film right through."

Gus glanced at the man's flashing blue eyes, and
noted the way they dulled at that. Obviously, it pained
the guy to think of damaging a film. Gus decided not to
tell him. "Okay, I get that. But tell me something. How
fast does the film stop when I push this knob?"

"It's instant. Whatever frame you're on, that's where
it stops."

Gus nodded slowly. "Okay, I think I'm ready."

"Remember, don't leave it stuck on one frame too
long or it'll burn."

"How long before it starts to burn?"

"About three minutes."

"I see." Gus thought about that. Three minutes was an
awful long time when a guy was coming after you with
a knife. "Thanks. And you've got your key to the door?"

"Right here." He patted his right pocket, and once
more his blue eyes began to sparkle.

"Good deal. Just remember, don't open this door for
any reason. No reason at all, all right? You wait until I
come out."

"Got it." Jefferson turned and made for the door slowly, thinking better of it before he actually put his hand on the knob. "I don't know what you've got planned, and I probably don't want to know. But good luck, okay?"

"Thanks. See you in a few." Gus gifted the man with a genuinely warm smile, and nodded.

The projectionist slipped out through the door, and for the first time since the whole thing had started, Gus had serious doubts about his plan. He knew for sure that there had to be a body in that one seat. The rest was all guesswork. Gus hated guesswork.

He drew in a deep breath and hooked one finger behind the film, pulling it out a little bit so the light would shine behind it. Tiny little frames, bits of people once alive, now dead, miniscule words printed across celluloid. When strung together, they made life out of light. Scattered amongst the frames of the living-dead actors and actresses, occupying every third frame, were the dark frames of a long-dead killer.

"Gotcha!" Gus whispered as he let the piece of film go.

He flipped on the lamp and focused the lens, watching the still-frame image on the opposite wall as it came into crystal clarity. Then he flipped on the motor, grinning as the gears clunked to life and the reels began to turn. Credits rolled across the white wall, the words large in the projected light, and somehow less white than they had appeared on the film itself.

Gus leaned back against the wall next to the projector and watched, one finger still on that motor control. If his hunch was right, he wouldn't have long to wait. As the credits rolled by, his smile widened and his palms began to sweat. His gun, tucked neatly into its holster, would be of no more use than his hands had been on those other nights. At that point, light was his best weapon.

Toward the end of the first reel, just before Mr. O'Toole had his big scene, the space between Gus and the movie image began to flicker and sparkle. Rather than winking into existence, the man popped in, appearing so suddenly that Gus shoved off from the wall, and for a moment his finger left the motor switch.

"Shit!" he hissed, and rested his finger on the switch again. He didn't want to turn it off before the man fully materialized.

The killer flickered one last time, the ghost of a hair crossing over his form from right hip to left shoulder, then disappearing. In his hand was the knife, appearing somehow larger and more menacing now that Gus could see it up close.

"What the—?"

Gus laughed and increased his finger's pressure on the switch. "Gotcha!"

The man looked more perplexed than anything else, but the expression disappeared as quickly as it had come over him, melting into insane glee. "No matter. I got no problem killing cops." The man took one slow, dragging step forward, smiling to reveal rotted teeth and a grayed tongue. "Aren't you afraid to be trapped in here, all alone, with a killer?"

"Me? Naw." Gus licked his dry lips and sighed. "I am curious, though. Why? And how?"

"I have no idea how I came to be trapped inside that projector. But I learned to work around it, now didn't I?" For the first time, Gus noted that the man had an Irish accent, and it made his leer all the more out of place. "As for the why, well, quite simply because I can. At first, I thought maybe I could trap someone else inside that thing and free myself. By the time I figured out it wasn't going to work, I simply couldn't stop the killing. I like it wa-a-a-a-y too much." He brought the knife forward, swooped his arm above his head, and targeted Gus with the tip of his blade.

"But you were real once, yes?"

"Yes, as real as you." He took one more lumbering step forward, slashing at Gus as if to unnerve him more than anything else. The knife cut through the air a foot in front of Gus with an audible *whoosh*.

Gus didn't move. The strike had never been intended to make contact. Besides, the man only slashed throats. Gus knew that. "And you were killed in this theater, in that very same seat, and that's why you come back to kill anyone who sits there."

The man threw back his head and laughed. It was deeper and more resonant than Gus expected. It made his spine tingle. "Oh, nothing as mundane as that, I assure you, m'boy."

"Then why that seat?"

The man leaned forward and whispered, as if to impart some secret. "I just like that seat. I can kill anyone I want, anywhere I want. For instance, I could kill you right here, right now."

Gus sensed that the man was lying. There really was

no reason for him to lie, but he had done it just the same. Gus's finger pressed down on the switch a little harder, ready to flip it off.

"Actually, you can't. As a matter of fact, you can't step outside the beam of light this projector gives off, can you? For some reason, a tiny bit of that light falls on that one particular seat. And you can only appear right there."

A hiss of air escaped through the gaps in the man's teeth, and he lunged toward Gus, leading with the knife. Gus took a step backward, farther away than the man's blade could reach, even if he stepped to the edge of the projector's beam. But the knife was just a little too close, and Gus fancied that he could smell the man's fetid breath, though he knew that to be impossible. For just a second, Gus thought he had waited too long, that even if he threw the switch instantly, it would be too late, and that knife would cut through his throat with ease. He threw the switch anyway, praying that he could outrun the man for the three minutes it took the film to burn.

The film stopped and Peter O'Toole froze in place, caught in the middle of a diatribe, looking for all the world like a crazed maniac. The man in front of Gus also froze, his face pressed into a mask of shock and horror. From the look of him, he had had no more idea than Gus that all his motion would stop if the film stopped.

Gus grinned. He leaned against the wall and watched, his arms folded over his chest and his eyes dancing.

Gus checked his watch and grinned some more. One minute to go.

The smell of smoke wafted up from where the man

stood, though it might just as well have come from the film itself. Then tendrils of the stuff spiraled up from the man's stomach and rose toward the ceiling, stinging Gus's nose.

Then the man simply burst into flames, igniting from the gut. The fire spread out across his body, parts of him charring and curling as the film curled and charred. There was no rancid smell of burning flesh and no sizzling sound. Gus had expected a scream . . . something.

Finally, the man's face disappeared in a huge, melted gob of image ash, rising toward the ceiling like a large spark at a campfire. Gus sighed and flipped off the bulb. Only then did he realize that someone was hammering at the door of the booth.

"Gus! Gus, open the damn door! Are you okay? Gus, say something!" Words passed between Stan and the projectionist, who apparently held his post better than Stan had, and was still refusing to open the door.

Gus crossed the room slowly, sidestepping the small pile of melted plasticlike goo that had collected on the floor where the man had stood. He opened the door on Stan's shocked face, and proffered a wink to the projectionist.

"Gus! We smelled smoke. Are you okay in here? What happened?"

Gus turned his back on Stan, and crossed the room to where an old microphone stand rested, minus its mic. "I'm fine. And what happened is that you abandoned your post. I told you to stay in your seat until I came to get you."

"We smelled smoke. . . ." Stan looked to the projectionist for backup and was sorely disappointed.

As they watched, Gus picked up the mic stand, raised it high above his head, and brought it crashing down on the projector. The projectionist screamed like a girl.

"What the hell are you doing?" Jefferson darted forward and made as if to grab the mic stand.

Gus brought the thing down on the projector once more, sending a hail of plastic and metal parts across the room. "Stopping a murder." One more strike and the projector began to spark and smoke. Gus reached down and pulled the plug, then set the mic stand back in the corner.

"Oh, my God!" The projectionist slapped both hands to his face and did a little dance of confusion among the parts. "Do you have any idea how old this thing was? It's been here as long as the theater has. It took me forever to get it working again."

"Well, now you can get a nice, shiny new one. Send me the bill." He clapped a hand on Stan's shoulder and smiled. "Come on, partner. I need a drink."

Stan allowed himself to be led out of the theater and into the night. He waited until they were safely on the sidewalk before he shrugged off Gus's grip and faced him. "Are you going to tell me what happened up there?"

Gus stared at the stars for a moment as if thinking, then inhaled slowly and let the breath out in a fast *whoosh*. "Nope! I'm not gonna tell you." He thought for a moment longer, and then shook his head. "Well, maybe over a bottle of good Scotch. Tell me something, Stan. Do you believe in ghosts?"

"Not really."

"Well, Stan"—Gus laughed, looping one arm around the man's shoulders—"let's hike on over to the Eagle and Anchor and I'll make a believer out of you."

DEVIL'S SMILE

By Glen Hirshberg

"In hollows of the liquid hills
Where the long Blue Ridges run
The flattery of no echo thrills
For echo the seas have none;
Nor aught that gives man back man's strain—
The hope of his heart, the dream in his brain."
—Herman Melville, "Pebbles"

Turning in his saddle, Selkirk peered behind him through the flurrying snow, trying to determine which piece of debris had lamed his horse. All along what had been the carriage road, bits of driftwood, splintered sections of hull and harpoon handle, discarded household goods—pans, candlesticks, broken-backed books, empty lanterns—and at least one section of long, bleached-white jaw lay half-buried in the sand. The jaw still had baleen attached, and bits of blown snow had stuck in it, which made it look more recently alive than it should have.

Selkirk rubbed his tired eyes against the gray December morning and hunched deeper into his inadequate long coat as the wind whistled off the whitecaps and sliced between the dunes. The straw hat he wore more out of habit than hope of protection did nothing to warm him, and stray blond curls kept whipping across his eyes. Easing himself from the horse, Selkirk dropped to the sand.

He should have conducted his business here months ago. His surveying route for the fledgling United States Lighthouse Service had taken him in a crisscrossing loop from the tip of the Cape all the way up into Maine and back. He'd passed within fifty miles of Cape Roby Light and its singular keeper twice this fall, and both times had continued on. Why? Because Amalia had told him the keeper's tale on the night he'd imagined she loved him? Or maybe he just hated coming back here even more than he thought he would. For all he knew, the keeper had long since moved on, dragging her memories behind her. She might even have died. So many did, around here. Setting his teeth against the wind, Selkirk wrapped his frozen fingers in his horse's bridle and led her the last downsloping mile and a half into Winsett.

Entering from the east, he saw a scatter of stone and clapboard homes and boardinghouses hunched against the dunes, their windows dark. None of them looked familiar. Like so many of the little whaling communities he'd visited during his survey, the town he'd known had simply drained away into the burgeoning, bloody industry centers at New Bedford and Nantucket.

Selkirk had spent one miserable fall and winter here fourteen years ago, sent by his drunken father to learn candle making from his drunken uncle. He'd accepted the nightly open-fisted beatings without comment, skulking afterward down to the Blubber Pike tavern to

watch the whalers: the Portuguese swearing loudly at
each other and the Negroes—so many negroes, most of
them recently freed, more than a few newly escaped—
clinging in clumps to the shadowy back tables and stealing fearful glances at every passing face, as though they
expected at any moment to be spirited away.

Of course, there'd been his cousin, Amalia, for all the
good that had ever done him. She'd just turned eighteen
at the time, two years his senior. Despite her blond hair
and startling fullness, the Winsett whalers had already
learned to steer clear, but for some reason, she'd liked
Selkirk. At least, she'd liked needling him about his out-
sized ears, his floppy hair, the crack in his voice he could
not outgrow. Whatever the reason, she'd lured him away
from the pub on several occasions to stare at the moon
and drink beside him. And once, in a driving sleet, she'd
led him on a midnight walk to Cape Roby Point. There,
lurking uncomfortably close, but never touching him,
standing on the rocks with her dark eyes cocked like rifle
sights at the rain, she'd told him the lighthouse keeper's
story. At the end, without any explanation, she'd turned,
opened her heavy coat, and pulled him to her. He'd had
no idea what she wanted him to do, and had wound up
simply setting his ear against her slicked skin, all but
tasting the water that rushed into the valley between her
breasts, listening to her heart banging way down inside
her.

After that, she'd stopped speaking to him entirely.
He'd knocked on her door, chased her half out of the
shop one morning and been stopped by a chop to the
throat from his uncle, left notes he hoped she'd find

peeking out from under the rug in the upstairs hallway. She'd responded to none of it, and hadn't even bothered to say good-bye when he left. And Selkirk had steered clear of all women for more than a decade afterward, except for the very occasional company he paid for near the docks where he slung cargo, until the Lighthouse Service offered him an unexpected escape.

Now, half dragging his horse down the empty main street, Selkirk found he couldn't even remember which grim room the Blubber Pike had been. He passed no one. But at the western edge of the frozen, cracking main thoroughfare, less than a block from where his uncle had kept his establishment, he found a travelers' stable and entered.

The barn was lit by banks of horseshoe-shaped wall sconces—apparently, local whale oil or no, candles remained in ready supply—and a coal fire glowed in the open iron stove at the rear of the barn. A dark-haired stable lad with a clam-shaped birthmark covering his left cheek and part of his forehead appeared from one of the stables in the back, *tsk*ed over Selkirk's injured mount, and said he'd send for the horse doctor as soon as he'd got the animal dried and warmed and fed.

"Still a horse doctor here?" Selkirk asked.

The boy nodded. He was almost as tall as Selkirk, and spoke with a Scottish burr. "Still good business. Got to keep the means of getting out healthy."

"Not many staying in town anymore, then?"

"Just the dead ones. Lot of those."

Selkirk paid the boy and thanked him, then wandered toward the stove and stood with his hands extended to the heat, which turned them purplish red. If he got about doing what should have been done years ago, he'd be gone by nightfall, providing his horse could take him. From his memory of the midnight walk with Amalia, Cape Roby Point couldn't be more than three miles away. Once at the lighthouse, if its longtime occupant did indeed still live there, he'd brook no romantic nonsense — neither his own, nor the keeper's. The property did not belong to her, was barely suitable for habitation, and its lack of both updated equipment and an experienced, capable attendant posed an undue and unacceptable threat to any ship unlucky enough to hazard past. Not that many bothered anymore with this particular stretch of abandoned, storm-battered coast.

Out he went into the snow. In a matter of minutes, he'd left Winsett behind. Head down, he burrowed through the gusts. With neither buildings nor dunes to block it, the wind raked him with bits of shell and sand that clung to his cheeks like the tips of fingernails and then ripped free. When he looked up, he saw the beach pocked with snow and snarls of seaweed, then the ocean thrashing about between the shore and the sandbar a hundred yards or so out.

An hour passed. More. The tamped-down path, barely discernible during Winsett's heyday, had sunk completely into the shifting earth. Selkirk stepped through stands of beach heather and sandbur, pricking himself repeatedly about the ankles. Eventually, he felt blood beneath one heavy sock, but he didn't peel the sock back, simply yanked out the most accessible spines and kept moving. Far out to sea, bright yellow sunlight flickered in the depths of the cloud cover and vanished as suddenly as it had appeared. Devil's smile, as the Portuguese sailors called it. At the time, it hadn't occurred to Selkirk to ask why the light would be the devil, instead of the dark or the gathering storm. Stepping from the V between two leaning dunes, he saw the lighthouse.

He'd read the report from the initial Lighthouse Service survey three years ago, and more than once. That document mentioned rot in every beam, chips and cracks in the bricks that made up the conical tower, erosion all around the foundation. As far as Selkirk could see, the report had been kind. The building seemed to be crumbling to nothing before his eyes, bleeding into the pool of shorewater churning at the rocks beneath it.

Staring into the black tide racing up the sand to meet him, Selkirk caught a sea-salt tang on his tongue and found himself murmuring a prayer he hadn't planned for Amalia, who'd reportedly wandered into the dunes and vanished one winter night, six years after Selkirk left. Her father had written Selkirk's father that the girl had never had friends, hated him, hated Winsett, and was probably happier wherever she was now. Then he'd said, *Here's what I hope: that she's alive. And that she's somewhere far from anywhere I will ever be.*

On another night than the one they'd spent out here, somewhere closer to town but similarly deserted, he and Amalia once found themselves beset by gulls that swept out of the moonlight all together, by the hundreds, as though storming the mainland. Amalia had pitched stones at them, laughing as they shrieked and swirled nearer. Finally, she'd hit one in the head and killed it.

Then she'd bent over the body, calling Selkirk to her. He'd expected her to cradle it or cry. Instead, she'd dipped her finger in its blood and painted a streak down Selkirk's face. Not her own.

Looking down now, Selkirk watched the tide reach the tips of his boots again. How much time had he wasted during his dock-working years imagining— hoping—that Amalia might be hidden behind some stack of crates or in a nearby alley, having sought him out after leaving Winsett?

Angry now, Selkirk picked his way between rocks to the foot of the tower. A surge of whitewater caught him off guard and pasted his trousers to his legs, and the wind promptly froze them with a gust.

Up close, the tower looked even worse. Most of the bricks had crumbled and whitened, the salt air creating blotchy lesions all over them, like lepers' spots. The main building still stood straight enough, but even from below, with the wind whipping the murky winter light around, Selkirk could see filth filming the windows that surrounded the lantern room, and cracks in the glass.

The keeper's quarters squatted to the left of the light tower, and looked, if possible, even more disheveled. Along the base, lime had taken hold, sprouting up the wooden walls like algae. Or maybe it was algae. This would not be something the Service salvaged. Cape Roby Light would have to come down, or simply be abandoned to the sea.

Selkirk rapped hard on the heavy oak door of the tower. For answer, he got a blast of wind nearly powerful enough to tip him off the rocks. Grunting, he rapped

harder. Behind him, the water gurgled, the way spermaceti sometimes did as it bubbled, and though he knew it
wasn't possible, Selkirk would have sworn he could
smell it—that faint but nauseating reek his uncle swore
was imaginary, because that was the glory of spermaceti
oil, the whole goddamn point: it had no significant odor.
Every day of that dismal fall, though, Selkirk's nostrils
had filled anyway. Blood, whale brain, dessicated fish.
He began to pound.

Just before the door opened, he became aware of
movement behind it, the slap of shoed feet descending
stone steps. But he didn't stop knocking until the oak
swung away from him, the light rushing not out from the
lighthouse but in from the air.

He knew right away this was her, though he'd never
actually seen her. Her black hair twisted over her shoulders and down her back in tangled strands like vines, just
as Amalia had described. He'd expected a wild, white-
haired, wind-ravaged thing, bent with age and the grief
she could not shake. But of course, if Amalia's story had
been accurate, this woman had been all of twenty during
Selkirk's year here, and so barely over eighteen when
she'd been widowed. She gazed at him now through
royal blue eyes that seemed set into the darkness behind
her like the last sunlit patches in a blackening sky.

"Mrs. Marchant," he said. "I'm Robert Selkirk from
the Lighthouse Service. May I come in?"

For a moment, he thought she might shut the door in
his face. Instead, she hovered, both arms lifting slightly
from her sides, as though she were considering taking

wing. Her skirt was long, her blouse pale yellow, clinging to her square and powerful shoulders.

"Selkirk," she said. "From Winsett?"

Astonished, Selkirk started to raise his hand. Then he
shook his head. "From the Lighthouse Service. But yes,
I was nephew to the Winsett Selkirks."

"Well," she said, the Portuguese tilt to her words stirring memories of the Blubber Pike whalers, the smoke
and the smell in there. Abruptly, she grinned. "Then
you're welcome here."

"You may not feel that way in a few minutes, Mrs.
Marchant. I'm afraid I've come to. . ."

But she'd stepped away from the door, starting back
up the stairs and beckoning him without turning around.
Over her shoulder, he heard her say, "You must be
frozen. I have tea."

In he went, and stood still in the entryway, listening to
the whistling in the walls, feeling drafts rushing at him
from all directions. If it weren't for the roof, the place
would hardly qualify as a dwelling anymore, let alone a
lifesaving beacon and refuge. He started after the
woman, up the twisting stairs.

Inside, too, the walls had begun to flake and mold,
and the air flapped overhead, as though the whole place
were full of nesting birds. Four steps from the platform
surrounding the lantern room, just at the edge of the spill
of yellow candlelight from up there, Selkirk slowed,
then stopped. His gaze swung to his right and down toward his feet.

Sitting against the wall with her little porcelain feet
sticking out of the bottom of her habit and crossed at the

ankle, sat a doll dressed as a nun. From beneath the doll's black veil, disconcertingly blue eyes peered from under long lashes. A silver crucifix lay in the doll's lap, and miniature rosary beads trailed back down the steps, winking pale yellow and pink in the flickering light like seashells underwater. And, in fact, they were bits of shell.

Glancing behind him, Selkirk spotted the other dolls he'd somehow missed. One for every other stair, on alternating walls. These were made mostly from shell, as far as he could tell. Two of them were standing, while a third sat with her legs folded underneath her and a stone tucked against her ear, as though she were listening. At the top of the steps, still another nun dangled from her curved, seashell hands on the decaying wooden banister. Not only were her eyes blue, but she was grinning like a little girl. Momentarily baffled to silence, Selkirk stumbled the rest of the way up to the lantern room. This time, he froze completely.

Even on this dark day, even through the dust and salt that caked the window glass inside and out, light flooded the chamber. None of it came from the big lamp, which of course lay unlit, assuming it still worked at all. Across the platform, a pair of white wicker chairs sat side by side, aimed out to sea. Over their backs, the keeper had draped blankets of bright red wool, and beneath them lay a rug of similar red. And on the rug stood a house.

Like most of the dolls, it had been assembled entirely from shells and seaweed and sand. From its peaked roof hung tassels of purple flowers, and all around the eaves, gull feathers hung like the decorative flourishes on a society woman's hat. On the rug—clearly, it served as a yard—tiny nuns prowled like cats. Some lay on their backs with their arms folded across their crucifixes, soaking up the light. One was climbing the leg of one of the wicker chairs. And a group—at least five—stood at the base of the window, staring out to sea.

And that is what reminded Selkirk of his purpose, and brought him at least partway back to himself. He glanced around the rest of the room, noting half a dozen round wooden tables evenly spaced around the perimeter. On each, yellow beeswax candles blazed in their candlesticks, lending the air a misleading tint of yellow and promising more heat than actually existed here. Mostly, the tables held doll-making things. Tiny silver crosses, multicolored rocks, thousands of shells. The table directly to Selkirk's right had a single place setting laid out neatly upon it. Clean white plate, fork, spoon, one chipped teacup decorated with paintings of leaping silver fish.

Selkirk realized he was staring at a crude sort of living sundial. Each day, Mrs. Marchant began with her tea and breakfast, proceeded around the platform to assemble and place her nuns, spent far too long sitting in one or the other of the wicker chairs and staring at the place where it had all happened, and eventually retired, to do it all over again when daybreak came. In spite of himself, he felt a surprisingly strong twinge of pity.

"That hat can't have helped you much," Mrs. Marchant said, straightening from a bureau near her dining table, where she apparently kept her tea things. The cup she brought matched the one on her breakfast

table—flying fish, chips, and all—and chattered lightly
on its saucer as she handed it to him.

More grateful for its warmth than he realized, Selkirk
rushed the cup to his mouth and winced as the hot liquid
scalded his tongue. The woman stood a little too close to
him. Loose strands of her hair almost tickled the back of
his hand like the fringe on a shawl. Her blue eyes flicked
over his face. Then she started laughing.

"What?" Selkirk took an uncertain half step back.

"The fish," she said. When he stared, she laughed
again and gestured at the cup. "When you drank, it
looked like they were going to leap right into your
teeth."

Selkirk glanced at the side of the cup, then back to the
woman's laughing face. Judging by the layout and contents of this room, he couldn't imagine her venturing
anywhere near town, but she clearly got outside to col-
lect supplies. As a result, her skin had retained its dusky
Continental coloration. A beautiful creature, and no mistake.

"I am sorry," she said, meeting his eyes. "It's been a
long time since anyone drank from my china but me. It's
an unfamiliar sight. Come." She started around the left
side of the platform. Selkirk watched, then took the opposite route, past the seaweed table, and met the woman
in the center of the seaward side of the platform, at the
wicker chairs. Without waiting for him, she bent, lifted a
tiny nun off the rug, whose bandeau hid most of her face
like a bandit's mask, and settled in the right-hand chair.
The nun wound up tucked against her hip like a rabbit.

For whom, Selkirk wondered, was the left-hand chair

meant, on ordinary days? The obvious answer chilled and also saddened him, and he saw no point in wasting further time.

"Mrs. Marchant—"

"Manners, Mr. Selkirk," the woman said, and for the second time smiled at him. "The sisters do not approve of being lectured to."

It took him a moment to understand she was teasing him. And not like Amalia had, or not exactly like. Teasing him hadn't made Amalia any happier. He sat.

"Mrs. Marchant, I have bad news. Actually, it isn't really bad news, but it may feel that way at first. I know—that is, I really think I have a sense—of what this place must mean to you. I did live in town here once, and I do know your story. But it's not good for you, staying here. And there are more important considerations than you or your grief here, anyway, aren't there? There are the sailors still out there braving the seas, and . . ."

Mrs. Marchant cocked her head, and her eyes trailed over his face so slowly that he almost thought he could feel them, faintly, like the moisture in the air, but warmer.

"Would you remove your hat, Mr. Selkirk?"

Was she teasing now? She wasn't smiling at the moment. Increasingly flustered, Selkirk settled the teacup on the floor at his feet and pulled his sopping hat from his head. Instantly, his poodle's ruff of curls spilled onto his forehead and over his ears.

Mrs. Marchant sat very still. "I'd forgotten," she finally said. "Isn't that funny?"

"Ma'am?"

Sighing, she leaned back. "Men's hair by daylight." Then she winked at him, and whispered, "The nuns are scandalized."

"Mrs. Marchant. The time has come. The Lighthouse Service—perhaps you've heard of it—needs to—"

"We had a dog, then," Mrs. Marchant said, and her eyes swung toward the windows.

Selkirk closed his eyes, feeling the warmth of the tea unfurling in his gut, hearing the longing underneath the play in the keeper's voice. When he opened his eyes again, he found Mrs. Marchant still staring toward the horizon.

"We named the dog Luis. For my father, who died at sea while my mother and I were on our way here from Lisbon. Charlie gave him to me."

After that, Selkirk hardly moved. It wasn't the story, which Amalia had told him, and which he hadn't forgotten. It was the way this woman said her husband's name.

"He didn't have to work, you know. Charlie. His family built half the boats that ever left this place. He said he just wanted to make certain his friends got home. Also, I think he liked living in the lighthouse. Especially alone with me. And my girls."

"Smart fellow," Selkirk murmured, realized to his amazement that he'd said it aloud, and blushed.

But the keeper simply nodded. "Yes. He was. Also reckless, in a way. No, that is wrong. He liked . . . playing at recklessness. In storms, he used to lash himself to the railing out there." She gestured toward the thin band of metal that encircled the platform outside the windows.

"Then he would lean into the rain. He said it was like sailing without having to hunt. And without leaving me."

"Was he religious, like you?" Selkirk hadn't meant to ask anything. And Mrs. Marchant looked completely baffled. "The . . ." Selkirk muttered, and gestured at the rug, the house. Sand convent. Whatever it was.

"Oh," she said. "It is a habit, only." Again, she grinned, but unlike Amalia, she waited until she was certain he'd gotten the joke. Then she went on. "While my father lived here, my mother and I earned extra money making dolls for the Sacred Heart of Mary. They gave them to poor girls. Poorer than we were."

The glow from Mrs. Marchant's eyes intensified on his cheek, as though he'd leaned nearer to a candle flame. Somehow, the feeling annoyed him, made him nervous.

"But he did leave you," he said, more harshly than he intended. "Your husband."

Mrs. Marchant's lips flattened slowly. "He meant to take me. The Kendall brothers—Kit was his best and oldest friend, and he'd known Kevin since the day Kevin was born—wanted us both to come sail with them, on the only beautiful January weekend I have ever experienced here. It was 1837. The air was so warm, Mr. Selkirk, and the whales gone for the winter. I didn't realize until then that Charlie had never once, in his whole life, been to sea. I'd never known until that weekend that he wanted to go. Of course I said yes. Then Luis twisted his foreleg in the rocks out there, and I stayed to be with him. And I made Charlie go anyway. He was blond like you. Did you know that?"

Shifting in his seat, Selkirk stared over the water. The sky hung heavy and low, its color an unbroken blackish gray, so that he no longer had any idea what time it was. After noon, surely. If he failed to conclude his business here soon, he'd never make it out of Winsett before nightfall, horse or no. At his feet, the nuns watched the water.

"Mrs. Marchant."

"He wasn't as tall as you are, of course. Happier, though."

Selkirk swung his head toward the woman. She took no notice.

"Of course, why wouldn't he be? He had so much luck in his short life. More than anyone deserves or has any right to expect. The Sacred Heart of Mary sisters always taught that it was bad luck to consort with the lucky. What do you make of that, Mr. Selkirk?"

Selkirk took several seconds to ponder the question, and as he sat, Mrs. Marchant stood abruptly and put her open palm on the window. For a crazy second, just because of the stillness of her posture and the oddly misdirected tilt of her head—toward land, away from the sea—Selkirk wondered if she were blind, like her dolls.

"I guess I've never been around enough luck to say," Selkirk finally said.

She'd been looking down the coast, but now she turned to him, beaming once more. "The sisters find you an honest man, sir. They invite you to more tea."

Returning to the bureau with his cup, she refilled it, then sat back down beside him. She'd left the nun she'd had before on the bureau, balancing in the center of a white plate like a tiny ice skater.

"The morning after they set sail," she said, "Luis woke me up." In the window, her eyes reflected against the gray. "He'd gotten better all through the day, and he'd been out all night. He loved to be. I often didn't see him until I came outside to hang the wash or do the chores. But that day, he scratched and whined against the door. I thought he'd fallen or hurt himself again and hurried to let him in. But when I did, he raced straight past me up the stairs. I hurried after, and found him whimpering against the light there. I was so worried that I didn't even look at the window for the longest time. And when I did . . ."

All the while, Mrs. Marchant had kept her hands pressed together in the folds of her dress, but now she opened them. Selkirk half expected a nun to flap free of them on starfish arms, but they were empty. "So much whiteness, Mr. Selkirk. And yet it was dark. You wouldn't think that would be possible, would you?"

"I've lived by the sea all my life," Selkirk said.

"Well, then. That's what it was like. A wall of white that shed no light at all. I couldn't even see the water. I had the lamp lit, of course, but all that did was emphasize the difference between *in here* and *out there*."

Selkirk stood. If he were Charlie Marchant, he thought, he would never have left the convent, as he'd begun to think of the whole place. Not to go to sea. Not even to town. He found himself remembering the letters he'd sent Amalia during his dock-working years. Pathetic, clumsy things. She'd never responded to those, either. Maybe she'd been trying, in her way, to be kind.

"I've often wondered if Luis somehow sensed the ship coming," Mrs. Marchant said. "We'd trained him to bark in the fog, in case a passing captain could hear but not see us. But maybe that day Luis was just barking at the whiteness.

"The sound was unmistakable when it came. I heard wood splintering. Sails collapsing. A mast smashing into the water. But there wasn't any screaming. And I thought . . ."

"You thought maybe the crew had escaped to the lifeboats," Selkirk said, when it was clear Mrs. Marchant was not going to finish her sentence.

For the first time in several minutes, Mrs. Marchant turned her gaze on him. Abruptly, that luminous smile crept over her lips. "You would make the most marvelous stuffed giraffe," she said.

Selkirk stiffened. Was he going to have to carry this poor, gently raving woman out of here? "Mrs. Marchant, it's already late. We need to be starting for town soon."

If she understood what he meant, she gave no sign, "I knew what ship it was." She sank back into her wicker chair, the smile gone, and crossed her legs. "What other vessel would be out there in the middle of winter? I started screaming, pounding the glass. It didn't take me long to realize they wouldn't have gone to the rowboats. In all likelihood, they'd had no idea where they were. The Kendall boys were experienced seamen, excellent sailors, Mr. Selkirk. But that fog had dropped straight out of the heart of the sky, or maybe it had risen from the dead sea bottom, and it was solid as stone.

"And then—as if it were the fog bank itself, and not Charlie's boat, that had run aground on the sandbar out there—all that whiteness just shattered. The whole wall cracked apart into whistling, flying fragments. Just like that, the blizzard blew in. How does that happen, Mr. Selkirk? How does the sea change its mind like that?"

Selkirk didn't answer. But for the first time, he thought he understood why the sailors in the Blubber Pike referred to those teasing, far-off flickers of light the way they did.

"I rushed downstairs, thinking I'd get the rowboat and haul myself out there and save them. But the waves . . . they were snarling and snapping all over themselves, and I knew I'd have to wait. My tears were freezing on my face. I was wearing only a dressing gown, and the wind whipped right through me. The door to the lighthouse was banging because I hadn't shut it properly, and I was so full of fury and panic I was ready to start screaming again. I looked out to sea, and all but fell to my knees in gratitude.

"It was there, Mr. Selkirk. I could see the ship. Some of it, anyway. Enough, perhaps. I could just make it out. The prow, part of the foredeck, a stump of mast. I turned around and raced back inside for my clothes.

"Then I ran all the way to town. We never kept a horse here; Charlie didn't like them. The strangest thing was this sensation I kept having, this feeling that I'd gotten lost. It was impossible; that path out there was well-traveled in those days, and even now, you had no trouble, did you? But I couldn't feel my skin. Or . . . it was as though I had come out of it. There was snow and sand flying all around, wind in the dunes. So cold. My Charlie out there. I remember thinking, *This is what the Bruxsa feels like. This is why she torments travelers. This is why she feeds.* You know, at some point, I thought maybe I'd become her."

Pursing his lips, Selkirk stirred from the daze that had settled over him. "Brucka?"

"*Bruxsa.* It is like . . . a banshee? Do you know the word? A ghost, but not of anyone. A horrid thing all its own."

Was it his imagination, or had the dark outside deepened toward evening? If he didn't get this finished, neither one of them would make it out of here tonight. "Mrs. Marchant, perhaps we could continue this on the way back to town."

Finally, as though he'd slapped her, Mrs. Marchant blinked. "What?"

"Mrs. Marchant, surely you understand the reason for my coming. We'll send for your things. You don't *have* to leave today, but wouldn't that be easiest? I'll walk with you. I'll make certain— "

"When I finally reached Winsett," Mrs. Marchant said, her stare returning, as that peculiar, distant smiled played across her mouth, "I went straight for the first lit window I saw. Selkirk's. The candle maker. Your uncle."

Selkirk cringed, remembering those hard, overheated hands smashing against the side of his skull.

"He was so kind," she said, and his mouth quivered and fell open as she went on. "He rushed me inside. It was warm in his shop. At the time, it literally felt as though he'd saved my life. Returned me to my body. I sat by his fire, and he raced all over town through the blizzard and came back with whalers, sailing men. Charlie's father, and the Kendalls' older brother. There were fifteen of them, at least. Most set out immediately on horseback for the Point. Your uncle wrapped me in two additional sweaters and an overcoat, and he walked all the way back out here with me, telling me it would be all right. By the time we reached the lighthouse, he said the sailors would already have figured a way to get the boys off that sandbar and home."

To Selkirk, it seemed this woman had reached into his memories and daubed them with colors he knew couldn't have been there. His uncle had been kind to no one. His uncle had hardly spoken except to complete business. The very idea of his using his shop fire to warm somebody, risking himself to rouse the town to some wealthy playboy's rescue . . .

But of course, by the time Selkirk had come here, the town was well on its way to failing, and his aunt had died in some awful, silent way no one spoke about. Maybe his uncle had been different, before. Or maybe, he thought with a sick quivering deep in his stomach, he was just an old lecher, on top of being a drunk.

"By the time we got back here, it was nearly dusk," Mrs. Marchant said. "The older Kendall and four of the sailors had already tried four different times to get the rowboat away from shore and into the waves. They were all tucked inside my house, now, trying to stave off pneumonia.

" 'Tomorrow,' one of the sailors told me. 'Tomorrow, please God, if they can just hold on. We'll find a way to them.'

"And right then, Mr. Selkirk. Right as the light went out of that awful day for good, the snow cleared. For one moment. And there they were."

A single tear crept from the lashes of her right eye. She was almost whispering now. "It was like a gift. Like a glimpse of him in heaven. I raced back outside, called out, leapt up and down—we all did—but of course they couldn't hear, and weren't paying attention. They were scrambling all over the deck. I knew right away which was Charlie. He was in the bow, all bundled up in a hat that wasn't his and what looked like three or four coats. He looked like one of my nuns, Mr. Selkirk." She grinned again. "The one with the bandeau that hides her face? I was holding her in my lap before. I made her in memory of that one moment."

Selkirk stared. Was the woman actually celebrating this story?

"I could also see the Kendall boys' hair as they worked amidships. So red, like twin suns burning off the overcast.

" 'Bailing,' Charlie's father told me. 'The ship must be taking on water. They're trying to keep her where she is.' "

Again, Mrs. Marchant's smile slid, but didn't vanish entirely. "I asked how long they could keep doing that. But what I really wondered was how long they'd already been at it. Those poor, beautiful boys.

"Our glimpse lasted two minutes. Maybe even less. I

could see new clouds rising behind them. Like a sea
monster rearing right out of the waves. But at the last,
just before the snow and the dark obliterated our sight of
them, they all stopped as one, and turned around. I'm
sorry, Mr. Selkirk."

She didn't wipe her face, and there weren't any tears
Selkirk could see. She simply sat in her chair, breathing
softly. Selkirk watched her with some relief.

"I remember the older Kendall boy standing beside
me," she finally said. "He was whispering. 'Aw, come on
boys. Get your gear on.' The Kendalls, you see . . .
they'd removed their coats. And I finally realized what it
meant, that I could see their hair. They hadn't bothered
with their hats, even though they'd kept at the bailing.
Remember, I've been around sailors all my life, Mr.
Selkirk. All the men in my family were sailors, long before they came to this country. My father had been whaling here when he sent for us. So I knew what I was
seeing."

"And what was that?"

"The Kendalls had given up. Less than a hundred
yards from shore, they'd given up. Or decided that they
weren't going to make it through the night. Either rescue
would come before dawn, or it would no longer matter.
The ship would not hold. Or the cold would overwhelm
them. So they were hastening the end, one way or another.

"But not Charlie. Not my Charlie. He didn't jump in
the air. He just slumped against the railing. But I know
he saw me, Mr. Selkirk. I could feel him. Even under all

those hats. I could always feel him. Then the snow came back. And night fell.

"The next time we saw them, they were in the rigging."

Silently, Selkirk gave up the idea of escaping Winsett until morning. The network of functioning lights and functional keepers the Service had been toiling so hard to establish could wait one more winter evening.

"This was midday, the second day. That storm was a freak of nature. Or perhaps not natural at all. How can that much wind blow a storm nowhere? It was as though the blizzard itself had locked jaws on those boys—on my boy—and would not let go. The men who weren't already wracked by coughs and fever made another five attempts with the rowboat, and never got more than fifteen feet from shore. The ice in the air was like arrows raining down.

"Not long after the last attempt, when almost everyone was indoors, and I was rushing about making tea and caring for the sick and trying to shush Luis, who had been barking since dawn, I heard Charlie's father cry out, and hurried outside.

"I'd never seen light like that, Mr. Selkirk, and I haven't since. Neither snow nor wind had eased one bit, and the clouds hadn't lifted. But there was the ship again, and there were our boys. Up in the ropes now. The Kendalls had their hats back on and their coats around them, tucked up tight together with their arms through the lines. Charlie had gone even higher, crouching by himself, looking down at the brothers or maybe the deck. I hoped they were talking to each other or singing—

anything to keep their spirits up and their breath in them. Because the ship . . . Have you ever seen quicksand, Mr. Selkirk? It was almost like that. This glimpse lasted a minute, maybe less. But in that time, the hull dropped what looked like another full foot underwater. And that was the only thing we saw move."

"I don't understand," Selkirk said. "The sandbar was right there. It's what they hit, right? Or the rocks right around it? Why not just climb down?"

"If they'd so much as put their feet in that water, after all they'd been exposed to, they would have frozen on the spot. All they could do was cling to the ropes.

"So they clung. The last healthy men came out behind Charlie's father and me to watch. And somehow, just the clear sight of the ship out there inspired us all. And the way the mast was tilting toward the surface got us all angry and active again.

"We got close once, just at dark. The snow hadn't cleared, but the wind had eased. It had been in our ears so long, I'm not sure we even realized it at first. The sickest men, including the older Kendall boy, had been run back to town on horseback, and we hoped other Winsett whalers might be rigging up a brig in the harbor to try reaching Charlie's ship from the sea side, rather than from land, the moment the weather permitted. I kept thinking I'd heard new sounds out there, caught a glimpse of the mast of a rescue vessel. But of course it was too soon, and we couldn't really hear or see anything but the storm, anyway. And in the midst of another round of crazy, useless running about, Charlie's father grabbed my wrist and whirled me around to face the water and said, 'Stop. Listen.'

"And I understood finally that I heard nothing. Sweet, beautiful nothing. Right away I imagined that I should be able to hear Charlie and the Kendalls through the quiet. Before anyone could stop me, I was racing for the shore, my feet flying into the icy water and my dress freezing against my legs, but I could hardly feel it. I was already so cold, so numb. We all were. I started screaming my husband's name. It was too shadowy and snowy to see. But I went right on screaming, and everyone else that was left with us held still.

"But I got no answer. If it weren't for the swirling around my feet, I might have thought even the water had had its voice sucked from it. And then . . ."

Finally, for the first time, Mrs. Marchant's voice broke. In a horrible way, Selkirk realized he envied her this experience. No single hour, let alone day, had ever impressed itself on him the way those days had on her, except perhaps for his few fleeting, sleet-drenched moments with Amalia. And those had cast an uglier, darker shadow.

When Mrs. Marchant continued, the quaver had gone, as though she'd swallowed it. "It was to be the last time I heard his real voice, Mr. Selkirk. I think I already knew that. And when I remember it now, I'm not even certain I really did hear it. How could I have? It was a croak, barely even a whisper. But it was Charlie's voice. I'd still swear to it, in spite of everything, even though he said just the one word. 'Hurry.'

"The last two remaining men from Winsett needed no

further encouragement. In an instant, they had the rowboat in the water. Charlie's dad and I shoved off, while they pulled with all their might against the crush of the surf. For a minute, no more, they hung up in that same spot that had deviled all our efforts for the past thirty-six hours, caught in waves that beat them back and back. Then they just sprung free. All of a sudden, they were in open water, heaving with all their might toward the sandbar. We were too exhausted to clap or cheer. But my heart leapt so hard in my chest I thought it might break my ribs.

"As soon as they were twenty feet from shore, we lost sight of them, and later, they said all they saw was blackness and water and snow, so none of us knows how close they actually got. They were gone six, maybe seven minutes. Then, as if a dyke had collapsed, sound came rushing over us. The wind roared in and brought a new, hard sleet. There was a one last, terrible pause that none of us mistook for calm. The water had simply risen up, you see, Mr. Selkirk. It lifted our rescue rowboat in one giant, black wave and hurled it halfway up the beach. The two men in the boat got slammed to the sand. Fortunately— miraculously, really—the wave didn't crest until it was nearly on top of the shore, so neither man drowned. One broke both wrists, the other his nose and teeth. Meanwhile, the water poured up the beach, soaked us all, and retreated as instantaneously as it had come."

For the first time, Selkirk realized that the story he was hearing no longer quite matched the one Amalia had told him. Even more startling, Amalia's had been less cruel. No rescues had been attempted, because none had been possible. No real hope had ever emerged. The ship had simply slid off the sandbar, and all aboard had drowned.

"Waves don't just rise up," he said.

Mrs. Marchant tilted her head. "No? My father used to come home from half a year at sea and tell us stories. Waves riding the ghost of a wind two years gone and two thousand leagues distant, roaming alone like great, rogue beasts, devouring everything they encounter. Not an uncommon occurrence on the open ocean."

"But this isn't the open ocean."

"And you think the ocean knows, or cares? Though I will admit to you, Mr. Selkirk. At the time, it seemed like the sea just didn't want us out there.

"By now, the only two healthy people at Cape Roby Point were Charlie's father and me. And when that new sleet kept coming and coming . . . well. We didn't talk about it. We made our wounded rowers as comfortable as we could by the fire on the rugs inside. Then we set about washing bedding, setting out candles. I began making this little sister here"—as she spoke, she toed the doll with the white bandeau, which leaned against her feet—"to keep him company in his coffin. Although both of us knew, I'm sure, that we weren't even likely to get the bodies back.

"My God, the sounds of that night. I can still hear the sleet drumming on the roof. The wind coiling around the tower. All I could think about was Charlie out there, clinging to the ropes for hope of reaching me. I knew he would be gone by morning. Around two a.m., Charlie's father fell asleep leaning against a wall, and I eased him into a chair and sank down on the floor beside him. I must have been so exhausted, so overwhelmed, that I slept, too, without meaning to, right there at his feet.

"And when I woke . . ."

The Kendalls, Selkirk thought, as he watched the woman purse her mouth and hold still. Had he known them? It seemed to him he'd at least known who they were. At that time, though, he'd had eyes only for Amalia. And after that, he'd kept to himself, and left everyone else alone.

"When I woke," Mrs. Marchant murmured, "there was sunlight. I didn't wait to make sense of what I was seeing. I didn't think about what I'd find. I didn't wake Charlie's father, but he came roaring after me as I sprinted from the house.

"We didn't even know if our rowboat would float. We made straight for it anyway. I didn't look at the sandbar. Do you find that strange? I didn't want to see. Not yet. I looked at the dunes, and they were gold, Mr. Selkirk. Even with the blown grass and seaweed strewn all over them, they looked newly born.

"The rowboat had landed on its side. The wood had begun to split all down one side, but Charlie's father thought it would hold. Anyway, it was all we had, our last chance. Without a word, we righted it and dragged it to the water, which was like glass. Absolutely flat, barely rolling over to touch the beach. Charlie's father wasn't waiting for me. He'd already got into the boat and begun to pull. But when I caught the back and dragged myself in, he held position just long enough, still not saying a single thing. Then he started rowing for all he was worth.

"For a few seconds longer, I kept my head down. I wanted to pray, but I couldn't. My mother was a Catholic, and we'd worked for the nuns. But somehow, making the dolls had turned God doll-like, for me. Does that make sense? I found it impossible to have faith in anything that took the face we made for it. I wanted some other face than the one I knew, then. So I closed my eyes and listened to the seagulls squealing around, skimming the surface for dead fish. Nothing came to me, except how badly I wanted Charlie back. Finally, I lifted my head.

"I didn't gasp, or cry out. I don't think I even felt anything.

"First off, there were only two of them. The highest was Charlie. He'd climbed almost to the very top of the main mast, which had tilted over so far that it couldn't have been more than twenty-five feet above the water. Even with that overcoat engulfing him and the hat pulled all the way down over his ears, I could tell by the arms and legs snarled in the rigging that it was him.

" 'Is he moving, girl?' Charlie's father asked, and I realized he hadn't been able to bring himself to look, either. We lurched closer.

"Then I did gasp, Mr. Selkirk. Just once. Because he *was* moving. Or I thought he was. He seemed to be settling . . . resettling . . . I can't explain it. He was winding his arms and legs through the ropes, like a child trying to fit into a hiding place as you come for him. As if he'd just come back there. Or maybe the movement was wind. Even now, I don't know.

"Charlie's father swore at me and snarled his question

again. When I didn't answer, he turned around. 'Lord Jesus,' I heard him say. After that, he just put his head down and rowed. And I kept my eyes on Charlie, and the empty blue sky beyond him. Anywhere but down the mast, where the other Kendall boy hung.

"By his ankles, Mr. Selkirk. His ankles, and nothing more. God only knows what held him there. The wind had torn his clothes right off him. He had his eyes and his mouth open. He looked so pale, so thin, nothing like he had in life. His body had red slashes all over it, as though the storm had literally tried to rip him open. Just a boy, Mr. Selkirk. His fingertips all but dancing on the water.

"Charlie's father gave one last heave, and our little boat knocked against the last showing bit of the Kendalls' ship's hull. The masts above us groaned, and I thought the whole thing was going to crash down on top of us. Charlie's father tried to wedge an oar in the wood, get us in close, and finally he just rowed around the ship and ran us aground on the sandbar. I leapt out after him, thinking I should be the one to climb the mast. I was lighter, less likely to sink the whole thing once and for all. Our home, our lighthouse, was so close it seemed I could have waded over and grabbed it. I probably could have. I leaned back, looked up again, and this time I was certain I saw Charlie move.

"His father saw it, too, and he started screaming. He wasn't even making words, but I was. I had my arms wide open, and I was calling my husband. 'Come down. Come home, my love.' I saw his arms disentangle themselves, his legs slide free. The ship sagged beneath him.

If he so much as touched that water, I thought, it would be too much. The cold would have him at the last. He halted, and his father stopped screaming, and I went silent. He hung there so long I thought he'd died after all, now that he'd heard our voices one last time. Then, hand over hand, so painfully slowly, like a spider crawling down a web, he began to edge upside-down over the ropes. He reached the Kendall boy's poor, naked body and bumped it with his hip. It swung out and back, out and back. Charlie never even looked, and he didn't slow or alter his path. He kept coming.

"I don't even remember how he got over the rail. As he reached the deck, he disappeared a moment from our sight. We were trying to figure how to get up there to him. Then he just climbed over the edge and fell to the sand at our feet. The momentum from his body gave the wreck a final push, and it slid off the sandbar into the water and sank, taking the Kendall boy's body with it.

"The effort of getting down had taken everything Charlie had. His eyes were closed. His breaths were shallow, and he didn't respond when we shook him. So Charlie's father lifted him and dropped him in the rowboat. I hopped in the bow with my back to the shore, and Charlie's father began to pull desperately for the mainland. I was sitting calf-deep in water, cradling my husband's head facedown in my lap. I stroked his cheeks, and they were so cold. Impossibly cold, and bristly, and hard. Like rock. All my thoughts, all my energy, all the heat I had I was willing into my fingers, and I was cooing like a dove. Charlie's father had his back to us, pulling for everything he was worth. He never turned around. And so he didn't . . ."

Once more, Mrs. Marchant's voice trailed away. Out the filthy windows, in the gray that had definitely darkened into full-blown dusk now, Selkirk could see a single trail of yellow-red, right at the horizon, like the glimpse of eye underneath a cat's closed lid. Tomorrow the weather would clear. And he would be gone, on his way home. Maybe he would stay there this time. Find somebody he didn't have to pay to keep him company.

"It's a brave thing you've done, Mrs. Marchant," he said, and before he could think about what he was doing, he slid forward and took her chilly hand in his. He meant nothing by it but comfort, and was surprised to discover the sweet, transitory sadness of another person's fingers curled in his. A devil's smile of a feeling, if ever there was one. "He was a good man, your husband. You have mourned him properly and well."

"Just a boy," she whispered.

"A good boy, then. And he loved you. You have paid him the tribute he deserved, and more. And now it's time to do him the honor of living again. Come back to town. I'll see you somewhere safe and warm. I'll see you there myself, if you'll let me."

Very slowly, without removing her fingers, Mrs. Marchant raised her eyes to his, and her mouth came open. "You . . . you silly man. You think . . . But you said you knew the story."

Confused, Selkirk squeezed her hand. "I know it now."

"You believe I have stayed here, cut off from all that

is good in the world, shut up with my nuns all these years like an abbess, for love? For grief?"

Now Selkirk let go, watching as Mrs. Marchant's hand fluttered before settling in her lap like a blown leaf. "There's no crime in that, surely. But now—"

"I've always wondered how the rowboat flipped," she said, in a completely new, expressionless tone, devoid of all her half-sung tones, as he stuttered to silence. "All the times I've gone through it and over it, and I can't get it straight. I can't see how it happened."

Unsure what to do with his hands, Selkirk finally settled them on his knees. "The rowboat?"

"Dead calm. No ghost wave this time. We were twenty yards from shore. Less. We could have hopped out and walked. I was still cooing. Still stroking my husband's cheeks. But I knew already. And I think his father knew, too. Charlie had died before we even got him in the boat. He wasn't breathing. Wasn't moving. He hadn't during the whole, silent trip back to shore. I turned toward land to see exactly how close we were. And just like that, I was in the water.

"If you had three men and were trying, you couldn't flip a boat that quickly. One of the oars banged me on the head. I don't know if it was that or the cold that stunned me. But I couldn't think. For a second, I had no idea which way was up, even in three feet of water, and then my feet found bottom, and I stood and staggered toward shore. The oar had caught me right on the scalp, and a stream of blood kept pouring into my eyes. I wasn't thinking about Charlie. I wasn't thinking anything except that I needed to be out of the cold before I became it. I could feel it in my bloodstream. I got to the beach, collapsed in the sun, remembered where I was and what I'd been doing, and spun around.

"There was the boat, floating right-side up, as though it hadn't flipped it all. Oars neatly shipped, like arms folded across a chest. Water still as a lagoon beneath it. And neither my husband nor his father *anywhere*.

"I almost laughed. It was impossible. Ridiculous. So cruel. I didn't scream. I waited, scanning the water, ready to lunge in and save Charlie's dad, if I could only see him. But there was nothing. No trace. I sat down and stared at the horizon and didn't weep. It seemed perfectly possible that I might freeze to death right there, complete the event. I even opened the throat of my dress, thinking of the Kendall boys shedding their coats that first day. That's what I was doing when Charlie crawled out of the water."

Selkirk stood up. "But you said—"

"He'd lost his hat. And his coat had come open. He crawled right up the beach, sidewise, like a crab. Just the way he had down the rigging. Of course, my arms opened to him, and the cold dove down my dress. I was laughing, Mr. Selkirk. Weeping and laughing and cooing, and his head swung up, and I saw."

With a single, determined wriggle of her shoulders, Mrs. Marchant went completely still. She didn't speak again for several minutes. Helpless, Selkirk sat back down.

"The only question I had in the end, Mr. Selkirk, was when it had happened."

For no reason he could name, Selkirk experienced a

flash of Amalia's cruel, haunted face, and tried for the thousandth time to imagine where she'd gone. Then he thought of the dead town behind him, the debris disappearing piece by piece and bone by bone into the dunes, his aunt's silent death. His uncle. He'd never made any effort to determine what had happened to his uncle after Amalia vanished.

"I still think about those boys, you know," Mrs. Marchant murmured. "Every day. The one suspended in the ropes, exposed like that, all torn up. And the one who disappeared. Do you think he jumped to get away, Mr. Selkirk? I think he might have. I would have."

"What on earth are you—?"

"Even the dead's eyes reflect light," she said, turning her bright and living ones on him. "Did you know that? But Charlie's eyes . . . Of course, it wasn't really Charlie, but . . ."

Selkirk almost leapt to his feet again, wanted to, wished he could hurtle downstairs, flee into the dusk. And simultaneously he found that he couldn't.

"What do you mean?"

For answer, Mrs. Marchant cocked her head at him, and the ghost of her smile hovered over her mouth and evaporated. "What do I mean? How do I know? Was it a ghost? Do you know how many hundreds of sailors have died within five miles of this point? Surely one or two of them might have been angry about it."

"Are you actually saying—?"

"Or maybe that's silly. Maybe ghosts are like gods, no? Familiar faces we have clamped on what comes for us? Maybe it was the sea. I can't tell you. What I can tell you is that there was no Charlie in the face before me, Mr. Selkirk. None. I had no doubt. No question. My only hope was that whatever it was had come for him after he was gone, the way a hermit crab climbs inside a shell. Please God, whatever that is, let it be the wind and the cold that took him."

Staggering upright, Selkirk shook his head. "You said he was dead."

"So he was."

"You were mistaken."

"It killed the Kendall boy, Mr. Selkirk. It crawled down and tore him to shreds. I'm fairly certain it killed its own father as well. Charlie's father, I mean. Luis took one look at Charlie and vanished into the dunes. I never saw the dog again."

"Of course it was your husband. You're not yourself, Mrs. Marchant. All these years alone . . . It spared you, didn't it? Didn't he?"

Mrs. Marchant smiled one more time and broke down weeping, silently. "It had just eaten," she whispered. "Or whatever it does. Or maybe I had just lost my last loved ones, and stank of the sea, and appeared as dead to it as it did to me."

"Listen to me," Selkirk said, and on impulse he dropped to one knee and took her hands once more. God, but they were cold. So many years in this cold, with this weight on her shoulders. "That day was so full of tragedy. Whatever you think you . . ."

Very slowly, Selkirk stopped. His mind retreated down the stairs, out the lighthouse door to the mainland, over the disappearing path he'd walked between the dunes, and all the way back into Winsett. He saw anew the shuttered boardinghouses and empty taverns, the grim smile of the stable boy. He saw the street where his uncle's shop had been. What had happened to his uncle? His aunt? *Amalia?* Where had they all gone? Just how long had it taken Winsett to die? His mind scrambled farther, out of town, up the track he had taken, between the discarded pots and decaying whale bones toward the other silent, deserted towns all along this blasted section of the Cape.

"Mrs. Marchant," he whispered, his hands tightening around hers, having finally understood why she had stayed. "Mrs. Marchant, please. Where is Charlie now?"

She stood, then, and twined one gentle finger through the tops of his curls as she wiped at her tears. The gesture felt dispassionate, almost maternal, something a mother might do to a son who has just awoken. He looked up and found her gazing again not out to sea, but over the dunes at the dark streaming inland.

"It's going to get even colder," she said. "I'll put the kettle on."

INSIDE THE LABYRINTH

By David Riley

Having paid his three and a half thousand drachma entrance fee, Beckett strolled with a studied nonchalance that all but belied his inner feelings of excitement down the gritty path towards the ancient Minoan palace at Knossos. Brilliant July sunlight seemed to bring out everything before him in incredibly sharp detail, as if his spectacles had been given even stronger lenses suddenly; so bright, in fact, that he had to narrow his eyes a little against the glare from some of the lighter stones of the excavated ruins.

He breathed out a sigh of utter contentment.

It had been his burning ambition for years to visit this, the home of one of the earliest and mightiest Mediterranean powers of the ancient world, a legendary civilisation that had already been forgotten long before Rome rose to power. Mesmerised, Beckett tried to take in the partially restored frescoes and dark blue pillars and tiers of solid, stone-built administrative buildings that made up the palace complex, his imagination only fitfully able to fill in gaps left by the violent ravages that had destroyed so much of this massive place, as a harsh-voiced peacock shrieked its strut across a paved courtyard less than twenty feet below the stone walkway he was on. It was a fitting sound, Beckett thought: a forlorn, rasping lament. It suited his mood as he gazed at the ruins; he felt saddened now, and at the same time awed by the sense of loss they inspired within him.

Tonight he knew he would get drunk when he arrived back at his hotel in Heraklion. Good, strong Cretan wine—that was the only thing he could drink after coming here. And plenty of it. In homage to Bacchus, if nothing else. Though in truth it was not often he felt need of an excuse to get drunk these days; the impulse was never all that far away. Though he blamed that as much on his failed marriage and the dead-end rut into which his career seemed to have dug itself in what fitfully passed for the history department at Mount Pleasant High School as much as anything else, even if excessive drinking had been one of several reasons Melanie had given for leaving their once so cosy shared abode in suburban Pire earlier this year.

Beckett let out a long sigh, then looked round embarrassed at the other tourists milling about the site with cameras and camcorders, to see if any of them had overheard him. The sigh had sounded overly loud even to him. Fortunately the nearest visitors, a middle aged couple with a scantily clad teenage girl, were too engrossed in sorting out who was to photograph whom against a brilliantly painted mural of a highly stylised octopus.

"It often makes me feel sad too."

Startled, Beckett turned at the comment.

A short, dark-featured, grey-haired man in a soft brown jacket that looked like very old suede, stood watching him from a few feet away with glittering, jet-black eyes, stubble almost thick enough to be a beard covering his chin and the sagging lines of his jaw. So pure was the English of his accent, Beckett would have not automatically taken him for a Greek.

"There is such an intense feeling of lost potential in this place," the man continued in a sad, almost wistful voice. "After all, as I am sure you are aware, it was neither war nor pestilence nor internal decay that finished them off, but the greatest volcanic explosion in recorded human history—that and the subsequent earthquakes and natural disasters which followed it." He shrugged his angular shoulders. "There was nothing they could have done to save themselves."

Unsettled by how the man could have got so close behind him so quickly, Beckett expressed his agreement with the man's comments. "Who knows what they might have achieved otherwise."

"Who knows, indeed?"

The man stepped nearer. Although the temperature was verging on one hundred degrees, he appeared at ease in his unseasonably heavy clothes, though Beckett noticed he wore no socks with his leather sandals, his thick yellow toenails like old ivory showing through the well-creased leather straps.

"Is this your first visit to Knossos?" the man asked.

"It's my first trip to Crete, though I've looked forward to seeing it for years."

The man nodded his head. "I come here often. At least two or three times a year. I am a teacher in Athens, and I like to keep abreast with the excavations still going on, so I can make my lectures about it back home as up to date as I can."

"You're a teacher of history?"

The man nodded again.

"That's a coincidence," Beckett exclaimed, genuinely pleased.

After that it was only minutes before they had exchanged names—the old man's was Demetrios Polydopoulos—and begun to discuss the various faults besetting their respective schools, before Demetrios suggested guiding his new friend round the ruins. "Since I know them so well, and you have limited time here, I can ensure that you miss nothing of interest."

"That would be great," Beckett enthused. "Just great."

As they walked about the vast ruins, it turned out that Demetrios was also staying in Heraklion, which was perhaps less than coincidental, since it was only a fifteen-minute drive from Knossos and an obvious place for someone interested in the excavations to stay. Unlike Beckett, though, who had come on a coach tour from his hotel, Demetrios had hired a car.

"Why not tell your tour guide you will return with me? You could stay here till the site closes at seven instead of going back earlier," Demetrios suggested. "And, unless you have already made arrangements for tonight with some of your friends on the tour, I know an exceptionally good restaurant where we could eat later."

Heartily despising most of his fellow tourists as a rag-tag mob of sun-seeking ignoramuses, Beckett very quickly assured Demetrios that he had made no arrangements with anyone at all. "I'm free to do what I please."

Demetrios smiled, for the first time revealing his small, nastily stained teeth. Like old, clotted blood in colour, Beckett wondered if the old man's gums had been bleeding.

Excessive queasiness about other people's personal hygiene being one of an admittedly quite long list of reasons Melanie gave for leaving him, Beckett could not help but feel suddenly less happy about his new friend's company. Despite this, though, he successfully managed to put most of his misgivings to one side as they toured the site. For all that the old man's teeth inspired nothing but nausea, he was a fascinating storyteller, more than capable of lending an extra-special magic to the ruins they looked at, as he plied Beckett with anecdote after anecdote about the place.

"This is a depiction of the man-bull, the minotaur," Demetrios explained; he pointed out the large, deep red fresco in question. "It is here the fabled creature was kept hidden in a deep labyrinth, where it was given human sacrifices by the king of Crete till it was eventually killed by the young Athenian hero Theseus. Though even death was no permanent thing for such a formidable creature. And every year sacrifices were made to its spirit, the greatest bull in the local herds being put to death to appease it. As, indeed, to this day there are villages where this is still carried out. I know. I have seen them."

Straining his eyes against the sunlight, Beckett said: "I wonder where the labyrinth was."

"It is wherever fables are," Demetrios replied. He tapped the side of his head. "In the wonderment and imagination of the human mind."

Beckett laughed. "I asked for that."

Demetrios laughed too. "As, indeed, you did."

By seven they were ready to leave. Though they had had a drink in the site cafe, the heat had given Beckett a thirst which it would take more than a couple of cokes to satisfy.

"I'll drop you off at your hotel," Demetrios said as they walked across the car park to a dusty, white Opel Corsa. "And meet you there at eight thirty, perhaps?"

Beckett said that would be great. "It'll give me just enough time to have a shower and get changed."

By eight twenty-five he was already waiting in the air-conditioned coolness of the hotel lobby, dressed in his most expensive brushed denim jeans and a green and blue Benetton T-shirt which had formerly belonged to his wife.

Demetrios arrived on time five minutes later. Unlike Beckett, he hadn't bothered to change; even the dust from Knossos still clung to his sandaled feet.

Leaving the hotel, they were within minutes on the seafront and heading past what looked at first glance like huge, derelict warehouses, the streets surrounding them cluttered with rows of badly parked cars. Leaving these behind they strolled towards the old town, a maze of short, disjointed streets filled with incongruously modern shop facades. At one point, making Beckett laugh out loud, they saw several tall, cardboard cutouts of Santa Claus leaning against the wall of a closed nightclub, as if they'd been abandoned. Beckett snorted at their high-heeled boots. "Looks like Santa's been doing a bit of cross-dressing," he joked to a puzzled Demetrios, whose grasp of English, Beckett deduced, was perhaps less proficient than his impeccable accent implied.

Then they were at their destination. On a particularly narrow street, otherwise filled with leather shops, boutiques and jewellers, an open doorway took them into a dimly lit taverna. Beckett breathed in the appetising aromas that filled its overheated atmosphere: garlic, tzatziki, tomatoes and onions. Small, comfortable-looking tables covered in spotless white damask filled most of the cramped space between the painted plaster walls, and old, Minoan-style vases stood on narrow shelves at head height, alongside "ancient" masks and effigies.

Perhaps too early even now for most of its regular customers, the taverna was disappointingly empty, apart from an elderly couple, sat hunched like gargoyles over what remained of lamb roasted in yoghurt.

Almost as soon as they stepped in, a waiter appeared from the back of the taverna, round face beaming a welcome to them as Demetrios addressed him in Greek. Nodding his head in assent, the waiter led them to a table several spaces away from the couple, then handed them menus.

"A drink?"

Demetrios glanced at Beckett, his thick eyebrows raised enquiringly.

"A lager for me," Beckett said. "I was going to have

wine, but this heat's given me too big a thirst for any of that just yet."

"But wine for me," Demetrios said. "Red wine."

While they waited for their drinks to arrive they took the opportunity to glance through their menus.

And so it began.

They chose light appetisers to start with—taramosalata for Beckett and stuffed vine leaves for Demetrios. Then, with Beckett's thirst momentarily soothed by two large beers, he finally agreed to order a bottle of wine to go with their main course: lamb and pasta for Beckett and macaroni pie with minced meat and bechamel sauce for Demetrios. As they ate, they drank, and their first bottle was soon replaced by another, then another, as the light darkened outside the taverna into night, with the faraway laughter of revellers on a neighbouring street. Inside the taverna, though, it was quiet. The elderly couple had long gone by the time Beckett and Demetrios were on their main course, and no one else had come in since they left. For all of this, though, there was an atmosphere of friendship and joyousness which struck Beckett as unique. Perhaps it was the wine, which he found himself drinking as if it was just a differently coloured cola. Or perhaps it was the company. For all that Demetrios was an odd-looking fellow with quite disgusting teeth, he was amusing and informative at one and the same time, filling Beckett sometimes with a sense little short of awe, when he discussed the ancient goings-on of some Cretan god or monster.

Before he had even finished his lamb and pasta, Beckett realised he was starting to feel drunk. Nothing unusual or even particularly unwelcome about this, it was only the speed with which it was happening that struck him as different, though he was, he knew it, throwing the wine back more quickly than normal. But so what? He was on holiday, with no need to get up early tomorrow morning—if at all. And he was in good company. He grinned at Demetrios, who was rounding off a tale about sacrificial bulls in a village on one of the Greek islands he'd visited, though Beckett had begun to lose track of what he was talking about minutes ago. Too much wine, he told himself. Or, perhaps, not enough. Whatever, it didn't matter. None of it did.

None at all.

He felt his grin broaden, become nonsensically wide, as if something he couldn't feel had gripped his cheeks and was drawing them farther and farther apart.

He reached for his wine glass, filled it once more from an already half-empty bottle, then took a long and leisurely drink, the rich wine filling his mouth with a taste of berries and herbs, of wildflowers and long, hot nights beneath the stars.

Beckett blinked. Now he knew he was drunk. There'd be poetry spouting from his lips next.

"I'm sorry," he muttered, his sense of balance sliding away as he pushed himself unsteadily to his feet. It wasn't just his balance, though, that was starting to slide away. As he put his hands on one side of the table, it began to tip over. He saw Demetrios suddenly leap to his feet as glasses tumbled and crashed to the ground.

Then someone took a hold of Beckett's arms.

"I'm sorry . . ."

With vertigo taking over, he wasn't even sure if it was his own voice he heard, or if someone else was talking. Confused, he saw Demetrios step round the table.

"Sacrificial bulls . . ."

Was that Demetrios? The voice wasn't clear. It could have been Beckett himself. Maybe . . .

"Put your weight on my arm."

This was Demetrios. He knew that now.

Beckett turned to him, suddenly angry at himself for not realising just how drunk he'd become till it was too late, till he was so far gone he couldn't even stand on his own anymore.

"I'm sorry, Demetrios," he heard himself say.

For a moment more he retained some semblance of consciousness, then oblivion set in. There were blurred patches in which he was aware of being led down a narrow, twisting street in the gloom, of rough plaster walls rising up on either side to dimly seen shutters high above.

Then he felt himself being guided into the passenger seat of a car. A hand protectively guided his head beneath the door arch. Then he settled back into the comfort of a well-sprung seat as the car set off, and closed his eyes.

He was not aware of anything else until the car came to a standstill. In the sudden silence after the engine had been turned off, consciousness returned, though the world still surged from side to side. He became aware of the scent of blossoms in the warm air as the driver opened his door and stepped out, and Beckett could hear the familiar drone of insects somewhere outside in the undergrowth.

"Time to get out."

It was Demetrios's voice. Were they back at Beckett's hotel, he wondered as he made an effort to pull himself together for the walk through the lobby to the lift and the last short stretch to his room on the sixth floor. Room 605, he remembered with a childish feeling of triumph as he rummaged in his jeans pocket for his key.

"You won't be needing that," Demetrios told him.

Only now did Beckett realise they were not at his hotel at all. Instead, across the road from the large gravel car park they had pulled up in, he recognised the souvenir shops and cafes that faced the entrance to the palace.

Why had they come back here?

Beckett turned to ask Demetrios what was going on, when he saw two overweight men in scruffy-looking jeans and dark T-shirts step out of the shadows beneath the trees along the edge of the car park and head towards them. Realising that something was seriously amiss, Beckett glanced across at the cafes for help, but they were in darkness and had probably been closed for well over an hour. Nevertheless, he thought, in some desperation, surely there was the chance of someone driving down the road in the next few minutes and seeing him if he dashed out into it. Realising his intention, though, the men suddenly hurried their pace towards him and quickly blocked his path with their bulk.

"What the hell are you up to, Demetrios?" Beckett asked, feeling suddenly, horribly sober again. "I thought we were friends. What have you done? Set me up to be mugged by a couple of your mates?"

"Be quiet," Demetrios said, as if to a child. "You have no choice anymore. So listen to what I tell you to do and make no fuss. Okay?"

"Okay, my arse!" Beckett made an attempt to break away from them, but the men yanked him back so hard they jarred his shoulders.

"Anymore of that and you will be hurt," Demetrios warned. As if in emphasis, the men, who were considerably bigger than either Beckett or Demetrios, with what could only be described as prodigious bellies and broad, sloping, muscular shoulders, tightened their grip on his arms painfully. "Understand?"

Beckett nodded. "I understand."

Demetrios nodded his acknowledgement, then strode to the main gates of the archaeological site. Producing a bunch of keys, he proceeded to unlock them. Then, after opening them a fraction and listening carefully for a few moments, he carried on into the forecourt beyond, pausing only to wave for the others to follow.

"What the hell's goin' on?" Beckett asked, but his captors ignored him. Perhaps they didn't speak English. Or perhaps—more probably, Beckett thought—they just weren't interested in whatever he had to say.

Inside Knossos the only light came from the sky. In the distance the perpendicular silhouettes of cypress trees stood out against the stars. There was an intense feeling of heat in the air. It seemed to throb, as if it came from something alive. But Beckett had no time to wonder about this as his captors pushed him ahead of them;

instead he had to concentrate on avoiding falling over stones and lumps of broken rock on the uneven surface of the path. As they passed into the ruins of the palace, though, he became aware of another source of light; it was as if its blocks of stone had somehow absorbed so much of the intense sunlight of the day that it was now beginning to radiate outward in a dull luminescence— pale, almost illusory, but nevertheless real. There was an eerie feel about the place now, and Beckett could have sworn it looked more different than the lack of sunlight should have accounted for. It wasn't just the additional shadows or the relative quiet of the ruins. Somehow it was as if the excavations were now even larger, as if there had been additions to it since he came here earlier. Even the two men beside him seemed different now. Grosser, their huge bellies swinging before them with belligerent power, while their necks looked even thicker, more sinewy. Their strength looked intimidating, like the innate primal power of a large animal—an ape or a bear.

Or a bull.

Sweat soaked Beckett's clothes as they progressed deeper into the palace complex, climbing down broad flights of steps that took them into deeper areas than he could remember seeing before. Dark frescoes covered the walls down here, but the intricate shapes depicted on them were indistinct in the gloom, though he found them disturbing even so. There was too much red about them somehow.

Demetrios strode ahead of them with a confidence that to Beckett seemed to rank as almost unnatural in the darkness, even with the strange light glowing from the stones, which lent a look of insubstantiality to every-thing, so that Beckett could have sworn even the inches-thick plaster that covered so much of it was in a state of flux, that buildings looked somehow subtly different if he looked away from them for a moment, then looked back. It was bewilderingly disturbing, and Beckett wondered just how drunk he still was, despite the sobering effects of fear.

Shortly Demetrios stopped.

They faced the entrance to a large, square-shaped chamber. Another doorway, barred by a metal gate, stood at the far side of it. The walls inside were bare stone for the most part; only a few patches of their original painted plaster adhered to them, though these hinted at a forbidding fresco. The floor was a dense mosaic, dark red against a mottled gray. Its design drew Beckett's eyes almost hypnotically, with its mad, interwoven swirls, dizzying in their psychedelic twists and turns.

"The labyrinth," Demetrios told him, pointing at the gate. "Beyond lies the original."

Beckett stared at him, puzzled. "That's a myth," he replied querulously "A legend."

Demetrios smiled. "To you, maybe. But that does not necessarily make it so." He strode almost reverentially into the chamber; his footsteps echoed. "But you will soon have cause to understand the reality of it all."

"You're bloody mad," Beckett heard himself shout, unable to believe that he had had the nerve to say it.

Demetrios inclined his head, a curious smile on his lips. Then he looked at his henchmen. "Bring him in."

Beckett found himself being bundled forwards, unable

to resist the overwhelming strength of the men gripping him. At the same time Demetrios strode to the gate at the far end of the chamber and pulled it open. Beyond lay a dank passageway lined with stone and remains of the ubiquitous plaster frescoes. Heading downwards at a slight bend, the tunnel-like passage had a damp, earthy smell to it, as well as the sour scent of something alive. Beckett was suddenly afraid they were going to throw him into a den of wild animals of some kind. He squirmed against his captors, but he could do nothing to weaken their grip on him. He felt like a child in their clutches as he glanced at their almost bovine features.

Demetrios stood to one side as the men forced Beckett toward the gate.

"What does it feel like to reenact a scene from legend?" the old Athenian asked as Beckett was finally thrown through the gateway. Demetrios swung the gate shut behind Beckett with a heavy clang, then fastened it securely with a padlock and chain.

"There is only one other way out," Demetrios went on. "And don't waste your time waiting till daybreak when the site reopens and tourists flock in. This place is not so easily accessible to those who do not already know how to enter it." He tapped his temple. "As I said earlier," he added cryptically with a further curious smile. With that, both he and the men retraced their steps across the chamber. A moment later Beckett heard the outer door slam shut, and there was silence.

And darkness.

Utter darkness.

Beckett's first instinct was to grab the metal gate and

try to shake it free from its hinges, but he quickly discovered that it was too sturdy for any efforts he could make to have any effect on it. His second was to shout for help, but who would hear him now apart from that treacherous bastard, Demetrios, and his fat henchmen? And why give them just cause for amusement? Beckett gritted his teeth in an effort to keep control of himself. He had to think. He had to act logically. Demetrios had said there was one other way out of here and, although he might be lying, it was obviously no use trying to get past the gate, so there was no choice: he had to go down the passageway and hope there really was another way out.

Beckett touched the cold stone wall. As he gingerly felt his way along it, the sour stench of animal grew even stronger. It was an obnoxious smell, and it was as much as he could do to stop himself from vomiting, especially in his weakened state from drink. Foot by foot, mindful of potholes, he crept down the tunnel, until, a short way farther on, the wall abruptly turned sharply left. After a moment's pause, Beckett cautiously crossed to the opposite wall. As he had feared, this one turned also, but to the right at ninety degrees. At the very least, he supposed, it had to be a T-junction, unless the passage continued straight on as well. He clenched his fists. Demetrios's description of this as a maze could be true, he realised despairingly.

Beckett stared into the darkness as his eyes began to fill with tears of fear and frustration. If he became lost in here he knew he would die. Or worse, weakened by hunger and thirst, any animals living in this dismal place would be able to attack him. The thought of ravening dogs or rats coming upon him in the dark spurred him on to move again. He had to get out of here. *I have to*, he thought, with a feeling of desperation.

For the next few hours he somehow managed to keep himself going. At first he tried to memorise the routes he had taken, but the place was too complex, and it wasn't long before he was thoroughly lost. He tried to tell himself that if he could just keep going, trying passage after passage, again and again, sooner or later he was bound to find his way out—if, indeed, there *was* a way out of this place. However hard he tried to suppress it, this debilitating doubt would not disappear, however much he dared not let himself believe it.

If only I could get out of here and get my hands on that treacherous Greek!

This thought alone helped to keep him going even when he began to feel like giving up and slumping into a heap on the floor.

If only . . . If only . . .

Suddenly the sour, animal smell that had been here all along became overwhelmingly, almost chokingly stronger. Beckett stopped in his tracks and fell into an instinctive crouch, as if to lessen his presence. Straining his ears, he heard something move. It sounded large and slow.

Then it breathed.

Fighting against hysteria, Beckett crept slowly forwards. There was a trace of light ahead of him, by which he could just make out the next sharp bend in the passage, black against grey.

Cautiously he peered round the corner into what he knew at once must be the hub of the maze. Lit by flames that rose from a pit in its absolute centre, he gazed in startled awe at the round, dome-shaped chamber. It was surrounded by the most fantastic frescoes he had ever seen in his life—of capering, grotesque, hellish creatures, part mythological, part nightmare, as if a psychopath had been given free rein to reinterpret various creatures from Greek legends. There were leering satyrs with massive, lethal, snakelike phalli, that leapt in an orgy of cannibalistic frenzy, entrails and hearts and limbs grasped in their blood-soaked talons. Howling centaurs threw themselves upon helpless dryads, choking them with massive, misshapen hands even as they ravished them. Hideously deformed harpies tore at their victims like maniacal vultures. The acts of violence went on and on. It was an astonishing scene. There was an abandoned savagery about it all which went far beyond the bounds of sanity. It was a Greek mythological hell, a Hieronymus Bosch from three thousand years before that artist was born.

Drinkett gasped with shock. It was a find which he was certain had never been revealed to any outsider before. Though no expert, he was sure he would have seen pictures, in some of the books he'd studied of the history of this area, of something so stupendously shocking as this. If he could only get out of here his name would rank alongside that of Howard Carter, the discoverer of Tutankhamen's tomb, and far beyond that of Schliemann, the discoverer of Troy.

Then he saw something move.

In contrast to the flamboyantly painted walls, it was almost indistinguishable from the mottled grey of the floor, looking no more than an ugly lump of what could have been old, rotted cloths. But old, rotted cloths didn't move. Not of their own accord. Nor did they proceed to rise up like a grim, greyish figure, with massive shoulders and a large, ugly, beastlike head.

Nor did old, rotted cloths turn round and suddenly gaze at you.

Beckett backed away from it, but the creature moved forwards, huge and terrible. Unlike the minotaur of legend this thing was not half man, half bull. There was a bestiality to its head—or parts of its head—but there was much that was neither man nor beast, something which Beckett could not recognise in its insane, mangled monstrousness. What he did recognise, as the leprous creature stalked towards him, its mouth overflowing with blood and drool, was its hideous malevolence.

Choking on a scream, Beckett turned and tried to run back down the unlit tunnel behind him, but the creature moved with incredible speed. He looked back as its bulk loomed over him. In sheer desperation he tried to leap forwards, but the monster's foot-long talons slid into Beckett's shoulders like grappling hooks and twisted him over onto his back to gaze up at it as its hot spittle fell on his face.

Demetrios Polydopoulos returned to the maze the following night, his two companions beside him. Again, as always whenever they came back to this place, they felt the subtle changes its evil influence began to exert upon their bodies.

"He has . . . not returned," one of the men said to him, his malformed mouth incapable of recognisable speech without great effort these days.

Demetrios nodded. Of the six of them who had chanced on this place more than ten years ago, two died in their first attempt to explore the maze, while the third returned incurably insane. Only Demetrios and his two remaining companions had somehow survived—though at a price.

At a terrible price.

Demetrios looked down at his thickened, almost bestial toenails as his tongue involuntarily slid across his filed-down teeth, tasting the blood that seeped from them. The others had fared far worse, of course, but they had always had more than their own fair share of the animal in them, he supposed.

He shuddered as he felt the hideous pull of the maze—that massive sense of inertia, which they could only resist by giving in to what *it* wanted, to what it told them to bring to it. And soon, he knew, another victim would have to be brought to this place—or they would feel that pull grow too intense to resist.

He looked up as, deep within the labyrinth, they heard its roar.

Its terrible, ageless, bestial roar . . . of hunger and lust and insatiable rage.

SKINS

By Gerard Houarner

Patrick spotted her by one of the ticket desks at the Central Park West entrance to the American Museum of Natural History. As Takisha had said, his blind date wore the black uniform of the downtown crowd, pants, boots and jacket accented by a red scarf and beret, and a shoulder bag made of alternating slick and pebbled strips of leather in shades of gray, charcoal and burgundy, interwoven in a pattern that made the bag seem alive and restless from a distance. She was blond, natural by Takisha's estimation, and straight, absolutely certified by Takisha, "because if you think I was going to let you at this little blond fish if there was any chance of my getting some, you are sadly divorced from reality."

"If she's so hot, why doesn't she have a boyfriend?" Patrick had replied. Looking at her studying a brochure on the other side of the canoe that dominated the lobby, tilting sophisticated, thin-frame glasses back as she looked down, he couldn't help but ask the question again. Was it because she was the type who wore glasses as an affectation, or was it that she didn't think enough of herself to get contacts?

"Because, like you, she spends too much time around people who aren't her type," was Takisha's answer. "But unlike you, getting hard-ons for lesbians, and chasing socialites and models who wouldn't piss on you much less let you buy them a drink, she takes control of her inhibitions. She chooses to hang with dykes she has no interest in. You guys are like two sides of the same coin. So give it a shot, big man: you two might have more in common than you think."

His blind date looked up at Patrick just as he approached, smiling only when he introduced himself, as if Takisha's description hadn't registered with her. Or she'd forgotten it or the fact that she was there to meet him. Or maybe, with his dress jeans, old dress shirt and unconstructed sport coat, he looked like every other loser nerd hanging out at a museum that wasn't even about art on a late Saturday morning, trying to pick somebody up.

"I'm Brit," she said, holding out her hand and fixing him with a pair of startling green eyes. "Just Brit; it's not short for anything."

A couple of lame lines almost spilled out of his mouth—so I see, neither are you—but the strength of her hand shake and her steady, disconcerting gaze froze him. For once, his discomfort around women—particularly women he was attracted to, and especially women who might reciprocate the feeling—saved him. He was thankful. She was beautiful. He wanted to preserve his chance with her.

When they released, they joined the short ticket line and got in on the museum membership he still shared with his sister, though she'd married and moved out of the city long ago. He filled the time babbling about the removal of his childhood favorite, the giant squid, and the new Hayden Planetarium, thankful the date was early: not only did they have time to ditch each other if things didn't go well, but most families and kids hadn't made it in yet, reducing the stress of crowds. The adventure of finding their way to the exhibition they had agreed to see together, walking past stuffed-animal dioramas and Native American relics, killed more time in which he might have made a fool of himself. By the time they went through the special gallery dedicated to spiritual artifacts from India, Patrick felt calm enough to ask her if she wanted to have lunch.

"No," she said, opening one of the small, wall-mounted shrines and smiling into the illuminated panels within.

Patrick's nervous, cautious mood slipped into darkness. Typical. He'd blown it again. Bored her. Probably the date had been a time-killing favor to Takisha before her real date later in the day. He dreaded having to see Takisha at the record company during the week and listen to her explain again how he'd blown still another opportunity. He hoped she didn't go back to thinking he was a closet case and set him up with guys.

Then Brit locked gazes with him again. With a slight smile, she whispered reverently, "Let's go see the bones."

He didn't understand for a moment, and scrambled to grasp the insult or brush-off implied in her request. With a touch of sullenness he didn't try to hide, they went upstairs to the dinosaur galleries. He let her walk ahead, afraid she was going to leave him with the fossils as a humiliating commentary on their date: a trick to brag about to friends like Takisha.

Before they entered the first hall, she turned suddenly, leaned against him, squeezed his bicep and said in a conspiratorial tone, "I have a thing about getting to what's underneath. Digging through the layers of the way things are and were makes me feel alive."

"You should've been an archaeologist," Patrick said, startled by her passion.

"Maybe you're right," she said, her smile fading. "I'd have the bones of dead things, then. But, of course, then I'd miss the substance of living things, wouldn't I?"

She turned away, leaving him breathless with the smell of her hair, the feel of her hand through his clothes; the memory of her body pushing against his, her body heat a fever infecting him. The brief contact had opened him up like a hunter's gutting knife. But instead of ripping out his heart, she'd filled him with herself, even as she turned her attention to things dead for millions of years.

He regretted her hand falling from his arm. Cold rushed in where her heat had warmed him. Whatever sparked and fueled the fire between them left with her. He shivered, and the loneliness that was his truest companion since childhood, closer even than his sister, Jessie, who'd tried so hard to be his friend and protector after their mother died, rose up like a mountain storm to engulf him in its selfish, jealous darkness. He wanted Brit. He wanted to be with her, and to bask in her regard, and to feel himself inside her as those eyes swallowed him and that voice told him he belonged to her.

But he also understood why she might not have a steady lover, and why Takisha's circle could accept her. There was wildness beneath the uniform of the repressed. A hint of ruthlessness, a requirement for survival when the tribe one belonged to was small and perceived by the larger nation as dangerous. He had no idea what she was talking about with her prattling about bones and getting underneath things. He couldn't fathom what the museum's dinosaur collection represented in her view of the world, but it was obvious her perceptions of the world and herself were skewed at best—perhaps bizarre, even dangerous.

He was startled to discover, as he followed her into the dim and quiet chamber, that he didn't care.

They didn't speak during their tour. Patrick followed her lead, pausing with her to study the sweep of rib cages, the curvature of spines, the arrays of teeth. In the quiet halls, he didn't dare interrupt her communion with whatever pure entity the bones represented.

By the time they were done with the upstairs galleries, Patrick had a mild headache from growing hunger and the rising level of background noise echoing through the museum's vast spaces. When he offered to take her to lunch again, she accepted. His spirits lifted, and he waded through tourists and their kids without complaint.

They ate at a tiny Middle Eastern sandwich shop, talking mostly of the neighborhood's burgeoning supply of upscale retailers and baby carriages, then went back to spend the afternoon cruising through the blocks of street vendors lined up against the Columbus Avenue side of the museum. He was surprised by Brit's tastes and even humor as she pointed out handcrafted frames, city photographs, antiques, and pins put together from odd pictures and tiny toys.

She gave him a wink when she lifted a multihued glass scarf ring from a display and dropped it in her bag. Then she watched him, keeping her distance, as he went from dealer to dealer, haunted by her attention, by the dare in her arched eyebrow and pursed lips, until he circled back and palmed the smallest of the playful pins, putting it in his pocket, and buying a larger pin in penance.

Patrick's heart was still racing when Brit caught up to him a few stalls later. She grabbed one of his arm with both hands, giving him a start, as if the vendor had realized the theft and seized him. She spun around him, laughing, her face and mouth and eyes all open and joyful and savage with triumph. They crossed the street. Kissed.

He was relieved by her approval, as if he'd passed a trial. He had never done anything like that in his life. A hard part of his shell, a rule of conduct that had defined him and his relationship with the world, had broken and fallen away. He'd been released from a prison he never knew existed.

They went to Central Park and spent the rest of the day walking, snacking on crepes and ice cream, commenting on the people passing by, joking and teasing and laughing, not dwelling on their pasts, living only for the present. It was the best day Patrick remembered having in a long time. When they parted in the late afternoon, Patrick didn't ask why she had to leave. They kissed, and she told him she'd see him later in the week, and that was enough for him. It was more than he'd gotten from anyone in his life.

"You know, I'm going to miss your candy ass," Takisha said, the next time he came to the record company to hand in work. She took a cursory glance through his files on her computer and, apparently satisfied that nothing major had gone wrong so far with the ad campaign she had hired Patrick to implement, let business go for a little while longer. "Like a homeless dog you get used to feeding out of the kindness in your heart, until someone with a kinder nature, and who isn't a cat person, takes him in."

"So you heard it went well," Patrick said, relaxing into Takisha's acceptance of his work and his newfound companion.

"Heard that, and nothing else. Girl dropped us like lead weights off a nipple ring. It's a shame, she was always fun on *Xena* night, playing that blond bitch, Callisto. But don't go thinking you turned her straight. She was just a pal with us. Not that we didn't try, some of us more than others. Looks like you were just the strange old soul she was holding out for. Gotta be, because I can't for the life of me figure either one of you out."

"Thanks for the introduction." Already, he was missing Takisha, as if he'd been too busy with Brit to check in with her for months. Something like what Jessie had done to him, when her Jack swept her up and took her away from him. Thinking he was having a premonition of guilt, he said, "But I hope we won't stop being friends."

"Absolutely not. As long as you keep turning in top-rate hip shit for peanuts, I'll be your pal. But I will say I won't miss running into your sad, horny face at Vendessa's or The Pipe Cleaner. It was getting so I was seriously considering giving you a pity fuck, myself." She gave him a grave look lightened by a touch of tenderness. "But then I'd throw up, and I find that always ruins the mood."

"Eat shit and die," Patrick said, with unexpected vehemence. His face flushed, and he laughed, as much at the unexpected comeback as at the flare of anger bursting, then quickly fading, inside him. He felt like a kid at a fireworks show, excited by the flash and noise of a pretend battle.

Regret came as Takisha's face registered a touch of shock. What he'd said wasn't him, and neither was the way he said it.

No. It was him, a part he'd never reached before. A part Brit had set free.

"Damn," Takisha said, her surprise dissolving into a smirk, "you haven't even scored yet and already you've got your balls back. Pretty soon you'll be bitch-slapping me for a raise."

"Would I get one?"

"Hell, no. Now come on, let's get this done," she said, turning back to the computer screen and mousing through screens of images. "I've got a couple of personal issues to take care of, and I need to go as soon as we're done."

"So do I, Takisha. So do I."

In the East Village club Brit took him to after dinner, Patrick was young again, younger than he had been when he should have felt as he did now. He'd taken her advice and scaled down his designer look, which made it easy for him to relax into a college mode more concerned with attitude than with money, carefree and living in the moment like the club's patrons.

A joyous bass beat carried him into the sour-smelling throng bouncing in a dark cave broken only by bright, neon-colored lights scattered across the ceiling, flashing out of synch with the music. Bodies bashed into one another, and no one held a drink far from the bar or the walls. He followed Brit to the dance floor, awkwardly at first. But as she pressed her body against his, and they bumped and banged into others, he found a connection with the beat, even with the flickering lights, and his legs, hips, shoulders, arms and head flowed as if possessed by an alien entity. Or released from bondage.

Brit laughed, clapped her hands. Kissed him again, long, hard, and they stared into each other's eyes as their tongues probed and teased and tasted. She'd lost the glasses. Affectation, he decided. A veil to sheath the piercing scalpels of her eyes.

They took a break, more for him and than for her. He got them beers. She took hers, but suddenly she seemed subdued, and pressed herself against the wall. She frowned, blinked at the lights, grimaced as the DJ switched briefly to a screeching, atonal track. Patrick almost laughed at her, seeing in her changing mood a reflection of the way he should have felt. He peered into her eyes, checking her pupils, to see if she'd done drugs while he was at the bar. She pushed him away, pointed to the bathroom, shoved the beer back at him and left.

Ten minutes later, he spotted her. He thought at first it was someone else, though the cut of her blond mane and her sliced, sleeveless long coat gave her a unique look. He stared. The woman embracing a taller, younger man, all muscular arms and leather and short-cropped hair and tattoos, was Brit.

He couldn't believe what he was seeing, or feeling. In that moment, he was naked. The innocence and childlike trust he had embraced in her company shattered. The connection to her, to what he thought she was, snapped like a brittle twig. Brit was a stranger, a lunatic he had allowed inside himself. He had actually opened up to feelings that were more than lust, more than fantasy infatuation. Not love, never love, too soon—things like didn't happen after a single blind date—no, never that. But something close to love. He'd taken a step on that bridge.

He slunk back to the wall, feeling everyone's gaze on him as if they expected a reaction. What—tears? Rage? Humiliation withered his flesh as his father's voice rose, hard and sharp like a machete, hacking with every word: wimp, faggot, pussy. For a dangerous moment, he was a child again, stripped of his mother's protection and forced to navigate the dangerous waters of adulthood.

He was a child fallen on the shards of his broken innocence, powerless, vulnerable, bleeding.

Of course, no one was looking at him. He took a deep
breath, taking in the smell of pot and sweat. Of course,
Brit had probably run into an old, or even current
boyfriend. The last swig of beer was warm, bitter. He
was nothing special in her life, not yet. Not now. Not
ever. What was he thinking, what did he expect? She was
obviously a flake. Takisha had warned him, if by nothing
more than the fact that she set up the blind date. What
did he expect from that circle? They were probably
laughing at him. He'd been suckered, like a little kid. Se-
duced, by the need for women he could never have, into
letting his guard down with a woman who'd never have
him. His life story. The one he'd spent a lifetime trying
to escape even as he sank deeper into its sanctuary from
risk.

Idiot. Moron. Fucking asshole.

He didn't even want to think about what his sister
would say: did Momma Lesbian let you down?

He started for the door. An argument broke out
nearby. Bouncers knifed through the crowd, toward Brit,
who was screaming at another woman. The young man's
lover? No, he wasn't around. The woman shouted back.
The woman wept, shook her fist at Brit. Patrick felt for
the woman. Understood.

Someone else with a broken heart. God, he sounded
like a country and western song.

Brit, unsteady on her feet, as if drunk, managed to absorb the woman's abuse with a grin.

Patrick couldn't leave until security had cleared away

the source of the disturbance. The DJ cranked up the sound, the beats per minute, whisking everyone's attention away from the little scene. Finally, Patrick was able to head for the exit.

Brit blocked his way.

"I thought they kicked your ass out," he screamed, barely able to hear himself. He wanted to punch her.

"How does it feel?" she asked, then gave him a hypnotic smile. Her eyes hooked into him, grabbed him by the nuts and the pits of his brain.

But for all her beauty, she didn't look in control of herself. Her face twitched. She kept moving to the music, but now she was stiff, uncoordinated, like a marionette, bouncing up and down. Her eyes were wide open and hardly blinked, like gates stuck in the open position, allowing floodwaters through.

Another fight broke out on the dance floor. The club was taking on an edge, but the people in it looked the same. Had someone started spreading bad drugs? Brit giggled. Stuck her tongue out between her lips and gently bit down.

"So many, all so ripe, so rich, do you feel them?" she asked after a moment, slurring her words.

He wanted to kiss her, but did he want to taste another man's lips? What would Takisha say about that?

She grabbed his arms. Shook him. Laughed crazily.

What did he care?

He grabbed her, drove his fingers into her back, bit her lip, her tongue. He wanted to make her feel a little of the pain he'd just felt. Their teeth clashed; bone butted on bone as they knocked foreheads and jaws. Her thigh mashed his groin, but she didn't knee him. Manicured nails drove into his neck, but didn't break skin. They parted for a breath of air. Both laughed.

"It feels so good," she said into his ear, then bit it. "But not as good as you."

They danced with each other, and then she spun away, landed in a man's arms. Danced with him. Enraged, confused, Patrick staggered to the crowd's periphery, debating whether he should fight and get thrown out of the club, or simply leave. A woman dancing by herself caught his eye. She grabbed hold of his hand, made him join her. Curiosity and sympathy mingled in her expression. Patrick hesitated, feeling exposed. Had he somehow become transparent to the women around him?

Brit bumped into them as she passed by with her new partner. The impact set off a blinding burst of white light in Patrick's head. He turned away from Brit, started walking off the dance floor. His partner came closer, held onto him until they couldn't possibly dance.

They groped and kissed in a corner for a few minutes, and she opened up to him as he had to Brit. Her layers peeled away for him, and he knew her name, Gina, and her five brothers in Ohio and her football-playing father, and her mad escape from all that maleness to find another kind of man, anywhere else. He knew she worked in a SoHo boutique, and went to Parsons School of Design, and drew all the time, and understood what the little curlycue characters she put on everything she owned really meant, and—

And a moment of peace in a field at night, underneath a million stars, with her mother at her side and the house, full of noise and lights at their back, peeled away from Gina, carved and served like a chocolate sliver directly onto Patrick's tongue by Brit's touch in a candlelit midnight romantic instant.

Gina cried out. No one noticed. She pushed Patrick away, gave him a startled look, ran off.

The taste of another reality melted inside Patrick. It was gone before he realized it didn't belong to him, before he understood he had consumed a piece of someone else. The encounter left him hungry for more, but not with Gina, or anyone else in the club. He wanted Brit. And he didn't want to take from her. He wanted to give, to offer himself up so she'd know, she'd understand, what he needed, and accept him.

Reality—his reality—snapped back into focus. He was Patrick again. Lost.

What had happened? What was that?

What the hell was that?

The club mob grew louder. More frantic, shouting, screaming, flailing to the music. The floor and walls and even the lights shook with their stomping.

The crowd's power swept him up, stripped him of the formal habits of his life as if they were clothes, or skin, leaving the way clear for savage urges to rise. He wanted to throw himself into the mob, to lash out, thrust himself into beautiful women, possess, take, hurt, use, control and throw away. Consume. He tried to hang on to the old feelings that would have him run away, hide, forget what he wanted, needed. The clash between the two instincts made him dizzy, nauseous. In the end, he wanted only to surrender, roll up into a ball and die.

Had someone slipped him a tab of LSD? Had he died and gone to hell? Was Brit a demon punishing him for— what? What had he done?

Who was he? What was he becoming?

His heart raced to the music's beat, but his legs locked into place while his arms and torso grew cold, numb. Mad currents tore at his stance, threatened to topple him. Terror dragged him out to a darkness that flooded his eyes and ears, filled his lungs, choked thought, crushed everything but fear.

Brit reappeared, her latest escort lost, her face breaking through the chaos in Patrick's mind. He sagged in relief. Forgiving her betrayals, he reached out for her, desperate for an anchor to the famliar. She threw herself into his arms, and he forgot questions and confusion and fear. He was whole again, and sane, and opened himself up to feel every inch of her body, all of her heat, every squirm of her body. She remained closed to him, unlike Gina. But he felt her inside him, moving, probing, an invisible eel gliding through all that he had just felt and more, going deeper, calling up random memories of Mom when she was still alive, reading him bedtime stories, giving him cookie snacks for school, kissing him on top of the head.

He tensed. Brit moaned. Her body felt so good.

"You see how it tastes?" she asked, her words running together in a drunken flurry. "You see what you can give me?"

What was she? He wanted to ask, but the words would not come. He didn't really care. How could she take what she did from others, or offer him a window into her world by getting him to taste Gina's life? Were there even more secrets in her?

Could he keep up with her?

She didn't leave this time, but drank from him. Devoured him. The serpent of her self swam through the strata of past and present, swallowing memories: his mother's perfume on Sunday visits to grandparents; the sun shining through trees on the morning school bus ride; Jessie holding him at their mother's funeral; his father gruffly shaking his hand at high school graduation. Bits and pieces, patches of a whole, snatches of conversation and experience, the thinnest layers of who he was. Yet he remained himself. Patrick. He remembered Mom, Dad, his sister. Takisha. The friends he'd made, the women he'd pursued. All the traumas and pain and fears with which he defined himself remained intact. What she took, he didn't need. What she took made her happy, made her more alive than he imagined anyone could ever be. What he gave promised him bliss.

He was certain he felt no different.

Brit led him to the exit. On the way, he caught his reflection in a mirrored wall. Though he was sure he was the same Patrick he always had been, he looked different. In what way, he couldn't specify. He was changed, there was no doubt. As if, in peeling away that layer of him, Brit had revealed something new underneath. Unfinished. Still raw. Bleeding.

What used to be there?

Outside, away from the bouncers, a drunken youth from the club staggered into him. Patrick hit him, in the cheek, then in the jaw, again in the stomach, then blindly, striking head and torso until the youth went down. He continued to kick away until one of the club's door checkers moved toward him, frowning. Brit dragged Patrick away. He resented her interference. He wasn't finished.

She took him to her place. He had no idea where it was or how he got there. He recognized her woven leather bag inside, by the door. They made love. He floated on her body, and beneath her, riding the current flowing from her eyes, steered by the hands on his shoulders, the thighs against his hips.

Later, he got up to go to the bathroom. He opened a door. It was a closet. As he shut it, the contents, only dimly illuminated by the night-light plugged into a distant electrical socket, registered in his mind. Full body suits, the color flesh, in the dozens, hanging like enormous spent condoms.

Brit laughed, far away. When he turned, she was beside him. She wasn't laughing.

He should have been afraid. He knew that much.

"What you want isn't in there," she seemed to say.

Whether or not he went to the bathroom, he couldn't say. He didn't wake fully until the next day, riding the train home in the late morning. Alone.

For a while, he wasn't sure who he was, or where he was going. When he finally recovered, it seemed to him there were still pieces missing from the puzzle of what had happened the night before, and who he really was.

"You look like shit," Patrick said as soon as he walked into Takisha's office and saw her looking down, holding her head with both hands.

She took the cartridge he offered and shoved it into the drive. "Like you look better?" she asked, giving him a raised eyebrow as she called up files.

He collapsed into the chair beside her desk and began playing with the paper clips on their magnetic holder. "But you're the office bitch. You're supposed to have everyone whipped, not the other way around."

She frowned, glanced at him, then back at the graphics displayed on her computer screen. "I'm having some issues right now, though I see I'm not the only one. Some friends of mine decided to go nuts on me, and frankly, it's a real pain in the ass." She threw down the mouse and leaned back in the chair. "What's this shit you're handing in?"

"The best I could do."

"No, I've seen the best you could do. And I've seen your regular stuff. The secretaries outside could do better than what you're giving me today."

"I'm the professional, that's what I'm handing in."

"Really? What is this, some ploy for a contract revision? More money? No way, little boy. This crap'll get you fired, breach of contract, not meeting your own standards." She removed the cartridge and slid it across the desk.

He put the cartridge in his jacket pocket, took off his tie, tossed it on her desk. "Then I guess I'm off the clock." He walked out of the office, feeling as if something had gone dreadfully wrong, but unable to put his finger on what. His actions felt natural. He felt justified. There was nothing more to be done, given the short deadline and his nights with Brit and the longer period of recovery he needed every day. What else could he do?

"Are you on drugs?" Takisha called out.

He kept on walking. Other office workers stopped to stare at him as he passed by. The question was one his sister would ask. He expected to feel comforted by Takisha's concern, but when he thought about the context, perhaps he should have felt angry. He had no reaction. Her words and tone bounced off of him as if he was invulnerable.

"Patrick!"

The tone, mimicking his sister's, and his mother's, brought him up short. He stopped, looked over his shoulder. It was only Takisha.

"You still seeing Brit?" she asked, holding on to the side of her office door. She was frowning again, her favorite expression, but this time a quirk of the lips made it seem as if she was worried instead of concentrating or worrying. She trotted up to him as he walked past the receptionist and pushed the elevator button. People in the office huddled, whispered. The hell with them, he thought.

"Listen," Takisha whispered, "about Brit. Be careful. She's not what you think she is."

Anxiety shot through him, and he pressed the elevator button again just to ground himself with the feel of cool metal against his skin. "What the fuck are you talking about?"

Takisha's head jerked back, as if poisoned by his venom. Anger fought with concern for control of her expression. "She was having affairs," she snapped back, barely able to keep herself to a discreet whisper. "With those friends of mine who're having little nervous breakdowns. They're not acting like themselves. It's like they have Alzheimer's, and they're forgetting who and where they are. Like you," she said, stabbing his chest with a finger tipped by a long, sharp nail. "She's not as straight as she seems, and she must have access to some serious drugs. So be warned, asshole. And let me know when you've come down from this trip you're on and you're ready to do business again."

The elevator came. "I thought you said she wouldn't go for your type," he said as he entered, looking back to see his parting shot hit its mark.

"I guess I was too much woman for her," Takisha fired back, giving him a look he took to mean he obviously wasn't too much of a man for Brit.

The elevator door closed. "Fuck you," Patrick said, to no one.

He was safe in Brit's apartment, as long as he didn't open the closet door.

"Are those uniforms in there?" he asked, once, when they were resting between bouts of lovemaking. They never went out anymore. He just came over, at night, and left sometime the day, when he found the strength. "Like athletes wear, to cut down resistance in the air or the water?"

"There's nothing there but my clothes," she said, without a smile, staring at him with dead eyes that were like ice he could skate on forever. Memory and a vague instinct told him he should be scared, he should run away. But she still felt good. And when he didn't bring up things she didn't want to talk about, she still drank him with her eyes, and bathed him in her attention.

"They were real thin," he said. Was he trying to find something out from her, or telling himself something important? "Like skin."

"Do you think I skin my lovers alive? Flay them, hang their hides up in my closet, like some kind of sex witch?"

"No, don't be ridiculous."

"Good. Because I don't. I'm not."

"Then what are you?" His tears surprised him.

She licked his cheeks, so that he could not tell the difference between the dampness from his weeping and her tongue. "Do you love me?"

The question carved a notch deep inside him, and he offered up what she'd cut out, like a sacrifice. To appease the gods, or atone for his sins, or just to rid himself of a thing that hurt, he couldn't tell. "Yes," he said.

"Would you leave me?" She snuggled close to him, and already his erection was growing, though they had been together half a dozen times during the evening. Her glasses were forgotten on the side table.

He was never tired with her. "No."

"Good," she said, still not smiling, not giving him any of the warmth he wanted. Because he was cold. Even under the covers, with her body half on top of his, he was cold. Trembling.

"Where do you come from?" He wanted to smell her, but her scent eluded him.

Her face was a few finger-widths away from his. Her

lips moved when she spoke, but it seemed as if nothing else on her face did. "Out of uncertain times. The past. Mist. Faraway places. You might call me an immigrant." She stared at him, unblinking, for a while. "Does it matter?"

"No." Desperation gnawed at the edges of consciousness. There was something he was missing. Voices, or the memories of those voices, spoke to him from holes inside him. Warned him. Groping like a deaf and blind man in heavy traffic, he asked, "What do you want?"

Her fingers traced lines across his chest. Her lips brushed the base of his neck, and then she filled his vision again. "Whatever you have. All the things you are. Is that what you want to give?"

"Yes." His head told him that was the wrong answer. But in his heart, it felt right. "Why?"

"To show myself I'm not a ghost, or a mirage or a figment of anyone's—or anything's—imagination. To live."

"You're not a ghost. I can feel you. Taste you." He held her tightly, put his face against her neck, breathing deeply, running his tongue along tendons.

She moved her head back. "You make me real."

"You mean, my love makes you real."

"No. Who you are, all the parts and pieces you give when we're together, make me real. I'm nothing without you."

"Me?" he asked, knowing that what he was about to ask should matter. "Or someone like me. A person, a man or woman, whomever you happen to catch?" The words sounded as if they'd been spoken by someone else, from a distant place, like a lost transmission bouncing around the atmosphere and finally being picked up by a radio.

"Do you want me to keep being real?"

"Yes." There were no more questions in him.

"Do you want to keep being the most important living thing in my existence?"

Her question made him shiver. He wanted to hold her, enter her again, surrender himself, but instead he said, "Maybe we should meet each other's families soon." He was not, apparently, out of warnings.

Brit smiled, and her smile lit him up from the inside, and the heat of her burned him, and he lived in that fire.

"Like a Sunday dinner, with everyone sitting around a table sharing gossip, a roast and wine?" she said. Her smile faded. "That would be an interesting party. A very interesting day."

Then she was on him, and he was with her, a part of her, and nothing else mattered.

"You're in love, right?" Patrick asked his older sister, Jessie, over the phone. It was a child's question. But he didn't care. He needed a child's reassurances. He needed answers, to save himself.

Jessie laughed. But it was a small laugh, her attention distracted by the sound of children playing in the background, a television blaring, adult voices booming. "Of course," she said.

"I mean with Jack."

"Yes, yes, my man Jack, who gives me nothing but

daughters," she screamed, and male laughter quickly drowned out her voice.

"What's it like?" A flash of irritation passed through him over Jessie's distraction.

"Oh dear, has it happened?" There was a moment of crackling, then the background noise quieted. "You've actually let yourself get into somebody? Somebody real?"

Patrick grunted, as if he'd received a blow. A normal response should have been, "Everybody I know is real." His situation demanded he answer, "I don't think so." What he said, instead, was, "I don't know. Things are little shaky." He bit his lip. That was not the response that would get him the help he had to have.

"You don't sound good, Pat," she said, voice lowering into the bass of concern. "You aren't using drugs or anything, are you?"

"No. Is that a mom question?" He rolled his eyes.

"When did I stop being your mom? Sorry. Practicing for when my kids get old enough to be asked that question. Which is when, by the way, these days?" An explosion of noise interrupted her.

"Did you ever do anything crazy when you first fell in love?" he asked, when quiet was restored. All he needed was a connection to her. Then he could be honest. She had to do her part, though. There were so many bare spots inside him for her to latch on to. Couldn't she tell he was opening up to her? Couldn't she save him?

"You mean like that time I ran away from home because I couldn't take Dad's yelling, and I tried to come back and kidnap you to live with me and my boyfriend?"

She laughed ruefully. "That was a long time ago. Love is different for me, for us, now. It's better. Love isn't supposed to hurt, but sometimes that takes a while to figure out. Why are you asking?"

"No reason," he said, struggling now with the idea of needing his sister to save him. Why couldn't he save himself? And what did he need to be saved from, he wondered? "I was just trying to remember, when I was younger, doing anything crazy, but I didn't. Not really. Not ever." He looked at her picture on the dresser, next to his mom's. His father's image was nowhere in the house.

"No, you were the good boy, that's for sure. I didn't have to work hard keeping you on the straight and narrow."

"Yeah, it was always like Mom was still alive and coming through the door any minute." He stared hard at his mother's picture. He didn't recognize her. He couldn't remember what it was like to feel like she was coming through the door at any minute. That seemed like a flaw to him. Like going to someone else to be saved, like not having the capacity to save himself.

A silent beat passed before Jessie spoke. "Maybe some of that was my fault. Maybe I protected you a little too much. Being what I thought was a mom, that sort of thing." She paused again. "What's going on, Pat? You afraid of getting hurt?"

"No," he said. He threw both pictures on his bed so he wouldn't have to look at them. Their lack of communication annoyed him. He felt like she was talking to the holes in him, the parts he couldn't find anymore. He was not a part of the conversation.

"Honey, you are a walking mummy, wrapped tighter than a dollar bill around Daddy's dick. You need to know everybody gets hurt. You can get over it. That's how you get to the good stuff. You've got to take risks, or else you'll never let anything touch deep inside where things hurt, and then you'll never heal."

Her words bounced off of him. Healing? What was she talking about? Why was he listening?

"You should've had a dog when you were young. Even a cat. Something alive. To teach you what it's like to be important to a living creature. You should've gotten married a long time ago, gotten yourself some kids."

"I didn't want to be responsible for raising someone like me." He was reaching without limbs, trying to feel something at his fingertips, when they were nothing more than bone covered in dead, dried-out flesh. His words rebounded off the wall in front of him.

Before Jessie could respond, he hung up. He didn't pick up when she called back, turned down the sound when she left messages on his answering machine. When she stopped calling, he thought he'd better leave before she camped outside his door.

He packed a few things and went to Brit's house.

The skins in the closet talked to him.

Whether in dream or reality, he couldn't tell. It didn't matter. The voices wouldn't stop. Like the pain of phantom limbs, the ghost sensations in charred flesh, echoes in the hidden chambers of buried pyramids, the voices haunted him.

He got up, leaving Brit sleeping on her side, facing away from him. The phone rang. Or had he dialed a number, and was he listening to the ringing on the other end?

"Hello?" a rough, drowsy voice answered.

"Dad."

"What? Who—? Pat?"

"Yes."

"Pat. My God. What happened? Are you all right?"

"I can't say."

"You can't— Son, where're you?"

"Did you ever love me, Dad?"

"What?"

Patrick breathed into the silence.

"Yes, Pat, I love you. And Jessie. And your mom. I love all of you. I always have."

"Why couldn't I feel it?"

"I—I'm sorry, I should've been a better—"

"Why can't I feel it now?" Before his father could answer, Patrick hung up the phone. He thought his father might try to call back, but Brit had blocked her number from being given out. Or at least Patrick told himself that was why the phone didn't ring.

He went to the closet.

The door opened before he reached it. Brit emerged. Patrick looked toward the bed. The lump of her body still rose and fell under the sheets. He knew he should run, even if it was a dream. His sister was waiting for him, somewhere outside. But love was here. What made him complete, where he belonged, was here.

"What are you looking for?" she asked, her face a blank mask. She closed the closet door behind her.

"What's missing," he answered. The skins, quiet during his talk with his father, murmured once more.

"But I'm here," she said, spreading her arms wide.

"Please," he said, "give me back what you took."

"I didn't take anything. You offered what you didn't want. Those things are gone. Spent. Consumed."

"But I saw things in the closet. Skins. They belong to me. The missing pieces of me. The layers of what I was. I know. I'm sure. I can hear them talking to me."

She opened the door. The closet was empty. "What you hear are ghosts. They'll fade away, in time. I know."

"I don't want them to fade away."

She was on him, again, melting him into her body, entering him through his senses. She seemed to carry him, carefully folded like a shirt, back to bed in the bag of woven leather strips that appeared alive the first time he saw her. He tried to move. The walls of his prison gave a little, but would not break.

He didn't bother leaving her apartment anymore. Or her bed. She came and went, but didn't ask him to leave. He didn't eat or drink. He never went to the bathroom.

"Am I dying?" he asked, once, as she came to kiss him.

"Your kind has so many skins," she answered. "So many layers. I can never get through them all, to the bone. Even at their simplest, life's experiences add too many for me to peel away."

"Will you love me?" It was the only question whose answer truly mattered to him.

She brought her lips to his mouth. Her eyes, green to depths he could never plumb, speckled by the play of light and shadow, were all that he was.

"To the bone, sweet," she whispered. "To the bone."

DESERT PLACES

By Matt Cardin

*Men with minds sensitive to hereditary impulse
will always tremble at the thought of the hidden
and fathomless worlds of strange life which may
pulsate in the gulfs beyond the stars.*
                                        —H. P. Lovecraft

1.

When Dr. Pryor told me that my friend Paul had been involved in a terrible accident, I was sitting in the heart of the Utah desert, fifteen miles outside Vernal, brushing away flecks of dirt from the leg bone of an as yet unidentified fossil. We only knew that it was some sort of dinosaur, right from the heart of the Jurassic period. Only a small portion had been exposed by our efforts. The bulk of it was still buried under the dry Utah soil. It would take many more days of painstaking effort to excavate the piece with all its secrets still intact.

The light of the early evening sun spilled over my shoulder like a flow of warm liquid, bathing the earth before me with a ruddy glow. That moment, with my eyes fixed on the long-buried bone of an extinct reptile and my brain reeling from the news I'd just heard, was burned instantly, irrevocably, into my soul. The feeling of being deeply and painfully marked was almost physical.

"I'm sorry," Dr. Pryor said. "The woman on the phone said I should tell you exactly what was going on. She said you'd listen better that way." His unreadable little eyes were even more opaque than usual behind his thick eyeglasses. He shuffled his right foot through the thick carpet of desert dust, and his work boot kicked up a brown cloud that lingered in the motionless air like a phantom.

I didn't have to be told who had made the call. No one else would have had the astounding boldness—or tactlessness—to pass the message through a stranger, nor would anyone else have had such a biting insight into my state of mind from across a distance of a thousand miles.

"Did she say how it happened?" I was oddly aware of the tone of my voice, which sounded as dry as the featureless landscape around us.

"Not exactly. Some sort of injury to the head. I guess it's quite serious." I knew I should have felt bad for my paleontologist employer. He was obviously discomfited by Lisa's awful judgment in giving the news directly to him instead of doing the sane thing and asking him to hand me the phone. But I couldn't feel anything besides a dullness that seemed to soak into me from the desert.

"I guess you'll be leaving?" His words were both a statement and a question.

"Yes." I took a final glance at the great leg bone, as thick as the trunk of a small tree back in my home state of Missouri, and willed the moment to stay with me. Something about its pain, its vividness, seemed crucial.

Something about the mystery of the buried bone seemed vital to my continued health and sanity. I wanted the pain of that mark on my soul, and the mystery of the dead monster, to stay with me forever, to remind me of the fact that I was indeed capable of feeling such a deep, pure emotion.

For an instant I had the impression of something flickering into existence—a brief, dreamlike mental glimpse like déjà vu. It was not the familiar sense of having experienced the present moment in a past dream, but more of a surreal certainty that if only I could become quiet enough inside my head and heart, I would be able to foresee something approaching, some momentous event that would prove to be the inevitable aftereffect of that very instant. It was a bit like looking through a window and watching some great beast lumbering past, and knowing that just as its head had come first, its tail must follow.

The image would not come clear, so I took a breath and rose to my feet. Dr. Pryor stood looking at me doubtfully. I knew I was abandoning him right when he needed me the most. But then, I had only been working with him for a relatively short time, whereas my roots with Paul and Lisa were old and deep.

"Sorry," I said. It was all I could manage. He shrugged and looked solemn.

"You have to do what you have to do. I'm sorry about your friend."

I started to say thanks, but then I just nodded and walked away to where we had parked our vehicles. The cloud I kicked up as I drove back to the road was like a fog of rust, as if the air itself had grown old and started to flake away. When some of it sucked in through the grill of my old Ford van and coughed out of the dashboard vents, it tasted hot and coppery, like a splash of blood on my tongue.

2.

The drive should have taken fourteen hours, but it took twenty-six. This was due not only to the fact that my battered old van with its badly unbalanced wheels shook like a minor earthquake when I exceeded fifty miles per hour, but also to the fact that I felt a sharp reluctance to arrive. I was heading back into territory that I thought I had left behind, and every mile I traveled was like fighting against a river current. I drove most of the distance at a speed of around forty, stopping by the roadside several times to catch my breath and stare up at the sky— dappled with silvery stars by night, then cloudless and harsh with heat during the day—while I struggled to divine my own motives. Did I really want to do this? Did I really want to go back and face the remains of my old life again?

When I finally arrived at the hospital in Farrenton, Missouri, it was eleven thirty at night and I felt like a walking dead man. My eyes throbbed with a pulsing ache and my back felt as if it could split in two.

True to form, Lisa displayed her talent for mind reading by greeting me in the lobby. There was no way she could have known when I would arrive, or even whether I would show up. But there she sat, waiting on a mahogany-colored sectional sofa with a crisp copy of the *Farrenton Beacon* spread open in her lap. When she saw me, she dropped the newspaper and ran to me as if I were a long-lost friend or lover. Which, of course, I was. Only she was obviously more at ease with our troubled past than I could ever be. The dark, midnight mood of the lobby, with its sleek contemporary décor and black-tinted windows, wrapped around me like icy fingers as she closed the distance between us.

"Oh, Stephen!" she cried, and buried her face in the breast of my tee shirt. As she heaved against me, I reflexively put my arm around her and then stood inhaling the scent of her perfume and looking down at the glossy black sweep of her hair. She watered my dusty shirt with her tears for a moment before stepping back.

"I'm sorry," she said, wiping her cheeks and attempting a smile. "It's good to see you. I've missed you."

I mumbled something in reply and tried not to notice that she looked delectable in a crimson turtleneck and auburn leather jacket. Her pants and boots were dark leather as well. Outside her sweater she wore a gold weave necklace that rose and fell with the curves of her breasts.

"I'm . . . sorry," she said again, and the falter in her voice caused me to notice for the first time how out-of-sorts she seemed. A sliver of pain was etched between her eyes, which still glowed an emerald cat's green, just as brightly as they ever had. The corners of her lovely mouth were taut with worry and her shoulders were drawn tightly inward. The social skills I had lost during three years of drifting through rain forests and deserts started to come back, and I took her by the arm and led her to the sofa, where I kept my hand on her until she was seated. Then I sat beside her and waited for her to make the next move.

"It's bad," she said. I knew immediately that she was referring to Paul. I had been gripped by a raging curiosity about his accident all during the long drive east, and more to the point, there was nothing else for us to talk about.

"He's not going to get any better," she said. "The doctor says he's brain-dead. He's just a vegetable." This brought on another bout of sobs, during which I again put my hand on her arm and noticed that I could feel the heat of her flesh all the way through the double layer of leather and cotton.

"Lisa," I said. It was the first time I had spoken her name in three years. She looked up at me with glassy eyes, and I knew that a part of me, a despised part that I would have given anything to be able to excise from my soul, still loved her. The question I then asked—"What the hell *happened*?"—referred to Paul's accident, but the vehemence with which I asked it arose from the fact that it may as well have referred to Lisa's and my sorry history.

The tale she related to me was absurd. That was what lingered with me, after she had explained everything and we were rising from the sofa. It lingered as she led me farther into the hospital, toward the elevators, toward the seventh floor, toward the sterile white room where my best friend and spiritual mentor, the wisest and kindest man I had ever known, lay attached to a respirator with a dent in his head from a wayward terra cotta planter that had fallen from a high metal shelf at a home supply store. He and Lisa had gone browsing there with idle thoughts of building a house together. Almost as an afterthought, they had wandered through the outdoor section, where a strong wind, a veritable mini-cyclone, had blown in from nowhere and toppled the fifty-pound planter off its perch and directly onto the back of his skull. He had never regained consciousness.

We rode the elevator in silence. Lisa's body glowed with warmth as she stood next to me in her red turtleneck. When the door opened, she led me in silence down a hallway, past a nurse's station, toward a room I dreaded to enter.

Paul lay under the sheets with a bandage wrapped around his head and various plastic tubes attached to his body like the limbs of a giant insect. The rasping of the respirator was dry and chilling. Several fresh flowers in plastic vases adorned the table next to the bed, along with a scattering of get-well cards. I stepped closer and looked down into his face. Even as he lay there unconscious, his dark eyebrows still endowed him with a placid, mysterious demeanor, halfway between brooding and peaceful. If it had not been for the tubes distorting his features, his expression would have been identical to the one I had seen a thousand times before, when we had sat beside each other in meditation.

Lisa showed uncommonly good taste by standing back and letting me absorb the reality of the moment. When I had drunk my fill of it, I turned to look at her.

"Lisa, I'm so sorry." And of course I really was.

Despite the fact that she had chosen him over me—devastating me with such a desperate sense of grief and betrayal that I had been driven to the brink of madness—I could not feel anything but anguish at Paul's fate. And I could not help feeling a momentary surge of protectiveness toward her, like the phantom sensation of a lost limb.

She stepped up beside me, and we both looked down at him. "Do you recognize that expression?" she said. "He could almost be meditating." A ripple of chills went down my spine at this latest display of her intuitive powers. I had never gotten used to that, not in all the years we had been lovers. She had always seemed connected to the universe in a way that I simply could not rival, no matter how hard had I worked to develop my spirituality. The fact that Paul, too, had possessed his own special kind of connection to the absolute, and had been not only my best friend, but also my informal guru, was more than just ironic in light of what had followed. It was downright brutal.

"I keep hoping," she said, "that he's experiencing things he's always wondered about. He always talked about death like it was a long-lost friend. He always expected it to tear away the last veil and bring him face to face with the great mystery." She looked at me and smiled a sad smile. "I don't have to tell you this. You knew him as well as I did." She had painted her lips red to match her blouse. They looked sweet as strawberry candy.

I was overcome by a sudden urge to get out of the room. There was no visible reason for it. I only knew that I had to step out for air. The memories and emotions were swirling too thickly beside Paul's bed. I said something about needing to visit the restroom, and she offered to walk down the hallway with me.

"No, it's okay," I said. "I just need a minute to wash the dust off. It was a long drive."

"All the way from Utah," she said. Her eyes were impenetrable when I dared to look into them.

"How did you find me?"

"I called your mother. She gave me your employer's number."

Of course. She had called my mother. How difficult should that have been to figure out? I had left Dr. Pryor's cell phone number with my mother, who had always loved Lisa, even after the two of them, Lisa and Paul, had betrayed me. The thought of these iconic women from my past chatting like old friends behind my back sent another chill down my spine. I hid my discomfort with a nod and made a hasty exit.

A sign directed me to a restroom at the end of the corridor. Most of the overhead lights in the main hallway had been turned off for the evening, and the beige walls and floor tiles gave off a chalky glow in the dim illumination. A woman was seated at the nurse's station on my left, reading a paperback novel by the light of a desk lamp. She glanced up at me, but I wasn't in the mood for casual contact, so I kept my gaze ahead and was grateful when I encountered no one else.

I spent a moment relieving my distended bladder, and then another washing my face in the utility sink. Then I paused to gaze at my reflection in the mirror. My tee shirt looked like a child had daubed it with clay. There were muddy streaks where Lisa's tears had wetted it. My face and arms were tanned. I needed a shave. My usually auburn hair was gray with desert dust. If I had not been the one living behind my own eyes, I might have done a double take, just to make sure I was really the same clean-cut person who had set out from this town only a few years ago.

When I got back to Paul's room, I found Lisa seated beside the bed in one of the guest chairs. Her eyes were closed and her lips were moving. She was holding Paul's hand, and I had the inescapable impression that she was uttering a prayer. Knowing something of her exotic spiritual proclivities, I didn't presume to venture a guess as to whom or what she might be praying to, or what she might be saying to them. In the silence, I looked around and noticed a small crucifix mounted on the wall above the bed. For a few seconds I tried staring into Christ's tiny face in an effort to find some kind of solace, but the sculpted look of agony only increased my uneasiness.

Presently, Lisa's eyes opened, and when I glanced down at her, my stomach seized with a sudden coldness. Something about her eyes was terribly wrong. It took me a moment to recognize it, but when I did, there was no mistaking it: her irises had darkened. Formerly a bright emerald green, they had turned a deep coal color while she had prayed, and even as I watched in shock, they appeared to be growing darker with each passing second. Her expression appeared unfocused, as if she were gazing not at the room around her, but at some other world that she discerned behind the surface veneer of plaster walls and vinyl floor tiles. The sliver of pain in her brow suddenly looked more cruel than wounded. Her entire demeanor exuded a kind of quiet menace that was simultaneously linked to her physical beauty, as if her loveliness were just a discrete facet of some other, wider reality whose overall character was awful.

Then the moment passed, and I realized she was looking at me. No trace of the sinister expression remained. She was offering me a wan half smile, and after wavering for a moment, I seated myself on the other side of Paul and tried to get a look at her eyes. They were their usual bright green. Without changing my position, I folded back into myself mentally and filed away the bizarre incident for later reflection. I had not experienced such a strong hallucinatory episode for quite some time. That it could come on so unexpectedly, without any warning, and in the midst of such an unlikely setting, disturbed me deeply.

We sat for a long time while I tried to figure out why I had come there, and why I was staying, and when I would leave. With a bit of surprise, I realized I wanted to take Paul's other hand, the one Lisa was not holding, and tell him that I had forgiven him. I wanted that to be his final memory of me, if indeed he was aware of my presence at all.

But it would have been a lie. Sitting there watching Lisa stroke his fingers with her face molded into an expression of loving concern, I could feel nothing but a semblance of the old shock and desperation—now stiffened with disuse like a crusted-over wound—that had been my parting feeling toward the both of them three years earlier. And beneath that, a cold fist of deadness that was slowly, subtly squeezing my heart with an ever-tightening grip.

After a while, the wheezing of the respirator began to sound like the wind scudding over the low desert hills. Its dry whisper filled me with an aching desire for solitude, and I breathed a silent sigh of relief that I had not taken Paul's other hand.

3.

"I want to ask where you've been." Lisa's voice, soft and smooth, woke me from a stupor. I blinked and realized I had been dozing. Paul was still unconscious, still a mere mechanism of flesh and bone. I looked around for a clock, and saw that the one on the bedside table read one fifteen a.m.. We had been sitting there for just over an hour, and I had spent most of it trying to stay awake. Apparently, I had failed.

"What?" My voice came out sounding thick and sluggish. The coldness had coagulated in my chest, and I was having trouble breathing.

"I want to ask where you've been and what you've done since you left town," she said. "You never called or wrote. We've been worried about you for three years. But I'm afraid you'll be angry if I ask."

I wiped a hand over my face, wincing at the sharp scrape of whiskers against my palm, and inwardly agreed with her. By all rights, I should have been angry. She had no right to know how I had chosen to live my life after leaving Farrenton, especially since my departure had been based solely on the fact that I couldn't bear to stay there and see the two of them together.

But something about her presence was acting like a magnet on me. I had spent a thousand miles and twenty-six hours steeling my resolve to remain aloof and distant. I had told myself that I was only returning to Farrenton because it would be cruel to refuse a summons under these circumstances. But as I sat there looking across the injured body of my comatose best friend and into the face of the only woman I had ever truly loved, I found I actually *wanted* to tell her what had happened to me. I wanted to shock her with the viciousness of it, force her to experience a living measure of the pain I had borne in solitude for three years.

The words began slowly but soon gathered momentum. Against my better judgment, and with growing amazement at my own willingness to open up to her, I began to tell her of my life without her, of how only a few weeks after I had fled from her and Paul, I had become involved with an activist group devoted to fighting the destruction of the Brazilian rain forest. The story sounded utterly foreign and ridiculous to me as I told it, as if I was talking about another person. Prior to joining that group, I had championed no causes. Although my self-conscious spiritual hipness had led me to pay lip service to environmentalism, I had done nothing concrete to support it. Nor had I ever imagined that this hypocrisy would be so simple to change. A chance encounter in a new city with a man handing out pamphlets on a street corner, an impulsive trip to the address listed on the cover, and one short screening session later, and I had found myself seated on a Boeing 757—I, who had never left the continental United States—headed for Brazil to join the protest. Even at the time, I had known that my impulsiveness stemmed from a desire to escape my past, to forget that my two best friends, who were also the two most spiritual people I had ever known, had betrayed me for each other. But this had encouraged rather than deterred me.

The memory of it made the experience of telling Lisa these things all the more painful, and also all the more delicious. I began to revel in recalling minute details of sight and sound, taste and smell, image and emotion. I told her of my first impressions of South America upon disembarking from the plane in São Paulo: of the stifling heat and humidity, the moist ripe smell of earth and jungle, and the way the humidity had seemed to focus the sunlight like a vast lens, which began to roast my flesh immediately as if I were a skinned lamb. I told her of the failed protest, the few friends I had made, and the eventual disillusionment I had felt when I realized that none of it made a difference.

Lisa asked no questions as I spoke of these things. She appeared virtually mesmerized by my account, and perhaps it was her enraptured expression that lulled me into such a state of self-absorption that when I arrived at the part of my tale I had never meant to relate to her— the part about the revelation or vision I received one night while sleeping in the open air under a mosquito net—I simply kept going, as if my words had cast a spell over both of us.

The fact was, after living for several weeks with the

constant assault of the jungle noises ringing in my ears—all the unidentified swishings and scrapings and screechings—I simply stopped noticing them. The pungent smells of earth and bark likewise faded from my awareness, until I noticed them no more than I noticed the stink of my own body in the tropical heat.

But on that single special night, three months into my stay, with no warning or prelude, it all suddenly became vivid again. I awoke from a dark, dreamless sleep and, after experiencing a strange episode of disorientation— as if I had forgotten not only my geographical location but also the very fact of being chained by a body to any specific locale at all—lay silently with the jungle saturating my senses. My ears tingled with all the secretive murmurings. My nose stung with the sweat of tree bark and beasts. My tongue stiffened with the tang of mold and grass. My skin inhaled the moist, rotten heat of hidden decay. I was overcome briefly by an impression of myself as a vaguely rodentlike organism crouched in the middle of a ring of wet foliage, helplessly exposed on all sides to an unknown terror, unable to escape from this exquisite animal sensitivity to the buzzing world of noise and color that enclosed me.

And I was sickened by the florid life all around me. For no cause that I could discern—and I tried long and hard afterward to divine a reason for the change—I was suddenly horrified by the organic eruption that was the rain forest. The one idea I recalled from reading Sartre in college came to mind at once: *de trop,* "too much." The jungle was *too much.* It was too ripe, too juicy, too pungent, too sharp, too *alive.* That was the crux of the matter: it was the principle of life itself, bursting and blooming all around me with scents and shrieks and hot lappings from rough little tongues, that horrified me.

After that, nothing could be the same. My acquaintances in the activist group, who liked to call themselves my friends but who in truth knew nothing about me, were shocked when I quit them without explanation and left the jungle to return to São Paulo. I flew back to the States and made an abortive attempt at resettling in the Missouri of my birth, but this proved to be in vain when I discovered that the midnight vision from Brazil accompanied me like a scar on my psyche. Leaving the original scene of its onset merely brought the new perception home to inhere in the things that were more familiar, as I quickly understood when the oaks, elms, cedars, and walnut trees bristling from the Ozark hills began to inspire the same reaction as the rain forest. I could not help thinking of those tree trunks as coarse hairs sprouting from a misshapen skull, nor could I stop thinking about the rodents and birds nesting in those trees, and the snakes and insects toiling in secrecy beneath the matted forest floors; and below that, the worms and grubs tilling the soil, consigning the whole pungent mass of nature back to the primal black mash that lay at the base of the eternal cycle.

After awhile, impelled by what had grown into a perpetual sense of loathing at my forested surroundings, I uprooted once again and drifted southward and westward into Oklahoma, then northward and westward into Kansas and Colorado, following no plan other than to survive with as little turmoil and social contact as possible. Eventually I found myself in Utah and in the presence of Dr. Malcolm Pryor, professor of vertebrate paleontology at Utah State, who hired me on the spot, on a pure whim, to serve as his informal assistant. I had no training in paleontology or archaeology or any other relevant field. I brought no necessary skills to his endeavor. My job was simply to help with the grunt work necessary to his ongoing excavation in the desert land outside Vernal. But he asked very few questions, apparently seeing in me a suitably solitary temperament for the lonely, dry work ahead.

I found to my grim delight that his assessment was correct. The arid land of the Utah desert proved a perfect environment for me, since its primary resident life was of the scaly, scrubby kind: junipers and sagebrush, lizards and vultures, the occasional mule deer and coyote. I could forget about the grubs and worms there. The desert soil was a baked crust that forced even the insects to work above ground. My job was to uncover carcasses long dead and buried, the remains of lives long desiccated and sealed off from the danger of rot and decay. I often felt a sense of yearning, so sweet it was painful, as I gazed at the rough desert floor and imagined the dead husks resting comfortably beneath it.

And the memory of this brought me to the present. I stopped talking abruptly. My mouth hung open for a moment before I thought to shut it. The respirator pumped dryly next to the bed. Paul's face appeared darker than it had before, as if he had somehow heard me speaking from the blackness inside his head. The spell of my words dissipated, and I realized that I did not know how much of my story had actually passed my lips. I had become so caught up in my recollection that I might have revealed far more than I had intended.

When I looked at Lisa, I found her watching me with a mixed expression of pain and something else, something that might have been wonder or terror. I feared she was reading my mind again, and this rekindled my anger.

"So what do you think of me? What do you think of your long-lost Stephen, who always wanted to be as spiritual as you and Paul?"

The idea that I might have misjudged her—that I might have *always* misjudged her—did not occur to me until she began to cry again. This time her tears were for me. And they were beautiful to behold.

"Oh, Stephen. Oh, my God. I'm so sorry." She sat with her hands in her lap and her head bowed. When she finally looked up, her cheeks glistened and her eyes flashed with a crystal film. "We both loved you. We both wanted you to stay. I know you only left because we betrayed you. I feel like everything you've suffered is our fault."

These astonishing words hung unchallenged in the air for maybe five seconds before the night nurse entered the room to check on Paul's vitals. She was an unpleasant-looking woman with a pear-shaped body and a face full of acne, and she gave me a look of muted disgust, as if she could not fully accept that someone with my ragged appearance would be sitting up late with an injured friend. I kept my face blank as she told Lisa that Paul was still stable, while Lisa, for her part, struggled to compose herself and show proper politeness to the woman.

When the nurse had departed and we were alone again, the moment of intimacy and amazement had passed, and whatever Lisa had been going to say next was lost. I tried not to care, but even when I had retreated back behind the mask of my habitual apathy, I could not shake the feeling that I would have wanted to hear her words, even though I knew they could have done nothing but increase the intensity of my personal hell.

4.

By three a.m. my hallucinations had returned. We had sat in total silence for over an hour, and my strung-out state had finally brought me to the point of full-blown delirium. In one of the visions, I thought I could see glowing bands of light connecting Lisa's heart to mine. The same golden strands also connected me to Paul, and Paul to her. We formed, I saw, three corners of a web of spiritual energy, but instead of peace or joy, the vision brought only horror. The last thing I wanted was to be connected to these two people in this intimate fashion, and I fought violently against the image.

My struggles only increased the force of the delusion, which was soon joined by a second in which I began to see Paul and Lisa as more plantlike than human. The transition was not subtle. I simply looked away from Lisa once, and when I looked back at her, her face had disappeared and been replaced by a beautiful multicolored blossom. When I looked down at Paul, the same change had taken place. Instead of looking into his face, I was looking into a nest of lush, satiny petals. Their bodies, too, had transformed, and were now delicate stalks of deep green, clothed with a translucent covering of cellulose skin that revealed a clear liquid circulating through a network of veins. When I looked down at my own body, I saw only a blackened trunk, like the remains of a gnarled tree after a forest fire. The blips and beeps of the medical monitors began to sound like screeches and caws, and soon I was unable to tell whether I was still seated in a hospital room or lying in a tent in the rain forest.

After an hour of feeling immobilized by these impressions—which, despite their surface beauty, were no less nightmarish than my earlier vision of Lisa's darkening eyes—I awoke as if from a dream and arose on shaky legs to see if the night nurse was still at her desk. A moment later, after bidding Lisa good night (and noticing with relief that her face had returned to normal), I followed the nurse down the hallway to a hospitality room, feeling Lisa's gaze caress my back the entire time, as she stepped into the hallway to watch me depart.

The hospitality room had a bed and bathroom, but I had left my bag of clean clothes out in the van, so I didn't shower. Instead, I just stretched out on the bed fully clothed and tried to sleep. But the mattress was too hard, and the pillow too hot, and soon I arose and went to the bathroom for a drink of water. It tasted bitter and musty out of the paper cup, and I poured most of it down the drain. When I returned to the bed, all I could think to do was to get in my van and leave, or else go back and sit with Lisa again. Both options were intolerable.

Finally, I did something I had not done for years: I laid the pillow on the floor in front of the bed and seated myself on it. Then I crossed my legs in a rather stiff half lotus, having lost most of my former limberness from lack of practice, and focused on my breathing.

Everything slowed down after only a few minutes. For quite some time I had been feeling like a river rafter borne along by a dangerous current. Now I began to feel safely in control of the situation, and a familiar inner image resurfaced from my meditative days: that I was safely away from the river, tucked back up on the shore in a protected cave from where I could survey my inner and outer landscape with a semblance of objectivity.

The pain I had tried to hold on to back in the desert was still there. That was the first thing I noticed when I tried to divine my inner state. It resided like a burned-out campfire in the middle of my chest. I stoked the coals by thinking about the desert and the bones beneath, and was rewarded with a few sparks of feeling. That was what I really wanted, just to return to the life I had been leading before Lisa had called me back in this nightmare. The pain was the only thing I trusted anymore, the only thing I could safely say I wanted without fearing a terrible reprisal meted out by the universe itself.

I spent maybe half an hour savoring the sweet sense of distance from my surroundings. Then the ache in my legs became too much to bear, and I had to stop. When I arose and stretched, the feeling of restlessness returned instantly.

I did not consciously choose to avoid Lisa when I ventured out into the hallway. I merely happened to notice a sign on the wall announcing the existence of a chapel at the end of the next wing, and before I knew what was happening, my feet had begun to carry me in that direction.

When I saw the open door ahead, I realized my feet must have been more intelligent than the rest of me, for my blood raced and the fire in my chest pulsed like a living heart. The sensation of returning life was a welcome one.

5.

I spent nearly half an hour alone in the chapel before Lisa found me. My first impression upon entering it was a sense of awe. I had known the hospital was a Catholic institution, but that had not prepared me for the elaborateness of what revealed itself before me. The very word "chapel" was inadequate, for the place was more like an entire church built seven stories above ground level. I stared up at the chiseled arches and saints, traced the lines of the sacred figures with their frozen gestures of holiness, and it seemed to me that a sense of the numinous spilled out from the gray stonework like a physical wave.

After basking for a while in the glow of the rich ornamentation, I began to skirt the perimeter of the church and study the depictions of the Stations of the Cross mounted high on the walls. This was an element of Catholic spirituality that had always seemed, at least in my eyes, to shine with numinosity. I studied Jesus' face in each scene, observed his expression of intense suffering, and tried to imagine the awesome depth of his sensations, both spiritual and physical, during the experience of his Passion.

At last I paused before the altar, turned my face up toward the giant crucifix where Christ hung in agony on the front wall, and then backed away and sat down in the third pew, where at last the enormity of recent events came home to me. My abrupt transition, in just over thirty hours, from the Utah desert to this hushed place of holy reflection seemed positively unreal, as did the fact of Lisa's waiting for me in a hospital room nearby where Paul lay dead for all practical purposes, having been reduced to a mindless engine running only by means of external aid.

In the silence, a memory spontaneously resurfaced: of Paul sitting before me on a cushion in the spare bedroom of our shared rental home, which we had decked out as a Zendo. He was smiling at me with that good-natured expression of peace and wisdom that I had come to cherish, and was saying, "It's so easy. This is all there is to it. The nowness of this moment is the point of everything. There's nothing to hold on to or hope for or regret. Enlightenment is right here, all around us and inside us." When I balked and said it was still beyond my ability to grasp, he laughed, squeezed my shoulder, and said "That's nothing but enlightenment, too." And amazingly, he actually made me feel better about my spiritual dullness. I felt lighter in his presence, more alive and aware, more capable of understanding the things I had always

longed to understand. He really seemed to regard his ad-
vanced state as something not to be coveted, but to be
shared freely with dullards like me, and more than anything else, this marked him in my eyes as the icon of
everything I had hoped to become.

The memory dissipated when I sensed the presence of
someone else in the chapel with me. I smelled her perfume riding the breeze ahead of her. Then she was sitting
beside me and I was raising my head from my hands. I
had not been crying, but it had been something like that.
My face felt twisted into knots by the forces struggling
behind it.

"I thought I'd find you here," she said. "I could see it
in your face. You needed to get away and reflect."

It was really too much, the way she read me as if we
had been together only yesterday. Somehow, she looked
even prettier when I was angry with her.

"*What* could you see in my face, Lisa? How the hell
do you always do that?" The sharpness of my voice
shocked me.

"I wish I could tell you. I really do." Her voice trembled, and her eyes begin to glitter with tears again. "It's
like seeing another level to things. Do you remember
learning to read when you were a child? First there was
just a jumble of marks on the page. Then, like magic,
they started to mean something. It's kind of like that."

"Well, it scares me. It's *always* scared me." I turned
my face away, searching for neutral space, and felt
pinned between her gaze and that of Christ above us.

"And you don't think it scares *me?*" she said. "How
much more of what's going on with Paul do you think I

can see than you can? Do you think I *want* to be able to sense where he's going? Do you think I like seeing the light die behind his face while he's drifting away?" She was crying for real now, and I had no reply.

"Please," she said at last, when she had regained control of herself. "I have to ask you something. It sounds insane. I know it will sound insane, especially since I know how much you must hate me. But I have to ask." She moved closer to me on the pew, and I tried not to smell her perfume or look at her breasts.

"First," she said, "I have to tell you something. Please just listen. Please don't make up your mind until I'm finished. Can you promise me that?" I avoided her eyes but said yes. Her breath was still labored from crying, and I could feel it on my face and hands, hot and moist, like a wet feather.

"Paul and I have been growing in new directions since you left. Our spiritual lives have taken a new turn. We've been exploring some things you may have heard of, certain pagan traditions with ancient roots. They're all about loving the earth and learning to feel at home with her. We've been trying to learn to see nature as a kind of enchanted garden that's powered by spirit and permeated with love." She eyed me then, and for once, in a moment of insight so intense that it caused my breath to catch, I knew what she was going to say before she said it: "I think what we've been cultivating is the exact opposite of the vision you had in the rain forest."

My revulsion was immediate. She had no right to speak of my experience. It was mine, my own special revelation and cross to bear. Every instinct I possessed told me that I did not want to hear where she was going with this, especially not if she was about to try and demonstrate some connection between what I had experienced in South America and my spiritual past with her and Paul. But in the face of her fresh-wept beauty, and under the piercing glare of Christ and the saints, I felt strangely helpless to protest.

"I really am afraid that what you've experienced is our fault," she continued. "I'm only just now learning about it, but there's a web of invisible interconnections between all of us. It's so intricate, and so beautiful. It's like a spiritual network that joins everything on the planet. Sometimes these connections are especially strong, like the ones between you and Paul and me." I thought of my hallucination earlier, but said nothing.

"I think," she said, "that when you left, we may have accidentally sent a terrible energy rushing in your direction. I think when Paul and I started trying to fall in love with the earth so soon after we hurt you the way we did, you received the opposite end of it. I'm not really sure how such things work, but I think you ended up seeing the opposite of everything we were trying to understand. When you described your vision in the jungle, it sounded exactly like the dark side of the beauty that we're convinced is the heart of nature."

That cold fist had begun to squeeze my heart again. I barely had time to register it before she did an extraordinary thing: without breaking the rhythm of her speech, she reached out a hand and laid it on my thigh. It was a simple gesture, but it sent shock waves rolling through my entire being. More specifically, it sent tingles crawling up into my groin, and a long-buried part of me suddenly lit up, glowing like a spark, at the thought that maybe, just maybe, Lisa's reasons for searching me out and asking me to return had been more complex than I had suspected.

"I'm not asking you to believe all this," she was saying. "I'm not trying to convince you. I just want you to know how we've thought of these things over the past few years, and how we've regretted doing what we did. Earlier tonight, when you told me what you went through, I realized the extent of the damage we've done." After a pause, she scooted even closer, and my slight spark of arousal ignited into a small flame. It was fascinating, really, to watch it all happening from a vantage point of objectivity. For I still felt that the greater part of me was tucked away back in that safe cave hidden high up on the riverbank. My flame of arousal, now growing into a bona fide blaze of lust, was something happening at a distance, something I was observing as a spectator. So was Lisa's beautiful face moving ever closer to mine, and also the feel of her delicate red-nailed fingers gripping my thigh with growing urgency. I knew the feeling of remoteness and safety had to be an illusion. But this did not take away from the reality of its seeming, nor the pleasure I derived from it.

Then she was leaning forward and speaking in a seductive whisper, like an actor leaning off the edge of a stage to share a forbidden wish with a solitary theatergoer. "But I do want to ask you something. Just listen to me before you decide." Her voice was husky and her eyes urgent and greedy as she said, "There's a way for us to get Paul back. The three of us share a special energy. I know you've felt it. Maybe you've even seen it. The thing is, we can *use* that energy. You and I can call out to Paul, wherever he is. We can send him a message. We can light a beacon to show him the way home, and we can give him the strength to make the journey." When she batted her eyes and assumed a kind of coy expression, her meaning was instantly clear, and the nature of her request would have been obvious even without her next words. "All we have to do is reconnect, you and I, on the most intimate level." When her red lips curled in what might have been the faintest of wicked smiles, I felt waves of warmth crash through me.

"Please," she said. "It will heal you, too. It will take away the vision of *too much*. We'll balance in the middle, and Paul and I will take back the energy we aimed at you. You can have your life back." If she did not send the next words directly into my brain as a telepathic transmission, then she must have spoken them without moving her lips: *You can have me back, too.*

By that point she did not need to say anything else, for I was hopelessly hers. She had worked her magic with consummate skill. I was consumed with lust, and its object was as much my former self and my own redemption as it was Lisa and her body. I wanted to possess her and regain possession of my soul in a single stroke. There was no distinction between the two goals. And if we could help Paul in the process, in some obscure way that made no sense to me, so much the better. Or on the other hand, if her ideas were simply the worst kind of lunatic self-deception, and all we would be doing was to commit adultery next to the body of my dying friend, then at least I could relish reclaiming what was rightfully mine and repaying Paul in kind for the perversity of his long-ago betrayal.

These thoughts seethed within me, whirling inside my head like a drunken haze, as she took me by the hand and led me from the chapel. The giddy feeling helped to augment the sensation of spectatorship, and so it seemed almost like a cinematic special effect when I experienced—I actually *experienced*, as a physical perception—the hallowed atmosphere of the chapel folding back in on itself like a flower, preparing to lie in wait for the next soul-hungry supplicant. I seemed to glide above the floor when she pulled me down the hallway and toward the room I had entered as a stranger only a few short hours ago.

The gliding feeling continued until she turned to face me beside Paul's bed, where I thought suddenly of the prehistoric bone lying partially uncovered back in the desert. The memory brought back a sweet stab of pain, and there was a moment of confusion during which the knotted ball of my resolve threatened to come unraveled. Why was I doing this? What did I think it would accomplish? It occurred to me that everything was happening too fast, it was all rushing ahead with a seemingly inbuilt logic that was really completely irrational. I had arrived only a few hours earlier, dragging my feet and dreading to unearth my buried past. And now was I really about to have Lisa again, and was I hoping that through it I would be healed of many years' worth of agonizing wounds? In the face of this turmoil of doubt, the dream of objectivity threatened to dissolve on the spot.

Then her hands were on me, pulling me down to the floor, and they banished all other concerns. The flesh-and-blood warmth and softness of the woman before me were irresistibly real. The memory of the dry desert bone with its accompanying dry desert sadness could not compete with this reality. Nor could common sense. I could not think about the fact that we might be discovered by the hospital staff. I could not think about Paul lying comatose beside us on the bed. I could think only of the heat of Lisa's body, and the pressure of her touch, and the wetness of her lips, like the petals of a flower in the rain forest, kissing first my eyes and then my mouth, drawing me out of myself and into a fleshy reality that was far more ecstatic than any experience of isolated spectatorship could ever be.

And soon, just as there had been in the rain forest, there were scents, and moans, and hot lappings.

6.

Time seemed to transform into a river of burning gold while I lost myself in a kind of primal rapture. Everything became liquid and surreal. The sound of my breath filled the whole universe like saltwater sizzling on a cosmic ocean shore. I had never been so sexually inflamed. All my repressed rage and bitterness flowed through my limbs like a torrent and focused upon the burning point of contact between us. She was on top of me, and I grappled violently with her back and buttocks, pulling her so tightly against me that I worried I might snap her in two like a china doll. She received it all with-

out complaint. In fact, her passion, if anything, surpassed mine. She swiped her tongue over my lips and
eyelids. Her nails scored parallel lines down my neck
and chest. Her hair whipped my face like the wings of a
frenzied bird.

When she had her orgasm, she arched so violently
that I thought my hip bones would break. A moment
later, my own orgasm sent my head spasming backward,
where the crack of solid floor tile against my skull set off
an explosion of stars in my sight. The impact dazed me
momentarily, and this became mixed up with the fiery
pulse of pleasure coursing through my body. Briefly, I
returned to the cave and the riverbank, where I floated
among black clouds and sparkling lights like a flaccid
swimmer in a sea of fireflies.

When I returned to myself, she had risen and was
bending naked over Paul's unconscious form. The air
was chilly against my cooling flesh, and my eyes felt hot
and gritty. I watched her caress Paul's face and speak
tender words to him. Her nudity, which only moments
before had been a veritable feast for my starving eyes,
began to look slick and rubbery. She cooed to him as if
he were a baby, imploring him to come back from what
ever dark dimension had swallowed him. Left to myself,
with the sticky evidence of our lust drying on my penis
and thighs, there was no way to feel that I was somehow
outside or above the situation. It was all too real, and I
was sickened at the thought of what I had just done.

But when I moved to sit up and cover myself, I found
to my astonishment that my limbs were stiff as a
corpse's. My arms felt as if they were shackled with lead

weights. It took all my effort just to raise my head an inch. My chest felt as if an invisible force were pressing down upon it, constricting my rib cage and forcing me to struggle for breath. Even as I began to worry that the trauma to my head might have been more severe than I had thought, the physical constriction gave way to a deeper one, and with astonished horror, I felt something begin to drag my spirit down within me.

Sex had never been an ultimately pleasurable experience for me. The feeling of lassitude afterward, as if I had been attacked by some kind of parasite and drained to the point of death, had invariably spoiled it. I had always felt like a walking dead man for days afterward. It had taken me years to connect my occasional feelings of an almost lethal sluggishness with my rare sexual encounters, and once I had made the connection, I had determined to try and forget that side of life altogether.

Now, it was as if all those former spiritual sappings had been mere preludes to this one great stealing of energy. I felt as if I were falling backward down a well. The ceiling receded. Lisa's naked form above me grew taller. The wheezing of the respirator began to reverberate like whispers in a cathedral. The feeling of heaviness in my limbs began to dissipate, not because I was coming to life, but because I was plummeting inward and leaving my body behind.

Above me, beside me, Lisa was looking more and more like an elongated figure in a surrealist painting. Still leaning over Paul's body, she reached down a rubbery stick-arm and probed between her thighs, gathering some of our fluids onto her fingers. Then she raised them to his lips and continued to whisper things that no longer sounded like language, but like a wordless chant, harsh and melodic.

A moment later I saw his hand twitch. I heard the rhythm of the respirator grow more insistent as it struggled with another rhythm that had begun to compete with it. And I heard Lisa utter a sharp cry of joy.

The room continued to recede. I continued to fall backward into a well of infinite seclusion. And yet I saw and heard everything around me. There was no end to the receding, no far edge of exile where I would find myself cut off from all contact with the external world. It was as if a hole had been punched in the back of my private cave to reveal an infinite, sucking blackness on the other side. The thought arose that in the hell of black emptiness opening out below me, I would not be allowed even the small comfort of forgetfulness. I would not be allowed to reside alone in a dank spiritual dungeon where I could forget that I had once tasted the air of a rain forest and smelled the dust of a desert. There would be nothing but distance—distance between the world and me, distance between everything I had ever loved and the possibility of grasping it, distance between my innate longing for spiritual wholeness and my ability to pursue it.

The restraint on my limbs let go abruptly. I blinked and rose to my elbows. Lisa was rushing to put on her clothes and throwing mine at me. In his bed, Paul was stirring with ever more vigorous motions. I knew I had just participated in some sort of rite, but I was totally ignorant of its nature. I only knew that my life force had been transferred to Paul, and that he had gladly accepted it. For this was, after all, nothing but the logical extension of the theft he had committed three years ago. The little moment of happiness unfolding beside me, where he had opened his eyes, and where he and Lisa were touching each other's faces with shared tears of reunion, was not meant for me. I was excluded by a gulf that now separated me not only from them, and not only from the happiness of my past, but from everyone and everything, from all things and beings in the whole vast, dismal universe.

I rose on legs that belonged to a dead man and finished putting on my clothes. With the eyes of a dead man, I surveyed for a final time the sight of a shared love that should have been mine. And with these new eyes, I *annihilated* it all. I took the sight within me and felt it slip away instantly, back through that hole in the cave wall, where it sparked out into ambient nothingness and disappeared forever. No memory was left, no feeling, no emotion or reaction to the things before me. The sight of Paul and Lisa was being born anew in my consciousness with each passing instant, and with each new instant I was devouring it and watching it be reborn again. It was like swallowing an ocean and finding that I was still thirsty. It was like eating the world and finding that I was still ravenous. I watched them press down under the weight of my gaze, trembling with an unknown terror that confused them both, and clinging to each other for warmth and comfort. Then I turned and left the room without looking back.

The hallway was still dim with nighttime illumination. The nurse still sat reading her paperback novel in a pale aureole of lamplight. When I looked at her, she shifted in her seat and glanced about her with a look of confusion and fear. She did not appear to see me when I passed right by her. I shared the elevator to the ground floor with an old black man pushing a janitor's cart. He did not seem to notice my presence, not even when I looked at him and saw his face blanch with dread as the visual impression of him passed through me on its way to everlasting oblivion. When I exited through the lobby and passed several people bound on early morning errands, none of them noticed me, but they gasped and nearly stumbled when I took the sight of them into myself.

A light rain was falling in the parking lot. I paused just outside the sliding glass doors to lift my face to the murky sky, where a delicate flash of lightning outlined a mountain of dark clouds. A moment later, a rumble of thunder rattled the windows behind me. I stood there with the rain spattering against my face and hands like tappings on a distant roof, and with the steamy air clotting my nostrils like a damp cloth. And from my fixed position there in the midst of it all, rooted at the center of my perceptual universe like the eye of a cyclone, I *annihilated* everything: the clouds and thunder, windows and pavement, even the slick, yellow reflections of the streetlamps in the myriad puddles dotting the asphalt. The depth inside me was bottomless, and the life around me to be devoured, infinite. I thought of Lisa's darkening eyes as they had appeared earlier, and of the sculpted face surmounting the cross in the chapel. The two images became confused in my mind's eye, and I saw Christ looking at me from beneath his battered brow with eyes that had become glittering pools of darkness. The mystical identification was instantaneous. An incontrovertible inner logic told me that his eyes were now mine, and that behind them lay the obscure powers that Lisa worshipped and had invoked to achieve her ends.

I stood there for a very long time, gazing out at a world that no longer had a place for me, and listening to Paul's words from long ago repeating over and over in my head. Indeed, he had been right, both in his perception of the truth and in his optimism about my spiritual slowness. For my eyes were now cleansed, and I saw that truly, there was nothing to hold on to, nothing to hope for, and nothing to regret. Everything was emptiness. Everything was now a vast desert whose surface concealed a mausoleum of desiccated lives. In place of my former longing, there was now only a desperate, dry sadness at the thought that I had at last surpassed my teacher, and had discovered a truth that I would have given anything to forget. I would have given anything to look around at the little patches of manicured grass dotting the hospital grounds, and to see them drinking their fill of the fresh rain that was beginning to fall more insistently, and to believe that among their roots, deep under the dark soil, an army of teeming life was working tirelessly to reduce everything back to the original substance, the viscous black stuff that formed the origin and end of all life. This thought, formerly a source of horror, now seemed a veritable consolation in the face of the dry emptiness that filled me. But the thought, too, had become a mere dead artifact, for I had graduated to the next level, and now knew beyond the shadow of a doubt that even the moist, dark life under the earth was ultimately nothing but dry bones and dusty flesh. Ultimately, the desert inside me and the desert of the world were inseparable, undifferentiated, identical, and would share the same fate.

The rain kept falling for hours while the eastern sky behind me grew gray with the approaching dawn, while I stood looking at everything with a new pair of eyes that would never grow old, and that would accompany me to deserts or rain forests or wherever I might go next, devouring and renewing all things in my path, and forever finding them insufficient.

The dawn, when it came, was cold.

MUGWUMPS

By Hank Schwaeble

No matter where he looked, Grant Lomax saw his fate hanging there in the balance, staring back at him. Not the fickle finger of an intervening deity or the character-determinism blathered about in philosophy classes; this was the obvious, cause-and-effect kind of fate, as predictable as it was preventable. There was a train wreck looming in his future, and avoiding it was simple: He had to find some way to rid himself of his client. And the quicker, the better.

Simple, but not easy. The balding, portly man in front of him, droning on about being a victim of circumstances as he solicited his lawyer's moral approval, was the only client he had. It had been that way since Grant left Winston, Peck & Hughes, accepting the man's offer to become his full-time attorney. It didn't take long for the golden handcuffs to start cutting off his circulation. After almost two years, he was almost ready to gnaw his hands off at the wrists to see them gone.

The real problem, hovering over him like a storm cloud, was that people didn't just rid themselves of Moscow Bain. If anyone was going to be dropped, it would probably be Grant by Moscow, not the other way around. And a six-foot drop, at that. He knew better than anyone that it was height of foolishness to lock horns with a man like Bain. And given the unsettling disappearance of Danny Alvarez, it was an understanding grounded in experience. Grant Lomax's shingle could easily change from Attorney-at-Law to Attorney-at-Rest.

"So, I'm asking you, Grant . . . am I wrong?" Moscow said, raising his bushy eyebrows. He was picking his teeth with an ornately designed toothpick as he spoke, reclining into the chocolate brown leather of a chair in Grant's office, his foot propped atop the lawyer's desk. Grant wondered where a person had to go to find toothpicks like that, ones that came individually wrapped, with intricately patterned grooving. He wished he still wondered what kind of person actually bought them.

"Am I?" he repeated.

Grant looked at the sole of the shoe staring back at him. Its heel was scuffing the otherwise flawless finish of his mahogany desk. God, he simply could not go on like this: a high-dollar whore, paid to be the screw*er*, rather than the screw*ee*.

"I can terminate the leases, if that's what you're asking," Grant said. That was certainly true. All the leases he drafted for Moscow contained provisions that were impossible for tenants not to breach. This was by design. Moscow Bain did not enter relationships he couldn't end at will, even though the other party was always bound, hand and foot, tighter than Faust. Grant's response to the question spoke to Moscow's legal position, even though that wasn't what the man was fishing for. Such was the way of their conversations.

"Of course you can. I can always count on you." Moscow looked down at his toothpick. A small, pasty lump of white food clung to the tip. He slid the wood through his fingertips, then flicked the glob away and rubbed the fingers against his pant leg. "Money-grubbing bastards. I can sell that property for seven million as a teardown. Seven million! Highest and best use, that's what that location demands. Some of those bastards have a five-year renewal right. Do you think any damn one of them wouldn't skip out for a *fraction* of that kind of money? Do you?"

No one who wasn't willing to pony up significant money in legal fees, only to face certain ruin in the long run, ever skipped out on a Moscow Bain lease or backed out of a Moscow Bain deal. But Grant knew better than to even hint at such a thing. Such was the way of their conversations.

"I can draft termination and notice-to-vacate letters tomorrow. We'll have most of them out in thirty days. Sixty to ninety if they put up a fight. But ninety days would be the max. That's the quickest you'd be able to close."

"Ninety days! *Jee*-zus. If somebody came to me and said 'Moscow, I need you to vacate because I've got a business opportunity,' why I'd be outta there in a week. A *week*, I tell you! I don't force myself on anyone. I'd tear up that lease and move on. But I'm old school. Old school guys, we didn't need lawyers to do up our contracts. It was all based on trust. If a situation changed and the other guy needed you to change the deal, to cut him a break, he could count on that trust to work things out. Not today. You can't hardly trust anybody nowadays. Nothing but money-grubbing bastards and *mugwumps*. Am I wrong? Tell me if I'm wrong."

Grant forced himself not to cringe. *Mugwump* was the term Moscow used for people he particularly despised. People like Danny Alvarez.

"I'll draft an opinion letter to the title company, stating that all leases are subject to termination, and that every unit will be vacant by closing. You shouldn't have a problem."

"You do that. *Ninety days*. I ought to sue any bastard who fights it, for my costs, for delaying my closing. We can claim conspiracy."

Grant rubbed his eyes, pinching the bridge of his nose between his thumb and forefinger. Everything that stood in Moscow's way was a conspiracy. It was almost laughable. The man was the target of more conspiracies than JFK.

"Something wrong, Counselor?" Moscow's tone, sarcastic and wry, suggested in its usual way that there had better not be.

"No. I'm just tired," Grant said, dropping his hand from his face and leaning forward to place his arms on his desk. He stretched the edges of his lips into what he hoped was a pleasant expression. "And I'm not feeling all that well."

It was the truth, he told himself. He was nothing if not sick and tired.

"Yeah, well, you better get some rest. But first, I got

something I want you to do for me." Moscow pulled his
foot from the desk and leaned forward, retrieving a slip
of paper from a rear pocket. "I want you to research
these properties. Find their owners' tax status. Most of
them are old and exempt from paying. This is a new gig
I thought of. If they owe anything on their house, I can
maybe buy the note and foreclose for letting the taxes accumulate."

"And if they're exempt?"

"Those are the ones I want to know about. You know
those taxes accumulate against the property until the old
people die. Most of the geezers with a mortgage, their
places are almost paid off. Got a couple of years left on
the note, maybe. But I bet you their loans don't allow for
taxes to go unpaid, whether they're exempt or not. Other
lenders may not care, but I can foreclose and pick up
those places for a song. A *song*, Grant."

Grant nodded, almost tasting the bile as it threatened
to crawl up his throat. Such was the way of their conversations.

When Grant led his client out of his office, his secre-
tary had already left for the day. Kyle Shaw was standing over the printer at her workstation, waiting for the
pages of a document to stop spitting out.

"Hello, Mr. Bain," Kyle said, smiling.

Moscow grunted a response, a hint of contempt tug-
ging at the pudgy creases of his face.

Kyle looked at Grant and hitched his shoulders.
"Well, have a nice evening, Mr. Bain."

Grant walked Moscow through a set of glass doors to

a bank of elevators. He pressed a button and waited with his client.

"When are you going to fire that kid?" Moscow asked.

"Kyle? He's okay. Besides, I need the help. You keep me pretty busy, you know."

Moscow pulled the toothpick from his mouth and stabbed the air near Grant's chest. "Well, I wouldn't trust him if I were you."

"Why not? He's harmless. A good worker, too."

"He's fake. A phony. There's nothing worse than a phony. Someone who smiles to your face, but secretly hates your guts. Know what I mean?"

"Yes," Grant said. "I don't think that's the case with Kyle. He's a good guy."

"You don't know shit, Counselor. You always say that about people. Other lawyers, *mugwumps*, people trying to screw me. I always have to educate you on the way people really are."

Grant inclined his head, placing a hand on the back of his neck and giving it a squeeze. "Are you insisting I fire him?"

"No, you're loyal. I respect that. Disloyalty is the only thing I hate worse than phoniness. I'm not gonna make you be disloyal." Moscow leaned back, peering past Grant and through the glass doors to where Kyle was tapping the bottom end of a clutch of papers against a desk, aligning them into a neat stack. "But I'm telling you, I wouldn't trust him. And I expect you to value my opinion."

"I always do, Moscow."

"You'd better. I'm the one who paid for that fancy suit you're wearing." The bell rang and the doors to an elevator car parted. Moscow stepped inside and turned back to face Grant, waving a hand in a loose sweep from left to right. "I'm the one who pays for all of this, and don't you forget it."

Grant wandered back through the glass doors into the reception area. Dark woods, green marble, supple leather. All in abundant supply. All bought with Moscow's money. Try as Grant might, forgetting it wasn't in the cards.

"Say, Boss, if it's okay with you, I'm going to kick out for the night," Kyle said, emerging from a small office opposite Grant's.

Grant glanced at his watch, a diamond-studded Rolex he bought himself the day he accepted Moscow's offer. The sweep of the second hand seemed both mocking and ominous as he checked the time, like it was happy to remind him that his was running out. It was almost seven.

"It's Friday, Kyle. You shouldn't ask. Get out of here."

"You okay, Boss? You look kind of . . . out of it."

"I'm fine, thanks."

Kyle curled the side of his mouth into a dimple. "I don't know why you're in bed with that guy. You must know you're *so* much better than this."

Grant eyed his clerk warily, saying nothing. The truth was, despite his defense of him, he didn't fully trust Kyle. There was something about his clean-cut image, his boyish face, his no-combing-needed, meticulously chaotic crew cut, that seemed . . . phony.

"I know it's not my business, Boss, but you can't tell me you don't think that guy is worse than awful."

"Mr. Bain pays the bills, Kyle. Don't forget it." Grant wasn't certain which was worse—saying it or knowing that it was true. It almost made him want to retch.

"Oh, there's no denying it. But I've been here almost three months now, and I can see it's killing you. Me, I'm just earning a paycheck. I can leave whenever. But you. You're stuck with him."

The kid was perceptive, he had to give him that. Then again, it had to be rather obvious. This wasn't the first time his clerk had made comments of this nature. It was, however, the first time he had seemed unwilling to let the subject drop without discussion.

"I've built a good practice around Moscow Bain. He pays me very well. I have no grounds to complain."

"All I'm saying is, you probably wish you could be free of him. Heck, *I* wish you could, and I only have to deal with his dirty looks and snide comments."

"What are you getting at, Kyle?"

"What would you say if I told you I had the goods on him?"

"I'd say you were insane. I'd also say you were fired. I'm his lawyer. I've got all kinds of stuff on him. I also have a fiduciary duty. Don't they teach that in law school anymore?"

The young man's eyes held Grant's for a long moment. "I'm not talking about privileged information. I'm talking about game-over stuff. Something outside the attorney-client relationship."

"I don't think I like the direction this is heading. And

you shouldn't, either. Moscow Bain is not somebody to fuck with."

"Look, Grant . . ." Kyle stepped up to place a hand on his boss's shoulder. Grant's eyes slid down to the hand, then back. The kid had never called him that before. He wasn't certain how to take it. "I haven't exactly been honest with you."

Kyle gestured in the direction of Grant's office. Grant regarded him for a moment, taking in his brown eyes and dark tousled hair, then led him through the door. Kyle took the seat Moscow had been using. Grant circled his desk and sat in his own chair. It was custom made from fine leather and expensive wood, with pneumatic lumbar support. Two thousand one hundred and twenty-nine dollars, he recalled.

"I'm listening."

"I took this job because you represent him. I came here to learn. To gather facts."

"About what? And why?"

"Let's just say I have my reasons. They have to do with my uncle. Let's leave it at that. But more importantly, if you want a way out, you definitely want to see what I have to show you."

Grant settled back into his seat and spread his hands. "Okay, I'll bite."

"Not here. Tomorrow. But first, you have to tell me something, and *be honest* about it. Do you want to be free of Moscow Bain? I mean really free? If you say no, I'll quit and we can pretend we never had this talk."

After studying the young man's face for several seconds, Grant let his eyes float around the considerable expanse of his office, pausing over a few unjustifiably expensive items as he contemplated how to respond. A four-thousand-dollar globe on a tall mahogany stand. A tapestry depicting a Persian archer on horseback—three thousand? A pair of ivory bookends that were at least a grand. Each.

"Okay, let's just say I *would* like to be free of him. What then?"

"Not good enough," Kyle said, shaking his head. "You have to let me know, one way or the other. Yes or no."

Grant's eyes dropped to the corner of his desk, where Moscow's scuff marks still remained. *The nerve of this kid*, he thought. *No way I'm going down this road, looking to some wet-behind-the-ears law clerk for salvation. No way.*

"Yes," he said. "I would like to be free of him."

Kyle let out a short, audible breath. "In that case, you need to come meet me tomorrow." He reached across Grant's desk and pulled a sheet of paper off of a memo pad as he grabbed a pen from its holder.

"These are directions to a place out Brenham way. It used to be my father's. Be there tomorrow evening around six."

Grant took the piece of paper from Kyle's outstretched hand. "Why can't you just tell me?"

"You need to see this for yourself," Kyle said, waving off further inquiry. "Believe me, it's the only way."

Shadows crept east as Grant made his way along the freeway from Houston. He had spent most of the day at his office, drafting callous letters in legalese to parties who stood between Moscow and money, haunted by thoughts of Kyle plotting and scheming against his client. He had changed his mind about going at least a dozen times, but now he was praying that whatever Kyle had to disclose would be big. Anything half-assed would place him in an untenable position, or worse. Blackmail ammunition wouldn't do. Not with what had happened to Alvarez lurking in his mind. For information to be helpful, it would have to guarantee Moscow Bain would be put away for a long, long time. Grant shook his head, wondering what the state bar would think. So much for his duty of loyalty.

By the time he turned off the freeway, the sun was a blazing ball resting atop the rolling tree line. The two-lane highway twisted through thickets of oak and pine, the tree trunks wading in tangles of underbrush. The road came to a fork, and Grant bore left, following the directions Kyle had written. After a mile or so, the densely wooded terrain opened into a stretch of fields. A stick-style farmhouse, its dull white paint tinged red by the dying fire of the sun, sat alone at the end of a long, unpaved drive.

Grant was glad to see Kyle's Mustang pulled up at the front of the house. He parked his Jag next to it and checked the time. A bit early, but not embarrassingly so.

The two-story house had the look of a rustic cottage, with clapboard siding and split-wood shingles. A veranda with a scroll-sawn railing sat above a foundation of short brick columns separated by lattice vents. The place could have used a coat of fresh paint, but otherwise seemed well maintained.

Grant climbed the steps and knocked on the door. He waited several seconds, then knocked again. He was about to knock a third time when he heard the thumping of footfalls and the sliding of a lock.

"You're early," Kyle said.

"I didn't know how long it would take to get here."

"No problem. Come on in. I was in the basement." Kyle stepped back from the doorway and beckoned Grant to enter. Once the door was shut and bolted, he led Grant into the living room. The furnishings were simple. Wooden tables, wooden frames. Cloth cushions hid behind lacy pillows, yellowed with age, and drab throw quilts. Islands of area rugs, ribbed ovals and rectangles, staked claims on the hardwood floor.

Kyle gestured for Grant to take a seat, then walked over to a television on a cart and retrieved a remote control. A white dot blipped in the center of the black screen when he pressed a button. The black screen eventually gave way to a blue one and a message appeared, telling the viewer to press PLAY to begin. Below the television, the time on a VCR blinked twelve a.m.

"This should be cued up," Kyle said.

"So, you brought me here to show me a videotape?"

"Sort of." Kyle turned back to face Grant. "I might as well get right to the point. What do you know about the disappearance of Danny Alvarez?"

Danny Alvarez. Grant told himself he should have known this would have something to do with him. Alvarez had made the mistake of investing in a limited partnership with Moscow, and Moscow played the game he always played, exploiting terms of their agreement to gain a financial advantage. But Alvarez refused to bend to Moscow's unyielding will, refused to let his percentage be repeatedly diluted through bogus cash calls. When Moscow tried to bury him in litigation, Alvarez's lawyer claimed his client had serious proof of tax evasion and loan fraud, and threatened to go to the IRS and other agencies if Moscow didn't back off. One day Alvarez's lawyer simply stopped returning Grant's phone calls. He was eventually found dead in a one-car accident. The police concluded alcohol was involved.

"I know he turned up missing, about a week after his lawyer wrapped himself around a tree. Nobody's seen or heard from him since, as far as I know."

"I assume you suspect Moscow was behind it."

Grant let out a humorless laugh. "Given the timing of it, well, yeah. I had my suspicions."

Kyle nodded. He pointed the remote toward the TV and VCR. "This should interest you, then."

The blue screen was replaced in a flicker with a grainy video scene. The image was of a man strapped to a chair, squirming and twisting. At the sight of it, Grant moved as far forward as he could without sliding off the couch.

"That's Alvarez?" Grant said, not quite certain.

"Yes," Kyle said. He turned up the volume with a press of his thumb. A moment later, he added, "Brace yourself."

Grant heard the tinny, hollow audio of a voice in the background, competing with the sound of Alvarez groaning as he strained to free himself. The voice sounded a whole lot like Moscow calling someone a *mugwump*. Then Grant heard a scraping noise, the clanking, grating sound of metal being moved. Or opened.

As if reading his mind, Kyle gestured for Grant to remain quiet, never taking his eyes off the television.

On the screen, Alvarez began howling curses, bucking his body up and down, back and forth, frantically trying to break free of the straps around his arms and legs. Then the convulsing stopped. His eyes widened and he drew back. Everything about his expression grew larger and the camera zoomed in slowly, expanding the image until the man's head and upper body dominated the center, his legs cut off at the knees. The lens finished refocusing just as he started to scream.

Kyle paused the tape. "You may not want to see the rest."

Grant glanced up at Kyle, then back to the frozen image on the tape. It was the face of a grown man, racked with dread, screaming like a terrified child.

"Keep going," he said.

The picture started moving again. Alvarez finished his scream and started another. A series of gasping cries followed, alternating between *no no no* and *please please please*. In the background, Grant thought he heard the word *mugwump* again.

Out of breath, Alvarez turned his head away, clenching his eyes shut, and something moved into the frame from the upper-right-hand corner. At first it looked like the boom on a soundstage, inadvertently caught on film. It continued to slide across the screen, dark and long, bobbing slightly. Trailing behind it was a large, egg-shaped bulb, and Grant saw the two were connected, one extending from the other. The bulb, pale and colorless, was connected to a thick, dripping appendage. The leading end, protruding from the bulb, gingerly touched Alvarez's recoiling cheek. Only then did it occur to Grant that it was a tongue.

In a sudden, violent motion, the bulb spread open, revealing itself to be a mouth. The mouth whipped forward and enveloped Alvarez's head, burying it down to the neck. His body shook, writhing and jerking in the restraints.

It was still shaking when the bulb snapped back, pulling out of view. Grant's heart skipped forward when he realized the bulb had taken a considerable amount of Alvarez with it.

From the base of the neck up, Alvarez no longer had any flesh. Or hair. Or muscle tissue. Only eyes and gums remained, exposed and raw, set in a glistening skull. Grant saw the man's eyes dart from side to side, and watched his tongue twitch as his fleshless jaw gaped. Grant turned away, covering his mouth with his hand, stifling a heave.

"Moscow did that," Grant said, still looking away.

Kyle turned off the television. "Yes."

"That tape's not enough to prove it was him. They may be able to do a voice print, but he's slippery." Grant ran a hand over his face, relieved the picture was gone. "Where did you get that? And what the hell was that thing?"

"The Australians call it a bunyip. As for where I got

the tape, we'll get to that. Look—there's more going on. A lot more. But first, I have to know. Are you in or out? I'll give you another chance. You can walk away now, if you want. We can pretend you were never here."

"After seeing that? How could I possibly keep dealing with him? Suspecting him of foul play is one thing. But *this* . . . and you say there's more?"

"Yes. Downstairs. It's only fair to warn you . . . you may regret this. Regardless of how you feel about Moscow Bain."

Grant took in a long breath. He swallowed to clear his throat. "Show me."

Kyle made his way to the center of the house and opened a door. Grant followed him down a flight of wooden steps. A damp, musty smell attacked his nostrils, becoming more pungent as he descended.

"This was custom built by my father. He had plans for a wine cellar."

The basement was much smaller than the first floor of the house. It was lit by a single unshaded bulb hanging from the ceiling. The walls were brick, but the one opposite the stairwell was hidden behind a dark curtain. In the middle of the room, Moscow Bain was bound to a chair, a handkerchief stuffed in his mouth.

"Oh, God. *Kyle,*" Grant said, pausing before he reached the bottom. "What have you done?"

Moscow rotated his head to look. He tried to speak, but could only manage a series of frantic hums and grunts. There was a volcanic ferocity in his eyes, but Grant noticed something else, too. Surprise, perhaps. Or fear.

"How . . .?"

"It's a long story. I'll explain it later."

Grant circled the chair to face Moscow, the man's head swiveling to follow him every step of the way. He looked at the straps, the chair, the floor bolts, then glanced at the walls. "Wait a minute. Isn't this—?"

"Yes. This is the room in the video. After my father died, Moscow bought this place. From the estate."

Moscow began grunting and humming again in a fierce display, whipping his head up and down and to the side. Veins were pulsing in his forehead, and Grant avoided looking him in the eye. He had to stop this, had to stop it now. He opened his mouth, searching for the words to tell Kyle this had gone too far when he heard the curtain slide open. He turned to see a huge tank, with glass panels over an inch thick. It was covered with a sturdy metal grate, hinged to a steel frame that was bolted to the walls. Inside the tank, a huge eye was pressed against the glass, blinking a transparent lid.

"And here's Moscow's little pet."

The creature bore a scorpion's general form, with paddle-shaped forearms and tentacles instead of legs. One giant eye dominated the dome of its squidlike head. A gaping, scooped lower jaw extended to the side, and seemed flexible enough to face any direction, independent of the eye. The thing's back curled into a long trunk with a bulbous end. It was using the bulb to pick things off the bottom of the tank and drop them into the huge lower jaw.

"As you saw, this thing eats people. Devours everything. Even the bones, by the time it's done. Doesn't leave a trace."

Grant thought of Danny Alvarez, and his eyes drifted over to Moscow, who was glaring at him and hurling muffled invective.

"Here's your chance," Kyle said. "Freedom. I unlock this lid, and all your problems are over. No more Moscow Bain."

Even the bones, Grant thought. No more Moscow Bain. No more evicting people who had done nothing wrong, no more screwing tenants out of leaseholds, no more suing innocent people to accommodate his client's greed or pride. And no more fear of becoming a target himself. It wouldn't even be murder. He wasn't going to lay a hand on him. He would simply allow the man to suffer the same fate he had inflicted upon Danny Alvarez. And who knows how many others.

"So, what do you say? Do I release the *mugwump* on him?"

Grant looked his client in the eye and watched as a sudden stillness seemed to claim the man.

"Yes, do it," he said, feeling a weakness shoot from his gut through his legs. Then he looked over at Kyle. "Hey, did you just call it a *mugwump*? I thought you said it was called a bunyip?"

"I said the Australians call it a bunyip." Kyle thrust his chin toward Moscow. "*He* calls it a *mugwump.*"

Grant's gaze shifted back to Moscow, whose beady eyes, still burning with anger, seemed ready to explode. "Why does he call it that?"

Kyle began to unfasten the latches that held down the

grate over the tank. "*Mugwump* was an Indian word that was used to describe Republicans who bolted the party in 1884, refusing to support the party's presidential nominee. Moscow thinks this thing'll turn on you the first chance it gets. He calls any person or thing he can't trust a *mugwump*."

"How do you know all this?"

"Oh, I neglected to mention," Kyle said, pulling open a latch and turning to face Grant. "Moscow's my uncle."

Grant felt a jarring thud in the back of his head. When his face hit the cement floor, he hardly felt anything at all.

The first thing Grant became aware of was the pain, a skull-crushing, throbbing ache thumping through his head. Eyes fluttering open, he tried to reach his hand up to his crown, but found himself unable to move.

"Good," a voice said. "You're awake."

It took his eyes a moment to focus. When they did, he saw Moscow Bain standing in front him. Kyle was off to the side, leaning against a wall near the tank, a smug, almost bored look on his face.

"My nephew," Moscow said. "He kills me. Always with the angles. Like when he comes back from bumming around Australia and says, 'Hey, Uncle, I want you to pay these guys for this thing, this rare monstrous thing.' I say, 'What do I want with some weird animal?' And the price! But he's always got a new angle. Never could say no to him."

Moscow turned and walked back a few steps to where a video camera was mounted on a tripod. "Take you, for example," he said, stooping to check the flip-out display panel and adjust the lens. "He says to me, 'Uncle,' he says. 'Uncle, why don't you let me check out that lawyer of yours? Can't be too careful,' he says."

Grant glanced over at Kyle, who lifted his shoulders in a lazy shrug.

" 'You don't need to do that,' I tell him." Moscow continued, leaving the camera and approaching Grant again. As he neared, he leaned forward, close enough for Grant to smell his rancid breath. " 'No, Grant's a stand-up guy,' I said. 'He's no fuckin' *mugwump*. If he wants out, he'll just tell me.' But I let him anyway. Then, when he says you *do* want out, he tells me I need to test you, for loyalty. That nephew of mine, he's always one step ahead. Just like when he told me how to deal with that other *mugwump*, Alvarez."

Moscow gestured to Kyle, who pulled on a length of rope that fed through a pulley above the tank. The metal grate shifted. "All set, Unc."

"You know," Moscow said, lowering his voice a notch. "I gave you every hint. I told you I wouldn't ever force myself on anyone, told you to listen to me and not to trust Kyle. But, like I said, you don't know shit about judging people." Moscow gestured toward the tank. "*Mugwump*? Meet *mugwump*."

Grant turned his head and stared at the eye, which pressed against the glass, wide with anticipation. He tried to tell himself it would be over soon, that at least then he'd be free. The eye seemed both patient and eager, like it knew it would get its way, but hated the wait. Grant wondered if this was what it was really like to stare down the eye of fate.

He also wondered whether that eye, naked and merciless, saw any of the same things in him that he saw in it.

LINKAGE

By Lucy Taylor

Leaning against the bar, Eric stared at the bright row of bottles and felt weak in the knees. They were lined up long and silky like the legs on a stage full of chorus girls, the colorful labels like bright, slutty thongs on their wet-looking loins and he fantasized—much as he might dream, in a Hefner-esque way, of choosing a lover from a line-up of centerfolds—about which bottle he'd command the barkeep to pour the first shot from. The Jack Daniels, always a classic—he could feel the hot blast of it smoking his throat—or the knock-you-on-your-ass gut shot of the Wild Turkey. He dreamed of the punch the tequila would deliver or the sweet, dark oblivion of a few shots of gin. They were hot and slutty and easy, like ten-dollar whores and elite and pricey and ultimately nasty as Kama Sutra–trained call girls who'd burn a man up in the process of laying him low, and he wanted to taste every fucking one of them, he wanted to drink himself into that place where he fled his mind and abandoned his physical form in an out-of-body experience that made near-death experiences pale in comparison.

But when he finally motioned the bartender over—a

narrow-jawed youth with skittish squirrel eyes who wore a short, matador-style coat and tight pants that made him look like a neutered show dog—he ordered another Diet Pepsi with lime, as though he could imagine no finer ablution to quench a man's thirst.

Then he pulled out his cellphone and called *her*.

Because he couldn't get her out of his mind.

Because the voice in those middle-of-the-night phone calls kept reminding him of her.

The calls had begun almost a month ago, in the dead of August, when the thick blankets of heat in his un-air-conditioned apartment thwarted sleep, and the prospect of another day framing tract houses in South Denver weighed on him like ten extra degrees on the thermostat. He wasn't sure if it was a man or a woman who called. There was something wrong with the voice. At first he'd thought it was simply muffled, then he'd decided the caller was using a device to alter the tone and pitch of their voice—he'd seen such things advertised in the backs of magazines aimed at amateur detectives and devotees of firearms.

"She talks about you all the time," said the androgynous voice, purring up from some neutral zone between female and male, and Eric, groggy, wrenched from deep sleep, muttered "Huh? Who?" thinking vaguely that the caller must mean his ex-wife, Gail, who still bitched that she got a bum deal on the alimony.

"She talks about your big, hard cock. She wants you to fuck her blind. She has all kinds of nasty, dirty fantasies," the voice singsonged, which at least established that whoever it was referring to wasn't Gail. "She wants to see you, but she's afraid—"

Sitting up now, wide awake: "Afraid of what?"

"You know. The outcome."

"I don't know shit. Who is this? Who are you talking about?"

"I'm a friend of Annette Doyle."

Annette Doyle.

He smiled for two reasons—pleasure at recalling the woman in question, and at the mere fact that he still remembered her at all. His time at the treatment center where he'd known Annette was a dark blur, a drugscape devoid of plotline or dialogue, a murky oblivion.

He hadn't dreamed about Annette in years—well, not in months anyway—but now a forgotten sky in his mind opened up and the images floated back like cobwebby clouds. Green eyes and a porno princess's body, the dirtiest mouth he'd encountered outside the wares of the adult bookstores he'd always enjoyed frequenting. Three years ago they'd fucked each other's brains out at Harmony, a rambling, one-time hunting lodge tucked away in the Sangre de Cristo Mountains in southern Colorado. A team of rich psychiatrists had bought it and converted it into a rehab center for the worst of the alkies and addicts, the ones who'd cycled in and out of other rehabs, the hopelessly mired and lost.

Most standard rehabs were for thirty days. Harmony was for ninety. Annette's stay there had overlapped his by six weeks. Sex between the so-called "students" was frowned upon in theory, but Eric couldn't remember any of the staff doing much besides looking the other way, and sometimes they hadn't even done that. Sometimes they'd watched.

Not that he could blame them, really.

Annette Doyle.

Even given his Swiss cheese of a memory, he realized the details he knew of her life were paltry at best—that she owned a cherry red Thunderbird, she'd been a stripper in Vegas, and that she frequented swingers' clubs because she wanted sex served up to her like a drink at a bar—no fuss, no fanfare, no wait. Instant gratification, immediate buzz. He could respect that.

In the muggy torpor of his bedroom, some sanity eked through. He thought: *Wait. Stop. I have a job. I'm sober. Annette will only be trouble. I don't even want to know how to find her.*

"So how do I find her?" he asked.

The voice gave a soft, jagged cackle, like someone crunching glass. "How badly do you want to know?"

That pissed him off. He started to hang up.

And the voice said, "She got married and changed her name to Benson. She's divorced now. But she's listed in the phone book."

"Who are you? Why are calling me?"

"Because she's an important person in your life and because she wants you. And you still want her. And I like people to get what they really want—eventually."

"Who are you?"

"A friend."

"Fuck you," he said, "I ain't calling her."

*   *   *

"I'm sitting at the bar at O'Shay's," he said into his cellphone. "I've got a shot of Jim Beam in front of me. I haven't touched it yet, but, God, it looks good."

He imagined her silence like a live thing cawing and ripping inside her throat. She'd hold it in for as long as she could. Then she'd open her mouth and say, *Hold on. Don't drink it. I'm coming over.*

After the silence drummed on a few beats longer than he expected it to, she said, "So? You want to drink, drink. What the hell am I supposed to do about it?"

"That's cold, Annette."

"The cold truth."

"I thought you'd want to know. In rehab they said we're supposed to call somebody if we're going to drink."

"Yeah? So why me?"

"You're an important person. Important to me, I mean."

"Yeah, right. That's why I haven't heard from you since rehab. It's been years, Eric."

He felt the first tendrils of rage sprout inside his skull. He was prone to rage, a therapist had told him, because of things his father'd done to him and things his mother hadn't, but he knew the truth. He was prone to rage because he liked it. Rage was fun and often the use of it got him what he wanted.

But not this time. If he unleashed on her now, he'd lose her. He knew that. So he kept his voice under control, even though she was disappointing him fiercely. In his mind, he'd already had her half of this conversation scripted, but she wasn't getting it right. She was blowing her lines. He wanted to scream, *Don't talk to me like that, you bitch. The voice on the phone says you talk about me, think about me—that you want to fuck me as much as I want to fuck you.*

Instead he said, "It's not like I *want* to drink. I can't help myself."

"*Jee*-sus!" Her voice soared up hard and high like a paper airplane lashed by a gust of wind. "You're sitting in a goddamn bar, what do you think they serve there, double lattes? Of course you want to get smashed. Otherwise why would you be in a bar? Why would you've ordered the goddamn drink? And why the hell would you've called *me*?"

"I'm sorry," he said, and for a strange, self-doubting moment, he genuinely was. "I've been thinking about you. I thought maybe you'd want to see me."

"If you're sober. I might want to see you if you're sober."

"I *am* sober. Now. But I need you here, Annette, or I'm going to drink."

"And if I come there, how am I supposed to stop you?"

"Because the only thing I can think of that would look better than this drink is you, stripped down and sweaty. On your knees with my cock in your mouth."

She didn't speak, but her breath changed—just a tiny, subtle hitch, as though someone had crept up behind her and held the barrel of a revolver to her throat. A surge of hot, electrical energy ate up the line between them. Only then did he allow himself to smile, because he knew the voice on the phone hadn't lied.

"So don't drink," she said. "And give me time to get changed. I'll be over."

The call disconnected. He waved the bartender over and was ordering another Diet Pepsi when his cell phone rang.

"Did you call her?"

The soft, sexless voice made the hairs on the back of his neck stand on end.

"Who the hell are you?"

"Did you *call* her?"

"You said she has fantasies about me. Didn't sound to me like she has any fucking fantasies. I think you're full of shit."

"It's just a game she's playing. She's so hot for you she can't stand it. Remember how it was at rehab—"

"I knew it. You're somebody from Harmony."

"Everybody pretended to look the other way, but we all knew. You were fucking each other's brains out."

"So the fantasies, what are they?"

"I can only tell you one of them. It's the same as yours. Her fantasy is to drink."

"I don't drink."

"Sure you do."

"I *used* to."

"You *do*. That's what alcoholics do: drink. Annette understands that. She wants it. Just like you do."

"I don't fucking drink."

"But you do now. You are being given permission. 'A' is for alcohol, Eric. Have you forgotten?"

"Who *are* you?" He kept talking into his cell phone, maybe a half minute past the point when he realized the caller had hung up. Talking to himself, really, explaining things, denying . . . *I can't drink, don't you get it? I'm an alcoholic. I lied about the Jim Beam. I only said that to get Annette to come here.*

But alcoholics drink.

He beckoned the waiter and ordered a shot of Jim Beam and sat staring at it, sipping the dregs of his Diet Pepsi, until Annette Doyle finally showed up. He didn't know what she'd been wearing during their phone call, but unless she'd been naked, it couldn't have been less than what she wore now—a slinky black-and-white checked halter top, high heels, and a denim skirt that rode up past midthigh.

She picked up the Pepsi, sniffed it, and eyed the shot glass.

"You're drinking."

"I am now," he said, and slammed back the shot. Liquid fire slid to the back of his throat and blazed up and ignited his brain. A line had been crossed that he'd forgotten was there until the first drink brought back the memory.

"Jesus, what the hell are you doing?" she said.

"I can do this," he said. "I can control it."

She made an "oh, puh-*leese*" expression, like someone had just offered to sell her swampland in Minnesota. "You're a drunk, just like me."

"Maybe, but you've never fucked me when I wasn't sober. Don't you want to see what it's like when I'm not? If I was good then . . ." He tilted his head toward the bartender. "How about a drink?"

"Club soda," she said.

"Me, I've always thought I fucked better after a few drinks. Less inhibition. You?"

She looked away, pretending to study a plant by the window, but he saw the smile twitch past her lips. "When it comes to depravity, booze isn't part of my equation."

"Bullshit, your equation's no different than mine."

"Fine. You want to sit here and drink yourself dead, don't waste my time."

She grabbed the purse that she'd laid on the bar, slid off the stool, and almost ran for the door. She was halfway across the parking lot, reaching for the door of that cherry red Thunderbird he'd once watched her drive away in, by the time he caught up to her. "I'm not wasting your time. Come home with me. Let me prove it."

She cocked her head to one side and put one hand on the edge of his shirt, the backs of her fingers stroking his chest, green eyes slanting up at him in the dark. Whatever perfume she was wearing, it reeked of sex.

She ran a hand down the front of his shirt to where the extra thirty pounds or so he was carrying swelled out in a spare tire. "You've put on weight. Aren't you afraid the fat will get in the way of your cock?"

"Try me and find out."

"And what the hell's this?" She peered at the tattoo that she'd discovered between his pectorals, a stylized letter "A" crisscrossed by thorn-bearing vines.

"You didn't have this before. What's it stand for?"

"Alcohol." He'd brought a fresh glass out of the bar with him—that was what had delayed his pursuit of her.

Now he raised it to his lips. " 'A' stands for alcohol. To remind me I'm not supposed to drink."

"Glad it's doing the job."

"*Another* one?" she said when they were back at his apartment, undressing one another in his bedroom. He'd stopped at Discount Liquors on the way there and bought a bottle, which she noticed he always kept within reach. He swigged from it while she sat on the bed, undid his belt and tugged down his pants. Along the curved expanse of his lower belly she found another tattoo, a black and green "S" that undulated up from his pubic hair like a snake from a patch of brambles. She traced it with her tongue.

"Sex," he said. " 'S' is for sex."

"Don't tell me it's like the 'A'—it's to remind you not to have sex?"

"Too late for that, isn't it? I've not only lost my sobriety, I'm getting ready to lose my celibacy."

A harsh note in his voice tugged at her, and she wondered if this was about to go bad even sooner than she expected it to.

Now that she was with him, memories of their time together at rehab were coming back—fragments of thoughts, like a jigsaw reassembling. She remembered that he'd been unstable, violent, twice getting into fights with male staffers, one time hurling a chair. And his brain didn't seem to see shades of gray. Everything was black and white, incontrovertible. Some people had real convictions about having or not having sex, didn't they? It was to be reserved for only important people, spouses, lovers. Casual fucking, that was only for—what had she heard once?—moral degenerates? Surely he hadn't morphed into one of those people who cared about such things.

"Are you a moral degenerate?" she said.

"I sure as hell hope so."

"Good. I like to play with my own kind."

He turned her over, stripped down her thigh-high hose with the seams up the back, ripping them both in the process. Then he shoved her skirt up, pushed the tiny thong bikini out of the way and entered her with no finesse and no preamble.

She saw stars. It had been a while since she'd fucked, and he was hung like something that ought to be running around in a paddock. She was pleased that she'd misjudged about the belly. It got in the way hardly at all, and the size of his cock more than compensated. She wondered why the hell she'd waited this long to have sex, anyway. She'd had plenty of offers. What was she waiting for? *Him?*

Drunk or not, he was as she remembered him, rough, insistant, greedy. Exhausted finally, she thought she understood why she had pretended to give a shit whether he drank or not, why she'd come to O'Shay's and then to his apartment. She wanted him. A final fuck for the road. . . . Why not?

When he rolled over to grab the bottle and refill the glass he'd set on the floor by the bed, she glimpsed something on the back of his neck. Another tattoo, but furtively placed, like a secret even from himself.

She pushed the hair aside to get a better look. Ripples of adrenaline chased up her spine.

"Jesus, you're a regular walking alphabet."

He looked surprised. "Huh?"

"The letter 'M' on the back of your neck."

"Oh. That."

"*That*. What's it stand for? Something else you're supposed to remember to avoid?" She giggled, but there was a thrill of fear behind it, something crisp and cold that zigzagged behind her ear like a tiny lightning bolt.

"Had a girlfriend named Michelle," he said. "It didn't work out."

He drained his drink, then crawled down to her feet and started to massage them. She flinched. "Don't do that."

"What's wrong?"

"You've forgotten, haven't you? I don't like my feet touched. My older brother used to tickle me and it drove me crazy. So as far as my feet go—don't even think about it."

"Gotcha. Anything else I need to know?"

"You knew a lot about me once."

"Yeah, but it's . . . I don't know . . . the whole time at Harmony, it's like a drug dream. Jesus, that'd be a trip. If they drugged us to get us off drugs."

"I thought that was standard procedure."

"You know . . ." He started to tell her about the voice on the phone, the one that had reminded him about her, that told him he could drink, but he didn't want to admit the whole thing hadn't been his idea entirely—the phone call and the drinking. Didn't want to admit he could be manipulated like that.

"So what should I know about you that I've forgotten?"

"I like to be scared."

"Yeah?"

"I been scared a lot. Things I don't even remember sometimes. But I like being scared when I know nothing really bad is going to happen."

"If you know you're safe, then you can't really be scared."

She traced her index finger around the "S." "It isn't logical, Eric. Nothing about how people deal with pain is logical."

"Yeah, I remember," he said. "At rehab, you told me that. Funny how little I remember about Harmony except bits and pieces. Like when a necklace breaks and beads go flying off in all directions and every now and then, even weeks after, you come across one and pick it up from behind a curtain or under a chair."

"I remember finishing up my ninety days and leaving," she said, "thinking I was going to make a fresh start, do things right this time, but not knowing what the hell doing things right meant."

"You will meet important people."

"What?"

"Dr. Kay said that. When you leave rehab and go out into the world, you will meet important people."

Annette felt that cold thrill up her spine again, less pleasurable this time. "Sounds like a fortune cookie."

"But she talked like that."

He sipped his drink. "God, this is good. Booze and sex, this is so fucking excellent." He held the glass out. "You're sure you don't want some?"

She got up off the bed and started fumbling around for her clothes. "I'm sure, Eric. And you shouldn't be having it either. You'll wind up back in rehab again. Or in prison. Or in the ground."

"Fuck," he said. "Life's a prison. And I'm gonna end up in the ground anyway."

"We all do."

He smiled engagingly and said, "Some of us sooner than others."

The blow came so fast and hard she barely felt it, and didn't see it at all. One minute she was standing there, talking to him, the next a hood of blackness crashed over her head and she was flat on her back, looking up at the cobwebs in the corners of the ceiling, wondering what had happened to her.

He got behind her, slid his hands under her arms, heaved her upright. Her knees wobbled, full of Jell-O. She ran her tongue around her mouth and tasted blood.

"Why? What did I . . .?"

"There is no why. Don't you know that? Because I like to. Because I can. Because I had the alcohol that leads to the sex that leads to . . . you figure it out."

"The 'M,' " she said. "It doesn't stand for Michelle."

"Smart girl. You remember."

He spun her around and hit her again, and she seemed to take flight, her body careening across the room, her head three times its normal size to accommodate all the ink-dipped cotton someone had stuffed in there. The bed caught her, buoyed her up like the sea.

His tattoos spun behind her eyes. This was out of control; it was moving too fast. What had she told him, that she liked to be scared? Why had she said that? She was scared now, and it was a brutal, stomach-churning fear, harsh and sickening. She folded her feet underneath her. It was important to hide her feet.

"Stop it, Eric, please. Why are you doing this?"

"Because I drank and we fucked and this . . . this is the next part."

"Part of what?"

"You are important," he shouted. "You are an important person, Annette."

"No, no, you're wrong. I'm not. I'm not important at all."

"You are! The voice on the phone told me you are!"

He turned away from her to rummage inside a drawer. She thought about making a run for the door, but then he had the gun out and aimed. It looked big and dark and brutal, starkly, almost pornographically masculine.

"The 'M,' don't you know what it stands for?" he said.

She glanced wildly around toward the door. There was still time. . . . "Murder."

He made a gun of his left hand and mimed pulling the trigger. "Correct. Buy that girl a drink."

"Please don't. Please don't kill—"

The shot roared in her ears. Red streaks exploded across the room as though someone had flung a bucket of paint, spattering the walls and the bedspread, and catching in her hair in long, gory ropes.

"Oh, Jesus! Oh, God!"

"It's all right, Annette. You're okay."

The woman stood over Eric's body, the gun aimed down as though she might shoot him again if he moved. But he wasn't moving.

"Jesus, you said it wouldn't get this far. I thought you weren't going to come. I thought you were going to let him fucking kill me."

She slid off the bed, felt her legs give way, and sank to her knees. Dr. Kay knelt beside her. She was a blond, sparrowlike woman with a thin, spartan mouth, dimpled cheeks, and brown eyes that looked like someone had run an eraser over them, diluting the color to the point of near lifelessness.

"Was Eric one of the important people you talked about when you called?"

"No, Eric wasn't important. He was just a test, a throwaway. The doctors who worked at Harmony when you and Eric were there, we're still testing the procedure, trying to figure out if the sequence of addictive response we taught actually works. Apparently it does." She pulled a tissue out of her pocket and dabbed at Annette's mouth, flicking away specks of blood. "This is why you must never drink—until I give permission. Because all things are linked in the addictive cycle. Because 'A' leads to 'S' leads to 'M.' "

"Look at his back," Annette said. "There's another tattoo."

She was looking down at Eric's body. He'd fallen

facedown, and she could see a second 'S,' smaller and starker than the first one, curling up like a tail from the base of his spine.

She knelt beside him and traced it with her finger. "What does it stand for?"

"It will come to you," said Dr. Kay.

"There's so much I can't remember."

"Understandable. All those years of drinking, Annette. It wipes out memory. Kills brain cells."

She reached down and turned her right foot up. Four letters were tattooed below the toes. ASMS. "Alcohol, sex, murder," she said. "But what does the second 'S' stand for?"

"You'll remember when the time comes."

Later, when the phone rang in the night, Annette wasn't surprised to hear Dr. Kay's voice. Not disguised the way it had undoubtedly been disguised for Eric. "There's going to be an important person in your life, Annette. You're going to enjoy fucking him. But first you need to have a few drinks."

Even though she knew there was nothing to smile about, she couldn't stop herself, as she imagined the pleasures to come, and found herself checking the clip on her gun, making sure there would be enough bullets.

SHADOWS IN THE SUNRISE

By Mark Dillon

My shadow on a wall, a sunrise in the western sky, a twelve-hour gap in time: how could I explain these things? And yet I found myself on the mountain road in the light of morning, whereas a moment before I had been crossing the darkened lawn in front of the Rexdale house; I had noticed my shadow moving on the wall— in the dark of night—and I had turned to see the maples thrashing in a sudden wind. And then I watched the sun rise on the wrong edge of the world.

But now I stood in the cold light of a normal day. Frost light gleamed from pebbles on the dirt road and glittered from the aspen leaves that fell around me in the stillness. I was bitterly cold, as if I had spent hours in the cold air . . . hours passing like a dreamless night. How could I have walked halfway home without remembering the trip? I checked my watch in disbelief: the date and time revealed a sudden loss of twelve hours.

I thought of returning to the Rexdale house but the idea sent a chill through me that was deeper than the morning cold. And it was cold: my face tingled painfully, as if with frostbite. So I continued on my way along the mountainside, then took the road down into the valley toward home. Away from the trees, between barren fields, I felt exposed beneath a cloudless sky, and the feeling remained even after I entered my house and shut the door behind me.

With a fire lit in the woodstove I warmed up quickly, but the cold lingered on my face. I peered into a mirror for any sign of frostbite but found, instead, a network of tiny red sores. At first I thought of measles, but as I examined my face and scalp I saw that every pore was inflamed, as if someone had stabbed at me with tiny needles—and then I suddenly vomited, repeatedly and helplessly, as if at the physical memory of a long-forgotten fear.

The day went by. With winter looming, I had vegetables to can and freeze, apples to store and wood to cut. Yet nothing I did could dispel the sense of strangeness that haunted me like an unrecollected dream. And I was very much alone: my parents had left the house years ago; they were down in the States, where they found life under martial law preferable to freezing to death in a Quebecois winter. "We're not allowed to leave the city limits," they had written, "but the weather's fine and we've got five hundred TV channels." That was life in America. Here, I was surrounded by abandoned farms; when the world economy had fallen apart it had dragged down all my neighbors with it. There was no one I could turn to for help.

That night, whenever I closed my eyes, I saw the

Rexdale house gleaming in the darkness. I had spent a lot of time there over the years, growing up with the Rexdale children as my closest friends. When the Great Deflation forced them out of the countryside, I agreed to maintain the house for them, even as the world around it fell apart—not for the money they sent (which had little value at any rate), but in memory of a time when there were people in my life.

Staring into darkness, I understood that memories were all I had . . . and I refused to have them poisoned by a mystery.

I left early the next morning, walked up the road that climbed the hillside and followed the winding route below the mountain. The day was milder, but the oblique sunlight, the wood-smoke tang of rotten leaves, brought hints of winter's rise, and the wind stung my healing face.

When I reached the spot where I had found myself the day before, I was tempted to turn back. The wind in the pines hissed like a tide retreating from a hidden shore, and the leaves scuttling over the dirt road sounded like dead things struggling into life. A lingering, indefinable dread had seeped through my mind, and it darkened everything around me.

The few farmhouses along the route were boarded up and empty. Staghorn sumac and hawthorns had spread across the fields; gray stalks of burdock and milkweed bristled on ragged lawns. I remembered how, as a child, I could see the sparse lights from distant farms at nightfall, or hear the faint barking of a neighbor's dog; these nights, the fields and hills were black, and the silence gave way only to the baying of the wolves.

On the far side of the mountain, the driveway to the Rexdales' weaved through a forest of gaunt maples and cedars until it reached the house, a white, one-storey building with a broad bay window that faced a long and narrow clearing. The surrounding woods were bleak: the scarlets and the orange-reds had faded to a dull copper, and the shimmering yellows of the aspen trees were spectral in the slanting light. Yet thanks to my maintenance work, the house felt unabandoned—an illusion that died as I peered through the bay window at the empty living room.

I studied the house, hoping to spur recollection, but nothing came. The western sky, pale blue with a streak of cirrus, brought nothing to mind, even as I waited at the exact spot where I had seen my shadow leap upon the wall the night before. There was nothing here to frighten me.

And how could a place so familiar be disturbing? As a child, I had played here many times with the Rexdale children. I remembered hide-and-seek, with the sheds and the encroaching woods as perfect spots to watch pursuers without being seen. But our favorite hiding place was the cubbyhole below the bay window, with a sliding panel built into the living room wall. If you lay down you could slide right in and close the panel until only your eyes were visible.

And then the shadows on the wall—
What?
As the shadow of a driven cloud darkens the fields and then fades away, something had loomed within my

memory and passed me by. I closed my eyes to the pale
sunlight and tried to see the darkness of the night before.

Shadows. Shadows on a wall.

I felt a sudden chill, the physiological memory of fear.
I touched my face and, prompted by a vague impulse,
ran my fingers over the irritated skin. They brought to
mind the fronds of a plant brushing against me, the sliding touch of wet ropes . . .

By now I was damp with sweat and my heartbeat
raced, yet I could retrieve only the vaguest hint of shadows looming high on a wall, seen from a low angle, as if
I were crouched on the ground.

No; as if I were lying on the floor, in the cubbyhole,
watching shadows on the living room wall.

I opened my eyes. The day was bright and clear: that
alone encouraged me to unlock the front door and step
inside.

Daylight shining through the bay window warmed the
empty living room, and because I had left the door open
whenever I worked outside, the air was neither stale nor
damp. Yet I could smell dust as I stooped at the cubby
below the window. The panel was open, and I noticed
scuffmarks on the dusty floorboards within; had I left
them the night before?

I lay down on my side, pulled myself into the compartment and slid the panel shut, leaving it open just a
crack, so that I could peer out at the wall on the other
side of the room. Then I closed my eyes and struggled to
remember.

Shadows on the wall . . .

*   *   *

*The sun has already set. I have just put the lawn-
mower into the shed and I am crossing the yard in the
darkness. Something moves at the edge of sight: I look
up and notice my shadow on the wall of the house. Then
I turn around to see the maples tossing in a sudden
squall, and there, in the western sky, the sun is rising.*

*Not the sun: a beam of light flickers through the nar-
row clearing.*

*My eyes are streaming in the wind but I can just
glimpse something moving through the woods: it looks
like a wall in motion. No . . . a scaffolding, a cage, a lattice of irregular shapes and sizes, glowing with purples
and magentas as deep as darkness yet somehow visible.*

*Descending from the sky—behind the trees, in front,
all around me—wall after wall of glowing lattices, a
cagelike framework facing all directions, too complex to
take in at once. Diamond shapes, lozenges, a mountainside of spikes, weblike panels set at every angle, greens
and blues and scarlets . . .*

*I run to the house, slam the door shut behind me and
lock it. Then I peer through the tiny pane as tall, swaying shapes approach from the light.*

*In a panic I crawl to the bay window, slide into the
cubby and pull the panel shut until I can barely see the
shadows on the opposite wall, shadows like the freeze-
frame snapshots of windswept trees. Despite the storm
they are motionless, and I can see their ropy boughs at
all angles, every bough divided into two branches, every
branch divided into two twigs, every twig divided into
two thorns, every thorn divided into two needles—*

Then light flares in the hallway just beyond my vision

as the front door crashes open. A shadow bulges on the wall and its wet ropes burst through the crack, fumbling at my face, stinging with a thousand pinpricks—

I wrenched open the sliding door and stumbled to my feet. The empty room was warm and sunlit, but I had to get out of there. Standing on the lawn, staring at the trees and sky, I found that nothing in the everyday world could dispel the cold fear that haunted me.

But that was absurd. These were not memories. Dreams, night fears, the fabrications of a mind that would come up with any explanation to resolve anxiety: these I could accept. But memories of actual events? Never.

Yet I found myself scanning the trees for broken limbs and peering at the ground for telltale holes and gouges. When I realized what I was doing, I turned away in disgust.

There had to be an explanation for the dazzling light, my wounded face, the lapse of memory. Had I been struck by lightning, had I wandered in a daze till morning? Or was my isolation driving me to madness?

Madness. A word I had avoided; there it was.

I noticed the front door gaping wide: in my rush from the house, I had left it open. As I went to lock it, that false memory of the door crashing open in a blaze of light nagged at me. Of course it was false. The door was undamaged; nothing had smashed it open.

Then I thought of infinitely branching ropes, splitting in two repeatedly from the size of a limb to the size of a molecule; no lock would keep them out. But that was nonsense. It had to be nonsense.

Two ravens leapt from the boughs of a cedar; I stood in the doorway and listened to their fading cries. There was nothing I could do but go home.

Hemmed in by the trees along the driveway, I felt naked beneath that wedge of sky; I glanced away from the boarded windows of the farms along the road. On the other side of the mountain I looked down into the valley and saw my house standing like a target amidst barren fields, exposed on all sides to any shadows that might loom with evening. Yet the darkest were already here.

Winter struck. I tried to focus on day-to-day work, but at night the stars looked down with enigmatic stares.

The telephone and power lines went down in the first blizzard. I lived in the kitchen, close to the woodstove. My supplies would last for a long time if I rationed every bite. In dreams I served at banquets, but always woke before I could steal any food.

Driving snow blotted out the world beyond my windows and hissed against the walls in a constant rush of wind. World War Three could have come and gone and I would have never known the difference.

One day I began the five-hour walk to the nearest village: I had to see if the outside world existed anymore. But visibility faded beyond the length of my arm and I had to give up. I stumbled back through a white cocoon of blinding flakes, terrified that the footprints I had left on the way out would disappear before I could find my way home.

That night I heard my parents struggling in the wind outside; they called my name with distant raven cries.

When I opened the door they gaped at me and backed away. Then I awoke, stumbled to the mirror and flinched at the sight of a stranger's hollowed face.

Last night I awoke to silence and realized that the wind had stopped. I scraped frost from the windowpane and saw moonlight glimmer through thinning clouds. Eddies of snow swirled across the fields, a thousand shades of white twisting in the darkness. And descending from the ragged sky, spanning the horizon, a wall of scaffolding, a glowing magenta cage sparkling with somber pinpoints of green and blue and scarlet.

Perhaps by now the world belongs to them: a world of shadows, drifting like the snow above abandoned fields, falling like the darkness on forgotten hills, awake and watching in the moonlight; a world that I could recognize but never own. My memory has returned and that, for me, is enough. There will be no spring.

THE OLD
NORTH ROAD

By Paul Finch

Forest of Lune: Northern England

Drayton was perhaps fifteen miles west of Barnard Castle when he came across the wrecked Peugeot 306 on the verge-side.

It looked to have come off the road at high speed: trails of melted rubber were smeared across the blacktop behind it, the hulk itself firmly wedged against the splintered trunk of an oak tree. Its bonnet was badly buckled, smoke and steam spurting out in jets through the shattered radiator grille. Only as he drove on past, however, did Drayton notice the girl standing beside the car.

He hit the brakes hard, then threw his vehicle into REVERSE.

A moment later he'd stopped and got out.

The girl was relatively young, probably in her mid-twenties. She wore a short denim skirt, a faded denim jacket over a pink T-shirt, and brown leather cowboy boots. She had longish blond hair, and was extremely pretty, with bright blue eyes, a turned-up pixie nose and sprinkles of freckles on either cheek. Drayton only approached her slowly, aware that a lone guy advancing on a marooned woman out here in the middle of nowhere could be deemed threatening. The girl didn't seem massively concerned, however. She was leaning back against the oak tree, hands in her jacket pockets.

"Hi," he said.

"Hi," she replied, smiling.

"Is, er . . . is everything okay?"

She nodded. "It's fine. Thanks very much."

"You're not hurt at all?"

"No."

He glanced round at the Peugeot. As well as the damage done to the front end, and presumably—by the gaseous emissions pouring out of it—to the engine, too, three of its four tyres had ruptured and gone flat. The windscreen had spiderwebbed with cracks.

"Looks like the motor's a write-off," he observed.

The girl nodded. "I think so."

Drayton couldn't help feeling puzzled by her apparently relaxed attitude. "Have you got help coming?" he wondered aloud.

Again, she nodded. "It's all taken care of."

He glanced back at the wreck, noting the fresh smell of burn that still wreathed it, not to mention the widening pool of petrol forming underneath. This incident had only happened in the last couple of minutes, he realised. It scarcely seemed possible that it could all have been, how had she put it . . . "taken care of." Not so soon.

"So there's nothing I can do?" he said, starting to wonder why *he* was the one feeling awkward about this.

"Nothing," she agreed, changing her posture, placing one booted foot up against the oak tree behind, unconsciously striking a cool and very sexy pose.

"Okay," he said, retreating towards his shabby old Chrysler Sunbeam. "No problem."

Just before he climbed back into it, however, he glanced around, suddenly aware of the deep stillness in the surrounding woods. It was mid-July, and though still far off dusk, the sun was steadily sinking. Shafts of fading orange light slanted down through the heavy green foliage. In all directions, only ranks of silent tree trunks were visible, the majority of them thigh-deep in dense, tangled undergrowth. Birds still twittered, but those twitters were growing fewer and farther between; vague blue shadows were starting to spread under the leaf canopy.

Despite the inclination he felt towards solitude these days, Drayton knew that he couldn't just drive away. He strode back over to the girl. "Look, I don't mean to be a pest. But . . . it's probably not a good idea for you to be waiting here on your own."

She gazed at him, as if trying to discern whether or not he was simply being kind or maybe had ulterior motives. Then she smiled, in a vaguely regretful sort of way. "It's okay . . . I'm not on my own. My boyfriend's with me."

"Oh . . . right." Drayton took a step backwards. That explained things a little. Not that he could see any boyfriend in the immediate proximity. "Gone to find a garage, has he?" he asked. "I mean, I can pick him up on the way, give him a ride."

"No, it's alright," the girl said. "But thanks anyway."

At forty years old, Drayton was experienced enough to know when somebody was trying to get rid of him. She was being awfully polite about it, but she clearly didn't want him around. And perhaps for *that* reason, plus of course his natural-born stubbornness, he felt less prepared to leave. "What's actually happened here, love?"

"We came off the road."

"Is your boyfriend hurt, maybe?"

"No."

Her smile had now faded, to be replaced by something else . . . a blankness of expression perhaps, which only thinly concealed distress. It wasn't as if she was in serious trouble—he could tell *that* much—but she clearly had a problem and was now putting on a brave face trying to cover it.

"If you must know," she finally said, her resolve suddenly cracking, "he's gone after the man."

"Man?"

The girl stood upright from the tree. Suddenly she looked tired, stressed. "Someone ran across the road right in front of us. We swerved to avoid him."

"And your boyfriend's chased after him?"

"Yes." She half smiled again. "Andy's like that. Gets cross easily."

Drayton eyed the encircling woodland. To the human eye, it was fathomless. The shades of evening were lengthening through its verdant depths even as he watched. "Probably not a smart move to go chasing some bloke," he said, "with no one else around to help."

The girl shrugged. "You can't tell Andy things like that."

Drayton got the impression that she'd already tried to but had failed.

"I think it's probably best if you just go," the girl added. "Really, it is."

Drayton wasn't normally given to helping people. He wouldn't have called himself a misanthrope, but the recent end of his fifteen-year marriage had soured him immeasurably, and the injustice of Sandra's decision to deny him access to the kids—now ratified by court order—had just about extinguished the last flicker of goodwill he'd felt towards the rest of mankind. There was something about this girl that moved him, however. It wasn't simply that she was good-looking, it was her predicament: stuck out here in the middle of nowhere, she was incredibly vulnerable, far more so than even *she* might realise. And from what Drayton had heard, this Andy—whoever he actually was—might only add to the problem.

Drayton took the mobile from his jeans pocket. "Can I at least call someone for you?"

Again, she shook her head. "It's alright. Honestly it is."

"But I don't like leaving you stranded. . . . Barnard Castle's the nearest town and that's a good twenty minutes' drive from here." He glanced at his watch, seeing that the time wasn't far off eight o'clock. "It's getting late, too. I mean, there may be nobody else along this road all night."

That was something she might not realise, he decided . . . especially if she wasn't native to the region, which he suspected she wasn't. This was the A66, the Old North Road, as it used to be called. For centuries, it had linked the former administrative capitals of Penrith and Durham—separated from each other by fifty miles of trackless moor and rugged woodland—but it was now defunct, thanks largely to the motorway networks build over the last fifty years. He himself had only happened to come along it because he wanted to call in at the remote ruin that was Laxholm Abbey.

The girl meanwhile was now looking at him in a faintly hopeful way. *Could he help me?* she was possibly wondering. Did he—this unkempt stranger, who was nearly twenty years her senior—have what it took to resolve her problem?

At length, she decided: "I honestly think it's better if you just go."

"Perhaps I should just wait till your boyfriend gets back?"

"That really isn't a good idea—"

"What's this fucking guy's problem!" came a sudden, aggressive voice.

Drayton turned sharply. The man who'd just emerged from the trees was an immediately intimidating presence. He was only about thirty years old, but of large, muscular build and perhaps three inches taller than Drayton's six feet. He was dressed in canvas pants and a white silk shirt that was open at the throat, showing gold neck chains. His head was shaved down to bristles and he wore a hard frown. In the parlance of the streets where Drayton had grown up, he looked as though he could "go a bit."

Immediately, the girl stepped between them. "Andy, this is, er . . ."

"Ralph," Drayton said.

"This is Ralph. He's offered to give us a hand."

Andy, who was flushed and sweating slightly, regarded Drayton with undisguised suspicion.

"Ralph," the girl went on, "this is Andy, my boyfriend . . . who I was telling you about."

Drayton nodded. "Hi."

Andy didn't say anything.

"I'm Shirley, by the way," the girl said, turning back to Drayton and offering her hand. "We were on our way to Edinburgh."

"Edinburgh?" Drayton was surprised. "Wouldn't it have been easier going up to Glasgow and cutting across by the M8?"

"We prefer the scenic routes," Andy replied. He'd relaxed a little now, but his tone was curt.

"Ah, right. So . . . looks like you've had a bit of a bump." It was an inane comment, Drayton realised, but the atmosphere was distinctly awkward. "Do you want me to give you a ride somewhere? I mean, there's bound to be a garage along here at some point."

There was a moment of silence as the younger guy considered this. He glanced fleetingly at his girlfriend, who, for some reason, looked as though she wanted to say no to the suggestion, but finally opted to say nothing.

She glanced down at the ground, wouldn't meet Drayton's gaze. Eventually, Andy nodded. "Not a bad idea . . . if you're sure it's okay."

"Yeah, course," Drayton said, somewhat distracted by Shirley's change of attitude, and now wondering if he'd been too hasty. Who was this bloke, anyway, this bloke who went running after people through the woods? Had it been a momentary road-rage incident, or did he make a habit of that sort of thing?

Andy meanwhile, had turned and was walking back to what remained of his car. "If we're coming along with you, there's some gear I could do with bringing," he said over his brawny shoulder. "Just for safekeeping, you know."

"No problem," Drayton replied. "I've got loads of room."

When Andy rejoined them, four large bin liners swung from his fists. They were bulging, clearly laden down with cumbersome contents. Drayton unlocked the Sunbeam's boot, but the younger man didn't swing the articles in, as he might have done with sacks of clothing, but placed them carefully, evidently trying to avoid bursting them. Drayton noticed that each bag had been fastened with a thick twist of duct tape, though he only had a glimpse of this, because once they were in there, Andy promptly slammed the boot closed.

A few moments later, they were driving, the two stranded motorists ensconced in the rear seat. Various untidy odds and ends, including an open sports satchel packed with Drayton's current project, had had to be moved first; it all now sat in a disordered heap on the front passenger seat. They trundled along in silence, passing endless sunlit glades.

"Did you catch him?" Drayton asked, just to make conversation.

"What?" In the rearview mirror, Drayton saw his male passenger go sharply alert.

"The bloke who crossed the road in front of you?"

"Oh." Andy seemed to chill again. "No, he'd gone. Stupid bastard . . . just running out in front of us. Fucking idiot could've ruined everything."

"Who was he, anyway? A tramp?"

Andy shrugged, stared out of the window. "Didn't see him properly. Looked like he had khaki gear on."

"Khaki?"

"Yeah. Camouflage stuff. Like a squaddie, or something." A thought suddenly struck the younger man. "Are we near a barracks round here?"

"I don't know, to be honest."

"You sound like you're from our part of the world?" Shirley said, in a transparent attempt to change the subject.

"Preston," Drayton replied.

"Thought so," she said. "I'm from Bolton. Andy here's a Manc."

Drayton didn't bother to mention that he already suspected *that*—the more the younger guy spoke, the whinier and more nasal his accent became. "You guys on holiday?" he asked.

"Business," Andy said simply.

They drove on.

"Hey!" Shirley suddenly exclaimed, making both men jump. "You're famous."

Drayton glanced into the mirror again, and saw that she was holding something up.

"This is you, isn't it?" she said. "On the back of this book?"

He realised that she'd found *Lore of the Land*, the last thing he'd had published. It must have been lying in the foot-well.

"Yeah," he said. "That's a few years ago, though. Fifty or sixty pounds, as well."

"So you're a writer?" she asked.

"For my sins."

"What . . . stories and that?" The girl was now flicking through the pages.

"Not my own," Drayton said, less comfortable explaining this now than he had been back during his hope-filled youth. "I write nonfiction . . . assess legends, fables, that sort of thing."

"Wow," she replied.

"Don't be too impressed," he advised her. "There's not much money in it."

He didn't bother elaborating on that . . . on how his obsession with pursuing so noncommercial a genre had actually *cost* him rather than earned for him; on how stepping out of the rat race in order to spend his time writing, and being arrogant enough to assume he was so good that whatever he wrote, it would someday be recognised as a work of genius and bring him fame and wealth, had been self-delusion in the most dangerous sense of the phrase. Not that it hadn't brought him a lit-

tle bit of wealth at one point, though Sandra and her so-
licitor had now neatly accounted for all that.

"Says here you're a family man," Shirley said, checking his bio.

"Was," he corrected her.

"Oh."

Drayton didn't bother elaborating on *that*, either—on
how his determination to work solely in the field he
loved, even though he knew that the chances of making
it pay were unlikely, hadn't just cost him a potentially lu-
crative career, but had cost him his marriage as well.

Sandra had endlessly nagged him to put his talent to
better use . . . to write a novel or play, to produce something marketable that his agent—another past-fixture
now—could have used to launch him towards the best-
seller lists. But no, the usual obstinacy and pigheaded-
ness had clouded his judgement. He hadn't left the
degrading world of nine-'til-five, he'd said, so that he
could just become a slave for someone else. He was an
author now, not a journo . . . that meant he could write
what he wanted, *when* he wanted. He would stick with
mysticism, his one true interest in life, resolute that he
would make it work . . . but even *he*—Ralph Drayton,
with his undeniable ability, and a vast, self-taught
knowledge of his chosen subject—had failed to pull off
that miracle. And at length, the pressure—of mortgage
payments they could no longer afford, of a wife who
now wanted to be at home with the children rather than
working herself, of in-laws who'd started to think him a
waster and a failure—had finally killed their relationship.

So here he was, at the start of middle age, embittered, lonely . . . and engaged in another futile quest for that one elusive project that might turn things around, knowing full well that he wasn't going to find it. On the cheery subject of which . . .

"Listen," he said, "I need to stop soon. I mean, obviously I'll drop you off first if we come to a village, but if we don't, there's a place I need to check out . . . just for research purposes."

Shirley leaned forwards. "Why, you writing a book now?"

The attention of so pretty and, yes, so *personable* a girl—he suspected, when Andy wasn't around—was undeniably flattering. Absurdly, Drayton, overweight and with a scraggy, greying beard and unruly, greying hair, began to wonder if her interest in him might owe to more than common politeness.

"That's why I'm all the way out here," he replied, slapping the satchel on the front seat.

"Can I look?"

"Be my guest. But it's mainly notes . . . more like a dog's breakfast than a finished text."

Shirley reached down towards it, only for her boyfriend to suddenly snap at her: "*Shirl, sit the fuck down!*" His tone was hard, ultra-aggressive . . . it was as though her burgeoning friendship with their would-be rescuer had suddenly worn out his no doubt microscopic patience.

Drayton stared into the rearview mirror. His own background was solidly working class, and briefly a more combative spirit arose. This passenger was bigger, younger and probably a lot fitter than he was, but the author had spent his entire adult life resisting authority, and he was damned if he was having the law laid down like that in his own car.

"It's okay, I don't mind," he said, quite firmly. "You can have a look if you want."

Andy met his gaze in the mirror, his face sullen but inscrutable.

"Here," Drayton added, grabbing up the satchel and shoving it backwards into Shirley's hands.

The two men watched each other for a moment longer, before Andy turned and stared out of the window again. Shirley meanwhile was now digging through piles of scribble-filled notebooks. She picked one up, and read the scrawled words on its cover: "*Rediscovering the Green Man.*"

"Yeah," Drayton said. "That's what it's going to be called."

"What's it about then?"

"Well, it's a long story—"

"And I'm sure we haven't got time to hear it," Andy said, butting in again. "Look Shirl . . . you wanted to read it, read it. But don't distract the man while he's driving. We've got to get on."

The girl stuck her tongue out at him, then flicked the pad open and defiantly began to work her way through Drayton's difficult longhand. The author didn't expect that she'd understand much of it, even if she found it legible. He intended this book to be his most scholarly to date. The aim behind it was to explore every aspect of the legendary "Green Man"—the mysterious woodland being of Britain's esoteric past—to cut out all the crap and, if possible, to restore the eerie individual to his correct place in the pantheon of ancient mythological entities. It seemed unlikely that a girl like Shirley would have any empathy with such a subject.

Her first question, however, rather surprised him, especially as she'd so far only read the first page. "So . . . the Green Man, he wasn't actually supposed to have existed then? He wasn't like a god or spirit?"

"Well . . . no." Drayton was caught on the hop: she'd clearly understood his introduction. "No, he's more of a symbolic figure. His original meaning, if there ever was one, is lost to us now. He's often associated with paganism of course, and fertility rites . . . but that's all bollocks. It's just New Age fantasy. In medieval times he was merely a representative of Nature . . . an embodiment of all its beauty and danger. The Church used him as an allegorical figure; an image of what Man could turn into if he didn't stay on the straight and narrow."

"Yuk!" the girl said, interrupting, and he knew immediately what she was looking at.

Among his notes, he'd inserted a variety of cutouts and original photographs, the majority of them depicting the so-called "foliate heads," the original and most common way in which the Green Man was presented to his mystified audience. These were invariably carvings, drawings or mouldings, usually found in religious buildings, and nearly always they'd feature a humanoid head that was either peeking out through dense vegetation or that had actually become part of that vegetation. In most cases, the semitransformed heads were quite beautiful, their normal human features melding flawlessly into concentric layers of crisp new leaves, their hair hung with fruit and flowers, though one or two—and these were undoubtedly the ones that Shirley had just found— were more gory; in their case, thick vines tended to uncurl from the face's gaping mouth, buds hung from the nostrils, branches often sprouted from the eye sockets, having first, presumably, popped out the eyeballs. They made for a very ugly sight, and the author had often thought them reminiscent of rotting corpses through which natural undergrowth had penetrated.

"That's the Green Man as a harbinger of doom," he explained. "The Middle Ages, when Green Man carvings were first made in Britain, were a time of plague. Death was all around, and clearly this affected some of the artists and sculptors who were working then. Just shows, the Green Man has a wide variety of meanings . . . something I'm trying to bring out in the book."

"Sounds cool," the girl said.

"I think so," Drayton replied, wishing that the world's paying readership would share her opinion, but strongly suspecting that it wouldn't. Still, it was a worthy cause, if not a profitable one (though he couldn't imagine many modern folks agreeing with *that* viewpoint, either).

"The Green Man's a more mundane figure these days," he added. "A clown who appears at village festivals, or a picture on pub signs. I'm just trying to give him back his dignity, I guess."

They drove on again in silence. Drayton glanced into the rearview mirror; Shirley was still reading his notes. The satchel was on her knee, and sitting in the open top of it was his camera, a state-of-the-art Ixus 400. It was about the only thing of value that he owned these days, and he felt a pang of sudden concern when he realised that Andy had noticed it.

"Nice piece of kit," the younger man said, not hesitating to pick the camera up and examine it.

Drayton watched him warily. "I *need* a good one." He nodded at the tree-lined lane spooling out before them. "There's a place somewhere along here, Laxholm Abbey. That's where I was planning to stop off. There are some bosses there that I want to shoot. It won't take us long, though . . . and there'll be no one around to get in our way."

At which point, he sensed that Shirley looked quickly up.

He switched his gaze to her. She was apparently considering what he'd just said, and as she did, for some reason, her enthusiasm for the book began to flag. A moment later she'd laid the notepad down on her lap and was staring into space. Andy, on the other hand, who now replaced the expensive camera in the satchel, shrugged and seemed content to accept the plan . . . which rather caught the author off guard. Drayton would have expected a bullish bloke like this to want dropping off first. In fact, Drayton had been rather hoping for that, too: it would have allowed him to fully concentrate instead of having to keep giving explanations. He'd even been contemplating driving on past Laxholm until they arrived someplace where the twosome could get out, then driving all the way back . . . though it now struck him that if he did that, he might lose the light, and that would be disastrous. He wasn't staying in this area after all. He had a hotel reservation in Durham for that night, and in the morning, he'd been hoping to start up work at the cathedral there.

He pressed on resignedly, passing no habitations whatsoever, and five minutes later they arrived at the medieval ruin that was Laxholm Abbey, though it wasn't an abbey as such. It was a former Benedictine priory, and though it dated from the thirteenth century, and was thus of considerable historic value, it had never been so large or grand as the term "abbey" might imply. In any case, it was nothing more now than a gutted relic, which wasn't even visible from the road. Drayton parked alongside a stile-type gate, with an ENGLISH HERITAGE notice affixed to it. Again, only green and tranquil woodland surrounded them, though the sun was now melting its way down through the western trees, and the birdsong had faded virtually to nothing.

"It's well out of sight, isn't it?" Andy remarked.

The author nodded, hurriedly getting his materials together, stuffing the notebooks back into his satchel, then grabbing his camera. "Most people don't even know it's here. Sorry folks, but I've got to hurry you."

"No problem," Andy said, as he and Shirley climbed out.

Drayton locked up the car, and a moment later they'd passed through the stile and were following a narrow footpath, which wound through several clumps of hawthorn before terminating beside a large information board. Beyond that lay open sward, upon which sat what remained of the priory; from this angle, it was little more than a roofless maze of high but crumbling structures, all clad in heavy coats of ivy. Here and there, though, portions of "olde worlde" architecture were still recognisable; the odd soaring arch, the occasional remnant of traceried stone.

The author strode forwards eagerly, already taking readings on his light meter.

Andy and Shirley followed slowly, ambling along side by side.

A couple of minutes passed, Drayton consulting his notes, and now exploring a part of the ruin that he assumed had once been the kitchens and refectory. According to his research, there were only three intact Green Men here, and the first—and best—was located over the entrance to what had once been the priory herb garden. He found it without too much difficulty. A turfed passage ran between the broken footings of two long-vanished walls, and led straight up to a freestanding arch, from the apex of which an alarming face gazed down. It was sorely eroded, but clearly a Green Man, being composed almost entirely of what was supposed to be leafy matter, though with two very human eyes wide open in the middle of it.

Drayton wasted no time in starting to take photographs.

"I can't believe it . . . this is a real stroke of luck," he gabbled, his zeal getting the better of him, even though it was highly probable that these two people, cooperative though they were, couldn't really have cared less. "The normal thing about the Green Man is that he's hidden . . . tucked away in corners, under chapel seats, that sort of

thing. It was a game the medieval artisans used to play.
Though the Green Man sculptures were always commis-
sioned by pious Christians, their very grotesqueness was
often associated with demonism, so they couldn't be
given pride of place like the angels and saints could."

Shirley and Andy now came up alongside him. The
girl was still strangely quiet . . . and the author wasn't so
engrossed that he didn't notice this.

"Okay?" he asked her, breaking off briefly.

She nodded, gave him a brave smile.

Suddenly, however, it was Andy who now seemed to
be troubled by something. "Shit! I, er . . . I couldn't borrow your car keys for a mo, could I?" he asked. "I need
to go back and check my gear for something."

The author glanced at the guy, unsure how to respond.
It was a simple enough request, but the daylight was fast
dwindling and, Drayton being Drayton, it was difficult
for him to conceal his annoyance. "Can't it wait a minute
or two?"

"Not really."

The author pulled a face but made to set off back, digging irritably into his jeans pocket, and silently cursing
himself for ever having stopped to help these people in
the first place.

"No, you just crack on," Andy said, halting him with
a hand on his shoulder. "*I'll* go." And he held out his
open palm for the keys.

"Er . . ." Drayton wasn't happy with this plan at all.
"I'm not sure about that."

"Why?" Andy asked. "You think I'm going to pinch
your car?"

"No disrespect to you, mate, but I don't know you, do I?"

Andy pondered this, then smiled broadly. It was evidently supposed to be a disarming smile, but there was something not quite right about it; it was almost as though he didn't know what a real smile was. "I'll leave Shirley with you," he offered. "Not going to go off without my bird, am I?"

The author was tempted to reply that he wouldn't be at all surprised, but instead decided to shrug and hand over the keys. First of all, he couldn't see why anyone would want to steal an old donkey wagon like his Sunbeam; secondly, time wasn't on his side . . . the sun was almost down, and he still had to locate and photograph the other two carvings. Andy nodded, clapped him on the shoulder, then turned and hurried back along the open passage, finally rounding a corner and vanishing.

Drayton watched him go before turning to Shirley. "He's a real piece of work."

Again, the girl just smiled.

"Shall we get on?" Drayton said, passing through the archway.

They strolled together across the garden, and then across what Drayton assumed had previously been the cloister—it still had a central grassy quadrangle, paved around its edges—finally entering the remains of the priory church. Again, it was open to the elements. The roof had gone, and large portions of masonry from above the windows had collapsed; only stumps were left of the pillars that had once run in neat rows down either side of its nave.

"According to my notes, the next one's at the top of the southwest tower," Drayton said. "Should be easy enough to find . . . there's only one tower left."

They spied it straight away and proceeded towards it, the girl still strangely subdued. Drayton wondered if this was perhaps something to do with the atmosphere. Like many ancient sites, there was a restful aura here, the ruins solemn and imposing rather than scary. The sky was now tinged with dusk, however, the lofty, broken structures leaving long dark shadows, with only a few patches of spectral sunlight interspersed between them.

"There's no such thing as ghosts, you know," he said, trying to make light of it.

Shirley gave him another brave smile, but said nothing. Whatever it was that was *really* bugging her, she didn't intend to come clean about it.

He turned back to the tower, an upright cylinder of stone occupying the southwest corner of the cloister. It stood maybe forty feet tall, and again, was clad all over with ivy. Even then, however, deep fissures were visible in its aged stonework. Its arched, ground-floor entrance had safety bars fixed across it.

"The boss is up near the top somewhere," Drayton said. "So I'll have to go up and look."

Whatever had been bothering Shirley, it was momentarily forgotten as she took in the tall, gaunt edifice. "But surely it isn't safe?" she said. "I mean, you can't even get into it . . . look."

"Oh, there's a way in," he replied. "Apparently, there's access through the undercroft on the other side. That building round there"—he indicated a squarish,

single-story annexe on the south side of the tower—
"that's the old dormitory. Some cellar door's recently
been excavated inside it."

"But is it safe?" the girl asked again.

Drayton shrugged. "Dunno. Never let it be said that
we authors don't take risks for our craft." He ventured
forwards, but then stopped abruptly. "I wouldn't suggest
you coming, of course. Best if you stay here."

She seemed to accept that, and stuck her hands into
her jacket pockets as she waited.

Drayton then circled around the base of the tower,
passing out through the church's formerly grand doorway—
nothing now but two decayed gateposts—and approaching the entrance to the dormitory. Like the rest of the
buildings here, it had no roof, though its outer walls were
largely intact. New work had recently been going on in
there, though, so English Heritage had erected a block-
ade of tape strips across its entrance, with a WARNING-
DANGER sign suspended between them. The author
paused for a moment, but then reminded himself that this
transgression was entirely in the interests of the histori-
cal aesthetic, and ducked under the tape.

Inside, various tools were propped up against the
wall, alongside two wheelbarrows, a pile of bricks and a
cement mixer. Immediately, however, he saw the doorway connecting with the undercroft. He crossed over and
poked his head through it. At first glance, the subterranean space looked black and airless, but at length his
eyes attuned, and he saw steps leading down into a wide
cellar area, its floor made of dank, beaten earth. Cautiously, he descended, and once at the bottom noticed

high apertures placed at regular intervals along the line where the eastern wall joined the ceiling. They were more like air vents than windows, all grated and set in deep embrasures, but they allowed in sufficient light to now illumine an aperture on the far side of the under-croft; almost certainly, this was the doorway connecting to the foundations of the tower.

He made his way over and, again, stuck his head through, seeing the foot of a steep stair, which spiralled upwards around a central pillar. Delighted, the author went hastily up. Like so many stairways in old castles and cathedrals, the steps had been worn at their central point by the passage of countless feet. Aside from that, though, the going was relatively easy . . . even to Dray-ton, with his hefty paunch and long-untrained muscles. About ten feet up, he passed the barred doorway leading back into the church interior. He'd expected to find Shirley still standing there. She wasn't, however. He paused for a second, wondering about this, but time was drastically short, so a moment later he hurried on up. At about eighteen feet, he passed a tall, narrow window which looked westwards, and then, at twenty-five feet, came to another one, which looked southwards, subse-quently gazing back over the cloister.

That was when he saw the girl.

She was standing in the very middle of the quadran-gle, in a rigid, frightened posture.

And instantly Drayton saw why.

Andy had reappeared. He'd passed in through the herb-garden arch and was now coming towards her, ad-vancing with a slow, heavy tread. In one hand, he was twirling Drayton's car keys . . . in the other, he held a firearm.

At first the author thought he was seeing things. He leaned forwards to look more closely, but there was no mistake. Even though the burly boyfriend was deliberately carrying his right hand down by his side, Drayton could see what was in it: a handgun, a black steel revolver. Andy casually, almost contemptuously, then tossed the car keys aside and fished something from his pocket: a magazine, which he promptly slid into the revolver's grip and snapped into place.

"Andy!" Shirley pleaded, sounding genuinely upset, as though all her worst fears were now confirmed. "Come on . . . please!"

"Where is he?" her boyfriend asked.

"For God's sake!"

"Just tell me where he is."

"I won't!"

"Damn it, Shirl, don't fuck about!"

"You can't do this!"

Drayton watched and listened, trying to tell himself that it was some kind of elaborate prank, but knowing in his chilled heart that it wasn't, that it *couldn't* be.

He'd let himself go to seed badly over the years; had been drunk and lazy, still suffered coughing fits due to a decade of heavy smoking, and was in all-round poor condition. But for once, just for once—probably because it was an absolute necessity for survival—his senses were in pitch-perfect form. He could clearly see and clearly hear everything that was happening below.

"He saw the bags," Andy pointed out.

"He didn't know what was in them," Shirley protested.

"And you had to give him our real bloody names!"

"Andy, he's just a decent bloke. He's trying to help us."

"Doesn't matter how decent he is. We're compromised."

Andy gazed around, no doubt scanning for his intended victim. As he turned towards the tower, Drayton ducked out of sight, and from this point on risked only quick, furtive glances.

"Andy!" the girl pleaded again. She took hold of him by his shoulders. "Think . . . please."

Andy's response was to thrust her backwards, then slap her across the face, a heavy blow that sent her tottering sideways. "I *am* thinking! It's you who's not, you docile, airheaded cow! Don't you understand? He's going to take us somewhere where we'll have to report the accident. That means it goes on file. You think Jack Deakin and his blokes haven't got coppers on the take?"

His voice rose steadily, despite his knowing that his prey was somewhere close at hand. "That's *my* frigging car back there! The moment it goes on the police computer, word'll get out. They'll be onto this guy in no time. That means they'll be onto *us*."

"Just let him go," she begged.

"We *can't* let him take us to some garage."

"Nick his motor then."

He grabbed her by the hair, yanked her head savagely from side to side. "He'll report it, won't he! He'll lead the coppers back to the Peugeot. It's a fuck-up, for Christ's sake! And all because of that bastard. . . ."

He gestured in the direction they'd come from, help-less, in a fury of impotent but clearly murderous rage. At which point Shirley saw her opportunity, reached out . . . and snatched the gun away from him. Andy turned abruptly, stood stock-still. The girl backed off.

"Gimme that," he said, starting to follow her.

Shirley looked terrified, but hid the weapon behind her back. "I'm not going to let you do it."

"Give it to me, Shirley."

"It's murder."

"That didn't bother you when I capped Forbin."

"*He* was a drug dealer."

"What am *I*, then?"

"Andy, it's not right."

"Right? Since when do *you* care what's fucking right?"

And now he was almost upon her, and Drayton could tell that he was about to strike.

"Andy, no . . ." she pleaded.

"*You silly idiot bitch!*" And he *did* strike, lashing out with serpentlike speed, again dealing a ferocious, flat-handed blow to her cheek: *whap!*

It echoed across the ruins.

The second blow was quieter, but in her belly, and this one was a fist, driven with merciless force. The girl dou-bled over, choking, gasping, then dropped to the grass, the gun landing beside her. Her boyfriend swept down and scooped it up, before kicking her twice, very hard, again in the guts. She rolled about in silent agony.

In the tower, the pit of Drayton's own stomach had gone cold. He was bathed in icy sweat, his heart thumping his chest wall. Again, he'd only stolen quick glances, but he'd seen everything. He thrust himself back out of sight, to try to think . . . and immediately spotted his camera, which he'd placed on the windowsill as he'd watched, and which was still there, sitting out in full view. He groped towards it, but his hands were treacherously moist, and shaking like leaves. Almost inevitably, instead of quietly removing the item from view, he fumbled against it.

And it fell noisily down the outside of the tower.

Drayton didn't need to look to know that Andy had instantly homed in on the sound. There was a deafening momentary silence, then: "I'll deal with you properly later. Stay there, if you know what's good for you." Followed by another brutal impact.

There was no point in staying hidden now. The author risked one more glance, and saw the madman heading eagerly across the cloister towards his position.

Drayton backed away from the window . . . but where could he go to from here? Suddenly his mouth tasted like bile. A frantic, helpless horror took hold of him. *Jesus, where can I go?* The only way out of this place was the only way in. . . .

Andy didn't know the layout of the priory ruins, yet it was easy enough to find the foot of the tower. The only problem then was how to get inside it. He stood baffled, staring at the barred-off doorway. Somehow that sissy dipshit Ralph had managed it, even though he had to weigh a good fourteen stone. In which case Andy could manage it, too.

He examined the bars. They were cemented into the stonework rather than fitted to some kind of frame that could be opened. He grabbed two of the steel shafts and shook them angrily, testing his gigantic muscles against them—to no avail—before finally giving up and heading around the base of the tower, hurriedly searching for another entrance.

Drayton had scrambled up the remaining flight of steps, only to find that they ended in midair. The topmost section of the tower had long gone, and the upper rim of its encircling wall was nothing more now than weeds and jagged-edged bricks. He hurried back down to the lower window, and peered desperately out again, sweating intensely, the heart trip-hammering inside him. Far below, Shirley lay where she'd fallen, curled in an agonised ball. But there was no sign of Andy . . . which meant that he was already here, trying to get in.

Drayton didn't want to face the reality of what that now meant. But what other choice did he have?

Andy was a hunter by instinct. He liked to think of himself as a wolf in human guise, and as such it didn't take him long to find the taped-off door to the dormitory, and beyond that, the door that led to the undercroft.

He paused before descending . . . to knock the safety-catch off, and to listen.

The underground place was dark, musty. He wasn't frightened as such, but he was a professional, and professionals always took precautions. So he paused for a moment longer, and he listened all the harder.

Still there was no sound, and at last he ventured down. The grip of his Beretta was slippery with sweat, but it was the sweat of tension, nothing more. This was a nobody he was up against here; a flyspeck below the level of amateur. Compared to Terry Forbin, Andy's former partner—into whom he'd put five bullets not two days ago, so that he could lay claim to *all* the cash they'd supposedly been delivering for Mr. Deakin— popping this so-called author would be as easy as swiping the proverbial candy. In truth, Andy could have done it beside the road, back where the accident had occurred, but that wouldn't have been clever . . . someone might have come along, and even if they hadn't, forensic traces would have remained that the pigs could immediately connect with the written-off motor. No, it was better this way, off the road in a nicely secluded location.

He reached the bottom of the steps. Now that he was down there, the undercroft was *dim* rather than dark. Before his eyes had adjusted fully to it, though, he heard the sound of feet.

He paused again, listening intently.

Then he spotted the doorway opposite, and on the other side of that, what looked like the bottom of a spiral stairway. Those feet were still approaching, meanwhile . . . and it sounded as though they were actually coming down that spiral.

Shit! Andy thought, falling to a crouch, taking careful, two-handed aim.

Easy as swiping candy?

This was going to be easier even than that.

It was the worse descent of Drayton's life, and that in-cluded the occasion as a kid when bullies had coerced him into jumping off the high-dive board at the local swimming baths, and the charity parachute drop he'd made in his early twenties when he'd only had a week's training.

All the way down, the ivy had felt as frail as paper. It had repeatedly torn away from the crumbling wall, each time threatening to let him plunge to his death. What was more, various horrible creatures had repeatedly burst out from it, from sparrows to spiders, scurrying over his hands, fluttering into his face. He'd rarely found a proper foothold, and had fallen on several occasions, grabbing frenziedly at the green stuff as he'd plummeted five or six feet at a time. Somehow, though, it had ulti-mately held. And when he'd finally reached the bottom, he'd slipped and swung down over the last ten feet in comical, uncoordinated fashion—like a drunken chim-panzee, he'd imagined—only to land on a thick cushion of springy elephant grass, which, though it had knocked the wind out of him, had spared him any serious injury.

Seconds later, having grabbed up the satchel, which he'd thrown down ahead of him, he was on his feet and running again, weaving his way back through the ruins. He stopped briefly beside Shirley, who had managed to get herself up into a sitting position, but who was white in the face and had blood seeping from the corner of her mouth.

"Hurry," he urged, trying to get her to stand.

She shook her head dumbly. "Leave me . . . just go, while you've got the chance."

"Don't be bloody ridiculous," he said. "I can't leave you here. He'll kill you."

"It's *you* he wants to kill."

"I don't care. I'm not leaving you."

She resisted his attempts to get her back to her feet. "You can't help me. No one can."

"There're too many girls who think *that* about the blokes in their life," he retorted. And now he had her under the armpits and was forcibly lifting her. "Come on."

At any moment, he expected to hear a guttural shout from behind, maybe a deafening gunshot.

"You're wasting your time," she groaned, though now she was upright again, albeit weakly, and allowing him to steer her back in the direction of the road.

"You tried to help me, I'm going to help you," he said, stopping only to snatch up his keys.

"He'll find me again."

"Not if *I've* got anything to do with it."

Shirley shook her head. She was still wan in the cheek, clearly nauseated by the blows she'd taken. "I know too much. He *has* to find me."

"*I'm* not on his network," Drayton replied, his confidence growing. Ahead, he could now see the signpost and the path leading back through the hawthorn. "Come with me and you're well away—"

And that was when they heard the shots.

There were two of them, fired in rapid succession,

and though they sounded far behind, they were frighteningly loud. They echoed in the lush woodland like a double blast of thunder.

Drayton's mouth dried as he glanced behind them. "He's going crazy back there."

"Leave me," the girl moaned.

"No chance." He continued to propel her forwards. They were now on the path. The road was just ahead. "We're almost out of here."

Seconds later, they'd climbed through the stile and were next to the Sunbeam. Drayton leaned the girl on its bodywork, as he thrust his key into the passenger door and wrenched it open. The central-locking system didn't work any more, so after he'd eased the girl inside, he had to hasten round to the driver's door and unlock that one manually as well. Before climbing in himself, he glanced back once into the woods enshrouding the old priory. Nothing stirred; dense masses of heavy, silent leaf concealed everything.

Drayton swallowed, fleetingly wondering what was going on back there, then jumped into the car. He switched on the ignition, gunned the engine and drove away from the verge.

Shirley still wasn't happy. "You're a very kind, nice man," she mumbled, "but . . ."

"But what?" he asked. "But you don't deserve someone like me? He's got you bloody brainwashed, girl. Anyway, I'm not as kind or as nice as you may think."

The endless reaches of trees flooded past them as they drove, though many were now lost in purple gloom. Twilight was finally infiltrating the forest.

"What's in those bags that's so important, anyway?" Drayton asked.

"Oh," she said, "about three hundred grand."

He hit the brakes instinctively. The car screeched to a halt in the middle of the road.

He looked slowly round at her. "Three hundred . . ."

She nodded painfully, but was now making an effort to sit upright again. She was recovering her composure, if nothing else. "All unmarked bank notes. Freshly laundered."

"Jesus God in Heaven. . . ."

"Why else d'you think he was on the run?" she asked.

Drayton was speechless.

"I wouldn't worry, anyway," she added, dabbing the blood from the corner of her mouth with a delicate fingertip. "It's yours now. You've earned it."

Drayton stared at her. "I can't take it!"

"Why not, it's all untraceable."

"That's not the point."

She shrugged. "Dump it, then."

"Dump it?"

"Well, you can hardly give it back." She rolled a shoulder experimentally, wincing in pain, but starting to look more her normal self. "It's mob money. Comes from dope deals, prostitution . . . if you want my opinion, it's better off with *you* than Andy and his like."

Drayton wasn't quite sure what to say. The incredible realisation slowly dawned on him that three hundred big ones wouldn't just solve his current financial problems, it would probably set him up for the next fifteen years . . . give him plenty of time to get his career off the canvas. But he couldn't just *take* it . . . not like that. It wouldn't be moral.

On the other hand, what else was he supposed to do with it? Like the girl said, it wasn't as if he could give it back. In fact, he couldn't even give it to the police. That would lead to questions, criminal charges, a court case in which he'd have to give evidence—lawyers and judges again, those bastards!—and then probably decades in some witness-protection scheme somewhere, constantly having to look over his shoulder. No bloody chance, not for him.

He put the car in gear and started driving again, this time at a more sedate pace.

They'd travelled perhaps a mile before he realised that Shirley was watching him.

"I'm not kidnapping you, if that's what you were thinking," he said. "Soon as we hit civilisation I'll drop you off somewhere safe."

"Do you beat women up, Ralph?" she asked.

He glanced at her. *"What?"*

"You heard."

"Well I'm a grouchy old git, but I've never *hit* a woman. *One* thing about myself I'm proud of, I suppose."

She was still watching him, very closely, with those lovely blue eyes of hers.

"Like I said," he added. "I'll drop you off somewhere. If that's what you want. I mean . . ." And now it was difficult saying exactly *what* he meant. "I mean, I didn't bring you along as some kind of prize." He tried to laugh off such a ridiculous notion.

She reached over and brushed a piece of ivy leaf from the collar of his T-shirt. "*I'll* decide whether I'm your prize or not," she said.

The laugh died on Drayton's lips. Had she really just said *that*? For a moment he had trouble keeping his attention on the road.

"Don't look too surprised, Ralphie," Shirley added, looking back to the front. "Everyone's entitled to a lucky day now and then."

Drayton's thoughts were suddenly racing so fast that he could barely contain them inside his head. *Three hundred grand sitting in the boot, and now maybe . . .*

"It's a luckier day than I thought it was about ten minutes ago, I'll tell you that," he stammered.

"Maybe it isn't luck," she replied. "Maybe you're being rewarded for something."

I can't think what, he was about to say, thinking of his past life, his various acts of selfishness, his arguments with Sandra, his self-pitying bouts of lonely, morose drinking (mind you, all of which he'd been punished for, he reminded himself).

And then, in a flash, he thought about the "camouflaged man" who'd suddenly sped across the road in front of Andy's Peugeot, causing this whole thing to happen in the first place.

Again, Drayton almost lost his grip on the steering wheel.

Shirley had to take him by the wrist to steady him. "Just keep your eyes on the road, eh," she said softly. "Everything's going to be fine."

*   *   *

In the bowels of the old monastery, the full blackness of night concealed the remarkable profusion of foliage that had taken root in the centre of the undercroft.

A massed tangle of greenery it was, growing almost to the ceiling and exploding in every direction with its myriad shoots and tendrils. Of course, for all its apparent size and strength, it was essentially a delicate object, and could never last long in this lightless, underground abode. In all likelihood, when the people of English Heritage came down here sometime in the future to complete their work, they'd find little left of it but a few dried and withered stalks mingled with the trampled earth.

There'd certainly be no trace of the decomposing mass at its centre; the sagging, deflated thing from which the hungry vegetation even now was voraciously drawing its nutrients; the drained, lifeless sack, which, if the truth be told, was already scarcely recognisable for what it once had been. Though, maybe, at the upper part of it, if one pushed the leaves and shoots aside and peered closely in, one might just identify a vaguely humanoid visage, though the illusion of this would quickly be dispelled . . . by the vines now curling en masse from its gaping maw, and the thick fibrous stalks sprouting from the empty sockets of its eyes.

WARM, WET CIRCLES

By Michael Kelly

Looking up from my desk, from the blinking green letters of the computer terminal, I watched the smoke-colored fog roll in and choke the building like a thick wool blanket. I gulped down the remaining tepid coffee from a Styrofoam cup and tossed the cup at a wire basket, but missed. There was a ring of condensation where the cup had sat. I poked curiously at it with a finger. The cheap veneer was still warm from the coffee. And it occurred to me, glancing around at my sullen coworkers with their disingenuous smiles, that they each wore a cheap veneer over their flesh and blood.

Bending to retrieve the wayward cup, my arm caught the edge of the keyboard tray and left a hunk of skin dangling from the corner. There was no blood. No pain. Indeed, there was only a minor scratch on my arm. But that strip of skin, that tiny piece of me, turned slowly in some phantom current, as if doing some delicate dance.

I peered out the window. The fog pressed ever closer.

I felt as if I were suffocating, so I went downstairs and around to the back alley for a quick toot of coke. That's where I found the dead man.

It was cool and misty, the air filled with a drear dampness. Downtown buildings stretched skyward, disappeared into ashen fog and dense smog. Gray. Always gray. And cold. A bit of nose candy was in order.

At first, I thought the dead man was just asleep. Just another drunk vagrant passed out in a downtown alleyway, blissfully unaware of anything but his own insular world. So I did a couple quick toots to clear my head, leaned back against the rough brick wall, and closed my eyes, waiting for the buzz. Once the edge was off, I opened my eyes and turned to head back to the office and the wonderfully exciting world of information technology. Back to the gray office with gray, unsmiling people. Back to lose another piece of myself to the corporate grind.

But the sleeping/dead man caught my eye. Something about the way he lay—facedown, stretched across the cement—seemed odd, unnatural, even for booze-laden homeless people.

So I sauntered down the alley, shoulders hunched, hands shoved deep in my pockets, trying for a casual, cool, nonchalant look, knowing I wasn't quite pulling it off, wondering why I cared to look cool, casual or nonchalant at all.

I gave the bloke a nudge with a booted foot. Nothing. I shivered, unsure whether it was from the cold or the coke. "Hey," I said, prodding him some more. "Hey. Get up." Still nothing. I squatted, leaned down for a look . . . and jumped back.

One great, bloodshot eye stared back at me. It didn't blink, didn't move, just stared. Steeling myself, I leaned in closer. That's when I noticed the rank smell of shit and urine, sweat and decay. It came off him in waves. Bile rose in my throat and I choked it down. He was obviously dead. Had been for some time. His clothes were a rumpled, uniform gray-brown. So was his hair. He lay splayed on the cold road, his fingers hooked, clawlike, as if he'd tried to crawl away from something, or tried to gain purchase from something that threatened to drag him away. That one staring eye looked at me reproachfully. The other half of his face lay hidden against the hard ground.

I'd never seen a real honest-to-goodness in-the-flesh dead person before.

Further down the alley something rattled, perhaps a garbage can. A plastic grocery bag appeared out of the fog, scuttled across the alley, caught on my leg and wouldn't let go. I snatched at it, shoved it into a pocket.

Shit, I thought. *What should I do?* Ideally, I should have called someone. But I didn't. I felt a strange detachment. After all, it wasn't my bloody problem. Someone else would come along shortly and find him. Wouldn't they? Let them deal with it. I had things to do. I didn't know the chap.

Or did I? What if it was someone from the office? A coworker or an acquaintance?

I chuckled at the absurdity. But to ease my troubled thoughts I reached down to turn him over and get a better look. At first, he wouldn't flip. I knelt down, grabbed hold of his greasy shirt and tugged. Slowly, he began to lift from the ground. But I saw the problem. It was his face, specifically the side that had been pressed to the cement. It was stuck. And as I pulled I saw his flesh string out like warm bubble gum that's been trod upon, the way thin, pink strands stretch between shoe and cement. Except this wasn't bubble gum, it was sallow yellow-gray skin with bits of dried blood, stretching, pulling.

Finally, with a wet snapping sound, I managed to yank the bloke free.

The wind moaned, but for a brief giddy moment I thought it was the dead man. Time to quit the nose candy.

Staring down at the dead man, I had to shake my head. If this was someone I knew, I didn't know how I was going to identify him. The skin had ripped off one whole side of his face. What a fucking mess. And . . .

. . . I was eight years old again, watching the puppy chase the ball into the road, hearing the squeal of tires, the tiny yelp of fear, and a soft thud. I stood, watched the driver get out, place a hand on the broken dog. Watched the tail wag once, the body twitch. Then Mom was there, grabbing my shoulders, ushering me into the house. And I didn't cry, didn't talk about it. The next morning I went out to the road. All that was left was a little blood and bone and fur. Then the rain came, washing away the remnants, and that's when I cried.

I trembled, wished I had another line of coke.

Breaking from my reverie, I noticed the skein of flesh stuck to the cement, how the taffy-pulled quality of it wavered, as if beckoning. A queer feeling came over me. Remembering the plastic bag in my trousers, I fished it out and, minding that no one was watching, used it as a glove. With a bit of effort I plucked the skin from the ground, turning the bag inside out so as to trap the tissue inside.

With one last look at the deceased, I stepped over his body and hurried back to the office with my prize clutched tightly in hand.

Curiously, the strip of skin on the keyboard tray was gone. Disappeared.

As was the case lately, I couldn't work, couldn't concentrate. I'd stare out the grimy window, at the sooty haze that choked the office tower like a great, gray hand, my thoughts jumbled, foggy like the outside world. Far below me, in that foggy outside world, a dead man lay in an alley. I had a piece of him in a drawer in my desk. A macabre memento.

Later, when I got home, I placed the dead man's flesh in an old, unused cigar box.

It didn't bother me at all that I had the skin of a dead man in a humidor in a dark closet in my apartment. There was something uniquely intimate about it that spoke to my peculiar sensibilities. A fragment; a puzzle; a thin, torn, membranous memory.

The following morning, before going up to the office, I stole a peek down the alleyway. Seeing nothing untoward, I strolled down the alley, whistling. The dead man, as I suspected, was gone. There were curious, brownish stains on the ground; ring-shaped, like moist, puckered lips. Otherwise, there was no other sign to tell me that a dead man lay here yesterday.

In a city this size there must be hundreds, perhaps thousands, of homeless. Where do they go? What happens to them when they die? Do municipal workers come by in big yellow trucks to scoop them up like roadkill? They can't just disappear.

The rest of the day (indeed, the rest of the week) was uneventful. I managed to perform even the most perfunctory of tasks without the benefit of any illegal stimulant. Wonders.

Then, early Saturday morning on my way home from the newsstand (where I picked up *The Guardian* and some Dentyne) I saw another dead man.

He was in a small side alley off the main street. It was still gray and dull and chill, a faint mist hanging in the air. The cold seeped into my bones. Christ, where was the fucking sun?

As I passed the tiny side street, I briefly glimpsed a dark, huddled mass in the periphery of my vision. It was still early enough that the streets were relatively empty, so I wandered down to the crumpled bundle of rags.

Indeed, it was another dead homeless man. *Were there no homeless women?* I wondered.

The man lay on his side, his sleeveless right arm tucked under his head as if asleep. Except he wasn't going to wake. This was the long, big sleep.

So I rolled him over onto his back. His arm gave some resistance, but pulled free, leaving clumps of gray-green skin on the ground. I didn't recognize him. He resembled the other dead man: bearded, greasy, unkempt.

Odd that life should be categorized and stereotyped. All the homeless looked the same. All my gray- and brown-suited coworkers resembled each other. What about me? Where did I fit?

His eyes were wide open, and a small Mona Lisa smile creased his face. My eyes were drawn to the patches of flesh—the pieces of him—that clung to the pavement. What a strange amalgam: flesh and stone.

Bending, I tried to grab hold of a piece of fleshy tissue, but it was too short, too ingrained in the cement, and I could gain no purchase. I grabbed a piece of cardboard that lay nearby and with shoveling and scraping motions managed to peel the majority of the flesh from the ground. Carefully, I placed the fleshy fragments into the bag alongside the newspaper.

When I got back to the apartment, I placed the skin in the humidor alongside the earlier remnants. Whereas the two dead men had seemed so similar, their skin, their remains, were completely different. One was thin and tissue-paperlike, the other a mix of small flakes and hardened little nubs. The irony wasn't lost on me. I wondered what the vestiges of me would look like.

The following day, Sunday, on my way back to the newsstand to buy Dentyne (one can never have enough chewing gum) I took a quick detour down the side street where I'd found my second dead man.

Gone. Nothing left but small, dark, circular stains that glistened suggestively. I bent, stroked the dark marks. They were moist . . . and warm. I was mildly aroused.

I went home, read the paper, chewed gum and drank tea. I tried not to notice the fog outside my window, thick and oppressive, pressing in all around me. Eventually, I closed the blinds and took to bed.

* * *

Days passed, one like the other, gray and unending. I withdrew from the small circle of friends (if you could call them that) and acquaintances that made up my world. They were cool and aloof. Or perhaps I was. Surprisingly, I stayed away from the cocaine.

One particularly dismal and rainy Tuesday I stopped in at a local pub. It was quiet, mostly empty, and the gloom outside pervaded the dark, smoky room. I was cold. Cold and alone.

I sat down at the bar, ordered a pint of the local brew. Sipping the bland ale, I noticed several rings of moisture atop the honey-colored wood. Remnants of the lives of ordinary people. Passing my hand through the residue, I wasn't surprised to find that they were warm, wet circles. I imagined them opening and closing like hungry little mouths. I imagined my penis in just such a mouth.

Later that evening, alone in my room, I took out the humidor, stared at the dead skin, rubbed my fingers over the texture. A pleasant quiver shook me.

I'd never been good with intimacy.

Early the following day I called work, told them I was sick and wouldn't be in. I tried to alter my voice, give it a coughlike quality, but didn't convince even myself. They wouldn't miss me anyway.

I didn't shower or shave. I skipped breakfast. I slipped on a windbreaker and wandered out into the streets. I headed downtown. It didn't bother me that I might pass by the office. I didn't fucking care. I just walked and walked. And as I walked the air became dense, moist, cloudy. The constant damp chill soaked into me, and I hugged myself for warmth. I passed people who seemed to be streaming by in a rush; all dressed in browns and grays the color of moths and rocks, gaping at me, their faces distorted. It was as if I was moving in slow motion. The fog got thicker. The streams of people dissipated. The streets became unfamiliar. I walked and walked, and it seemed that all the streets were alike, that I'd walked this same stretch over and over, twisting and turning through dark back alleys, wading through gasoline-choked puddles that glimmered with a strange fishlike iridescence. And I was reminded of little fish mouths gasping for air. Reminded of odd, dark stains and warm, wet circles.

Finally, I found him, in a greasy cardboard lean-to in an anonymous back alley. He lay facedown, arms stretched wide, palms pressed to the ground as if he'd just done a set of push ups and needed a rest. Smiling, I grabbed hold of one hand and tugged. It was spongy and gummy, but pulled free without much effort. I fished a sandwich bag from my pocket (the type that zips neatly shut) and scraped the decaying flesh from the ground, scooping it into the waiting bag. The skin was wet and smelled faintly of smoke or ash. I zipped the bag closed and made my way back to the apartment, making a mental note of the main intersection closest to this side alleyway. Once safely home, out of the gray fog, I deposited the new flesh into the humidor. The moist, rank skin contrasted nicely with my other pieces.

Satisfied, I fell into bed with my clothes on. Just before succumbing to slumber, I recalled I hadn't eaten anything all day. I wasn't hungry.

And when I woke bright and early the next day, I still wasn't hungry.

I left the apartment immediately, not bothering to call in to work, though it was only midweek. Chances are, they wouldn't even miss me. In a city this size, people go missing every day. I wore the same clothes as the day before, and I still hadn't shaved or brushed my teeth. It was damp outside, the air heavy, seemingly thrumming with queer electricity.

The alley wasn't hard to locate once I found the intersection. I hurried down it, searching for my dead man, though I knew he'd be gone. There was no sign of him. The rain had destroyed the cardboard lean-to, rendering it a sodden mess. I got down on my hands and knees, brushed away the detritus of cardboard, dirt and old newspaper. There, on the wet cement, hundreds of circles—like suckers from an octopus—pulsed and writhed. I smiled. I was ready.

Pressing my face to the pavement, I lay down on the warm, wet circles.

I always wondered what happened to homeless people. They just seem to vanish. Yet, if you look hard enough, you can find remnants of them.

I wondered if I would disappear without a trace.

JUST BEYOND THE MIDDLE OF THE JOURNEY

By Joseph A. Ezzo

Elizabeth grew extremely despondent the day after they visited the Choeung Ek killing fields and the Tuol Sleng Museum, and Turk sensed it immediately, felt her slipping through his fingers into a private reserve of detachment and inaccessibility. Her spirits of the first three days in Phnom Penh—bubbly, wildly energetic, filled with exclamations of ebullience at the outwardly friendly demeanor of the locals (particularly the groups of boisterous children who appeared at every turn)—had dissipated completely, and now, as they strolled in the miasmic heat of Sisowath Quay, dodging motos and cyclos and the clusters of tourists, her withdrawal was so profound that he could not really think of anything useful to say that would reach her. As they walked, they passed family-run shops, food stalls, fruit stands where women and their daughters prepared smoothies at the cost of about a quarter ("Pretty much what Wally

Cleaver used to pay when he took Mary Ellen Rogers to
the malt shop," Turk chortled when the two of them
stopped and purchased a tall, fabulously sweet jackfruit
shake to share, savoring the experience with relish), the
travel offices offering discount fares and tours, the boys
in clean shirts selling newspapers; they heard the groaning hum of the traffic, horns constantly blaring, the dare-
devil moto drivers, lithe young women seated sidesaddle
behind them, darting in and out between the larger vehicles. By Turk's reckoning, he and Elizabeth should have
been wholly sucked up in the sheer, heady vitality of it
all, just as they had been the past three days. Now, if
Elizabeth was absorbing any of this, it did not register
one whit in her behavior.

They passed Chiang Mai, reputed to be one of the
finest dining experiences in the Cambodian capital, and
with its prices, just about the best value around. Turk
glanced at his watch, then pointed to the restaurant.

"What do you think?" he asked, trying to make him-
self sound in high spirits. "Supposed to be outstanding
Thai food. The *Lonely Planet* guide says so, and so did
Luong."

Elizabeth wrinkled her nose.

"The very helpful, very friendly woman at the front
desk of our hotel. Anyway, it's almost two. You up for
some lunch?"

Elizabeth paused on the sidewalk, looked at him as if
she did not understand what he was talking about. Then
she twisted up her mouth, gave Turk the slightest of
nods, and headed inside. When a slightly bent, middle-
aged man came to take their order, Turk gestured to Eliz-

abeth, but she used her hand to indicate that he should order first.

"Chicken in red curry, with rice," he told the man. He looked up at Elizabeth, but she was staring off to the side. "Elizabeth?"

She shrugged, not changing her position. "Nothing," she muttered.

When Turk looked up, the man had already left. He returned shortly with a large bottle of water, very cold, and one glass. Turk started to ask him for a second glass, but the man left the table again as soon as he set them down.

Turk sighed. "Elizabeth, I know yesterday was disturbing. It really frightened me, too. That's one of the reasons why I bought those books before we left. To try to understand the whole thing a little better." He poured water into the glass, took a long drink. As he looked up, he saw she now had her eyes on him. "I'm very upset by what I saw, too. But isn't it better than we went there, that we at least saw—"

"Do you know that they opened that museum barely a year after the prison was discovered by the Vietnamese?" she asked distantly. "That the Vietnamese sent their best museum expert, Mai Lam, to begin setting up less than two months after they first came upon it?" Her voice grew louder. "Mai Lam, that was his name. Isn't it something when you can put names—the real names of real people—to such things? The first visitors who went there got to see the pools of dried blood on the floor and the stairs, the swarms of flies that lived in them. What *can* you make of that?" Suddenly she started to laugh; Turk heard bitter sarcasm in it.

"I saw you reading from a number of the books last night. In fact, I don't recall you even coming to bed, you seemed so engrossed—"

"Yes, yes, two of them I stuck in your backpack this morning. Have a look at them. Part of the reason the Vietnamese did it was because of their traditional hatred for Cambodians. Absolutely. They wanted to show just how barbaric their enemies were, not to mention what lousy Communists they turned out to be. Don't you get it, Turk? Don't you see what we saw? We saw hatred stacked on top of hatred. If the Khmer Rouge had not been so full of hate for their own people, no such prison would ever have existed. If the Vietnamese did not hate the Cambodians they way they do—or did, I don't know—there'd be no museum to commemorate the perversity of the prison. We come here and file through like it's Disney World or whatever. Human suffering becomes our little sideshow to delight and entertain." She looked at him with a crooked, pained smile. "And"—she waved her hands frantically—"look around you. Everybody here is so happy. We're happy. The other tourists are happy. Those slimeball foreigners who go to the nightclubs to pick up underage Cambodian prostitutes are happy. And so are the local people themselves. Happy, happy, and happy! We're all just one big happy—" She broke off, began to sob. Then she got up and left the restaurant. The waiter came to their table, set down an empty plate in front of Turk, then a dish of red curry chicken in the middle of the table. He came back immediately with a bowl and a large metal container of rice. By the time he finished spooning rice into the bowl and refilled the water glass, Elizabeth had reentered, stood with hands on hips, facing Turk. He lowered his eyes, unable to find the courage to see if she would sit down again. He began to pick at his food, then stopped and reached into his backpack, extracted the two books she had mentioned. He saw that she had marked a spot in each book with a piece of tissue. He opened one book to the mark and noticed that a passage from the page had been circled in red ink.

Duch, the head of S-21, did not preside over torture sessions and executions. This was left to a trio of brutal guards who answered directly to him: Peng, Tok, and Huy. According to the testimony of the few who survived S-21, these three men delighted in inflicting savage punishment on prisoners. They were possessed of no moral sense whatsoever, but undertook their work with a cold and vicious efficiency. They were the true butchers of Tuol Sleng, as each of them was directly responsible for the killings of more than 2,000 people.

Turk glanced up, could not see Elizabeth. He set down the book and cautiously collected the second one. A much longer passage was circled, with two pairs of three large exclamation points penned on either side of the text.

I was standing a short ways inside the entrance with Nath, Tuon, Meng, and Chan, watching visitors filter into the weedy ground toward the Build-

ing 1. It was then I spotted a limping, gray-haired man, his face drawn, body very thin, and bent forward in a strange way, as if he were carrying some very heavy on his back. He wore large dark glasses and did not move his head at all as he walked. Despite the shriveled form of his body, and the sunglasses, I knew I was looking at Tok, one of the most vicious butchers at Toul Sleng. What in the world was he doing here, after all these years? As he passed us, I held up a hand and called out to him.

"What business do you have here?" I asked angrily, staring intently at him. "Look at us. Do you remember who we are? Do you think I don't recognize you?"

He stopped, turned his head slowly in my direction, and, to my surprise, removed his sunglasses. "What business do you have with me, brother?" he asked then, his voice husky and very hoarse.

"Don't pretend you don't recognize me, Tok. I know you well, just as you know all of us. Now, what are you doing here?"

He ran a hand over his mouth and chin. "I've come to see the museum." He spread his arms. "Like everyone else here."

"So, you've come back to relive the days of your glorious slaughter of thousands of innocent Khmer, is that it?"

He drew up straight and bared his teeth. "I don't know what you're talking about, brother," he said indignantly. "I'm a respected Phnom Penh businessman and have every right to be here."

"Don't play this game with us, Tok. We know who and what you are."

"My name is not Tok, so please stop—"

"How many people do you think you killed here, Tok?" I asked furiously. "Two thousand, three, maybe five thousand? Did you and Peng and Huy have a competition to see who could kill the most?" Now I was sweating heavily, and shouting so that many people had turned and were staring at me. "Well, Tok, look at me. And Nath, and Meng, and Tuon, and Chan. You didn't get us. We lived through it, and now neither you nor anyone can stop the truth from being told. So, Tok, how many innocent people, how many children and babies, how many pregnant women, did you torture and slaughter here?"

Tok shrunk back from me, perhaps afraid that I was going to attack him. Tuon and Chan were at my side, ready to grab my arms if I struck. Then Tok ran his hands down the front of his shirt and sleeves, put his sunglasses back on again. "I live and work here in Phnom Penh," he said evenly. "My name, brother, is not Tok, but Seng Meanchey. You can ask anyone who knows me." With that, he turned and walked away, toward the first building of Tuol Sleng Museum, where he had murdered several high-ranking Khmer Rouge cadres during the final days of the prison.

When the man was clearing the dishes, Turk looked up, and saw that Elizabeth remained near the entrance, staring at him once again. He held up the books half-heartedly, a searching expression on his face. *I read the passages you highlighted,* he wanted to say. "Can you explain to me why you wanted me to see them?" he did ask, but she did not appear to hear. Turk sighed and returned the books to his backpack, then rose and paid the bill.

When they got back out onto Sisowath Quay, heading south, he took her hand, determined to hold it despite how lifeless it felt. Overhead, heavy clouds were building up, and a hot, sour-smelling wind was wafting from the Tonle Sap River, suggesting that a summer thunderstorm was perhaps only minutes away. Now the street was lined with hotels, restaurants, more travel offices, Internet cafes, the sidewalks more congested. When they reached Phlauv 178, Turk pointed to the right. "The National Museum," he remarked. "We could always have a look in there. Weather's starting to look serious."

They walked up the street, but as they neared the museum, Elizabeth seemed intent on continuing rather than turning onto the museum's grounds. Turk did not force the issue, and within a few minutes the impressive, deep red terracotta structure passed out of view. A low roll of thunder rumbled overhead. As they had experienced walking along any number of streets that radiated off of Sisowath Quay, they found themselves in a jumble of vendors. These were primarily artists and dealers of artwork. After passing a block of stone sculptors, then another of shops specializing in woodcarving and textiles, they reached a succession of open-air establishments sporting brightly colored paintings of a variety of sizes, most of them depicting the ruins of Angkor Wat. As they passed the first of these vendors, Turk felt raindrops conk him on top of the head. The wind had picked up, spraying sand across the road, and pedestrians were hurrying to shelter.

Before them was a shop that stood out from the others. Unlike its neighbors, with their gritty, bland exteriors, this establishment was highlighted by a lush presentation of hanging plants. In the outer area of the shop stood paintings, like the others, and there was also a glass counter featuring small brass and bronze statues of mythological figures from the *Ramayana*, one or two of which might have been genuine antiques. Behind the counter, Turk could see an inner chamber, well lighted and ringed with additional glass counters. He indicated to the place to Elizabeth.

"What do you think? Looks as good as place as any to wait out the rain." He nodded to her, waiting for her approval. Elizabeth cocked her head to one side, then sighed. For all Turk could discern, she appeared more content to remain on the sidewalk and allow the coming storm to drench her. "Elizabeth? You want to just step inside there for a few minutes, at least until we can figure out what to do?"

She looked around the place, clearly distraught over something about it. She chewed on her lip for a few seconds, then sighed. "Yeah," she said absently, although it sounded to Turk as if she were answering a very different question. She folded her hands tightly against her belly, then proceeded.

As they reach the doorway to the inner area, the rain now beginning to fall in earnest, an elegant Khmer woman inside was smiling and waving at them to enter. "Hello, sir!" she called out in a friendly voice. "Please, come in. Would you like to see the jewelry I have? I have some very nice pieces; excellent quality. Gold, white gold, diamonds, rubies, blue sapphires." She was dressed in a dark sleeveless dress that hugged her slender frame. A thick gold chain hung around her neck, and similarly stylish bracelets gathered on her wrists and forearms. She moved with polished grace from behind the jewelry counter to the center of the room.

Turk guessed she was probably in her forties; her large dark eyes and lustrous hair, her high cheekbones and full lips (not to mention her poise) all commanded attention. "Is there anything in particular you might be looking for?" she asked, looking into Turk's eyes. He turned his head slightly, saw Elizabeth in the entryway, eyes darting back and forth between the shop and the street. Then she slipped into the outer area of the shop and he lost sight of her.

Turk glanced about at the cases, but his eyes did not focus on anything. "Your first time in Cambodia?" the woman asked.

Turk nodded. "Yes, and we're having a wonderful time."

"You will go to Siem Reap? To visit Angkor?"

"Oh, yes. Day after tomorrow."

"Ah."

"Everyone here is . . . well, we're really amazed at . . . I don't know how to say it, but the people here must be so strong to have rebuilt everything since . . . well, I've bought several books about Cam . . . about your country . . . to learn more." He looked up at the woman helplessly. "Everyone is so kind here, so friendly. It's really . . . I've . . . we've"—Turk pointed back and forth between Elizabeth and himself several times— "never quite experienced this before."

The woman smiled knowingly. "We like to work, and we love to smile," she said pragmatically.

Turk looked back at the entryway, saw Elizabeth pass once, arms still folded against her midsection. He rubbed his forehead and surveyed a section of a jewelry case. "You have much very beautiful jewelry here," he remarked rather vapidly. "And also you speak English well."

The woman laughed, blushing slightly. "No, I don't. I only pick up English from tourists since I start my business."

Turk found that he had to make an effort to prevent himself from uttering a profusion of compliments about her looks. "How . . . long have you had this business?" he asked to divert his attention.

"Four years now. It's okay. I like to work here very much. Normally I have my sons, my nieces and nephews to help me. But today they tell me it's too hot, so they all go to the swimming pool." She laughed as she revealed this. "I tell them they must go early, before the rains, but they don't listen, so they will likely return soon, without much chance to swim."

"You have this business with your husband?" Turk

asked, glancing at the entryway. Elizabeth was passing by again; she stopped, glared at him rather sharply.

The woman shook her head. "No, just me. My husband gives me the money to start the business. He has several businesses in Phnom Penh. But this is mine. If there is anything you want to look at, please let me know."

"Thank you." Turk turned to Elizabeth, who remained where she was, apparently oblivious to the merchandise. "Is there anything you want to look at?" he asked gently, cautiously. "There is a lot of nice stuff here. Maybe if I see something I might like to buy for you, you'll be willing to have a look. What do you think?"

By way of reply, Elizabeth met his eyes for a few seconds, a look of distraction on her face, then turned away and disappeared beyond his line of sight.

A muffled tune began to play, and the woman stepped away from the counter and collected a handbag, from which she extracted a cellular phone. She opened it and began speaking in a low voice. Turk likewise moved away from the jewelry cases and went to the entryway. Elizabeth was standing nearby, watching the rain.

"Elizabeth, honey, snap out of it," he purred in her ear. "I know you're hurting inside, but you can't let this get you so down." He put his arm around her shoulder, felt her stiffen slightly as he did. She continued to stare out to the street, where the rain was falling in thunderous sheets. "Elizabeth, talk to me, tell me something. Look, you want to go somewhere else? I could ask this woman to call a taxi for us. We could go back to the room, if you want, or to the National Museum, maybe somewhere for ice cream. How would that—"

She murmured something then, and shivered. Her body had turned so cold that he pulled his arm away from shoulder. He could not be certain what she said, but it sounded something like, "This place is dead for me," or perhaps, "This place is dead in me."

Turk leaned over and kissed her cheek, which felt repulsively cold also. He glanced back at the cases, saw that the woman was no longer on her cell phone, but was busy arranging some pieces in one of the cases. She smiled as she worked, and moved with such grace that Turk was absolutely certain he had never seen a woman who moved like her before. He turned back to Elizabeth. "Come and look at the jewelry with me," he implored in a whisper, leaning close to her ear. "Let's find something really special to buy for you. I'm sure this woman will give us a good price."

"Her?" Elizabeth asked suddenly, staring wide-eyed into Turk's face. "Do you know who—" she broke off, turned back to the rain. "I'd rather be standing in that," she spat, pointing out at the street.

Turk frowned, shrugged. "Why?" he asked. "Please, Elizabeth, let me know what you want. We can get a taxi and—"

"It isn't *right* here. Don't you get it?" She spoke with teeth clenched, grinding her words torturously.

Turk sighed deeply, walked back to the counter opposite the woman, smiled. "Okay, I'm ready to do some serious looking."

"Do you have something in mind? Is there a special lady you to buy for?"

Turk frowned, cleared his throat. "Yes," he replied rather emphatically. "Of course. I think . . . earrings. Let's have a look at some earrings. Something with a precious stone, set in gold. White gold, if you have it."

The woman laughed softly. "Of course. Just here, I have four pair of white gold. Three of them have stones." She pulled the three pair out and set them on the glass countertop. She pointed to each with a sleek, manicured index finger, the nail long and painted bright red. "Rubies, blue sapphires, and topaz. They are all very beautiful, excellently crafted. And all made here in Cambodia. In Phnom Penh. We have many very gifted craftsmen of jewelry in our city now."

Turk leaned closer to the countertop. "Yes, indeed," he replied, not really knowing what he was looking at or why. "They are indeed exquisite. The ruby set is certainly . . . well, elegant. Hmmm. I just don't know"—he glanced back at the entryway, which was vacant—"if they'll work on my . . . Now the blue sapphire . . . My, this is a lovely stone, isn't it?"

The woman nodded rapidly. "The stone comes from Thailand. But it's cut and prepared here in Phnom Penh. Blue sapphires are very popular among Khmer ladies." As she spoke, Turk noticed a very thin ring on the small finger of her hand, highlighted by a dark blue stone. He wanted to take her slender, brown hand in his—just feel the life there, assure himself all of it was authentic. Perhaps if he could take Elizabeth's hand and place it in hers, she would feel the life that pulsed through this city and would snap out of her state of distress, allowing them to continue the remainder of their trip in high spirits.

"Then it's the blue sapphire set," he stated firmly, tapping his fingers on the top of the glass case.

"I'm sure your lady will look beautiful wearing these," the woman noted as she pulled out a small case and began to fit the earrings carefully into it. When she had the small package wrapped securely, she handed it to Turk, then took his money and made change for him. "Here," she said, pulling a business card from a small stand on the counter. Turk held it up to his face. TONLE SAP JEWELERS, it read in a flowing script. He looked at the fine print at the bottom. "So, you are . . . Seng?" he asked.

"My family name. By marriage. In Cambodia we write family name first. So, I am Seng Sokhim. Or just Sokhim. Ah," the woman then extolled, eyes widening. She smiled broadly and waved, her head turned toward the back of the shop. "My husband."

Turk turned, saw a slightly bent, white-haired man moving soundlessly out of the shadows toward the woman. He face was brown and leathery, deeply creased, and he looked much older than his wife. He made eye contact with Turk and nodded; Turk responded with a smile and held out his hand.

The man accepted it at once. "Mmmm," he mumbled, pumping Turk's hand. He smiled to reveal a mouth of yellowed, broken teeth. A loud gasp rose behind them, then a piercing scream, followed by the crash of splintering glass. Turk wheeled around to see Elizabeth, a look of abject terror on her face, bolt from the entryway and down Phlauv 178. Seemingly oblivious to the downpour, she sprinted in the direction of the river.

Turk looked back once at Sokhim, who smiled crookedly—perhaps an expression of helplessness—then he nodded to her husband and likewise left the jewelry shop at a run. As he jumped across the entryway, he could not see any of the broken glass. The street was deserted in the downpour; Turk caught sight of Elizabeth a few blocks ahead of him, spraying water with each retreating step. As he passed the entrance area to the National Museum, he saw her reach Sisowath Quay, then disappear behind a recently remodeled building as she headed in the direction of their hotel. Rain drummed down on him, soaking his hair and clothes almost instantly. He found running through it a laborious task, as if he were slogging through a swamp. Elizabeth, as near as he could tell, seemed to be having no trouble at all running through the storm; he got the impression that she was almost born to it. By the time he reached Sisowath Quay he was out of breath, and when he turned in the direction she had run, he could not see her. He was surprised to see a large number of motos operating on the street despite the weather, and wondered briefly if perhaps she had flagged one down to ferry her back to their hotel. After taking several deep breaths, he broke into a run again, and as he did, he thought he glimpsed her, now several blocks ahead of him, her pace, if anything, having quickened.

At some very weary point the Chiang Mai came into view, and, as Turk passed it, the man who had waited on them was standing in the entrance, staring at him with a profoundly puzzled face. Turk could no longer see Elizabeth, and his patience had worn thin; as upset as she was, he decided, there was no call for this kind of behavior, and she owed him both an explanation and an apology for it. Fortunately, he was no more than a block from the hotel now, and, satisfied with his attitude about this business, he slowed to a walk, no longer caring about the rain, as it could not possible make him any wetter.

In the lobby of his hotel he saw Luong at the front desk, smiling sympathetically at his waterlogged condition. "Did my . . . Did Elizabeth . . . come in? Is she here?"

Luong frowned deeply. "I'm sorry, I didn't understand," she replied cautiously, holding out his room key.

Wiping rain from his eyes and forehead, Turk accepted the key and charged up the stairs, taking them three at a time until he reached the second floor. The door of the room was slightly ajar. Turk pushed it open, found that the place had been ransacked. The bedclothes had been torn up and heaped on the floor. The pillows had been gutted and lay in feathery mounds on the mattress. Clothes littered the top of the dresser, the floor, and hung across the TV screen, which was shattered and smoking. The books purchased at Tuol Sleng were strewn about the room, their spines crushed, clusters of pages—some flat, some wrinkled into balls—scattered across the bed and nightstand. Moisture hung and dripped from the walls and ceiling as if it had been raining inside as well as out.

The mirror above the dresser was cracked, spiderwebs of ruptured glass emanating from behind a page from one of the books that was tacked to the center of it. A short passage was circled in red ink. When Turk inspected it more closely, he saw that the page was affixed to the surface of the mirror with an earring—identical to the pair he had just purchased. He glanced down at his hands, found they were empty. He must have dropped the earrings in the rain.

Turk shook his head, trying to dislodge the unnerving image of himself, alone in the room, very recently in fact, shouting and cursing over the absolute brutality of what he had read, shredding the books: all part of a prolonged tantrum brought on by a glimpse of the horror of sheer madness. A second page—tacked by the other earring to the bathroom door—was from a different book than the one on the mirror.

His head against the bathroom door, Turk then heard vicious sounds of destruction coming from beyond it. The sounds beckoned him, as if he were part of something of which he was unaware. Heavy things were being broken and shattered, and amidst the crashes were screams so visceral that he was certain they could not have come from human beings.

Turk pounded on the bathroom door. "Elizabeth!" he shouted, then understood that the name did not have the meaning he thought it did—had not one of the books' authors borne such a name? The door flew open. A raw, foul odor filled the room. The crashing and screaming was replaced by the muted grating of a buzz saw. The bathroom was steamed up, and awash in blood; it covered the sink, walls, shower curtain, toilet. It was so deep on the floor that his shoes sunk into it. Chains, ropes, and bizarre, blood-soaked wooden devices dangled from the ceiling. For an instant Turk thought he was standing in a slaughterhouse, for there were no fewer than ten lifeless masses, attached to massive hooks, piled along one wall. A phenomenal swarm of flies droned about them. Through the steam Turk made out the mirror above the sink, saw that it alone was not covered in blood. There was however, dripping blood on it, shaped into a message:

YOU SHOOK HANDS WITH HIM

As Turk discerned the words, he heard a commotion in the doorway of the hotel room. A shadow fell next to where he was standing, and he turned to see Luong standing just outside the bathroom door. Two maids were busily cleaning up the room. Luong did not look the least bit surprised. One of the maids slipped silently past her, trailing behind her a bucket and mop. Luong offered Turk a thin, supportive smile, then shrugged slightly.

"We're not yet free of it," she said wistfully, taking him by the hand and turning from the doorway.

SOMETIMES I THINK IF I STAND BY THE PHONE IT MAY RING

By Robert N. Lee

She's whispering and the connection keeps dropping. By this time she's babbling. Still, he holds the phone hard, listens harder, makes fitting responses and never says, "I can't hear you" or, "You're breaking up," because that might mean missing something. This may be the last call, the last one ever like all the calls today, and he figures if there's any time in life to just shut up and mostly listen, now's the time. If your girlfriend calls you from a hijacked plane, you shut up and listen like that was God on the phone. If she calls from the middle of "What the fuck is going on, the world would like to know," you listen like it was God's boss.

Earlier she called for a couple of minutes and told him that her mother was, then was not. That's the way she phrased it, like Bible talk. He can barely remember the rest of what she said, he's so wrung out and it was so crazy. Something about a corner that was no longer a corner and her mother, who was and then was not.

He never ate his lunch. He wonders when last he ate.

With a start, he realizes that he's spacing out, not listening to what she's saying. *Oh Jesus, what a time to—*

"Eight eight eight eight eight eight . . ." *How long has she been saying that?*

"Eight eight eight eight eight eight . . ." He can't even tell if she's actually saying that at this point or panting or something, she's speaking so quietly. He juggles the "no interruption" policy for a sec, figures your girlfriend having a psychotic break rates an exception.

"Honey, you're not making any sense. Are you saying 'eight'?"

On the other end she stops, and there is silence that sounds like a dropped call, the cell mike on the other end cut off in the absence of close ambient noise. He waits and hopes that's all it is and the call hasn't dropped.

"Eliz—"

A wail and she screams his name and then she barks it. "JIMMY!" Panic shoots up him and he stands. Then she barks it again, her voice not her voice anymore, nothing left of Elizabeth Katherine Ivans, who liked Vietnamese food and going out dancing and Michael Mann movies and Jimmy Barnes a whole lot, God only knew why. He doesn't know who this new voice is, but it scrapes at his brains and his heart and he's pretty sure the owner hates everything Elizabeth loved and mostly *him.*

And then it starts again, the bark maddening and running

and blurring. "Eight eight eight EIGHT EIGHT EIGHT EIGHT EIGHTEIGHTEIGHTEIGHTEIGHT—"

A little while later, he picks up the phone and, cautious, hits the TALK button. Listens. Nothing but dial tone. He sighs and feels stupid and breaks down sobbing again.

If you could sleep until noon any day of your life, Jimmy Barnes figured, the day after you lost your job was that day. He stumbled around the small kitchen, blinking, assembling cereal and toast, still in his underwear just because he could be. He pushed aside the small pile of bills Gary had obviously left on the table, given the sticky note on them shouting "JIMMY!" in bold red ink. He sat and considered his options for the day.

One, Jimmy was hung over. He and some of the other layoff guys and some of the guys who were staying, too, had tied one on and then another, and his head was both tender and expanding hourly. Limiting travel was essential. Two, Jimmy'd gotten a twenty sack off an ex-coworker last night at the bar. Three—fuck three, get stoned and watch movies sounded like a plan.

One bong hit before leaving, and he never noticed how empty the streets were as he headed to Blockbuster. He noticed on the way back, but that was after the clerks at the video store looked at him weird when he came up with his pile of tapes and DVDs. He'd tried to make a joke of it, looked around at the ceiling-mounted TVs and apologized for interrupting their Jerry Bruckheimer movie, and they stared at him even harder then and he got out fast.

The clerk at the convenience store, where he bought beer, was sad-eyed and sympathetic and Jimmy began wondering if the predrive bong hit had been such a hot idea.

So it was that he did notice, on the way back to the apartment, that the streets were unnaturally devoid of cars. He had no idea, however, whether he was seeing things correctly or was suffering extreme pot-induced paranoia, so he forgot about the whole thing as fast as he could.

He was in the middle of *Henry: Portrait of a Serial Killer* when the phone rang the first time. He was taking a hit and decided to just let it go.

"Fuck you," he yelped, exhaling, to whatever stranger was on the other end of that shrieking phone. "I lost my *job*."

He pictured her pinned under something, something big, something of hers crushed, delirious from the pain. Nothing else explained most of what Elizabeth had to say, in her voice mails or when he finally did get through to her on her cell.

Jimmy had immediately groaned when he first checked his voicemail and heard, "seven new messages." He knew who it was, he knew she was calling to bug him about finding a new job, but . . . *seven times*? What the hell was that?

So it was that Jimmy hung up without listening to his voice mail messages and put in another movie and popped another beer and decided it could wait a while longer.

His guilt caught up with him halfway through *2 Fast 2 Furious* and if he'd expected absolution in finally giving in to duty, he didn't find it. The first message was about twenty seconds long, if that, and it sent his heart right into his feet.

"Jimmy? Are you there? Pick up if you are, I'll call back in a minute. Something happened." Sad, panicked, an edge in her voice he'd only heard once before.

Oh, great, her dad or her grandma died or something and I've been ignoring her calls.

The second was worse.

"Jimmy. I loved you, remember that."

The third one made no sense at all.

By that time, he'd hung up and was frantically redialing her cell number and scrambling for the remotes, switching from DVD to cable.

Oh, fuck.

That wasn't a Jerry Bruckheimer movie.

"A PLEA FOR SANITY" read the subject line, the thread pinned to the top of the board. Jimmy opened it, reading what he'd expected, "Some of us and some of ours are in harm's way." "Please can we be civil to one another across party . . ." He backed out, checked the whole site, or the first page anyway.

The rest of the messages on the front page of the board all said "DC" or "Washington" or "Beltway" and had lots and lots of responses. Jimmy didn't bother with any of them. He'd just wanted to see if anybody was in chat, and nobody was, and he didn't feel like calling everybody in.

Then, almost done with the page, he saw it: "Weird Call from My Mom in VA."

The first post read:

"My mom got through to me about half an hour ago, and I talked to her for ten minutes and I still have no idea what's going on in there. She must be hurt or something, because nothing she said made any sense. She spent the first half of the conversation reminding me of bad things I'd done as a kid and the second half talking about the light of the world and the false light or something like that. I'm so scared right now."

The followups broke down into two categories: messages of sympathy and support and iterations of "I talked to my father/brother/niece/whatever and he/she said almost exactly that."

Jimmy decided the thread didn't need another "me too" post from him. He'd heard the seventh voice mail message by then.

He continued hitting REDIAL and headed for some news sites.

It was nearly four when he finally got through. She didn't pick up. He left a message asking what was going on, begging her to call back if she could.

By then he'd seen the same video clips of sudden fire and destruction and read the same stories about a hundred times apiece. Nothing new since before he'd woken up. Nobody could get within thirty miles of the DC area. The same shots, over and over, of the handful of emergency vehicles and news vans that had tried this morning.

So he spent half his time frantically reloading news sites, in case something did happen, listening for any sudden change in CNN, out in the living room. The other half he spent on message boards, having finally broken down and decided to read the speculative arguments on the subject, in the absence of new information. He never responded, just read, and so he learned that this was clearly the fucking towel-heads again, that this was *Reichstag II: Electric Boogaloo* from Bush and friends, that this wasn't really happening, that it was aliens, that it was God, that it had something to do with Clinton getting a blow job and Rush-goddamned-Limbaugh.

He never responded, but he kept reading and staring at the phone.

When it rang, he surprised himself with his calm. He picked it up after the first ring and said "Hello?"

"Hello, Jimmy." If his calm had surprised him, hers floored him, especially after those increasingly bizarre messages.

"What's going on, honey? I didn't watch the news or anything this morning, and then I got all these messages from you."

"I'm not sure what's going on. There were these noises and then light and then I was down here in the cellar and about an hour ago I accepted something."

Jimmy frowned. "You what? You accepted something?"

The phone was silent a moment. "Yeah. I tried not to, but it was too big so I had to take it."

"Uh, honey . . ." How do you ask somebody, *Were you raped?*

"You'll accept it too. A lot faster than I did, I think."

"What?"

"You were always weak. I dealt with it, but I don't need to do that anymore."

Okay, Jimmy thought, *she's dying. She's trapped under something, maybe she's been attacked, maybe she's* dying. *Hurt and sick and dying people lash out at people around them sometimes.*

"That's not what's going on, Jimmy."

"What isn't what's going on, Elizabeth?"

"What you're thinking. I'm not hurt."

He couldn't respond.

"But I'm going to hurt you. I'm going to have a long time to hurt you. He said."

She hung up.

And then she called back to tell him about her mom and hung up again.

On the news, again and again, phone calls from inside the "DC Disaster" on CNN, the "Hell Zone" on Fox News. None of the calls were from after eleven that morning. All of the voices were scared and concerned, reaching and loving. Nothing weird about noises, lights or corners, none of the spillage of resentment he was getting from Elizabeth and reading about, increasingly, on message boards.

"I can't believe she brought that up. It happened when I was eight, and I'd totally forgotten about it. I guess she didn't . . ."

"I know I've talked about him a lot here, how proud we are of him and his accomplishments. I finally got to talk to Randy earlier, and he . . . I'm having trouble just typing this. He told me he'd always hated me, that I was a horrible mother, and then he told me exactly why. The worst thing was that everything he said was true. . . ."

"I started crying hard, and it was like she didn't even hear me, she just kept talking, telling me how miserable I was. . . ."

"A few hours ago, all I wanted was to hear his voice, and now I don't pick up the phone most of the time."

Elizabeth was calling every ten minutes or so by this point. Jimmy was not, however, ignoring the phone. Sighing, he'd pick up, say, "Hello?" and subject himself to a few minutes of abuse, no personal stone of his left unturned. She laid into his laziness, his bad work habits, his deficiencies in bed, his ridiculous family, his lack of real goals, his drug use. She suggested alternately that he was a homosexual and a raging satyr and a psychopath.

"Sigh," he typed.

"She just called again, didn't she?" This was followed by an animated smiley face becoming ill and throwing up. Somebody had finally posted a "come chat" message and he had a private window open with Andrea, one of his better friends on the board.

"Yeah, she did."

"Maybe you should think about skipping some of those calls."

"I can't do that."

"Okay. Sorry." Frowny, embarrassed face.

"You don't have to be sorry. I just can't."

"Yeah."

"I gotta go."

Beat.

"C YA."

He interrupted only once, before the end, to ask why she hadn't called him for hours and was suddenly calling all the time.

"I couldn't call you again until you invited me, Jimmy."

"What? That doesn't make any sense at all."

"After I . . . accepted what I did, I couldn't come in unless you asked me to."

"Come in?"

"Oh, I will," she said and hung up again.

After that was the call where she kept saying "eight" and after that there were no more calls. He fell asleep in his chair and dreamed vividly of Elizabeth. She was neither barking nor ranting, but standing in front of him wearing nothing but his Ramones shirt and telling him that she was all right and he shouldn't worry about her. When he woke with a start he knew she was dead and he waited for that dream hangover to fade, waited to know it was just a dream and go on. But it never happened, the certainty never faded.

Numb, he made coffee and wondered where Gary was at this hour, and found himself back at his desk, hands on keyboard and mouse, without any sense of time having passed, unsure how he'd gotten here, even.

He read.

Around eleven o'clock, the messages online took a turn for the ugly. It started with a few board regulars without family or friends in and around DC, most of them formerly very nice people. They began complaining that they were being "swamped" with posts about people's personal history with their loved ones, and they were tired of that shit. This was a national emergency, after all. Naturally, the insulted and bereaved were aghast at this and hit back, and both sides gathered support, and many threads and posts were locked and deleted.

Then the personal attacks began, so much like the phone calls from Elizabeth that Jimmy couldn't stand to open another thread like it for an hour or so. After that, he opened another one and after that, that was all he read. Everything, every argument ever held in public and every no-longer-secret private encounter thrown out, board members challenging each other on the pettiest and largest things, and Jimmy just could not stop reading. The moderator of one board shut the whole thing down after a member revealed that he'd raped her on their one real-world date. The admin of another board posted a message stating that he would not be locking any more threads, as he thought this was an important discussion, and then he continued on and tore apart half a dozen souls he'd seemed bosom chums with until that moment.

By the time those who'd posted earlier about agonizing phone calls from loved ones began posting lists of the offenses said loved ones had committed against *them,* and who the hell were they to talk, anyway, Jimmy was long past refraining from response. He'd fanned the fires of a few dozen raging feuds, started a handful of his own and was readying his own thread about what a total cunt Elizabeth had been. He felt no shame at this; it seemed only right to him, with what she'd put him through all day, after all.

At some point, someone posted a "What The Hell Is Going On?" message with a call to the chat room, and Jimmy logged in, but it was more of the same. Andrea got on after a while and ripped into him for never noticing how much she obviously liked him and he ripped back with, "I noticed, you're just too ugly and geeky for me." Things got really good after that, and he wasn't sure, but he thought Andrea had killed herself.

At another point, Gary called, but that was just more of the same, only real-world, and they screamed at each other for a few minutes and somebody hung up.

So it is that when the trumpets sound and light that isn't real light blares everywhere and there are no shadows left, Jimmy Barnes is not particularly surprised.

When the flames roar around him and catch hold of him and he begins to burn, he looks down and falls to his knees and begins to try to catch the voice and make it his own.

She was right; he is weaker than she was.

He seeks it out, flesh crisping yet not consumed, screaming now, trying to align with the voice urging him to hate hate hate hate hate hate hate hate hate hate hate hate hate hate hate

Copyrights

About the Editor

A Bram Stoker Award winner, **John Pelan** is a prolific editor of horror anthologies and the coauthor of several novels, short stories, and film and comic scripts. He is also an active member of the Horror Writers Association. One of the founders of the Northwest alternative publishing revolution of the eighties, he also founded Silver Salamander Press, an imprint with a reputation from uncompromising dark fiction. He lives with his wife in Seattle.

THE ULTIMATE IN
SCIENCE FICTION AND FANTASY!

From magical tales of distant worlds to stories of
technological advances beyond the grasp of man, Penguin has
everything you need to stretch your imagination to its limits.

penguin.com

ACE
Get the latest information on favorites like
William Gibson, T.A. Barron, Brian Jacques,
Ursula Le Guin, Sharon Shinn, and Charlaine Harris,
as well as updates on the best new authors.

ROC
Escape with Harry Turtledove, Anne Bishop,
S.M. Stirling, Simon Green, Chris Bunch, Jim Butcher, E.E.
Knight, and many others—plus news on the
latest and hottest in science fiction and fantasy.

DAW
Mercedes Lackey, Kristen Britain, Tanya Huff,
Tad Williams, C.J. Cherryh, and many more—
DAW has something to satisfy the cravings of any
science fiction and fantasy lover.
Also visit dawbooks.com.

Get the best of science fiction and fantasy
at your fingertips!